4/14 FM 3 50

ST. MARTIN'S

MINOTAUR

MYSTERIES

D1024255

I dropped to my knees onto the cool, rough, weed-infested grass before the graves . . .

Then I remembered. Yesterday Miss Maggie had asked me to close my eyes. My heart thumped wildly as I did so now.

Immediately, I saw five crosses, each with a pyramid of stones and broken brick supporting the base, keeping them upright. Evan's was most weathered, the wood silky gray, but it was also the most carefully constructed, the cross-pieces flush with each other, the lettering neat . . . A coffin-sized rectangle of earth in front of each marker was sunken in an inch or two . . .

No wall enclosed the plot, no forest stood beyond, only grayish, tangled growth. I clearly saw the Rapidan, its water a rusty café au lait, both banks barren, punctuated with tree stumps. The pungent odor of burning hung thick in the air.

Another faint scent made my nose itch, reminiscent of a local petting zoo back home . . .

And even as I thought it, the whinnying and snorting were back, loud this time, with the stamping of hooves.

Right behind me.

By Blood Possessed

Elena Santangelo

St. Martin's Paperbacks

Author's note: All versions of historical events, persons, and places in this novel are either fiction or used fictitiously, as are all other names, characters, incidents, and locales. Any similarity to actual events, places, or persons, living or dead, is entirely coincidental.

BY BLOOD POSSESSED

Copyright © 1999 by Elena Santangelo.
Excerpt from *Hang My Head and Cry* copyright © 2001 by Elena Santangelo.

Library of Congress Catalog Card Number: 99-15936

ISBN: 0-312-97723-9

Printed in the United States of America

St. Martin's Press hardcover edition / October 1999
St. Martin's Paperbacks edition / January 2001

St. Martin's Paperbacks are published by St. Martin's Press, 175 Fifth Avenue, New York, NY 10010.

10 9 8 7 6 5 4 3 2 1

To the memory of my uncle,
Joseph B. Chicco

⊲ ACKNOWLEDGMENTS ⊳

This novel wouldn't exist if not for my brother Tom, who tossed me the dare I needed to get it started, then let me raid his personal library and make off with all his Civil War books. So I not only thank him publicly, I forgive him for everything he did to me when we were little. My best friend, Linda Gagliardi, never stopped believing I'd make it into print someday—for all her support and for letting me use her computer when mine crashed in the middle of Chapter Thirteen, I'll be forever indebted. Also deserving of my gratitude are Jeff Gerecke and Kelley Ragland, for giving me a chance; and, of course, my parents, for all their worry and patience.

Much thanks to all the friends, extended family, and mystery-writer colleagues (one in particular—you know who you are) who provided encouragement, advice, and research help. I wish I could mention each name, but there'd be no room for the rest of the book.

By Blood
Possessed

If one Confederate soldier kills 90 Yankees, how many Yankees can 10 Confederate soldiers kill?

Math problem from *Johnson's Elementary Arithmetic*, published in Raleigh, North Carolina—1864

MAY 1, 1864—CLARK'S MOUNTAIN, VIRGINIA

Against the satiny ribbon of river below, bathed blood red by the setting sun, the horse and rider appeared as little more than shadows of the lone toy cavalryman my brother Lane let me have years before.

The rider coaxed his mount away from its refreshment of Rapidan water, toward the sea of white, conical tents that seemed to stretch clear back to Washington. As he cantered between the Yankee watchfires on the far bank, their glow picked up the yellow of his sash.

An officer, maybe even a general.

I was stretched out flat, snug against the cool, damp earth. Good Virginia clay that should have given off the heady smell of late spring bounty. This year it reeked of sweat and urine, blood and death. All the world did. I breathed in the stench, welcoming its reminder of mission.

The ground itself seemed to respond, cradling me like a familiar lover, angling my arms, bracing them, until Pa's heavy old fowling rifle formed a true line between my eyes and that toy soldier pausing to speak to his pickets.

Keeping his blue-coated shoulders in my sights, I ran my palm along the gun stock, letting it warm beneath my fingers. His horse pranced nervously, as if sensing the danger, but the rider was too intent upon his business. I could hit him square, I knew. I'd practiced nearly every day for two months after coming home from Richmond last fall. Then the armies had returned, bivouacking once again on either bank of the river, and it proved safer for me to stay huddled in the cellar until nightfall.

My fingertips traced the rifle's contour, savoring the grooves fancily etched into the metal by some long-dead gunsmith, caressing the grip until my hand became one with the wood, stroking the inner crescent of the trigger as if it were the most delicate crystal.

"Bang," I whispered, a parody of the game played with my toy warrior long ago. "Bang. You're dead." And I conjured up a vision of him toppling from his saddle, his foot caught in one stirrup, the great steed rearing up in terror as foot soldiers rushed to his aid, striving vainly to catch the wayward reins.

Across the river, the rider raised his head, scanning warily the thick forest carpet on this arm of the mountain, assuring his mount with a pat of his gauntlet. An emotion overtook me that moment, strong and exhilarating. Fear had been dispatched and received. He knew something in these woods held his doom in balance. He realized my power over him.

When the time came to face my true nemesis, I would desire that sensation again.

"What in blazes you doing a-way up here, boy?" Someone dropped to the ground beside me. I couldn't see much more of him in the fading light than an outline of rags hanging loose from his emaciated figure, but his speech proclaimed him a fellow Virginian. He didn't startle me— I'd already identified him as the gristled veteran who'd taken me under his wing, who carried with him permanently the aura of a skunk he'd had the misfortune to disturb.

"Look yonder," I said, nodding to the opposite bank. "A general, you reckon?"

"Mebbe." He pushed my rifle barrel down. "Ain't the time, son. No honor in it 'cept in battle."

Honor? I wanted to shout. To the devil with "honor" and "glory" and all those high-sounding words that send men to war. The only honor comes in admitting we're all assassins, revelling in havoc and devastation. And always will be, until the Final Armageddon.

But the old man was shoving his upturned hat under my chin, and a more appealing scent fought its way through the pungency of the skunk. "Here. Blackberries. Found 'em down along that little spring you told me about, hidden under a mess of sumac. Go on, fill yourself up. No telling when we'll get better'n goober peas again."

I took one to roll around my tongue. Wasn't ripe, wouldn't be for a while, which was why the animals hadn't found them yet. But pure heaven to an army living on peanuts and wheat bran. "Any more where these came from?"

"Whole bush, only I didn't have anything with me 'cept my hat and pockets to carry 'em."

"Show me where. We'll fill up my pockets too, bring them back, make up a soup so they go farther."

"Best watch out, son. They make you chief quartermaster for notions like that." He laughed, and his nearly toothless grin pleated the long whiskers around his mouth.

As we made our way down the gully above Long Branch, he started in talking once more, now solemn and shrewd. "I was like you once. We all were four years ago. Hankering to get into the fight, itching to shoot my first Yank. Wanted a general too. Settled for a private what should never'a left his mama's knee. Though a darn sight older'n you, boy."

I let myself smile, knowing he couldn't see it in the dark. I'd aged a millennium in—was it little more than two years? But I'd never been young. Neither had this old gnarled specimen at my side. Old, though no more than ten years my senior, looking out of eyes that had viewed more than men thrice his age ought in one lifetime. This was our one similarity. He'd never been like me otherwise. "The Army of Northern Virginia can't be too particular these days," was how I answered him.

"No, it can't. Friends I grew up with, men I did business with, almost all dead now. Even those what survived Manassas and Sharpsburg, I watched mowed down in that final charge on Gettysburg." His voice caught, and I resisted a childish urge to touch him. Gettysburg had also taken my dearest brother, Lane, but I'd not seen the carnage firsthand like this man had.

"And now those Yankee devils won't exchange prisoners," he continued, recovering himself. "Soon we'll be stealing babies right out of their nurses' arms. 'Stead of walking, we'll teach 'em to charge. 'Stead of talking, we'll learn 'em the Rebel yell. 'Stead of sucking at teats, we'll let 'em suck hardtack. Lord, they won't ever want to go home."

"Things keep up, none of them'll have homes anyway," I murmured.

"True enough." He stopped to clap me on the shoulder. "Seen the way them bluecoats been a-bustling of late? You'll get your first taste of battle right soon, son. Mebbe kill yourself that general."

I intended to, if I could, but not the one I'd had in my sights tonight. There was only one general worth killing, whose death would pay for the lives of my family, the ruin of my home and land. And before I pulled the trigger, I'd make sure he knew who dealt his fate, and why.

⚔ 1 ⚔

MAY 1, PRESENT-DAY—SOUTHEASTERN
PENNSYLVANIA

Against mauve cubicle walls, Herb's bald spot gleamed
pale, almost jaundiced, like an old softball left up in the
attic too long.

His phone was ringing. We all knew it was his, the
ringer set louder than anyone else's. If you didn't know
him, you'd assume he wanted to be able to hear it when
away from his desk, say, at the copier. But Herb never used
the copier, never left his seat except for two daily sojourns
to the little boys' room. Yet he'd always let his phone ring
three and a half times. Sat there watching it like a starved
raptor, chubby forefinger poised over the speaker button. A
nanosecond before voice mail could snatch the call away,
he'd jab his talon at his prey, intoning, "Dawkins-
Greenway Corporation. Herbert J. Kruminski speaking.
How may I help you?" Every time. Even on in-house calls.
Like he was CEO or something. And because he always
used his speaker, always cranked up as loud as it would
go, the rest of us got the special treat of having to listen to
both sides of every blessed conversation.

This call was from Shipping. Herb had left a bunch of
blank spaces on a customer's order change. Again.

I rested my hand on the rim of the bust-high cubicle,
palm down, thumb lined up with Herb's off-white dome of
brain wrap. Slipping one of those thick, paper-ream-sized
rubber bands over the thumbnail, I slowly eased it back,

feeling the tension increase until I had to bend my thumb knuckle against it.

"What the hell are you doing, Pat?"

The band snapped back at me, whacking the tiny quasi-funny-bone in the soft spot below my forefinger. "*Ma-donne!*" I jiggled my hand to relieve the pain as I turned to my cube mate, Denise-of-the-Oh-So-Perfect-Timing. "What's it look like I'm doing? I'm wishing I had a gun."

Her attention had been fixed on an e-mail message on her computer monitor up to that point. Now she gazed at me over her glasses like some wise old woman. With her twenty-five-year-old baby face and body I would have killed for a decade earlier, the look wasn't convincing. "For Herb or me?"

"Does it matter?"

"If it's Herb, I'll dig my dad's old starter pistol out of the basement for you."

"No thanks. If I'm going to do this disgruntled employee thing up right, I should have an assault rifle. And I wouldn't start with peons like you and Herb. I'd open up on Burt first. Use up a whole ammo cartridge on him and his fancy office." Want to hear the scary part? I wasn't kidding, folks. My imagination spent the better part of each workday iron-ing out the details.

"Do me a favor," Denise said, swivelling back to her e-mail. "The morning you reach into your closet and pull out jungle fatigues instead of a business suit, call me so I can take a sick day."

"Can't. They'd make you an accessory."

"In that case, I want matching fatigues. Designer. Some-thing showing cleavage and leg, you know?"

"We'd look like Charlie's Angels."

"Who?"

She was serious. I'd always expected a generation gap when and if I ever had kids, but it gets you in the gut when it happens with a co-worker. For Denise, Jaclyn Smith was simply a name on K-Mart clothes. "Sorry. Before you were born."

"What was it like back then, living in caves? Eating dinosaur McNuggets?"

The rubber band soared straight and true this time, halving the four inches between Denise's screen and nose.

She didn't even flinch. "Call me crazy, but something tells me it's a good thing it's Friday and you're on vacation next week. Where'd you say you're going?"

"Virginia."

"What's there? A beach or something?"

Beaches are where people in our office go on vacation: the Jersey Shore, or if you managed to save a few bucks, a coast with white sand and water sans hospital waste. Mexico, Bermuda, the Caribbean. If you had kids, you did Disney World. California and Hawaii were also acceptable. Any other state drew frowns of puzzlement unless it had a beach, famous golf course, or relatives you couldn't get out of visiting.

I hate travelling alone, so on my off-time, I usually hole up in my apartment with take-out food and a stack of videos. The only reason I was headed for Virginia this time was that I'd received a bizarre letter from one Joel Peyton, Attorney-at-Law, saying a ninety-one-year-old woman named Magnolia Shelby was leaving me her land. The catch was, I had to go stay with her during the last week of April and first week of May.

Since I didn't know anyone named Shelby, nor had ever heard my parents mention the name or anyone else in Virginia, I'd checked the letter out, phoning Mr. Peyton to ascertain the size, situation, and certainty of the bequest. A couple hundred acres. Non-swampland, in fact prime real estate, already surrounded by development. Peyton assured me old Magnolia wasn't loony, either in the senile or psycho sense. She'd written the will thirty years earlier, and it'd taken that long to track me down. He refused to discuss the "Why Me?" aspect of it, but he did say this Shelby woman had no relations who'd contest her will and no intention of changing her mind. Neither was she anywhere near her deathbed.

Still, I could put up with even *this* job another ten years if the sale of two hundred acres could mean early retirement.

All I had to do, apparently, was go suck up to the woman. What the hell?

So I'd put in for the vacation time. Burt, control-bastard that he is, refused to let me have both weeks off. Having foreseen this possible snag, I'd asked Mr. Peyton which days were most crucial. I put in again, this time for April twenty-ninth through May fifth. Burt, on one of his worst omnipotent-being jags yet, insisted he had a critical project due the first of May, but he'd let me take the week of the fourth, out of the decency of his heart. The project, I'd discovered yesterday, turned out to be a simple client list. I could have run it Tuesday afternoon. Or in the extreme unlikelihood that we signed on another client in two days, Denise could have run the list without me.

More incentive for early retirement. Or the jungle fatigue option. Whichever.

Luckily, Mr. Peyton had been very understanding.

But, for obvious reasons, I hadn't told Denise or anyone else about this deal. It could still fall through, making me look gullibly stupid.

"Sure it's got a beach," I said. "Virginia Beach."

Denise nodded her approval. "Send me a postcard. You know the kind. Guys in bathing suits. Lots of tush."

⇲ 2 ⇱

I hate driving. Twelve years of rush hour has pretty much sapped the fight out of me. You'll notice, people with kids can drive anywhere. They become experts in the fine arts of impatience and intolerance. Me? One hour on an interstate and the temptation to close my eyes and whimper is overpowering. So one of my stipulations was for someone to meet me at the nearest Amtrak station. Peyton had put a round-trip ticket to Fredericksburg in the next day's mail.

So, on the morning of May fourth, as I exited Fredericksburg station, I expected to see someone holding a card with my name on it. What I didn't expect was the someone himself. Build-wise, he could have been the Incredible Hulk's stunt double, except with red hair, matching mustache, and no green skin. His expression was more stoic than the Hulk's, but his body language, as he leaned against an old white Ford Escort, said he'd rather be swimming in shark-infested waters—after slitting his wrists.

When I dropped my suitcase before him, the look changed to disbelief. "*You're* Patricia M—"

"Montella." I couldn't handle a Southern accent mangling it this early on.

"Mun-*del*-la?" he aped in a fair imitation of the dialect, though he still looked skeptical.

"What? Do I have to show ID?"

"No, I just didn't think you'd look so . . . so . . ."

Had he been rooting around for a compliment, I would have let him take his time. After all, he wasn't hard to look at, in a raw physical-power kind of way. Admittedly, I was basing this solely on his arm and neck muscles. He might have been all flab under the loose, double-extra-large polo he wore. I wasn't about to ask him to take it off so I could check. Not when the tone of his voice, on searching for words to describe me, made it obvious that "beautiful" and "alluring" weren't even remote likelihoods. "Didn't think I'd look so *what?*"

He shrugged. "Italian, I guess."

"The last name didn't give you a clue?" Was this some antebellum prejudice against short, dark people? I hoped it was, for his own good, because if he was being personal, referring to, say, my hips, I intended to make him regret it. "I take it you're not Mr. Peyton?"

"Joel?" A smug grin crept onto his face and a ounce of sarcasm into his voice. "Why, I'm nothing but your chauffeur, Miss Mun-*del*-la. Fitzhugh Lee, ma'am, at your service."

Fine one to make fun of my name. His was backwards. Tempted as I was to point that out, I didn't want to be stranded, so I kept my mouth shut and let him take my luggage. As he moved away from the car door, I noticed the insignia he'd been obstructing. "U.S. Mail?"

"When I'm not driving around important visitors such as yourself, they let me work at the post office."

"Really?" For a moment, a very *brief* moment, I wondered if he might be a kindred soul. "Is it true what you hear about postal workers?"

He tossed my suitcase carelessly into the hatchback. "What would that be?"

"Ever feel like bringing a gun into work and shooting everyone?" I enjoyed the color that brought into his face.

"Since I'm the only one manning the little satellite office at Bell Run, I can honestly say no, that particular urge has never come over me." He glanced warily down at my bag as if he now suspected a bomb, but he slammed the hatch shut and motioned me into the passenger seat.

* * *

On first impression, Route 3 west of Fredericksburg seemed a clone of my daily commute through King of Prussia: shopping malls, motels, restaurants of the fast and slow ilks, badly timed stoplights, and way too much traffic. Virginia drivers, however, actually knew how to use turn signals, and more than one politely made room when the Escort changed lanes. Very little predatory fervor whatsoever, though they seemed to have a regular lust for vanity plates.

My driver, looking cramped like big men do in small cars, at first resisted all my attempts to get him talking and spill his guts about why I was here. So I was surprised when he suddenly asked, in a tone of near friendliness, even genuine interest, "What exactly do you do, Miss Montella?"

"I'm a business analyst." My standard, glib reply. True, this was my official title, but it meant absolutely nothing. I did mindless office work for mindless people. The only thing I analyzed each day was my motivation for not quitting. Minimal health-care benefits and a minimal salary, to be specific.

"Which company?"

"Dawkins-Greenway. You've probably never heard of them."

"They make office furniture, don't they?" It wasn't a question. He could have easily said "They make toxic waste" in the same tone of voice.

"Right. That's them."

"Executive furniture. Big, fancy, polished-wood desks, tables, credenzas. High-back chairs wide enough for two people. Cutting down trees to build up egos."

During my employee orientation, while watching a propaganda video about D-G's exclusive product line, that same thought had occurred to me, in almost the same words. After I made the first payment on my student loan with my first paycheck, my conscience had shut up. It snickered now, piping in with a muffled "told you so." Time to change the subject. "Do you know Magnolia Shelby?"

"Everyone in this part of Virginia knows Miss Maggie." Said as if I should know her too.

Evidently a notorious oddball. Swell. "What's she like?"

"If you're looking to prepare yourself, you're probably too late." He chuckled to himself, as if they were all playing some elaborate joke which I was falling for completely.

Not that I was paranoid or anything. "Too late?"

"Joel should have told you to get plenty of rest. Miss Maggie'll keep you hopping."

I conjured up a bedridden hypochondriac, making me her slave. Well, I'd come to suck up. If that meant waiting hand and foot on the woman for a week, so be it. "I don't mind helping her around the house. At her age—"

More laughter, louder, not unpleasant, but it made the car shake a little. "Don't mention the word 'age' to her, whatever you do. What do you know about the Civil War?"

I could tell he didn't want the recitation of the Gettysburg Address I'd memorized in fourth grade. Not that I could have spit out more than ten words now anyway. "Like what?"

"Ever been to a battlefield?"

"Gettysburg." A field trip as part of that same fourth-grade unit. I recalled seeing a gigantic map with little lights all over it, then riding around on a bus all afternoon, accompanied by the deadly dull drone of a pre-recorded tour guide. My most vivid memory was the stone monuments—what had seemed like thousands of them, every size and shape—dotting the landscape helter-skelter all along the route. On the test, I'd said that Gettysburg was a big cemetery. My teacher had thought I meant the National Cemetery, where Lincoln made his famous speech, but I'd meant the whole battlefield. That's what the place had looked like.

"You realize you're on a battlefield now?"

I'd tuned out the scenery. Swiftly blinking it back into focus, I expected to see cannon lining the road. All I spotted were real-estate offices. Doing a quick brain scan, I tried to wring out any bit of data leftover from the *North and*

South miniseries I'd seen years ago. Guess I'd been too busy salivating over Patrick Swayze to absorb much history.

"I'll give you a hint. Salem Church is coming up on our left. A shame you missed the reenactment yesterday. They do it Saturdays and Sundays now, regardless of when the battle really was. Too many of the volunteers have regular jobs."

If the name or building had been featured in the miniseries, I must have been in the kitchen getting a snack at the time. Didn't look like a church at all. No steeple. More like a big brick schoolhouse, or like the Quaker meetinghouses back home. Thinking I could sneak another hint, I asked, "When exactly was the battle?"

"Salem Church was May 3 and 4—1863." This last was added to show he knew I was totally ignorant. "But this skirmish was only a small part of the Chancellorsville campaign—April 27 through May 6."

"So that's why Miss Shelby wanted me here last week?"

"She did? I didn't know that." He chuckled again but seemed to think better of it mid-snicker. His brow creased in thought. "Likely. Chancellorsville or—ever heard of The Wilderness?"

Could you resist a straight line like that? "Where the buffalo roam and the deer and the antelope play?"

The only reward for my wit was a patronizing smile. "That's where you're headed."

"Oh, the name of a town." A religious name, no doubt, like some of the Amish towns back in Pennsylvania: Paradise, Lebanon, Mount Joy. Or maybe a literal description. This part of the country had to have been wilderness at one time, back when John Smith was making eyes at Pocahontas.

"No, not a town," he said, crushing what I thought were brilliant deductions. "Not yet, anyway. I mean the battle."

I revised my conception of Magnolia Shelby. A matron of the Old South, straight out of *Gone with the Wind*. Black high-necked gown à la Queen Victoria. Confederate Battle

Flag over fireplace. "Dixie" playing interminably on an antique, wind-up music box. Probably still hadn't heard who won.

But hey, if the old bat wanted to relive her favorite battles, I'd hold her hand on the sidelines and cheer on the Rebels.

As the roadside became less commercial with each mile, my driver returned to his persona of the strong, silently rude type. He roused himself just once, lifting a forefinger from the steering wheel to point out a grassy lot behind a zigzag rail fence on our right. Low stacks of bricks were visible between two trees.

"That's where Chancellorsville Inn used to stand."

I opted for a polite, generic, "Oh, yeah?"

He might have been offended by my indifference because he didn't speak again until I asked him a question. We'd turned off the main road, passing under a canopy of tall trees. The grove continued along on the left while the right side boasted one of those new upscale housing developments, complete with impressive monolithic entrance. Brass letters on black stone spelled out BELL RUN.

Hence my question. "This where your post office is?"

"Not inside." The snide utterance of a servant not permitted to eat in the dining room, who'd rather barf than do so anyway. "Let me show you the real Bell Run."

He made an abrupt left down a bank. Three full, frantic heartbeats later I realized we weren't careening out of control but were actually on a road. A very narrow road, one car wide. I could have reached out and touched the tree trunks in passing. A wild jungle of vines wove itself between trees and undergrowth, seeming as ominous and animate as any evil *Star Trek* alien. I visualized the vines twisting about the car, choking the life from us, digesting us slowly, burping up only the oil filter before settling down to await another victim.

The greenery parted slightly and, with a hollow-sounding thump followed by an agonizing groan, the Escort came to a stop. Both sounds had been produced by an unsafe-looking wooden bridge, now directly beneath us. Three feet beneath that was a shallow, gurgling, swirling creek.

"Bell Run." He put the car in park and yanked on the brake. "Not much now, but I've known her to surge up over this bridge in a good downpour."

My increasing claustrophobia from the trees, his talk of flash floods, the chronic groaning of the planks, and a new realization—that this was a very lonely spot to be marooned with a complete, not to mention very large, stranger—were all playing havoc with my panic button. I couldn't suppress the tell-tale squeak in my voice when I asked, "How much further to Miss Shelby's?"

"We're here."

"Here?" Not being a Stephen King fan, I didn't have a field of reference, but I was sure this was where the villain switches personalities as he takes a meat cleaver from under the car seat.

"On her property. Everything this side of the road." He was eyeing me with speculation, probably deciding whether to rape me or kill me, or in which order to do both. "So, what do you think?"

I was thinking there was nothing outside my door but a three-foot drop into shin-deep water. I was cursing myself for wearing heels instead of sneakers. I was wondering how I could go so totally blank on the words to the Hail Mary when the nuns in catechism class had made me repeat it ad nauseam for four years straight. "I think we shouldn't keep Miss Shelby waiting."

Having seen once on the news how you shouldn't look an attacker in the eye, my own were focused straight ahead, so I only heard his reaction: half grunt, half snort, conveying the sentiment that I'd lived up to every one of his predictions.

I hoped that was good.

He released the parking brake as I released the breath I was holding. "It'll be rough going from here on."

The road became gravel just beyond the bridge, actually seeming to narrow as we bumped and skidded our way up the incline. The undergrowth, now uninhibited by mac-adam, had sent long tentacles of green snaking across the path. Wouldn't have surprised me to hear screams as we ran over them.

That we were headed deeper into this forest concerned me no small amount, though, after sneaking a glance at my companion, I relaxed a little. His demeanor was more that of a mailman delivering a gift package of Washington ap-ples rerouted via South America and a month past ripe. I almost wanted to apologize. For what, I had no idea.

Around the next bend, the woods seemed to have taken a giant step back, letting blissful sunlight radiate all the way down to the road. Optimistically it could be called a clear-ing. We turned onto a dirt pull-off, stopping under a tall shade tree saturated with pale greenish-yellow flowers as big as grapefruits.

"This is it." He cut the ignition and got out before I could ask, What was it?

I saw the house then, peeking out from behind the tree. Not the Tara I'd envisioned. More like John-Boy Walton's farmhouse, except smaller, or it seemed smaller within this setting. An H.O. house in a Lionel-scale forest.

What drew my attention to the house was the woman who banged through the porch screen door. Her T-shirt and sweatpants matched the tree's blossoms. She was elderly, yes, but not feeble or doddering or any of the other adjec-tives that came to mind on hearing her age. She moved stiffly, a little bent over, taking each of the three porch steps right-foot first, clutching the railing, but none of that slowed her down. Before I could close my car door, she'd grabbed my shoulders and spun me around.

We were about the same height, though I was willing to bet she'd been a good head taller in her youth. The hands that held my arms were gnarled with arthritis but felt in-credibly strong. Her eyes, sunken deep into her skull, glowed with green fire as they traveled over every inch of me.

"Not what you expected, Miss Maggie?" Fitzhugh Lee came up beside me, toting my suitcase, a cynical grin stretching his mouth wide.

"I'm not so much a fool as you think, Hugh." Her voice matched the rest of her, sharp, raspy, full of energy, but her mild accent stole away the edge, leaving the possibility—remote as it seemed—of humor.

Her grip eased as her gaze ran one final audit of me. "Joel was supposed to tell you to bring comfortable clothes."

"I did," I said hastily. "In the suitcase." I'd worn my navy-blue suit and ruffly ivory blouse to make a good first impression. The standard job interview outfit, recommended by *Business Week* and the *Wall Street Journal*. Then again, though I'd worn the suit to eight interviews in the past half year, I was still doing time at Dawkins-Greenway.

"Bring her luggage up to the back bedroom, Hugh. She has to change before we can get started."

"I'll take it myself." I was afraid he'd spout off some b.s. about Southern chivalry, but he surrendered the bag almost gratefully. Anxious to get away from me, I supposed.

My host called after me as I walked toward the house. "Wear long pants, a light color if you have 'em. Helps keep the ticks off you."

Not a house nor a fence, not a tree was to be seen for miles, where once all had been cultivated farmland, or richly wooded country. Here and there, a stack of chimneys or a broken cistern marked the site of a former homestead, but every landmark had been destroyed.

One of General Grant's aides, on seeing Virginia—1864

MAY 4, 1864—CLARK'S MOUNTAIN, VIRGINIA

I hadn't slept a night through in nearly eighteen months but was surprised to find this same condition in my fellow infantrymen. I'd supposed a body got used to war. In a way, it does. If a barn mouse knows an old tabby's sharing his territory, he doesn't stop living. Comes out to forage his supper same as before, only he learns to keep watching over his shoulder. These soldiers are like that, every mortal fiber of their beings constantly at the ready, looking over their shoulders for Death Himself.

We all spent this night watching the signal fire flare up on Clark's Mountain summit. The Yanks were on the move for sure, though no one cared to speculate which way. We'd be marching at them in good time. No need to prophesy how soon either. Orders had come through day before yesterday to pack up everything we couldn't carry, to be sent for storage in Richmond. I'd had nothing but some provisions rolled in a blanket and my rifle when I came into camp. My blackberry hunting friend—Cobb was his name—had procured me a haversack for my food and ammunition, and a canteen. Rummaged, no doubt, from the bodies of those past thirst or want.

At daybreak, we could make out the roads north of the river choked with bluecoats, dust rising up behind in great brown clouds. They were parading downriver, toward the same fords that half a year earlier had served as their access to Mine Run, and a half year before that, Chancellorsville. This time they brought their supply wagons, white muslin covers brightening in the sunlight as it nudged aside the morning mist.

A year ago on this side of the river, they'd found fields of tender young sprouts, a thriving grist mill, and a stately brick dwelling where their officers had, uninvited, made their quarters.

Now they'd find only the burnt ruins of my home and barren expanse of our farm. Nothing to pillage or set torch to this time but the paltry wood crosses of our family plot.

3

After the air-conditioned train and car, I hadn't realized how warm Virginia was until I lugged my suitcase up the stairs. The upper landing was a square floor of yellowed hardwood surrounded by one bathroom and three bedroom doors, all of which were open. A pleasant cross-breeze cooled the sweat on my forehead.

The back room was furnished with odd pieces from different sets. Art Deco desk in a dark walnut veneer. Antique colonial nightstand, cherry wood, good workmanship. Simple maple dresser with plain wooden drawer handles, probably homemade. Hung above the dresser was a mirror in a wicker frame. The bed was modern, queen-sized, with a perfectly flat mattress—none of the hills and valleys my ancient Beauty Rest boasted. I sat down, bouncing to test it out. Good and firm; in fact, it felt brand new. At least I'd sleep well.

I couldn't waste any more time exploring. Miss Shelby obviously had an agenda for me. Gardening came to mind, considering her comments.

I crossed to the nearest window. The back of the house was much like the front with only a mowed strip of—no, it couldn't be called lawn. A weed-fest of dandelions, clover, and unidentifiables created a carpet of color almost all the way to the roots of the trees. But no garden. Too bad, I liked gardening. One of my happiest memories was helping my dad each summer. We'd grown tomatoes, eggplants, green peppers. He'd always let me plant the circle of marigolds around the basil to keep out pests.

Now, come April each year, I yearn to be outside getting dirt under my fingernails, and hate apartment living all the more.

Figuring I was in for *some* sort of outside work, I donned jeans and sneakers. The top was a major decision, but I finally chose a white, long-sleeve button-down, despite the heat. The sleeves could be rolled up for now, down if I encountered any poison ivy.

I found my host going through her mail at a table in the lower hall. She was reading a letter intently, paper practically touching her nose, though she wore reading glasses. When she heard me on the steps, both letter and glasses went into the table's single drawer before she turned to inspect me once more.

"Sensible," she said, giving my clothes a nod of approval. "Just your hair is all."

My hair was short, collar-length. What'd she want me to do? Shave my head?

Toddling over to a closet beneath the stairs, she pulled out two wide-brimmed straw hats and tossed one to me. "Keeps the sun off your neck and the skeeters out of your hair."

As she spoke, she was already moving toward the back of the house. I followed her through an old-fashioned kitchen as big as half my apartment, then out the back screen door. To my dismay, she made straight for what I'd begun mentally calling "the Forest of No Return."

I ran to catch up—had to, she walked that fast. She plunged right into the profuse undergrowth, and miraculously, it seemed to know her and part before her.

That's when I saw the trail, little wider than a shoe width, double A at that. After the first vine sent tiny needles into my forearm, I rolled down my sleeves and stuck my hands in my pockets in self-defense. "Miss Shelby?"

"Heavens, don't call me that. I taught junior high for over forty years. Still get shell-shock every time I hear 'Miz Shelby.' "

"What should I call you then?"

She shrugged. "Magnolia, Maggie, whatever."

"The man who drove me called you Miss Maggie."

"Hugh's one of my former students. Never could get him to drop the Miss. Use it if it makes you feel better. Or you could call me Mary. My christened name. Hardly anyone knows it, except Joel since it's my legal name, too. Wouldn't mind *you* calling me Mary. Only when we're alone, though."

"Why me? I mean, Mr. Peyton said—"

She stopped walking abruptly and swung around. "Can't tell you. Not yet. Joel says to wait until you sign the papers. He'll be over with them tonight." Again she canvassed me, toe to head, sighing when she reached my nose. "Say your name for me."

"Patricia Montella."

She repeated it, sounding as Italian as my grandmother. "Pretty name. Melodic. You prefer Patricia?"

I shook my head. "Pat."

"Suits you." Turning her back on me with a nod, she resumed her brisk pace.

Not ready to give up, I tried a roundabout approach to my mysterious benefactor. "How'd you come to be named Magnolia?"

She laughed. "My granddaddy called me that because I loved to climb that old cucumber magnolia in front of the house."

"You said you taught junior high. What subject?"

"History." As she said it, we stepped out of the forest, into another semi-clearing.

Before us rose a mass of vines, in places twice my height and three times as wide as the farmhouse we'd come from. I supposed that association made me say, "This was a house, wasn't it?"

Her eyes widened in surprise. "Beats me how you could tell. Burned during the Chancellorsville battle. Most of the original bricks have been hidden by this jungle long as I can remember."

I was barely listening. A powerful feeling had come over

me, almost as if those long-concealed bricks had suddenly sat up and greeted me. And the single word that came into my mind, and stuck there, was "home."

"Come on." She was walking along a mowed path encircling the ruin. "Something else I need to show you."

Only too anxious to leave, I hurried after her, telling myself it was nothing but a case of nerves. Early PMS. Bad cream cheese on the bagel I ate on the train. But I warily kept the old house in the corner of my vision.

We reentered the forest on the opposite side, wading through another sea of brambles until the ground sloped downward. Through a break in the tree branches, water shimmered blue-green in the sunlight.

"That's the Rapidan down below. North border of the property." Another trail intersected ours, and Miss Maggie veered off to the right onto it, following the top of the ridge. We came to a hip-high stone enclosure, inside which were five neatly tended graves.

"Your family?" I asked, marvelling how the forest seemed to crouch outside the wall, ready to rush in should it disappear.

"Not mine." She entered the enclosure through a small gap on the river side. "My granddaddy brought me here when I started asking questions. 'Who lived in that house back there?' 'Why did they go away?' 'Where were they now?' He said I was the only one in our family who cared about the past the way he did. So he showed me these graves. The Bell family. All killed during the Civil War."

Standing at the gateway, my back toward the river, I felt exposed. The forest was getting to me, I presumed, but the rationale didn't keep me from scurrying over to Miss Maggie's side.

"When Granddaddy decided to settle here after the war, he found rotted wooden crosses on this spot with only names and dates of death carved into them. He replaced them with stones and built this wall. Said it was the least he could do for the family for taking over their land."

I could picture those crosses vividly, the small family

plot muddy and unkempt, wood splinters biting into the hands of the carver. Balling my own hands into fists, I diverted my attention by studying the present graves. Having buried both parents in the last decade, I knew something about tombstones. Though these had been styled after the kind you see in old cemeteries, they were polished granite, inscribed by machine, I was sure. "These stones aren't that old."

"Had these put here myself, after I traced the birth and death records. Took me a long time to find out this much."

The two graves in front, by their birth dates, must have been the parents.

Armstead Bell
BORN 1818   DIED DEC. 1862
MORTALLY WOUNDED AT MARYE'S HEIGHTS
FREDERICKSBURG

Clara Shackleford Bell
BORN 1823   DIED MAY 1863
KILLED BY FIRE IN HER OWN HOME
DURING THE BATTLE OF CHANCELLORSVILLE

In the shadow of these were three children:

Evan Bell
BORN 1843   DIED AUG. 1862
KILLED AT BRISTOE STATION
NEAR MANASSAS

Lane Bell
BORN 1841   DIED SEP. 1863
MORTALLY WOUNDED ON CULP'S HILL
GETTYSBURG—JULY 1863

Julia Bell
BORN 1845   DIED NOV. 1863

Miss Maggie walked over and laid a hand on this last stone. "Still haven't found out much about Julia. No death certificate. No mention in the local papers or church records about a funeral. Granddaddy said she must have been buried in a hurry—no coffin and only a few feet down. Two years of winter rains had brought her bones part way out of the ground again. He made her a pine box and buried her proper. But he said she had a hole in her skull, so we know she didn't die naturally. If the date of death's correct, could be she caught a stray bullet in the Mine Run Campaign. Just a guess though. Didn't seem right to put it in stone."

"Mine Run? Another battle?" I was feeling dazed, my imagination working overtime, conjuring up images worse than anything on network news. At least they give you the "following contains graphic footage" warning. My brain wasn't so considerate. I gave in to the weakness in my knees and sat down on the wall.

"What's wrong?" Miss Maggie's voice snapped me back to the present.

"It's the heat." Nothing could be further from the truth. There were goosebumps all over me. I sternly reminded myself what I was doing here. "Please go on. It's interesting. I don't know much about the Civil War."

She smiled and shook her head. "After forty years of teaching, I know brown-nosing when I hear it, Pat."

"But I didn't mean—"

"Don't think you were brought here to indulge an old woman's passion for her favorite subject." That struck her as funny and she cackled loudly. "All right, maybe you were. But before this land becomes yours, I intend to teach you everything I know about it."

That's when it hit me. This godforsaken forest, that little farmhouse, the vine-covered ruin, these five melancholy, nightmare-inducing graves—this was my legacy. What had I expected? Cleared lots, already subdivided, with sewage and water? "I'm listening."

"Stand up and face the river."

I did, wishing I could see her out of the back of my head.

"Now, envision yourself in the center of a big clock, facing twelve. Turn to face one o'clock. Right there, perfect. If you walk in a straight line, you'll reach Washington, D.C. after about ninety miles. And you're asking yourself, why would you want to?"

Of course I was, but I made myself play along, reaching for the mindset of a nineteenth-century Virginian. "Because that's where Abraham Lincoln is?"

She clapped. "A-plus, Miss Montella. Now spin around to face six o'clock. If you walk about seventy miles, you'll reach Richmond, where Jefferson Davis is. Federal capital one way, Confederate capital the other, and us here, almost smack dab in between. Know how many times the North tried to advance on Richmond?"

I shook my head, but she wasn't waiting for an answer.

"Seven times! Under seven different commanders. The last three, the Federals forded the Rapidan right near here and marched over Bell Run. Three times in little more than one year! Chancellorsville on April 29, 1863, Mine Run in November, and finally, the Wilderness campaign on May 4, 1864."

"May fourth? That's today. And April twenty-ninth was the date you originally wanted me here."

"Not that anniversaries matter. Time of year's more important." Miss Maggie spun me around to face the river again. "If you'd been standing right here the night of April 29, 1863, you could have looked up river and down, and seen about forty thousand Federal troops. . . . Ever seen forty thousand people in one place before?"

"I went to a rock concert at Vet Stadium once."

"Close enough. Picture that many trying to wade across. After a season of rain and thaw, the river was running swift, chest deep and icy. All their possessions were stuck on a bundle on the tip of their bayonets. Yet I don't believe the Bell family, if any of them witnessed the crossing, would've felt much sympathy."

My darned imagination called up a film clip of it, obligingly reducing the trees to stumps so I'd have an unobstructed view. "They'd have laughed themselves silly every time a soldier fell in."

"Think so?" Miss Maggie also had her eyes trained on the river, but she was frowning.

I realized I was, too. Scowling, feeling oddly violated, as if an army were actually invading my land. "And they'd be angry . . . and . . . and frightened, most of all."

Miss Maggie nodded. "Same way during Mine Run, only twice as many troops. That battle didn't amount to much . . . the Confederates were too well fortified, so the Union called off the main attack. Wilderness was different, though. Morning of May fourth, the Federals built pontoon bridges. No wading this time. They sent over the whole army, one hundred and fifty thousand men. Artillery and supplies drawn by more than fifty thousand horses and mules. Why, the Yankees had more mustered on four legs than the South had on two."

I shuddered, instinctively ready to flee back through the woods.

But no army crossed the river. The only one invading this place today was me. And back then, no one was left alive on this farm to care.

I said as much, more to put myself in perspective than anything else.

Miss Maggie shook her head. "Well, then. Who buried Julia? Who carved her cross?"

I shrugged. "A neighbor?"

"Possible. But she had another brother. Gabriel. Would have been about fourteen years old at the time."

After her dramatic pronouncement, Miss Maggie suggested we go back to the house for lunch. Like a laundry-detergent ad right after the final suspenseful chord of a soap opera. Talk about anticlimactic.

Maybe she expected me to ask questions. Not that I knew what to ask. Or maybe she thought I needed time to ruminate. Whatever, she remained silent and walked slower on our return trip.

I *was* ruminating, sort of. Alternately thinking things like, "History's not so bad. I lucked out. She could have been a biology teacher," or "Why couldn't I win the lottery instead?" or "This forest shouldn't give me the willies. It's better than Burt's office on a good day."

When I caught myself thinking, "As if my life isn't complicated enough," I stopped ruminating. What complications? I had no kids, no family, no mortgage, no man even on a temporary basis at present—Mr. Right was taking his good old time knocking at my door—and no health problems. I was the most complication-free person in America. All I had was a job I hated and, far from making things worse, my present circumstance should eventually provide me a means of escape.

As we reached the farmhouse's backyard, Miss Maggie dropped back, slipping her arthritic fingers into the crook of my elbow. "Just how much of an Italian are you, Pat?"

The question, out of left field, caught me unawares. "My father's whole family, and on my mother's side—"

"No, not that. I already know your family tree."

"Did you know my parents? Is that why—"

Shaking her head, she patted my arm with her other hand. "Patience. I will say that I didn't simply pick your name from a hat. I know quite a bit about your background. What I don't know is . . . can you make tomato sauce from scratch?" She sounded so hopeful.

"I used to watch my grandmother make it but—"

Miss Maggie closed her eyes against the blow. "Please don't tell me you eat the jarred stuff."

"No. I compromise. Canned tomatoes and paste, dried basil and—"

"Perfect!" Squeezing my arm tighter, she stepped up her pace, practically dragging me to the kitchen. "Pasta tonight. Joel needs fattening up anyhow. Oh, Pat, you don't know how much I *love* Italian food."

I was only too happy to oblige. Cooking's my favorite hobby. After a full day at D-G, it's pure therapy. If I didn't spend an hour a night creating something, even if it's only a concoction of leftovers, I surely would have donned those jungle fatigues long ago.

We reached the back porch in time to see a young woman tiptoe around the side of the house. She was on her toes in order to keep her two-inch spiked heels from sinking in the loose dirt. The fingertips of her right hand gingerly prodded the clapboards to maintain her balance. She reminded me a little of Denise, maybe a couple years older, but the same enviable build and brassy shade of blond hair. And she was wearing a navy blue business suit, giving me a taste for how out of place I must have appeared earlier.

"Miz Shelby! Have I caught you at a bad time?" Her voice oozed molasses, and she punctuated the question with a beauty contestant paste-up smile.

"Why no, Flora, honey," Miss Maggie oozed right back. "Any social visit from you couldn't possibly be at a bad time." There was hidden meaning in it, but I didn't own the proper decoder ring.

"Flora Shifflett." Stepping onto the porch, she extended her hand palm down, as if I should kiss her ring. She was wearing a beaut, too—a cranberry-sized ruby. "Miz Shelby was my favorite teacher in school."

Something about the whole scene made me want to hook my thumbs behind my suspenders and rock back on my heels with an amicable, "You don't say!" In the absence of suspenders and a certain amount of gall on my part, at least around strangers, I merely shook her hand and said my name.

"You're not from around here." Said with exuberant delight. Was she delighted at her own deduction? Or was there something so horribly wrong with the natives that any outsider was welcomed with open arms?

"Pennsylvania," I mumbled. "Near Philadelphia."

Miss Maggie pinched my arm in warning. "Pat's an old friend of the family, come to visit for a few days."

"How nice for you." Whether Flora meant me or my host was unclear, but "nice" was stressed a little too potently. "I can't stay long, Miz Shelby, much as I'd love a leisurely chat, but I wanted to let you know, still *another* buyer has come forward, inquiring about your property."

"I trust you told this one the same thing I had you tell the other two?"

Flora's generous smile broadened. "Having your best interests at heart, Miz Shelby, I felt I should come see you personally about it, before definitely turning down the offer."

"So *thoughtful* of you, Flora, as always, but I won't be changing my mind. Too bad you can't stay. Pat'll walk you around to your car." She released my arm, nudging me off the porch the way my mom used to nudge me toward eligible men at my cousins' weddings.

With two sets of eyes on me, Flora's blue, revelling in her good fortune, and Miss Maggie's green, the leer teachers use when announcing a pop quiz, I agreed readily. I'd need to be in touch with Flora and her chums sometime in the future. A little networking wouldn't hurt.

Flora tiptoed back along the side of the house, me in her wake, rolling my sleeves up again, now that I was under the hot sun once more. As soon as we were out of earshot of the porch, Flora turned her polished smile my way. "Miz Shelby's so *amazing,* don't you think? Living out here alone at her age?"

Considering Miss Maggie had more than a half century on me, my own amazement stemmed from the fact that she was living at all. Flora's tone, however, was one of condescension, making me defensive. "She seems more than capable of taking care of herself."

"Oh, she is, honey, don't you worry. But as an old friend of the Shelbys, you already know that."

Caught in the web again. "Actually, it's the other way around. Miss Maggie's an old friend of the Montellas."

"Really? She never mentioned knowing anyone in Pennsylvania."

I suspected Miss Maggie mentioned as little as possible to Flora Shifflett, or anyone else for that matter. We reached Flora's car, a recent-looking Mercedes in mourning-dove grey. "The real estate business must be booming."

Flora caressed the fender possessively before opening

her driver door. "The market's ripe for development. Good interest rates."

"Guess that was a developer asking about this place?"

"You can bet on it." She leaned both arms on the top of the car door, like a neighbor about to impart juicy gossip. "Look, honey, we're not fooling each other. All of Stoke County knows Miz Shelby's bent on leaving this property to some out-of-state stranger. Namely you. Maybe I'm the first to come by and check you out, but there'll be others. Hell, you'll be a regular tourist attraction while you're here. All I want to know is, once you get your hands on the place, are you putting it on the market?"

"*If* Miss Maggie leaves it to me," for I still couldn't believe anything good in life was that certain, "yes. I have every intention of selling. To the highest bidder."

The smile that took over her face now was genuine, if thoroughly predatory. "You're a businesswoman. I can appreciate that. Here, take my card. 'Course, like I said, the current market's hot, but even if the economy sags before you're ready, you won't suffer. This area's a developer's dream: right outside Fredericksburg, halfway between D.C. and Richmond. It's turning into Suburb City for all those top management wannabe types. I'll get you a real handsome price."

She left me there, holding her card, as she circled the car around me on the pullout and drove back down the dirt road, using slow prudence to keep that new German suspension from getting nicked.

Lost in thought, I walked after her as far as the edge of the clearing. Her "top management wannabe" line had hit a nerve. Only last month, Burt had bought a house way out in Lancaster County, a big rambling villa for his Barbie doll wife and two-point-seven rug rats. A house like that, one half hour closer to work, would have cost him three times as much.

I'd have the chance to make big bucks off ambitious jerks like Burt. My revenge-seeking dark side giggled with glee. Better than an M-16 any day.

Stonewall Jackson...was the true type of all great soldiers. He did not value human life where he had an object to accomplish. He could order men to their death as a matter of course. Hence, while he was alive, there was more pride than truth in the talk of his soldiers' love for him.

General Lawton, as told by Mary Chestnut—1863

MAY 4, 1864—CLARK'S MOUNTAIN

"If they never intended to give us sufficient time to cook three-days' rations, why order it at all?" The command to fall in had come in the midst of our baking, and I watched the camp hustle to obey. Cooking fires were snuffed out, steamy dough shoved into haversacks, blankets and tent flies rolled and slung over shoulders.

"This is how it always is," Cobb said. "Five-months' leisure, then one hour to do everything. Stow your meal for now, Gabe. We'll get respite before the day's out. Mebbe."

The half-baked wheat paste in my haversack felt uncomfortably warm against my hip. "Seems to me those generals would know better if they did their own cooking."

"Wouldn't that be something?" Cobb chuckled merrily. "Fancy Dick Ewell hobbling about on his one leg, waving a stirring spoon. Or Marse Robert hisself, using one long grey coattail to pick up a hot kettle."

"They're men. Put their trousers on each day like anyone else."

Cobb, frowning now beneath his whiskers, shook his head. "They's different. Me? I'm ready to give my life for the cause. Been ready three years now. But if it came to making someone else do it—ordering a thousand men on the right to die so a hundred men on the left succeed? Not a job I'd ever want."

That's what I couldn't fathom. How could these generals decree a battle won when ten thousand lay dead on the field? Killed, while they sat up high and mighty on their steeds, far back from the action, electing who would act as sacrifice to the god of war that day.

Yet men follow them, eagerly, like—I could think of no parallel in nature. Animals can be lured, fooled, but will not go willingly to their deaths. They have no high ideals.

Except family. Didn't I, only the other day, watch a blue jay attack a turkey vulture when the larger bird flew too near the jay's nest?

"Hey, you Virginians!" called a Georgian as General Early's division filed past. "Y'all going to miss the cotillion if you don't hurry yourselves along."

"Naw," Cobb hollered back. "We're just waiting for you'uns to warm up our dance partners for us."

"Plenty to go 'round," another Georgian said good-naturedly. "I hear we each get five Yanks apiece."

"Lordy," Cobb yowled. "Can't wait to fill up my dance card."

Our column fell in behind, everyone bantering and laughing, the biggest joke being how badly we were outnumbered. Anyone not knowing our business might have thought we were on our way to an afternoon tea.

I, for one, would have preferred a place further back in the order. I had no intention of getting killed before achieving my purpose, nor could I afford to be caught deserting. But I'd outsmarted the whole Army of the Potomac once already. These Confederates wouldn't be much different.

Cobb turned his face to the noonday sun as we tramped down the rutty track leading to the Orange Turnpike. "Nature's smiling on us today, Gabe. Yes, sir. Marse Robert's army's in motion again. Never to be conquered."

4

A rustle of movement came from the underbrush to my left. A *big* rustle, big enough for the word "bear" to come to mind, accelerating my heartbeat to escape velocity.

I caught a glimpse of red fur. Not a bear after all. A fox. I'd never seen one and couldn't for the life of me remember if they attacked anything but henhouses.

Beneath the red fur, I spotted black T-shirt material. A fox wearing a T-shirt? Only in Saturday morning cartoons, at least in my day, before fantasy characters were expected to morph into dinosaurs. My fear turned to anger. "Who's there?"

Back home, in a similar situation, I would have run inside my apartment, dialed 911 to report the intruder, and cowered behind my sofa until the cops showed up. Here I was, possible danger between me and the only house within screaming distance, and I was standing feet apart, hands on hips, looking for a fight.

The interloper stood. A teenage girl, and a young one at that, though already taller than me. Her Greenpeace T-shirt sported a white wolf silhouetted against a night sky, the fabric pulling a little too taut over her blossoming breasts. Partially blanketing the shirt was a stunning mane of red hair, giving the impression that she was once as spirited and lithe as that wild wolf, before puberty caught up with her, changing her agility to awkwardness and her spirit to defiance.

"What were you doing there?" I asked, knowing she

ought to be in school and letting that justify how confrontational I felt.

"I've got more right to be here than you," she spit back, with a scowl that would intimidate a Philly bus driver.

"Yeah? What's your name?"

Her eyes darted in her first sign of apprehension. "None of your business."

"How can I tell if you've got a right to be here if you won't tell me your name?" A couple hours and I was acting like I owned the place already. Disturbed, I changed tactics. "Or maybe you're afraid I'll report you to whatever school you should be attending?"

"My father was right. You're nothing but a city bitch."

Father. Red hair. Attitude. Ah-ha! "Your last name's Lee?"

"You bet it is!"

Her vehement pride threw me. Teens are not usually proud of their parents. Embarrassed by them, yes. I certainly had been. Italian parents can be mortifying well after you pass twenty-one and aren't supposed to care anymore.

Then it dawned on me. I hadn't asked if she were Fitzhugh Lee's daughter, but if her last name was Lee. And, forgive me if I'm slow about these things, Lee in Virginia was like Rockefeller in New York and Kennedy in Massachusetts.

That made me angrier, all my Italian immigrant blood surging up in resentment. What right had she calling me names simply because her ancestors got here two hundred years earlier? "Tell your father I don't care for the language he uses in front of his daughter."

She crossed her arms over her bosom, theatrically, reminding me of Yul Brynner in *The King and I.* Her lower lip pushed forward another centimeter. "Tell him yourself."

"Don't think I won't." I met her embittered glare with one of my own, confident in that moment that I could stare down a cat. Not fair to her at all. I'd been playing mind-poker at Dawkins-Greenway before this girl was potty-trained.

She blinked her misgivings, her eyes wavering away from mine. "He didn't say it to me. I overheard him."

"So, you eavesdrop, too?"

Her gaze settled, stonily, on the business card still in my hand. "Only when he's right. Bitch." She waded out of the brush, seemingly oblivious to the brambles scratching her arms. As she reached the road, her glower was so fervent I expected her to spit in my face. Instead she swung her back to me, tromping off down the path as if trying to start an earthquake with her feet alone.

I knew as long as I stood there, she'd continue tromping, so I stared after her, letting her feel my eyes on her back until she rounded the bend and left my sight.

Then I wondered what had come over me. Doing battle with a kid, for Pete's sake.

Miss Maggie was waiting behind the front screen door. "I see you made Beth Ann's acquaintance."

"That her name? She wouldn't tell me."

"No. Don't suppose she would."

"Said her last name's Lee. Fitzhugh's daughter?"

"She is."

"Shouldn't we phone him? Let him know his darling's playing hooky?" I had a few other things I wanted to say to him, too.

Miss Maggie beckoned me toward the kitchen. "You've never dealt with kids, have you, Pat?"

That brought me up short, cooling my anger, but I parried. "I thought you knew everything about me."

"I know you've never been married and don't have children of your own—"

The fact never bothers me until someone throws it in my face.

"—but, I mean, do you spend any time around kids? At a friend's house? Neighbors?"

"I don't have much leisure time." That sounded like an excuse, but it was true. I leave for work before the school buses in the morning and usually don't get home until six-thirty, seven o'clock. By then all I want to do is have a decent meal and veg in front of the TV until bedtime. Weekends are for all the domestic chores saved up from the week. Just try fitting a social life into that schedule.

"I figure, in my years of teaching, I had maybe five thousand kids. All around Beth Ann's age. Tuna okay for lunch?"

We'd been standing in the kitchen, and yet her question took me by surprise. "Sure. Let me help."

"Suit yourself. Get the tuna and bread out of the pantry over there. Pumpernickel for me. There's a loaf of Italian if you'd rather." She plunged her head into the fridge and began pulling out lettuce, tomatoes, pickles, and mayo. "Out of those five thousand teens, there were, oh, two, three of them you could actually classify as mean. The rest had bad days, mind you, but they were—trying on themselves, so to speak. Seeing what fit, what felt right for them. I imagine you did quite a bit of trying on at that age, Pat. Didn't you?"

I felt my face grow warm. The woman was a regular gypsy mind reader. "I never played hooky." Granted, I'd cut a few algebra and chemistry classes, hiding in the janitor's supply closet with my two best friends, but it wasn't the same thing. I hadn't left the building.

"First time for Beth Ann, far as I know. Probably wanted a look at you is all. Here, better let me open the can. Toast the bread, will you?"

I'd been trying to hook the opener onto the right side of the can rim. Miss Maggie clipped it onto the left with no trouble. "Flora said I'd be the star of the local freak show this week."

"Did she now? You two hit it off okay?"

"I guess." Dropping two pieces of pumpernickel in the toaster, my hand absently tried to push the plunger down on the right side. Problem was, the plunger was on the left.

Miss Maggie grinned impishly. "My kitchen takes some getting used to for you northpaws."

"Obviously." I did a closer visual inspection of the

room. The innocent, old-fashioned-looking kitchen was anything but. Tall, glass-fronted, stenciled cupboards held every culinary gadget ever invented, if not left-handed, ambidextrous. I suspected the kitchen was an outward manifestation of its owner. Miss Maggie certainly wasn't all she seemed at first glance. "Why did you insist I walk Flora to her car?"

"Figured you two had some business to talk over."

"She asked me if I intend to sell this property . . . if it ever becomes mine."

"It will, Pat. Don't think I'm leading you along. Though, God knows, I'd be just as doubtful in your place." Miss Maggie calmly shook the water out of the tuna as she spoke, as if we were talking about the weather instead of my future.

"Is there something wrong with the land, that you've never sold it? High radon levels or something?"

"No, no. Nothing of that sort. Flora give you that idea?"

I shook my head. "She seemed to think it'll be snatched up as soon as it hits the market."

"Flora'll get you a good price—bigger commission for her—but keep your eye on her, Pat. She's not the most honest person you'll meet."

Flora's card had been burning a hole in my jeans pocket. I couldn't get out of my mind the way Beth Ann had glared at it. The girl had, I assumed, overheard our conversation. "Beth Ann didn't like me talking to Flora, did she?"

"I'd say you've hit the nail smack on the head, Pat."

Silly, but I felt better. Beth Ann's wrath hadn't been directed at me personally, for no reason, but at my actions. I reran the conversation in my head one more time. "She doesn't want me to sell? Why? What business is it of hers? It's your land."

Miss Maggie was still standing by the sink, though the tuna can had long since stopped dripping water. She was looking through the window or, more likely, looking within, at a remote memory. "Beth Ann grew up in these woods. Knows every inch of them."

That stirred a memory of my own. When I was a kid, we had a little municipal park a few blocks away from our row home. I wasn't allowed to go to the park by myself, but it was a treat when Mom or Dad took me to play on the swings and walk along the creek. That and Girl Scout hikes at Valley Forge constituted my sole encounters with nature. Yet I could distinctly recall the taste of the wild raspberries I picked with my junior troop up on Mount Joy thirty years ago. "Like losing her own private park."

"No, not private." Miss Maggie turned to me, a sheepish apology on her face. "I let school groups come each year. Used to bring my own classes and before I knew it, other teachers were asking and—it started long before I'd decided what to do with the place."

School groups. I'd be inheriting an outdoor classroom. The PTA probably already had my picture pinned to their dartboard. What I didn't understand, other than why Miss Maggie was so determined to give me the land in the first place, was why she was apologizing for doing with it as she pleased.

"I don't mix the mayonnaise in with mine anymore," Miss Maggie said, giving the can one last shake before returning to the table. "A dab on each piece of bread is all. The light stuff, low fat, no cholesterol. With a dribble of pickle juice in the tuna to moisten it up. 'Course, you can do what you like with yours."

She was changing the subject, resolutely. I didn't mind. Gave me time to mull it over. "Are you on a special diet, Miss Maggie?"

She laughed. "Think you get to my age eating junk food? 'Course my diet's restricted. All the lows: cholesterol, fat, salt, caffeine. Not sugar though. Not yet anyway. Thank God for small miracles." Her smile vanished abruptly. "Oh, my. You *can* make sauce without red meat, can't you?"

"Don't worry. My dad had a heart condition for ten years before he died. I know the drill."

We talked about egg substitutes, making nonfat sour

cream that tasted better than store-bought, and food in general through lunch and as I began making tomato sauce. Her specialized kitchen stymied my normal cooking routine to a degree, and Miss Maggie made me slow down so she could record my every move on a laptop computer she'd set up on the table. But somehow I managed to get about a month's supply of basil sauce simmering on the old porcelain stove by two-thirty.

This was my idea of a pleasant way to pass the day, certainly closer to what I'd call a vacation than the morning had been. But the whole time I was cooking, I could have sworn I heard someone, something, shuffling around out in the yard. When I glanced out the window over the sink, more and more often as the afternoon wore on, I saw nothing that could account for the sounds. Very bizarre.

Miss Maggie didn't seem to hear, so at first I said nothing. I figured maybe some animal lived under the porch, and Miss Maggie was used to the noise. But as the sounds grew louder and more distinct, I wondered if she had a hearing problem.

"Afraid Beth Ann'll come back?" Miss Maggie asked after I'd scanned the yard for what seemed the hundredth time.

"I thought I heard—you didn't hear anything outside?"

Her eyes blinked in surprise, and she strolled over to join me at the window. "What'd you hear?"

This particular noise had been the loudest yet, sharp, and repeated four times. "Like—like metal hitting wood."

Frowning, she crossed to the door, banging through the screen as, I was learning, was her habit. I followed and stood beside her on the porch. "Hear anything now, Pat?"

I shook my head. In fact, the woods were absolutely silent, almost unnaturally so. No birds singing, no breeze. A mugginess clung to the air, weighing it down.

I would have welcomed any break in the stillness. A plane flying overhead. A siren going off. Anything.

When Miss Maggie answered the phone shortly after that, I ran for the powder room. Nature wasn't calling, at least, not especially urgently, but I felt the need for a good heart-to-heart with my reflection in the mirror.

What was going on? This morning I'd gone completely paranoid. Now I was hearing things. Worse yet, I was hearing things in front of the woman who wanted to give me a fortune in real estate.

Miss Maggie had murmured soothing assurances about poachers chopping firewood on the property, but her laser-beam eyes had burned a hole through me until I had to escape. Was she having second thoughts about making a crazy woman her beneficiary? Who wouldn't?

I studied myself critically. The dark eyes studying me back were worried. Was there madness in them? How could you tell? Maybe I was a bona fide psycho. I mean, I fantasized about killing my boss every day, didn't I?

But all I saw in the mirror was a new wrinkle, making itself at home between my brows. I tried to evict it, widening my eyes, stretching my forehead muscles.

As I performed these calisthenics, another thought popped into my head. Did Miss Maggie hear those noises and pretend she didn't? Why?

The ghosts of every scam story I'd ever seen on *60 Minutes* floated before my eyes. Step one, feed the victim some get-rich-quick scheme. Check. I'd been suckered in. Sure, I'd called Joel Peyton, but did I know he was actually a lawyer? Did I know for sure that Miss Maggie owned this land?

I pulled Flora Shifflett's card from my pocket. *Member, Stoke County Board of Realtors*. Looked official, but anyone could have cards made up. Of course, I could check her out with a phone call, but even if she was a realtor, couldn't she also be a con artist?

But that meant Fitzhugh and Beth Ann Lee must also be in on it.

Too many players. Besides, what could they possibly hope to get out of a victim like me? I was no rich retiree. My salary put me in a low-income bracket, and I had a pitiful little 401K pension plan tied up in mutual funds that always seemed to lose more than they earned.

I let go of the scam theory, reluctantly, because it meant admitting I'd heard sounds that Miss Maggie hadn't.

"Pat? Are you all right?" came her ratchety voice through the powder-room door. Guess I'd overstayed my welcome.

"Coming." My reflection told me to cook her meal and meet her lawyer, but not to sign anything until I understood every word. And to keep my eyes, and ears, open.

Miss Maggie was waiting for me as I stepped into the hall. "That was Wilma Rae Boutchyard on the phone," she said, lips pursed like she'd bit into a bad grape. "Wanted to come by, look you over. I told her to hold off 'til to-morrow, but I doubt we can avoid her longer than that."

"Why? Who is she?"

Miss Maggie sighed. "If we had a mayor, she'd be his wife, if you get my meaning. Head of every civic group around." She placed a hand on my shoulder, then slid it down my arm to squeeze my hand. "The heck with being diplomatic. The woman's a pretentious busybody. Ever seen *The Wizard of Oz*?"

"Every year since I was born." I could sing verbatim all the parts of the Munchkinland scene, even way up high for the Lullaby League.

"Picture a Miss Gulch of the Old South."

"Oh." The sinking feeling in my stomach must have registered on my face because her grip tightened, though not as reassuringly as she probably intended.

"Well, no use worrying about it now. Let's go talk cooking instead."

We hadn't taken two steps toward the kitchen when a chugging noise floated down the hall from the front of the house. I recognized it as a car engine, though I wouldn't have been surprised to find a guy playing steel drums under the hood.

"Sounds like Beau," exclaimed Miss Maggie, heading for the porch. Since she still had hold of my hand, I had little choice but to follow.

A baby blue pickup, dented and scratched from many years of service, but gleaming as if just washed and waxed, came to a grudging standstill on the pullout. One last wheeze and the steel drum concerto choked off midphrase.

The driver, disembarking as the engine creaked and sighed, was elderly, though probably a couple decades younger than my benefactor. Tall and lanky, he seemed all bones inside his white short-sleeve shirt and tan pants, both of which were frayed around the hems. The bowtie at his throat was plaid, but the style was thin, not showy. He approached Miss Maggie in a friendly but formal way that put the words "former student" into my head.

Relinquishing my hand and pushing me forward, Miss Maggie introduced us, ending with, "Now, don't you say a word, Beau Dillard. Joel says she's got to sign papers before I can tell her anything," so I knew this man was more in her confidence than Flora Shifflett.

He bowed, clasping my hand as if I were royalty. " 'Pleasure, ma'am." He added a wink. "Now you make sure you sign everything and make it proper and legal, Miss Montella. Magnolia's been looking forward to this for a long time. You'll make her one happy woman."

Oh Lordy, another one, I thought. Assuring him that making Miss Maggie happy was number one on my to-do list, I gave my hand a little yank, indicating I wanted it back.

Taking the hint, he let go. "Came by for that kitchen chair you said needed fixing, Magnolia. If you won't be needing it."

"Not unless you want to stay for dinner, though I'd as soon give you a folding chair than trust that wobbly leg." The invitation was smooth and, I was fairly certain, sincere, so apparently this man was trusted enough to sit in as we discussed legal matters. I was willing to bet it wasn't just because he'd been a straight "A" student.

Beau waved both his hands as if warding off temptation. "My daughter might stop over later. Thanks, anyway. Let me go get that chair."

When the screen door swung shut behind him, I ventured, "One of your five thousand kids?"

"Not Beau. His family didn't move to these parts 'til he was in high school. Things might have been different if he'd been here longer." That faraway look stole into her eyes for a few seconds, but then her mouth crinkled up into a grin. "I'd say you passed inspection, Pat."

"So he really only came to check me out?" Like I hadn't guessed that the moment his truck pulled up. I'd be skeptical of every caller at Miss Maggie's door for the next week, even the mailman. Though, come to think of it, the mailman had already checked me out, found me wanting, and was probably telling every blessed person who tried to buy a book of stamps today.

Miss Maggie's eyes were still focused on the front door. "I'm glad his excuse was to finally come get that chair. Been saying he would for weeks."

I shrugged. "Some people procrastinate—"

"No, no, that's not it. Oh, I don't care two cents about the chair. No one's sat in it since the leg came loose ten years back." She sighed. "I've been trying to get Beau to do some odd jobs around the place, so I can slip him some money without him feeling like it's charity. You'd have to be blind not to notice how much he needs it."

I let my gaze stray over the old pickup, which was still muttering a sporadic complaint beneath the muggy sun. Why was this woman leaving a complete stranger her land when she admittedly had a close friend—or whatever he was—who was poor? I tried to ask just that, without seeming ungrateful, but Miss Maggie cut me off.

"Even if I had a choice, Pat, Beau can't wait 'til I die. He works two days a week now at the County Archives— can't work more or he'd lose his Social Security—but he used up most of his retirement savings last year when his wife came down with leukemia. Medicare didn't cover everything, especially some of the experimental drugs. Helen Dillard suffered a long time before she died and their daughter—"

Beau returned, backing out of the house through the screen door as he supported the old maple chair with both hands. "Shouldn't need more than a finishing nail and some carpenter's glue to make it good as new, Magnolia."

"Now don't you skimp on the job, Beau Dillard. I want it done right." .

"Yes, ma'am." Chuckling, he swung his burden into the bed of the truck. "Nice meeting you, Miss Montella. I'll be by later in the week, after all Joel's legal mumbo jumbo's out of the way."

I implied that his return would be the high point of my visit. The way things were going, it might be.

After he'd driven off, Miss Maggie sighed again. "Wish I could get him to stay for dinner. He's too skinny."

"I'm sure he'd have stayed tonight if his daughter—"

"That's what I was trying to tell you. His daughter hardly remembers to call him anymore. I don't think she's been to see him since her mother died. No, it's just stubborn pride."

⊿ 5 ⊾

I'd had enough local gossip for one day, though I couldn't honestly say that any of Miss Maggie's comments had the ring of idle chatter. More like a teacher summarizing material for an upcoming exam. I remembered the tidbits she'd told me earlier, regarding Beth Ann, Flora, and that "Booshard" woman, and it struck me that they'd all been warnings. Still, wanting more time to think, I kept my questions to myself and concentrated on dinner.

One thing I'll say about Miss Maggie's kitchen: It was stocked. A green-grocer's dream in the fridge. A pantry crammed with rice, pasta, cereals, beans, fruit, you name it. A freezer stuffed with fish, fowl, and low-fat frozen dinners. And a *full* spice rack.

I whipped up a sweet-and-sour dill dressing for the salad, letting Miss Maggie think it was an old family recipe. In fact, I'd learned it from a Pennsylvania Dutch cookbook. For dessert, I threw together a skim-yogurt concoction, layering it in wine glasses with crushed nuts, honey, and cinnamon, an ad-lib rendition of a dessert I'd once sampled in a Greek restaurant.

At five-fifteen, I let Miss Maggie do the taste test on the sauce.

"Ooh, Pat," she practically swooned, "I don't have to die now 'cause I've already been to heaven."

Hoping that meant she'd forgotten my phantom noises, I transferred enough sauce for dinner to another pan and pulled a zucchini out of the fridge.

"My goodness," Miss Maggie exclaimed. "We'll have to freeze the rest of this, and I don't know if there's room in the cellar icebox." She made a beeline for a door in the corner, which I assumed led below. "I'll clear some space and bring up the freezer containers. We'll need a dozen at least."

"Need any help?"

"No, no. I wouldn't dream of taking you away from the miracles you're performing at that stove. I may chain you there permanently." Flipping the light switch, she descended, leaving me to peel and chop with her left-handed implements.

I was dumping the zucchini rinds into the garbage when a man's voice from the next room made me jump.

"Lord Almighty, what smells so good in here?"

As I turned, he came into the doorway, hands in the pants pockets of his pin-striped, three-piece suit. The first thing I noticed was how superbly he filled it out. The second was his face—angular jaw, full lips, lively gray eyes—topped by a mass of ash-blond hair, short on the sides, but luxuriantly thick from ear to ear. His vest was unbuttoned, tie missing, two top shirt buttons undone, and he had such a relaxed manner, I couldn't picture him ever totally dressed up.

"Patricia Montella?"

Wiping my fingers on a dishtowel, nodding, I came forward to shake the hand he offered, self-conscious of possible sauce splatters on my shirt. "And you are?"

"Joel Peyton, ma'am. We spoke on the phone." His grip was like a warm, cozy blanket.

"I didn't expect—I mean, Miss Maggie said you were coming for dinner, so I figured we wouldn't see you for another hour, at least." I was babbling, I knew, but he had the most disarming grin, and his hand still held mine.

"I'm here strictly on business, Miss Montella. We have a few things to talk over, and I thought we'd get some of it out of the way before supper." His eyes contradicted the formality of his words. "Then again, I hadn't anticipated my client would have bonded you into slave labor so soon."

"Oh, I volunteered. I want to—"

Miss Maggie interrupted, her voice ringing up out of the nether regions, "That you, Joel Peyton?"

"At your service, Magnolia."

"Get down here, then, and give me a hand. Leave Pat alone. She's busy."

" 'Scuze me, ma'am. Duty calls." Letting go of my hand—reluctantly? or was that my optimistic imagination?—he went below, leaving a subtle trace of cologne in his wake.

I didn't think twice about eavesdropping. Tiptoeing over to the cellarway, I stood with my back to the wall beside it. They were right at the bottom of the steps.

"What do you think you're doing, Magnolia Shelby?"

"What's it look like? Here, put your arms out. I'll load them up."

"That's not what I mean, and you know it. You've got her working like a hired hand. She's supposed to be your guest."

"Pat likes to cook. And I like to eat. Begrudge me that much, Joel. This business is hard enough."

"You tell her anything yet?"

"Just took her around the place a little is all. Showed her the cemetery. She doesn't seem to know beans about the war. But she saw *something,* Joel. I'll swear she did."

Did I? Was she referring to the property's potential? Or did she mean literally? And if so, what had I seen? The only portion of the morning's walk I remembered was the fiction I'd conjured up. Had I let my imagination run away when I should have been paying attention?

"Don't go getting your hopes up, Magnolia. She's young. Got her life ahead of her." He probably meant "young" in relation to Miss Maggie, but I pretended it was a compliment.

"I know, Joel. Go on. That's all you can carry without dropping them."

Hearing him on the stairs, I made a quick dash back to

the stove, adding my chopped zucchini to the sauce as he reached the top. He held old sherbert, margarine, and whipped-topping receptacles, balancing them like a circus performer, managing to get them to the counter before they toppled.

Seeing me hold back a laugh, he grinned. "Magnolia has saved every reusable food package ever to cross her threshold. Ever see three-pound coffee cans? Original Coke bottles? Planters Peanut jars? The Smithsonian would kill for her collection."

Miss Maggie was right behind him, toting three more plastic tubs. "Hush up, Joel Peyton. Remember now, they only started recycling this decade. I couldn't see throwing out perfectly good stuff. And I've never had to buy a piece of Tupperware my whole life."

"Don't mind him, Miss Maggie. My mother did the same thing. We had cabinets full of ricotta-cheese containers."

"There, you see? People who went through the Depression understood frugality. You young'uns waste too much."

"Youth has nothing to do with it," I protested. "My boss is ten years younger than me, and I yell at him every day for not using his recycling basket."

"Do you, Pat?" Miss Maggie's interest seemed way out of proportion.

I shrugged. "He throws everything in his trash basket. What extra effort would it take for him to toss his office paper and soda cans in the can beside it? It's like he's proud of his selfishness. Like he's so important, he thinks it's beneath him." I could feel my hair bristle. Just thinking about Burt raised my blood pressure. I took a deep breath. "Besides, I'm kind of fanatical about it. My cube mate calls me a militant terrorist recycler."

"Terrorist?" Joel didn't stop grinning, but his eyebrows went up warily.

I assured him it was only said in fun, crossing my fingers behind my back, hoping he'd never find out about the

cleaning man I'd threatened when I caught him putting re-
cyclables in the trash Dumpster.

Joel seemed relieved. "I need to talk with Miss Montella
privately, Magnolia, if you can see your way to letting her
out of the kitchen for a half hour."

I headed off any objection she could have made. "The
zucchini will take a while to cook anyway, Miss Maggie.
All you have to do is stir it occasionally."

But Miss Maggie apparently had no objections whatsoever. "I'll do up the salad in the meantime. You two go
have your chat."

Joel stripped off his jacket and vest as we passed through
the lower hall, dangling them carelessly from the stair bannister post. "Mind if we go outside? I've been cooped in a
stuffy law office all day."

I agreed, thinking he meant to sit on the porch rockers,
but we bypassed them and his car, a sporty red Lexus.
Taking long, slow strides, as if it felt good to stretch his
legs, Joel sauntered over to the road, waiting for me to
come alongside, before continuing his stroll.

The clearing was swathed in long shadows now. The
sun crouched behind the frilly treetops before us, illuminating the west side of the house and trees beyond. I could
hear birds in those branches, boisterously enjoying the
warmth, but none flew to our side of the clearing. These
empty trees seemed cloaked in gloom, already prisoners to
the approaching dusk. Back home I'd have expected three
more hours of daylight. Here, I felt, night would come
early.

"So, what do you think of your little corner of Virginia,
Miss Montella?" Hands back in his pockets, Joel walked
with his upper body turned to me, like the moon always
facing the earth. He didn't look comfortable, but did wonders for my ego.

"Please, call me Pat." I gave my corner of Virginia another cursory glance before replying. "The forest took me
by surprise, I guess."

"Suppose I should have warned you, ninety percent of

the place is covered with thorns. Still want it?"

"Of course I do."

"I'll be frank with you, Pat. When Magnolia decided to make you legatee of her property, I had you thoroughly investigated."

I didn't particularly like the thought of anyone delving into my private affairs. Not that I had many. "Must have been a pretty short report. I've led a dull life."

"Your lack of a police record is commendable." His grin lingered, teasing but professional at the same time. "I was more concerned with your financial status. Pardon my saying so, ma'am, but you do tend to live paycheck to paycheck."

"It's the car payment. I'll be able to save more once it's paid up." That is, if my old refrigerator didn't up and die in the meantime.

"I'm not criticizing. I'm only saying I recognize your need to dispose of this property as soon as it passes into your hands. I'll do my best when the time comes to hurry along the paperwork for you. But I need to know—is there anyone who could make a claim or demand against the estate?"

"You mean, someone I owe money to?"

He nodded. "That's one possibility. As I've said, I've seen your financial records, and the only large debt outstanding is your car loan. That is, unless you've made a private arrangement with someone?"

I laughed. "Don't assume all Italians have organized crime connections."

"Okay. No loan sharks. How about friends?"

"My cube mate, Denise, loaned me two bucks for a slice of pizza last Friday. I'll pay her back next week. Swear to God."

"Are you . . . involved with anyone?"

My reaction—drawing in my breath like a vacuum cleaner, jerking my head up to stare, wide-eyed, into his face—led him to reassure me hastily. "I'm not prying. You'd be amazed how many people don't consider sharing an apartment a financial arrangement. Until one of the parties comes into money."

I shook my head. "No live-in. No one at all."

He grinned triumphantly, didn't even try to be subtle about it, so I knew the question hadn't been entirely business.

Now, what about him? "Not fair. You know all about me. I know nothing about you."

Fascinating how many different moods he could convey with that singular grin of his. I'd seen it friendly, professional, joking, honest, victorious. Now it went completely mischievous. "Like you, I too have a car payment."

"Just one? I thought you lawyers made megabucks."

"Corporate lawyers maybe. Mine's but a modest country practice inherited from Dad a few years back. I expect to be paying off my law school loan 'til I'm Magnolia's age. And I just put a down payment on a condo for me and Sadie."

My bubble deflated. "Sadie. Oh."

"Faithful friend, confidant, and the prettiest little goldfish a man could ask for." He couldn't hold in his laughter any longer.

"You tell your innermost secrets to a goldfish?"

"She's a good listener. Not real sympathetic though. I'd consider trading her in for—what's wrong?"

I'd been enjoying our little bout of flirting so much, I hadn't realized we'd entered the forest until a thorn attacked my hand. We hadn't come far, but the shadows were spookier than I could handle. "Nothing. I should be getting back."

He did an about-face, shrugging, abandoning the banter, probably figuring my hesitation centered on him.

Just as well. I had questions of my own. "A realtor stopped by today. Flora Shifflett?"

He nodded. "I know her."

"Said she's had several buyers interested in the place. Miss Maggie never sold even a portion of the land. Why?"

"Lots of reasons. Three I can think of right off. She grew

up here, born in that house, lived there with her husband—"

"Husband?"

"Jake Shelby. She didn't tell you? He died almost twenty years ago. Stomach cancer. She gave birth to a son there, too. She tell you about him?"

I shook my head. "How'd he die?"

"He didn't."

"But you said she had no relatives—"

"None who'll contest the will. He won't." A silent interval, broken only by the crunch of gravel beneath our feet, told me it was all he'd say on the subject. "Magnolia's whole life's bound to this place. She'd rather die in her own bed than in a hospital. Another reason she never sold is, simply, she's never needed the money that badly. Her school pension and the income from her books—"

"Books?"

"She didn't tell you she writes? What did you talk about all day?"

"Food."

His grin returned. "That's Magnolia, all right. Well, she's written four history books and a slew of articles for magazines. Did you watch that Civil War documentary on PBS a while back?"

I shook my head, ashamed to admit I rarely forsake my sitcoms for a little education.

"Her name was in the research credits. They wanted to put her in front of a camera, but she turned them down flat. Said the viewers would rather see gory Matthew Brady photos than her old parchment face, and hear Garrison Keillor read a soldier's diary than listen to her scratchy voice. Said she didn't need fifteen minutes of fame. I told her if people saw her on TV, they'd rush out to buy her books. Didn't faze her. Said the folks watching would've already learned what the books could teach them. The extra money didn't matter to her."

"What's the third reason?"

Joel put his professional grin back on, with a hint of a

grimace this time. "She'll tell you herself tonight. I wouldn't want to ruin her fun."

I remembered the eagerness on her face that morning. The third reason had to do with me. "She said you had papers for me to sign first."

Joel nodded. "Formalities. Protecting my client's interests."

"Like what?"

His gray eyes scanned me shrewdly, all lawyer now, so I assumed I'd asked an intelligent question. Made me feel as if I had business savvy. Considering I was usually a pushover—Girl Scouts with cookies knew they could make a killing at my door—the feeling was one to be savored.

"In a nutshell, you'll be promising not to make any claim on the land until after Magnolia's death."

"That's not standard procedure, is it?" I had no experience with wills. My parents, being properly superstitious Italians, hadn't written them. But I'd never heard of a pre-will agreement.

"Mitigating circumstances."

"Like what?" The question worked before, I figured.

"Like the third reason."

We'd arrived back at the house and stood in front of his car, eyeing each other cautiously but with interest. I was wondering if he were friend or foe, hoping for the former, that the legalities would turn out to be, as he said, just protocol. Nothing to worry about.

Dinner came off without a hitch. Pretty astounding when you remember I was in a strange—in more ways than one—kitchen, and hadn't cooked more than single servings in ages. Joel had two helpings of the penne I tossed with the zucchini sauce. Miss Maggie had three.

We cleared the table and loaded the dishwasher. Yes, she had one, hidden behind a pair of raised-panel cabinet doors. Left-handed controls, of course. Had to have been custom-made.

When I tried to do more, Miss Maggie shooed me away.

"Take her into the war room, Joel. I'll be along shortly. Bring your coffee with you."

Joel had just poured himself a second mug. Since it was decaf, and therefore guiltless except for calories added by two spoons of sugar, I followed suit. He led me into the front room off the hall, which was a kind of parlor.

A TV with a thirty-inch screen hogged the corner to the right of the fireplace. To the left was a computer desk smothered in paper and books, a state-of-the-art PC and laser printer just visible through the mess. Four oversized, mismatched recliners—blue velour, tartan, flowered, and yellow paisley—were arranged randomly, as if whoever de-livered them simply set them down facing every which way, and no one had bothered to move them since. Small tables, also mismatched, were scattered between the chairs.

The two walls without fireplace or windows were veiled in maps of every type: Virginia highway, topographical, detail maps of seven counties, facsimile maps from the nineteenth century, photocopies of hand-drawn maps. All stuck to the wall with masking tape. All scribbled on in various colors with felt-tip pens.

"Here. You can read this over while we wait for Mag-nolia." Joel was already sprawled back into the blue re-cliner, briefcase open on his lap, holding out a multipaged, legal-length document.

I set my mug on a coaster and took the draft from him. Small print. Every other word "wherefore" or "insofar as." It'd take me a week to decipher all the gobbledygook.

Miss Maggie came scurrying in, her green eyes blazing. "Are we ready?"

"Soon as Pat signs on the dotted line, you can blab to your heart's content." Joel held out a pen.

I didn't take it. But not wanting to screw up my chances, I snatched at excuses. "Aren't you supposed to have two witnesses?"

"Just a simple agreement," Joel said. "Kind of thing you sign when you open a bank account."

"Hugh's a notary. I'll give him a call." Miss Maggie

moved toward the desk. There was, I observed, a phone cord making inroads through the mountain of paper. "He'll come right over and—"

"No." That's all I needed. More pressure. "I . . . I haven't had a chance to read the whole thing yet."

Miss Maggie scowled at her lawyer. "Didn't Joel explain it to you, Pat?"

"I did. Before supper." He sat forward on the recliner, pushing the footrest down with a thud.

I set the document next to my mug. "Truth is, I want a few days to look it over. And I want to know everything there is to know before I sign anything." Cowering, I wondered if I'd botched it.

Joel whistled. "Brains, too. You sure can pick 'em, Magnolia."

"That agreement was your idea, Joel Peyton." Miss Maggie turned to me. "You're a hundred percent right, Pat. I should have told you everything this morning. Or put it in a letter to you before bringing you all the way down here. Durn-fool lawyers. His father was the same—"

"Now wait a blessed minute, Magnolia." Joel also turned to me. At least I was the center of the universe. "If you won't sign that, you're going to have to give us some guarantee that you won't use anything Magnolia says against her."

"Don't you listen, Pat. Promise you'll take the information and do only what's best for you—"

"Whoa." I held up my hands, feeling as if I had to fend both of them off physically. "I'm not promising either of you anything. I'm not doing or signing anything until I know what's going on." Italian bullheadedness can have its advantages.

Joel rolled his eyes and, letting his briefcase slip to the floor, slid back into the recliner again. "Do what you want, Magnolia. I won't be responsible."

Miss Maggie slipped an arm around me and, squeezing me tight, led me over to a chair. "Sit, Pat. Time you knew why I chose you."

I sank down, suddenly not sure I wanted to know anything. I could feel my heart thumping in my throat.

Miss Maggie held my hand as if she were afraid I'd disappear before her eyes. "Only three of your grandparents have Italian backgrounds, correct?"

I nodded. "My mother's mother—we called hers the mongrel branch of the family."

"Her maiden name was Souder. A common name in Pennsylvania, isn't it?"

"I guess. I didn't know her. She died before I was born."

Miss Maggie let go of my hand and began moving around the room. "*Her* mother's mother was named Clarissa Howard. She was born in 1862, in Richmond, to seventeen-year-old Julia Bell."

Talk about dropping bombshells. "The same Julia Bell that's—" I gestured nebulously to the north side of the house, seeing in my mind's eye the lonely cemetery by the river.

"She returned home that fall to bury her brother, Lane, leaving Clarissa in Richmond with a family named Howard. When I found all this out thirty-some years ago, I realized there might be descendents, and if I could, it was only right that I return the land to the family."

The family. *Me*, I thought, not at all ready to believe it.

"You are, apparently, the only living direct descendent, Pat. Clarissa had one child who lived to adulthood, a girl. Eight grandchildren, but between the influenza outbreak and World War One, only two survived. Your grandmother's sister and her four children were killed in a fire. Your grandmother died during the birth of her second child—"

"And Uncle Sal never married." My mother's younger brother had died of heart disease a year before his sister.

Miss Maggie nodded, adding gently, almost inaudibly, "You had a brother, too."

I reacted as I always do, with guilt that I should feel something, with rationales why I don't. "I never knew him. He went into the Air Force when I was four."

"Shot down over North Vietnam."

I nodded, but Miss Maggie's gaze was no longer focused on me. Glancing over my shoulder, following her line of vision to the mantle, I saw a framed, black-and-white photo. Leaning proudly against a big solid sedan like you see in old gangster movies, was a smiling, dark-haired, young man. A sailor in dress whites.

MAY 4, 1864—NEAR LOCUST GROVE, VIRGINIA

We weren't to have our battle that day after all.

When we came upon Mine Run, some of the veterans made for the old earth-and-log trenches of last November's engagement, assuming we'd be holding the same line as then. We were told no, keep marching. A great cheer had gone up, as if this were a good portent. But not two miles further, and only eight or so from our starting point, we were ordered to camp for the night in the high brush to the right of the turnpike.

At the skillet wagons, each of us received a few hard crackers and a pathetic slice of bluish meat. I saved the hardtack and ate the meat slowly, along with some of my ration which I finished cooking. Each mouthful fell heavily on my churning depths.

Overhead, in a circle of sky framed by scrubby branches, stars blinked through the smoke from our meager fires. Constants in a world where only change seemed certain. The same stars shone everywhere, over my family's graves at Bell Run, and over Richmond.

Over little Clarissa.

The war had taken nearly all I held dear—my parents, my siblings, my home, my very soul. All but Clarissa. For her sake, my mission *must* succeed—that she might be safe. This gave me courage.

What would they tell her of her Uncle Gabe? That he stopped the madness? Would they brand Gabriel Bell hero or villain? Saint or sinner? Not the latter, I prayed.

Still, this world's opinion would bear no weight on the Day of Reckoning.

⤳ 6 ⤺

An hour after I'd put my head on the pillow, I came awake again, wondering where I was at first, then remembering as my eyes focused on the luminous numerals of my watch. Only 11:37.

I'd left the windows open, as I always do as soon as the weather warms up. Breathing in stale, machine-channeled air day in, day out at work gave me a genuine appreciation for the fresh stuff. One of the sweetest fragrances I know is a spring breeze coming into a room that's been shut up all winter.

But tonight it wasn't spring I inhaled. Wood smoke. Not the noxious, house-burning-down variety. More like some-one cooking outside. Mingled with the smokey pine were the aromas of coffee and roasting pork, dredging up a child-hood memory of New Year's Eve celebrations with my Sicilian relatives. Except there was no garlic and fennel this time. No sweet smell of barbecue sauce either.

Pushing off the chenille spread, I padded across the rag rug to the window, wincing as the floorboards creaked, hop-ing the noise wouldn't wake Miss Maggie. Outside, the night seemed too dark. I reminded myself this was the country. At home the sky was sidelit by shopping malls and street lamps. When I looked out my apartment's bed-room window, I could see only the security beacons on the backs of the houses across the parking lot.

I heard what sounded like a train off to the west. I'd grown up with trains, their tracks just two blocks away from my house. A long diesel freight would pass by at two o'clock each morning, its steady clicking on the rails like a soothing lullaby; the whistle, a low lament. The train I listened to now was also rhythmic, but instead of a whistle, there was a hissing sound. After a few seconds I placed it— a steam locomotive.

I'd read about a weekend-getaway train, done up in Victorian opulence, pulled by a steam engine. Granted, this was Monday night, but it had to be the same kind of deal.

Strangely enough, the chugging wasn't fading into the distance, or getting closer for that matter. But it *was* getting faster.

My initial thought was to push up the screen, try to see something through the trees. The little spring catches locking the screen in place foiled the plan. By the time I got the screen up and leaned out, the engine had stopped.

All at once though, I heard movement below in the yard. Squinting into the blackness, I could make out nothing further than the edge of the porch roof. I told myself I was hearing an animal—a deer maybe. Did deer stay out this late?

Something—I couldn't tell what—whizzed past my eyes, and I heard a loud, sharp whack against the clapboards beside my head.

I dropped to the floor, facedown, willing myself to scream, but my throat was closed tight with fear. My heart was thumping so loudly, it's a wonder I heard anything else. Yet I distinctly caught the soft footfalls of someone running across the yard, the rustling as he . . . she . . . entered the underbrush. Then silence.

I let that peace stretch on to an eternity before I got the guts to push myself up on my knees. Poking my head just over the sill, I saw a small, dark lump on the porch roof. Since it wasn't ticking, I decided to let finding out what it was wait until morning.

Still kneeling, I pulled the screen back down. The steam engine was gone, as were the cooking odors. The night smelled of rich earth and honeysuckle.

Shifting my knees to one side, pulling my nightshirt down over my legs as far as it would go, I rested my arms on the sill. Ahead, through the forest, lay the burned-out building that was my ancestral home. And five graves overlooking the river that held a great-great-great grandmother, two quadruple-great grandparents, and a pair of uncles—I had no idea how many "greats" to assign them.

None of it seemed real. When I thought "family," I pictured the Montellas, the Muscarellas, the Giamos. When I thought "ancestor," I pictured turn-of-the-century laborers working in quarries, on railroads. Living in Pennsylvania immigrant communities like Mogee Town and Norristown's East End. Fighting language and culture barriers thrown up by—by people like the Bells.

Or the Lees. I remembered what I'd been thinking when I confronted Beth Ann that morning. Were her ancestors really here before mine? Maybe the Bells had come over on the Virginia equivalent of the Mayflower. Maybe they'd fought in the American Revolution. Maybe I had as much right to a DAR award as the blond, blue-eyed girls who'd walked away with them each year at my school.

So, if I was a product of the Founding Fathers—or the Old South—why was someone using me for target practice?

Though it didn't take an Einstein to guess who. And, as if to prove I was no Einstein, I dozed off.

I jolted myself awake after my arms slipped off the sill but before my head hit the floor. Cold and stiff, I crawled back into bed.

I overslept my usual six o'clock wake-up by three hours. Far from feeling rested, I had a headache the size of Delaware and a professional tailor's crease between my shoulder blades. Rubbing my eyes, I shuffled over to the windows.

No surprises. The thing on the porch roof was a rock. How unimaginative. Not even a note tied around it.

The sun hadn't gotten to this side of the clearing yet. At

least, not down to the grass—the treetops were waxy green with it. Right on the forest fringe, two deer seemed to fade in from the grayish shadows, like objects in those Hidden Picture puzzles—once you see them, you can't understand how you missed them at first. Oblivious to me, the deer nibbled at wildflower blossoms, the smaller of the two still spotted and, to my eye, vulnerable. I watched until the larger one raised its head—perhaps it heard a noise or sensed me. As if reading each other's minds, they bounded into the forest in unison.

After a good steamy shower that didn't do a thing for my aching head and back, I found Miss Maggie at the kitchen table, slaving over a hot laptop, reading glasses almost hanging off her nose. "Sleep well?" She didn't look up from the screen, but the query was perfectly timed with a gargantuan yawn on my part. "Help yourself to breakfast. I don't usually brew coffee in the morning, but you can if you like, or there's instant in the pantry. Tea bags, too."

All the choices were decaffeinated, unfortunately. I heated a mug of water in the microwave and stirred in a spoon of the Folgers crystals, remembering too late how the burnt-toast smell of instant always made my nose itch. Holding my breath, I sipped the hot liquid.

"I have a few questions," I ventured. Boy, was that an understatement. I had so many I'd mentally made file folders for them: Family Roots, Missing Link Generations: Civil War to Present, Property Specs, Locale Info.

Miss Maggie nodded. "I knew you would. I dug out a copy of this for you." She slid a book across the table, an inch-thick paperback, the textbook kind, big with heavy white paper. *Wilderness Voices: The Civil War Letters of the Armstead Bell Family* by M. Shelby. "There's a short family history in the preface, and the rest'll bring you up-to-date to where my research was in the seventies. I've filled four notebooks since then. You're welcome to read them."

This was becoming a more academic vacation than I'd bargained for, but I decided to give the book a chance and

ask my land-related questions. "Yesterday you said the
north border of the acreage was the river. Hugh said the
paved road was the east border. That leaves west and
south."

"The south border parallels the drive, fifty yards beyond
it, through the trees. If you follow the drive about another
half mile, the woods and road both end at a parking lot."

"What's the lot for?"

"Industrial park. Not tenanted right now, but the road's
posted, so if anyone does move in, the workers won't be
able to avoid rush hour by driving through here."

"That's why you've never paved the road?"

Miss Maggie laughed. "I haven't driven in fifteen years.
Even so, I've no reason to go out on bad days since I fax
or e-mail my work in by computer. That reminds me, let
me see if my fax to New York went through." She scurried
off to the parlor.

An interesting paradox. Who needed paved roads if you
had your own private on-ramp to the information super-
highway?

Miss Maggie returned, continuing as if she'd never left.
"The industrial park could be a selling point for you. Good
access."

"Is there a railroad off to the west? I heard a train last
night."

She raised her eyebrows. "Must be fifteen, twenty miles
away."

"It *sounded* like a train—a steam engine, actually. Nothing like that around?"

Puzzled, she shook her head.

"Are there houses to the south?"

"A farm right now. Flora told me he's selling to a developer, though. Won't be long."

"So your closest neighbor at the moment is that development, Bell Run, across the road." I was trying to estimate
how far those houses were. Too far for the breeze to carry
grilling aromas, I thought.

"Hugh and Beth Ann are closest, this side of the road, then the development."

I told her about smelling someone's cooking. "Couldn't have been anyone camping in the forest, could it?"

Miss Maggie's eyes had come forward, almost out of her skull. "Coffee and pork, you say? And you heard a steam engine?" She dashed off to the parlor again, this time bringing back a thick book. She paged impatiently back and forth, then squiggled a finger down one long paragraph. "Here, read this."

More homework.

The passage described Union troops eating a dinner of pork and coffee, then for entertainment, pouring the rest of their coffee water into a sawmill's steam generator to see how fast they could make it go.

Miss Maggie was so excited she could barely get her breath. "Happened the night before the Wilderness campaign. May fourth. The mill was on Flat Run, just west of here. Troops were camped all over, even here where this house sits now."

Knowing I wouldn't like what she was thinking, I was determined to find a rational explanation first. "So who was in the forest last night? Living-history people? I thought reenactments were only held on weekends."

"I didn't give anyone permission to camp here last night, Pat. Even if I did, the sawmill's long gone." Miss Maggie sat, staring at me as if I were the Hope diamond.

"Maybe they brought their own generator."

"You heard noises yesterday afternoon, too. People moving around in the yard? Chopping wood?"

"I don't believe in ghosts." Yeah, right. I was as superstitious as my parents.

"No, not ghosts. Somehow, you've looked through a window back into the past."

"I didn't see anything."

Miss Maggie brushed away my literal interpretation. "Listened through a keyhole, then. You experienced a piece of hist—" She froze, scowling, snapping the book shut.

"Did you know any of this before you came?"

"No, I swear." Bad enough she suspected me of having Walkman earphones plugged into "the Other Side," now she was accusing me of fraud.

She wasn't convinced. Who could blame her? Here I was, heir to her real estate, all of a sudden claiming to smell coffee whose grounds went through their compost cycle a hundred and thirty years ago. I tried logic again. "What if one of my teachers told that story to my class? Maybe I wasn't paying attention enough to remember, but my subconscious stored it away. Yesterday, when you mentioned the battles and the army crossing the river, it came back in a dream last night."

"You're saying you dreamt it." This wasn't a question. More like an unflattering dress she was trying on me to see if it looked better off the hanger.

"Sure. It *had* to be a dream."

Miss Maggie might have heard the desperation in my voice. I thought it was pretty obvious myself. Whatever the reason, she dropped the interrogation. "Get yourself breakfast while I finish up some work in the war room. We have plenty to do this morning."

I also had something I wanted to do, though I wasn't sure when I could get around to it. One thing was certain. Neither dreams nor ghosts throw rocks.

General Lee was to have a grand review the day we left Richmond, and quantities of people were to go up by rail to see it. . . . They came back faster than they went. They found the army drawn up in battle array.

from the diary of Mary Chestnut—May 8, 1864

MAY 5, 1864—SAUNDERS' FIELD

I'd supposed when the bluecoats were met, a battle would ensue. A naive assumption, I found.

These generals much prefer to set their men in place, like pawns on a chessboard. To move them accordingly, as if they could remove a man's very soul, turn him into a dispassionate piece of whittled wood.

And so we were ordered not to attack the Federals, but to fortify the impenetrable copse north of the turnpike, below Spotswood Road. I assumed the bluecoats were similarly employed, for only the intermittent clatter of skirmish fire interrupted the monotonous din of our digging and chopping.

Those of our corps set on either side of the turnpike had an easier time burrowing in. Their defenses were far superior to ours. Yet, the brilliant Federal officers centered their assault there, advancing their men recklessly up the exposed incline. Their Zouave uniforms of blue, red, and yellow were easy marks, and as if determined to oblige us further, they presented their unprotected flank to our division. With a shrill yell, the men 'round me rained lead into them without mercy.

Repulsed, I unloaded my weapon into the dust this side of the enemy's feet. No one observed: My comrades were occupied by the passion of the massacre. Our officers were enthralled by their good fortune, behaving as if their intelligence, and not Providence, had brought it about.

When the smoke of our weapons dissipated, the dead lay in a straight line, as if some ghostly undertaker had set them thus.

This they call "honor"—the butchery of souls unable to shield themselves.

Was this how my brothers died? Slaughtered by cowards who refused to look them in the eye?

7

Miss Maggie insisted on light colors again. "More so today. Won't be trails some of the places we're going."

Oh, lovely. I'd packed a pair of white stirrup pants in case I needed casual wear that was decent-looking. Today I'd get grass stains on them. All for the cause. The air felt muggier than yesterday, so I donned a large, white T-shirt earned at a walkathon a year earlier. All that white made me look five inches wider.

"Bring your wallet," Miss Maggie called up the stairs.

Why? I wondered. There wasn't likely to be a refreshment stand back in the woods. I had no pockets—even if I had, my wallet had a severe case of obesity caused not by money or credit cards, but by slips of paper with unidentified phone numbers, coupons, and other people's business cards. In the end, I decided to take the whole handbag, which wasn't much larger than the wallet and had a long strap to go over my shoulder. Besides, I wasn't likely to be mugged by a deer.

Miss Maggie was waiting in the lower hall, straw hats in hand. She led me out the back door again, this time off to the right, to a trail more trampled and almost wide enough to walk two abreast. The grade was downhill, more than moderate, less than steep. Every ten yards or so, a log had been sunk in diagonally across the path.

"Hugh did that," Miss Maggie said. "Directs water run-off into the underbrush. Protects the trail from erosion."

We came to the creek, which was spanned by a narrow

bridge of wooden boards nailed to logs. No handrail, but the expanse was no more than a dozen feet. Crystal water flowed beneath, skirting around moss-carpeted rocks while a crowd of resplendent green ferns seemed to cheer the stream on from the sidelines.

"Hugh's work too?" I asked, nodding toward the bridge.

"He fixes the planks if they rot out or come loose in a flood, but my husband, Jake, laid the logs." Miss Maggie stopped midspan, her eyes misting over as she gazed down into the eddies. "He built it for my fiftieth birthday. Said an old woman shouldn't be trying to balance on slippery rocks. I made him sleep on the porch that night. Never called me old again."

"Joel said you have a son," I ventured.

"Frank," she said, nodding, then abruptly she turned downstream pointing to a spot where the creek narrowed between two boulders. "If you sell to developers, they'll probably put a dam there. Make a pond, put the houses around it. That's how they usually build in these parts. Almost all the old mining and mill runs are now lakes and ponds. Brings more mosquitoes, but they attract water birds, so it's not too bad."

Miss Maggie walked on briskly, and I hurried to catch up. She and her son must have had some kind of falling out, I assumed, for her not to want to speak of him. Not to mention going over his head to give her property to me.

Then again, I reminded myself, I was the rightful owner. Miss Maggie's kin had been trespassing on my land all these years.

What was I thinking?

That I could take her to court? Take over the place right away? That's why Joel wanted me to sign the agreement, I realized. And here I was, contemplating it. A hostile take-over, the sort of thing Dawkins-Greenway clients lived for.

Another visit from my dark side. Just what I needed today.

Up ahead loomed the back of a trailer, a big double one that had been there awhile, from the size of the azaleas growing around it. Their pink and lavender blossoms were a welcome break from the endless green forest.

As we walked around it, I realized we'd come to the paved road. A wide gravel shoulder ran in front of the trailer and parked on it was the little postal service Escort. A plain white sign beside the trailer door read, U.S. POST OFFICE, LOCUST GROVE ANNEX, 22508.

"They'll want to build a regular post office here sooner or later," Miss Maggie said. "When we're big enough for our own zip, I guess. They lease the land from me now. I'll have Joel show you the papers. It's only for the area under the front trailer and parking lot. Hugh and Beth Ann live in the back section, and I don't charge them 'cause Hugh's always doing work for me."

"Water and sewage?"

"Well and a septic tank for the back. Front section's nothing but P.O. boxes and a counter. They pay their own electric and heat. Come on, I'll show you." She was already clambering up the wood steps, opening the glass door.

As Miss Maggie'd said, most of one side of the trailer was, floor to ceiling, post office boxes. The other side sported commemorative stamp posters on the dark paneling between the windows. Across the width of the opposite end was a bust-high Formica counter, and on it a stand-up cardboard sign and a push bell. The sign said the counter was manned noon to four, Monday through Friday. The bell implied someone would help you other times.

Miss Maggie tapped the bell, and Hugh came out from behind the boxes, his red hair softened today by the blue of his uniform. I could have sworn he'd grown since yesterday. The counter seemed too small for him, giving the impression that he, like Alice in Wonderland, had chugged half a bottle of enlarging potion.

" 'Morning, Miss Maggie . . . Miss Montella." With his greeting, I got a grudging nod at no extra charge. Reaching into his pocket, he brought out a key ring and dropped it in Miss Maggie's waiting palm. "There's a half tank of gas. Should do you fine."

"We're taking the Escort?" I asked. "Isn't that illegal or something?"

"No, the car's mine," Hugh said. "Postal Service pays me expenses when I use it for work. I had the decals put on so I could park in the developments without the security guards bothering me."

Miss Maggie passed the keys to me. "You won't have any trouble with it, Pat. We aren't going that far. Thanks, Hugh." She turned toward the door, but he called her back.

"Miss Maggie?" He glanced at me, annoyed, as if trying to figure out how to ignore me. "Miss Maggie, did you see Beth Ann up around your place yesterday afternoon?"

"The school called you, did they?"

"Yes, ma'am. Only I had customers and couldn't go look for her. She came home her regular time, but when I asked where she'd been, she got all bent out of shape and gave me the silent treatment. She *was* at your place?"

Miss Maggie nodded. "Part of the time. 'Round twelve-thirty, quarter to one. She met up with Pat, got acquainted."

His gaze drifted to me once more. "She civil to you?" He must have already known the answer, though he seemed to want to hear it from me. Probably wanted me to get my back up over it.

Still, eager as I'd been to tell him what I thought of his daughter's behavior, something about the way Miss Maggie had said "Hugh and Beth Ann" nagged at me. The girl obviously didn't have a mother and, for some reason, that weakened my resolve. "She was fine," I said evenly.

"Just going through a phase is all." Miss Maggie shook a finger in Hugh's face. "Don't you be hard on Beth Ann, Fitzhugh Lee, or I'll tell her what you were like at her age."

That brought a slow, roguish grin. "Why, Miss Maggie, how could you forget what an angel I was?" He laughed. "Don't worry about Beth Ann. Got me wrapped around her little finger. She's grounded 'til the weekend, that's all."

Was she? I was willing to bet she'd already sneaked away from the trailer since his edict. Late last night.

And I hadn't forgotten that she'd overheard her father

calling me names. Soon as I got the chance, I intended to let him know exactly what I thought of him spouting off his opinions to customers.

Miss Maggie directed me south onto Route 3, then west on Route 20. "This road used to be called Orange Turnpike, because it leads to the town of Orange, about twenty-five miles southwest. Morning of May fifth, the Federals marched down it, this direction. Had to stay on the roads—all the mining and industry in the area had used up the big trees. Second-growth thicket filled in the old forest—twenty, thirty feet high in spots. So dense, you couldn't see more than sixty feet through it. That's why people called it The Wilderness."

I was trying to rein in my imagination today, but on the fringes of my vision, her verbal portrait came alive. The trees shrank, the underbrush grew to monster proportions.

"Turn in that lot, up on the right."

The trees parted, and a grassy meadow appeared on both sides of the road. The parking lot was for a Park Service pavilion, its sign proclaiming it number ten on the auto tour: Saunders' Field. I had my choice of parking—the lot was deserted—so I picked a nice, shady spot.

Miss Maggie grabbed my arm as I began strolling toward the shelter. "You don't need to read their maps and things, Pat. That's what I'm here for." She surveyed the whole length of the meadow. "We'll start at the lower end. Looks like they mowed the grass some, but it's still knee high. If you don't want ticks on you, better put your socks outside of your pants and tuck your shirt in." Miss Maggie proceeded to take her own advice.

Since no one else was around to see how silly it looked, I did as she asked, which, with stirrup pants, was more trouble than it was probably worth. Then we crossed the road and waded diagonally downhill through the grass.

"Careful where you step," Miss Maggie warned. "Easy to twist an ankle in a gopher hole."

As she said this, my foot went sideways, but I managed

to wound only my self-confidence. From then on, I kept my eyes to the ground.

Miss Maggie stopped at the foot of the forest, about seventy yards in from the road. "Turn around."

I did. The slope was blanketed with wildflowers that I hadn't noticed on the way down.

"Pretend you're a Union soldier, hidden back under these trees." She pointed up the incline to the other end of the road. "You're watching the Rebels up there as they dig trenches, making their position stronger and stronger each minute you sit here waiting for the order to advance."

Why did I feel she was setting me up to be the victim here? "Why are we waiting?"

"Remember I told you how big the Army of the Potomac was? 'Course, they weren't all here—most were further south. 'Spite of that, they outnumber those troops up there more than four to one. More troops to move around. More officers making decisions. So everything takes longer."

"Gee, and I thought bad management was something new. I assume they were eventually ordered to attack?"

Miss Maggie nodded. "They sent men up across this field for three hours. Then, seeing the Confederates were pretty well fanned out on either side of the road, they brought in more divisions and spread out, too, until their line was nearly four miles long. And they stormed the Southern line another two hours."

As good a storyteller as Miss Maggie was, and as impressionable as my imagination could be, I simply couldn't envision tens of thousands of men trying to kill each other for so many hours on end. Even if I could have understood what drove them ethically and emotionally—which I couldn't—I had no reference point for the sheer physical exertion required. The most strenuous thing I'd ever done was shovel my car out of its parking spot after the Blizzard of '96. "Did they accomplish anything, besides mass suicide?"

"In the military sense, almost nothing. Most that can be said of either army is that they kept a third of the enemy forces occupied so they couldn't aid the fighting further south. But they all changed history. Know how?"

"No." This was way out of my realm. Besides, what did it have to do with my inheritance?

Instead of answering her own question, Miss Maggie tugged on my shirt. "Let's go on up to the Confederate end of the field."

We walked back along the road, past the parking lot, and up to the trees opposite. Miss Maggie tromped off to the left into the grass, over to an unnatural hump set at right angles to the road. After maybe forty yards, it made another right angle, curving away from us before disappearing into the trees below.

"Before the Civil War," Miss Maggie began, "earthworks were used primarily to protect artillery. The infantry would march out in front of it in shoulder-to-shoulder ranks, facing the enemy on an open field. Ever seen eighteenth-century reenactments, Pat?"

"What?" I was barely listening, having been struck by my first-ever case of déjà vu. But something wasn't right. "Eighteenth century? Like the Revolutionary War? They do demonstrations at Valley Forge sometimes. Always thought they were pretty dumb, standing and shooting at each other like that."

"The technique was a result of the technology. Muskets can barely hit the side of a barn from further away than, say, thirty yards. The only way to intimidate the enemy effectively with them was to line up and have everyone fire at once. But weapons changed. Rifles could be loaded faster and easier, so the musket became obsolete. And the North poured big money into the new repeating rifle."

Miss Maggie gestured to the mound. "The South, already outnumbered as it was, had to find some way to even up the odds. Robert E. Lee was an engineer—designed forts as a young officer in the U.S. Army. And in 1862, he witnessed how a simple stone wall in a good location had won him the Battle of Fredericksburg. So he gave his troops axes and shovels, had them build walls for themselves out of logs and dirt. And in the process, invented trench warfare—Pat, what *are* you looking for?"

I'd been glancing over my shoulder, leaning uphill, drifting that way, trying to make the landscape look the way I thought it should. Like trying to recall the words to a tune that's been running through your head all day, driving you nuts. "I . . . Can we . . . can we cross the road?"

Her ears came forward like a terrier on the scent. "Do you hear something?"

"No!" I said testily. I took a deep breath to contain my frustration. "I just want to see what the meadow looks like from over there."

"Come on, then." She grabbed my arm and propelled me to the macadam. I think she would have run out in front of a Winnebago barrelling down on us, but she changed her mind at the last moment, figuring I wouldn't be fast enough.

Once the road was clear, we ran across, up onto the grass beyond. I faced downhill again, expecting the feeling to have vanished in the mad rush, but it came back stronger than ever. The view still wasn't what I was looking for, though. Not that I could have said what that was.

"Go on," Miss Maggie urged. "Do whatever you need to."

I followed the tree line, sidestepping, going backwards, diagonally, Miss Maggie at my elbow every inch of the way, catching my arm before I could trip over a vine or step in a hole. The trees squared off at the highest point, turning to parallel the parking lot, the land dipping slightly. Right behind the shelter it rose again where a trail entered the woods. I backed down the trail as far as I could without losing sight of the field.

This was my best vista yet, and I was beginning to realize what was familiar about it. The trees were all wrong, the grass, too, but the land itself—or what I could see of it past the shelter—

The slope wasn't perfectly straight. Low swales had formed where a millennia of runoff cut veins into the grade.

This texture, the roll of the ground, was very close to right.

"I've been to a place like this," I murmured, feeling Miss Maggie needed some explanation for my odd behavior.

"Where?"

I shrugged. "Maybe Valley Forge." But I knew that wasn't it. Had my parents brought me here when I was young? Not likely. Dad had chronicled every vacation, every outing, with his eight-millimeter movie camera. We had reels and reels of Wildwood, New Jersey, and every tourist trap in the Poconos, but neither he nor Mom had been big into history.

"You want to go further up this trail, don't you, Pat? Know which brigade was positioned back up in there?"

I shook my head, not really caring. All my concentration was directed toward the field before me.

"Walker's Virginians. The Thirty-Third. Mean anything to you?"

Again I shook my head. Although the shapes of the land were what first got my attention, they weren't important. What mattered were the trees down below. Yes, I was sure.

"What do you see, Pat?"

"Nothing!" I snapped.

"Close your eyes. See it with your mind."

Afraid of losing my hold on the feeling completely, I hesitated, but in the end, did as she asked.

The landscape rearranged itself to my mind's specifications. I saw motion in the high scrub below, like a wave rising up out of the ocean, brightly colored in reds, blues, yellows. As it crashed up the slope, I saw blinding flashes of fire on my right. The wave receded, then gaining energy, surged once more. This time the flashes intensified, seeming to ignite on all sides of me. The wave tumbled laterally, and in it I could suddenly make out men's faces, all deformed by powerful emotions—hate, terror. And all too often, agony.

8

My eyes flew open. *"Madonne!"*

"You saw it, didn't you, Pat? Saw what happened here clear as bottled water."

"No—" I hugged my arms to myself to stop my hands from trembling. "—No, it couldn't have been this battle. The uniforms were all wrong. They were—like something out of an old Rudolph Valentino film."

Miss Maggie slipped an arm around my waist. "One of the first regiments to advance over this field were Zouaves from New York. Ever heard of them?"

I shook my head, not really wanting to hear her next words.

"Remember, Pat, these people lived in the Victorian era. They were big into romance. Not the love story kind—I mean they loved the exotic, the ideal. Legends, myths, bigger-than-life sagas. They got caught up in visions, deliberately turning their backs on reality. Men went off to war to *play* soldier, and the recruiters liked uniforms that encouraged fantasies. The Zouave regiments wore Turkish-style outfits—baggy pants, boots, short jackets with fancy, tasseled trim." She gave me a squeeze of encouragement. "Now, Pat, are you going to tell me the same history teacher told you all about them, and your subconscious just kicked in?"

"I . . . Sure. Why not?"

"He must have told you they were in this particular contest of this particular battle. If I'd gone into that much detail in my American History classes, I'd never have gotten past the first battle of the French and Indian War before the school year ended."

"There's no other explanation that makes sense." I made up my mind to do STUBBORN. She had no idea what she was up against.

Miss Maggie gently swung me around. "The entrenchments back along this trail were Gabriel Bell's last known address. He enlisted in late April, right before this battle."

"What are you saying? That I saw what he saw?"

"Maybe he's trying to tell you something, Pat. Considering the sounds you heard yesterday—"

I snatched at the incongruity. "That proves it. You said he enlisted in late April, so he couldn't have been up near the river on May fourth."

"Still, you came right over to this spot today. You saw the beginning of the battle—"

"I didn't see anything," I shouted, pulling away from her. "I imagined it, that's all. Or maybe I saw it in a miniseries. But Gabriel Bell's ghost did not come back and show me his last minutes on earth."

Miss Maggie pursed her lips, patiently waiting for me to calm down. Feeling guilty, I muttered an apology.

"At any rate, you didn't witness Gabriel's last minutes, Pat. He survived the first three-hour assault, according to the diary of Josiah Cobb, another soldier in the unit. I only said it was his last known address because he was among the missing at the end of the day."

"Missing in action?" That stirred up some uncomfortable feelings whose expiration date should have run out long ago.

"Armies have been misplacing personnel since war was invented. Your brother was MIA for quite a while before they found his plane, wasn't he, Pat?"

"Four months." I'd only been in first grade, but I remember more details about those months than any other part of my childhood. Every time the phone rang, my parents would freeze, paralyzed with fear, afraid to answer it.

Every time a plane flew over, my mother would break down, sobbing uncontrollably.

Then came Christmas and our house was the only one on the block without lights and decorations. We had no tree, no stockings, only a ceramic nativity set on the server in the dining room, with a St. Jude votive candle burning beside the manger. I approved of this last innovation, since the baby Jesus was dressed in nothing but a cloth diaper while every other person in the scene wore heavy robes. Nothing else made sense to me, though, and when word came soon after that they'd found Lou's body, it'd been a relief to a six-year-old who wanted parents and security back again.

Miss Maggie had been silently watching me—now she turned back uphill. "It's possible Gabriel died in the late afternoon fighting. Might have been wounded and crawled off into the underbrush, never to be found. Or he might have been one of the unidentified corpses. Always plenty of them, though toward the end of the war, the veterans had come up with a system—wrote their names on bits of bark or cloth, fastened them to their uniforms. Homemade dog tags."

"Gabriel might not have done that."

"Maybe. Two other possibilities though." She held up one bony finger. "He might have been taken prisoner. His name didn't appear on any of the lists, but slip-ups in red tape also happened back then. Two," another digit joined the first, "he might have deserted."

"He *was* only fourteen. Who could blame him?" I would have deserted, too, after three hours of the kind of carnage I'd just glimpsed.

"Don't go thinking Gabriel so innocent. The war'd been going on nearly three years, almost half of it in this part of Virginia, the boy's backyard. He must have seen, experienced, an awful lot before this battle." Miss Maggie wheeled around to face me again. "I've been trying to track down Gabriel Bell most of my life. The trail always ends here at Saunders' Field. If you've got him on the line some-how, ask him where the hell he got to."

Her grin told me she was kidding, and I managed a weak smile in return. "If he calls again, I'll let you talk to him."

She took my arm. "Come on, Pat. You've had enough for one day."

As I walked with her down to the lot, I wondered if I hadn't had enough for a lifetime.

Miss Maggie didn't say a word until I pulled out of the lot and left Saunders' Field behind. "You never talk about your job, Pat."

"I'm on vacation." It came out more vehement than I expected.

"Doesn't stop most young people. All wrapped up in their careers, most of them. Flora'll talk real estate all day and night if you let her. Joel likes to chatter on about un-usual law cases. Hugh—"

"Commemorative stamps? Postage meters?"

She gave me a look that could have withered steel. "I can tell, Patricia Montella, that you were the kind of student that got record detentions for interrupting the teacher."

I grinned. "Sorry, Miz Shelby. Didn't think you'd want me to raise my hand while driving."

She couldn't maintain the stern gleam in her eye any longer but, even laughing, she didn't let me off the hook. "Hugh talks about people. He knows everyone with a box and what mail they're getting. Knows if they're in for good or bad news when they walk in. Doesn't break any confi-dences, mind you, but manages to drop a hint if he thinks, say, old Mrs. Adkins might appreciate a visit. Come to think of it, Sarah Adkins will talk your ear off about an-tiques—had her own shop for forty years. Maybe it's not only young people."

"The subject of history has come up once or twice in the past twenty-four hours, Miz Shelby. Oops, sorry, forgot to raise my hand again."

"You made your point. I'm guilty as the next person

when it comes to my favorite subject. You're the exception."

It was a question, a vacuum that needed filling.

I shrugged. "I don't do anything interesting. Answer phones. Handle customer complaints."

"And you don't like it?" Either Miss Maggie was being tactful or had a real talent for understatement.

"Wasn't so bad back when all the execs had secretaries. When they called, most were polite and efficient. Some were even human. Now, most of the secretaries and admin assistants have been laid off. Corporations figure, if a manager has a PC that does everything except fetch his coffee, he shouldn't need a secretary."

"So the executives call you direct?"

"God forbid. Shitwork like that gets passed down to the lowest flunky, who nowadays has an MBA and considers it below his dignity. Not a good preliminary for enjoyable conversation, let me tell you."

"You have a liberal arts degree, don't you, Pat?"

I kept forgetting this woman knew my life's story. The degree had been an object of pride the day they handed me the diploma, but the business world had quickly made me ashamed of it. "I took some night courses in computers, too," I added, as if to justify my presence on earth.

"I didn't know that. And what about hobbies?"

"Hobbies?" I racked my brain. Vegging in front of the TV wasn't what she wanted to hear, I was sure. "I don't really have time for hobbies—"

"Right. You don't have a lot of leisure. I remember. But, I mean, what will you do after you quit your job?"

The question dumbfounded me, in more ways than one.

"Don't tell me you haven't thought about quitting, Pat. That's the first thing people say they're going to do when they hit the lottery. When the property passes to you, you'll sell it and tell your boss what to do with your job. Right?"

"The notion has occurred to me."

"Well, I'd do it in your place. But you must have something to do. You have to keep your mind active. Trust me, Pat. I *know*."

I kept forgetting Miss Maggie was ninety-one. While her contemporaries were being spoon-fed in nursing homes, she was faxing articles to New York from out in the middle of nowhere. Apart from stiff joints, a strict diet, and a few microscopic pauses in her speech, she showed none of the outward behavior I associated with advanced age. Apart from an eccentric streak, the woman had all her marbles, maybe even more than she started with. And what she was saying was, if I wanted to end up like her, I'd better get a life.

I shrugged. "Haven't had a chance to think about it yet. I will. I've got plenty of time to try new things. Don't I?"

Miss Maggie chuckled. "Durn-tootin', missy."

I pulled up in front of the post office and cut the ignition. Popping open my seat belt, I decided not to bother pushing the driver's seat all the way back. The image of Hugh banging his knees on the steering wheel was too seductive. "I'll run the keys inside, Miss Maggie."

"Get my mail, too. Take your time. I'll wait around back."

Now, if the postmaster had no customers—no other cars parked out front, so it looked good—I'd get my opportunity to speak with Fitzhugh Lee alone.

He was hunkered down in front of the counter, tacking up a poster about sending postal orders instead of money. The poster showed a Hispanic family, all grouped around the kitchen table, wide-eyed with wonder at the postal order Papa held up delicately, as if it might turn to fairy dust and blow away. I envied them the generous, rich relative. I had cousins who were doctors, lawyers, and plumbers. Did they ever remember me this way? Not once.

"Here are your keys." I tossed them over his head onto the counter. Even hunkered down as far as he could go, his head was even with my breasts, so this was no easy feat. "Don't worry about the fender. The guy driving the semi said he'd bring it back as soon as the body shop pries it out of his grill."

Most men I know—Herb, for instance—would have dashed out to check. Not Hugh. He gave me an amused once over.

I realized I'd never untucked my T-shirt or put my socks back underneath my pants. Picture my face, above all that white cloth, as red as a ripe plum tomato.

His hand reached out without warning, pinching my buttocks.

I jumped back three feet. "What the hell are you doing?"

"Sorry. Friend of yours?" Between his fingers was something that looked like a big, shiny, black pinhead, except with squiggly legs.

"What's that?" I'm not afraid of bugs. Really I'm not. I frequently grant amnesty to little brown spiders in my apartment. Unless, of course, I find them in my bed. Then death row, no appeal. Denise says this attitude must somehow account for my bed being empty of higher lifeforms, too. I argue that men don't fit that description.

"Dog tick. Don't fret. Worst you could get from her is Rocky Mountain Spotted Fever."

I won't share the mental picture that conjured up.

He clamped the wiggling critter between two fingernails, and its little back cracked like a tiny nutshell. I actually felt pity.

Hugh went behind the counter to inter the remains in the trash basket. "You'd best look yourself over for more when you get back to Miss Maggie's."

I nodded, feeling suddenly itchy, wanting a shower right away. "She told me to pick up her mail."

He nodded. "I'll get it. Wait here."

What else could I do? I hadn't exactly taken hold of the conversation. I started to untuck my shirt, but it occurred to me that my glossy little interloper might have co-conspirators. Bad enough they were on the *outside* of my clothing.

Hugh came back before my imagination could send me

into an orgy of wanton scratching. In one hand was the mail, in the other was a quart-sized plastic bottle half-filled with a golden liquid sloshing thickly from side to side. "Beth Ann swears by this stuff. If you put it on your exposed skin and around your socks and shirt cuffs, it'll keep most insects off you."

Taking both offerings, I popped up the lid on the bottle, sniffing warily. The odor was sweet, not perfumey, sort of reminiscent of coconut oil, but not that either—didn't smell like bug repellent at all. If anything, I'd have expected it to attract insects.

"Ask Miss Maggie for a little container to put some in and bring the rest back when you get a chance."

I saw an opening. "What time does Beth Ann get home from school? I'll make sure to bring it back down before she needs it."

"Quarter to four, but it doesn't matter. She won't be going any place she'll need it for a while." Hugh leaned both arms on the counter, decreasing the difference in our heights. "Now that Miss Maggie's not here, you don't have to be diplomatic. What kind of hard time did my daughter give you yesterday?"

Is it my fault he asked for it? "She passed on your opinion of me."

I enjoyed how much that shocked him. He actually blushed. "Opinion?"

"Apparently she overheard you telling a customer all about me."

"Couldn't have. Not if she was up Miss Maggie's before one." He was mumbling, thinking aloud. "She left school during her lunch period—would have taken her a while to walk home. Even if she came in the back, I only had four customers in the first hour and none of them asked—What exactly did Beth Ann say?"

I levelled my stare at him as I had his daughter the day before. "She said you called me a city bitch."

He shifted his eyes down as she had, accompanying the motion with a sigh of exasperation. Or maybe embarrassment? "She overheard me talking to myself. I didn't know she was there. I apologize."

That made me madder. "For her or you?"

His silence implied that his opinion had been honest and founded in fact. "I'll speak to her."

"What for? She agrees with you. At least she had the courage to tell me to my face." Furious, I swung around, and stormed out of the door, barrelling into an older man coming in.

Miss Maggie pursed her lips at my red face and tense muscles but said nothing as I approached. Taking her mail, she nodded a question to the bottle I held.

"Bug repellent," I replied, a little too tersely. "Sorry I took so long."

She waved away my words like they were annoying mosquitos. "Come over here. I'll show you what I was looking at." I followed her around to the north side of the trailer, where another path entered the woods. A few yards in, clusters of bell-shaped blossoms burst from the thicket in lavender-blue cascades.

My bad mood evaporated. "They're beautiful."

"Virginia bluebells. Always were my favorite. Never told Jake though, or he'd have picked them for me. I'd rather see them in this setting."

I saw what she meant. The flowers had somehow transformed the underbrush. No longer space aliens, the vines and brambles had become noble guardians of precious treasure. I brushed my fingertips lightly along one blue fringe. They felt as silky as they looked.

"What shall we do with the afternoon, Pat?" Miss Maggie asked as we retraced our steps to our path home.

I shrugged. "Depends how complicated you want dinner to be."

She stopped dead in her tracks. "Dinner?" Her palm smote her forehead. "I clean forgot. You have a date tonight."

"What?"

"Joel called this morning, before you came downstairs. Asked if he could steal you away for dinner. He's picking you up at seven."

"You said yes for me? I don't have anything to wear."

"I told him that. Said, 'What are you thinking, Joel Peyton? We told her to bring comfortable clothes, and here you are, wanting Pat to get all prettied up.' He promised to take you somewhere casual. I probably have a top I can lend you, and those white knit things you're wearing will do all right."

Had she told me this morning, I wouldn't have worn the stirrup pants to traipse through high grass with her. Then again, maybe the jeans would have attracted more ticks. Grass stains were a small price to pay to avoid infestation worthy of an Indiana Jones movie.

My intention, as soon as we got back to the house, was to head straight for the upstairs bathroom, where I could strip under a fluorescent light bright enough for insect inspection. However, Wilma Rae Boutchyard was waiting for us on the front porch, occupying a rocker as if she were a queen on her throne. In looks, she wasn't anything like the Wicked Witch of the West. More like a fiftyish Auntie Em, though her hair was black with a purple tint, a sure sign of henna gone horribly wrong.

The car parked in the turn-around was midsized, sensible, and American. A midsized man stood by the driver's door, smoking a cigarette, the expression under his black baseball cap blank, zombielike. Classifying him as a chauffeur, I was surprised when Miss Maggie introduced him as Wilma Rae's hubby, Elliott.

"Pat, go fetch Wilma Rae a glass of iced tea, won't you?" Miss Maggie handed me the door keys, since we hadn't yet gone inside.

I wasn't sure if she wanted to talk to the woman alone, or if she was giving me a chance to make myself presentable, or if she simply didn't want to leave me alone with Wilma Rae while she fulfilled her hostess duties. Wondering which, I opened the screen and unlocked the inside door, scooping up a junk-mail flyer that had been stuck between the two. Not until I was beside the hall table about to set the flyer down did I notice the paper had "For P.M." neatly laser-printed in big, bold Times Roman.

The sheet was plain white, folded in half. I opened it and inside was an editorial quoted, it said, from the *Stoke Vindicator,* 1868:

> The rumors of Yankee carpetbaggers being shot or stabbed in Stoke County are entirely without foundation. However, Northerners who have come to Virginia to seek their fortunes and swindle the good citizens of this state would do well to return from whence they came. Any Yankee requiring a more formal invitation is likely to be presented a fine suit of tar and feathers as a farewell memento.

Below the paragraph were the underlined phrases *Newspaper Index* and *Back to Reconstruction Main Page.* A web site printout, I deduced, though any headers or footers giving the address or date of access had been carefully snipped off.

More imaginative than throwing rocks at me, at any rate. I suspected the same hand had done both. Not having time to mull it over further, I refolded the page and stuffed it in my pocketbook, which I parked at the bottom of the stairs.

When I returned to the porch with the iced tea and more orderly clothing, Miss Maggie waved me into the other rocker. I was learning that, despite her nine decades, she wasn't much for sitting down, as if she'd used up her sitting allowance years ago.

In contrast to Miss Maggie's constant energy, Wilma Rae looked as if she never unbent her knees. I could picture her in a sedan chair, being lugged around by a couple of Nubian Hulk Hogan types.

Wilma Rae opened her mouth and julep-tinted basso profundo tones rolled out. "So *you're* Patricia Montella."

It was all I could do not to recoil, her enunciation was

that horrible. Not only my last name but my first as well. Even Miss Maggie, behind the woman's back, produced a grimace worthy of a Kodak moment. Unsure how to react, I nodded.

"Just what sort of name is Montella?" Wilma Rae's eyes dared me to come up with an acceptable reply. Lavender eyes she had, making me wonder if the color in her hair was natural after all. Maybe she had some purple pigment chromosome, handed down as proof of royal blood.

Obviously, to answer "Italian" would only dig my social grave deeper. Or as Wilma Rae would no doubt say, "Eye-talian." Mind poker, I told myself. Pretend she's Burt. Better yet, think of her as a nice change of pace. "We're the Montellas from Campania. Surely you've heard of us. Purveyors of fine marble for generations. All the famous Renaissance sculptors got their stone from us." It might even have been true—after all, my great-grandpop had worked in a marble quarry.

"Yes, of course." Did I mention? The woman never smiled. Even when she was bluffing.

Miss Maggie rewarded me with a grin.

"On your mother's side," Wilma Rae continued, with the air of someone finally getting to the meat of the matter, "you're a descendant of the Bells and Shacklefords."

The Bells and Shacklefords. Sounded like an Olde English pub. I almost blurted out "And the Giamos," though I knew she wouldn't view my Sicilian blood as an enhancement to the gene pool. Even the Montellas had been against Dad marrying a Sicilian. Three of his aunts never spoke to him again.

I shoved my Mediterranean pride aside and slipped a pinch of Dixie into my voice. "Yes, ma'am. Why, I feel like I've finally come home."

Miss Maggie's cheeks reddened and tears glistened in her eyes. It wasn't the sentiment—she was desperately trying not to laugh. Over by the car, Elliott lit up another cigarette.

Wilma Rae sipped her tea for the first time. "I'll see to your application myself, Patrice."

Patrice? Miss Maggie's warning cringe told me not to correct her. "Application, Mrs. Boutchyard?"

"For the Daughters of the Confederacy. After all, three of your ancestors fought bravely for the cause. I'm sure Magnolia can provide you with all the documentation you need."

Here I'd been speculating about the DAR, not realizing the Confederacy had its own little quilting circle, apparently ready to welcome me cheerily to their bosoms. So why did I want to toss my breakfast?

"Now—," Wilma Rae tabled the discussion and moved on to new business, "—the Historical Preservation Society has some recommendations regarding the restoration of the Bell House."

I realized she meant that pile of vine-covered bricks in the woods. "Restoration?"

"We feel the public should see it as it was in its heyday, furnished, of course, with reproduction period pieces, and displaying items of historical importance from local collectors. The Boutchyard collection of antique firearms, for example."

The woman was on controlled substances. "Have you seen the house, Mrs. Boutchyard?"

"A grotesque eyesore, Patrice. It will have to be rebuilt from the ground up, naturally. Let me give you the name of an excellent architectural firm in Fredericksburg—Maguire and Rhodes have restor—"

"It'd cost a fortune."

Wilma Rae sipped her tea calmly, as if we were talking about the weather. "You may, of course, pass the restoration costs on to whichever developer purchases the property. The house, you see, would be a *focal* point for the new development. This is quite a common way of preserving the past, I think you'll find."

I knew it was. Lots of the big estates back home in Pennsylvania were now retirement communities, condo complexes, office suites. On all of them, the manor house had still been standing, lived in right up until the builder brought in the bulldozers. "I don't think it's feasible here."

"We're having a historical easement placed on the lot, so that no development may take place unless the main house is restored."

My stomach lurched. "This Historical Society of yours, if they're so concerned—they're welcome to bid on the property when it comes up for sale. Restore it themselves."

"The Historical Preservation Society does not function in that capacity." You'd think I asked the U.S. Surgeon General to write out a prescription for antacids. Wilma Rae stood, handing her half-empty glass to Miss Maggie. "I'll bring the recommendations by later this week, Patrice."

After she'd gone, Miss Maggie poured the remaining iced tea off the side of the porch. "I hope it doesn't kill the grass."

"Can she do what she said, Miss Maggie?" I asked.

"You mean make you or some developer rebuild Bell House? Not likely. For an easement you have to prove the house is architecturally one-of-a-kind, or that somebody famous lived there, or that something important happened there." Miss Maggie held the front screen door open for me. "Let's forget Wilma Rae and go have lunch, Pat."

But I couldn't forget her. She might make it impossible for me to sell the place. Was the Battle of Chancellorsville an important enough event? Hadn't I seen a historical marker out on Route 3 that said Stonewall Jackson had been mortally wounded practically in Miss Maggie's backyard?

Wilma Rae was Miss Gulch, all right. I felt like she'd stuffed my little dog into her picnic basket, and I'd never see him again.

I never had a clear conception of the horrors of war until that night. . . . I could hear on all sides the dreadful groans of the wounded and their heart piercing cries. . . . Friends and foe all together . . . I assure you I am heartily sick of soldiering.

Texan, A. N. Erskine to his wife—1862

MAY 5, 1864—SAUNDERS' FIELD

Relentlessly, as the sun fell from overhead, the Yanks sent men up that gradient into the strong center of our ranks. I witnessed the final moments of hundreds, the abomination of the day etched into their sallow faces by horrifying death.

Yet, our troops remained relatively unmoved throughout, losing ground only where the field and forest burst into flame. No army cared to claim those acres then. Both withdrew, leaving the screaming wounded behind to await their demise in the inferno. By mid-afternoon, Hell's battalions held as much terrain as both mortal forces combined.

Finally came a lull, the cries of the wounded growing clearer, more disturbing, as the din of gunfire was quelled. They called for water mostly, some for loved ones, many for Mother. This last I found difficult to abide. They took for granted those women who'd borne them—raised them to these high precepts, sanctioning murder—those women resting safe in their Northern homes.

Whose name could I evoke in my hour of death? Not Mother, lest it be to petition her intervention that I might somehow gain Heaven's refuge. But no, I belonged with Lane and Evan, with my father, and with these newly perished souls on Saunders' Field today. I deserved damnation and would embrace Hell's torment throughout Eternity.

"Get ready, Gabe." Cobb's voice broke through my meditations. "They're coming again."

Sure enough, the forest below spewed forth a line of blue sharpshooters, coming right at us this time.

General Stafford, whether truly seeing an opportunity or caught up in the exhilaration, hurdled his horse over a furrow, brandishing his saber, signalling his men from the shelter of their trenches forward to meet the advancing enemy. Howling, they charged from our right, General Steuart's Louisianans close behind, across our volleys, forcing us to desist and watch their idiocy.

Confounded by the action, our General Walker faltered, not knowing if he should have sent us along the left of Stafford's men. But it was plain he had to move us someplace now. Screaming to his captains, he commanded us right, to span the increasing gap between Stafford and Steuart.

Such obvious suicide. Bluecoats had already breached the opening and more were storming around Stafford's other side. Yet someone sounded the Rebel yell, and hundreds of surrounding voices took it up, until it became so shrill I yearned to clap my hands to my ears. I was carried out of the trenches by the sheer delirium of the mob.

Because I was so much smaller than most of the men, it was easy to fall to the rear overlooked. Not fifty yards out, flush with a tract of gangly, dense thicket on our flank, I fell to the ground as if wounded.

Cobb, who must have been looking back for me, called out, but I waved him on, holding my leg as if I'd wrenched it in a fox hole. He nodded, gestured me to keep my head low, and raced off into the midst of the bloodshed.

I slithered, prone, facedown, to the undergrowth, burrowing deep beneath, feeling its barbs snag and rip my clothes, drawing blood from my head and neck. I had no time to ponder how safe this haven would prove, for posthaste I heard a thunderous commotion of gunfire near at hand.

A panicked stampede of gray and tan legs traversed the ground over which I'd just crawled, followed closely by limbs swathed in blue and red. They were on all sides and so many, I was sure the thicket would be mowed down by the force of their numbers and I trampled to death, as insignificant as an ant.

Closing my eyes, shielding my head with my arms, I lay frozen through an eon of bedlam, the ceaseless roar of musketry, the deep, robust hurrahs of the Yankees as they took our original line, the piercing Rebel yells that prophesied each countercharge.

Amid all, the stenches of sulphur and blood, and the salty taste of my own tears.

9

After Wilma Rae left, and after finally making sure no tick
stowaways had hitched a ride from Saunders' Field, I pulled
a container of chicken broth and a carton of egg substitute
from the freezer to defrost for Miss Maggie's dinner, despite her protests that she could fend for herself.

"You wanted Italian food this week," I pointed out.
"This is Grandma Montella's recipe."

Miss Maggie stopped protesting. Her salivating got in
the way.

I ate a hurried lunch, then chopped some Italian bread
into half-inch cubes, and finished defrosting the egg substitute in the microwave. Miss Maggie, bless her soul, had
real Locatelli cheese, hand-grated (with her left-handed
grater). I beat maybe a tablespoon of cheese into the egg,
dunked the cubes, and fried them like French toast in a few
drops of oil. When they were done and the grease sopped
off them with a paper towel, I popped them into the fridge
in one of Miss Maggie's ubiquitous storage tubs. The cubes
don't fall apart later on if they're cold first.

Then I played dress up, feeling like a Barbie doll, if you
can picture one in her thirties with generous hips. If only
Joel hadn't reminded me so much of a bleached-blond Ken.
Granted, his hair was probably never combed into perfect
rubberized plastic waves, nor did he seem the boxer-shorts
type, though researching this wasn't out of the question.

I finally settled on a V-necked top from Miss Maggie's
closet: light blue and, of course, her favorite color, pale

yellow, with white lace trim separating the colors. It hung loose over my butt—a miracle—with elbow-length sleeves and padded shoulders to bring my upper into proportion with my lower. Also among her handouts was a gold necklace, its round pendant of bright blue and amber stones enhancing the bare skin framed by the vee, bringing attention to my gold hoop earrings.

With everything settled by three-thirty, I changed back to my jeans and T-shirt. Miss Maggie provided a travel-sized squeeze bottle that had once held shampoo. I filled it half full of Beth Ann's golden ointment and dabbed some onto my arms.

I was determined to talk to the girl, needed to, before trying to sleep another night, and before I told Miss Maggie or Hugh about the rock throwing or the suggestive newspaper quote. I might be wrong, and Beth Ann might be innocent. If she hadn't been the rock thrower, maybe she knew of kids who hung out in the woods at night. Kids throwing rocks, while not on their best behavior, I could somehow understand. Adults throwing rocks scared the hell out of me.

I thought I'd have to steel myself to enter the forest alone. Surprise, surprise. I found myself actually enjoying the walk down to the creek. Sunbeams slanted through the trees from right to left, hanging a hazy curtain of warmth.

I began to notice details that had escaped me before. Orange mushrooms fashioning a ladder on a dead log. A pair of chipmunks playing tag to and fro across the path. Heart-shaped hoofprints—deer, I supposed. And wildflowers of all shapes and colors.

Perhaps I was getting used to the place. Or maybe only the part of the forest leading back to the old ruin and cemetery was spooky. Or all the ghosts had gone south to participate in today's phantom reenactment at Saunders' Field.

Then again, I could be encountering ghosts right now and never know it. My other brushes with "Ouija-World" hadn't been especially frightening. Not until Miss Maggie opened her big mouth to tell me what I'd been hearing and smelling and seeing. Maybe I was viewing this forest now through the eyes of Gabriel Bell. If I was, he must have loved it.

As Miss Maggie had that morning, I paused in the middle of the bridge, this time on the upstream side. It was all I could do to resist the urge to get down on my knees and plunge my hand into the clear water. After ten seconds of self-discipline, I gave in to the desire.

My fingers tingled in the cold water. A tiny tadpole, swimming out from between two smooth green rocks, was startled to find large, pink, wiggly limbs in his path. He darted side to side before deciding things were safer upstream.

I don't know what made me look up—certainly no sound or movement—but there on the right bank, crouched like a gnome beside a huge rotted-out stump, Beth Ann watched me over her shoulder. She was as motionless as the deer in the backyard had been when they sensed danger. And for a very brief moment, her eyes seemed as vulnerable.

Then anger flashed across her face and, gathering up her school knapsack, she lunged toward the creek, trying to ford it over the moss-covered rocks. One foot slipped, her leg sinking up to the calf, but regaining her balance, she forged on.

"Wait," I shouted. "I have something of yours."

Beth Ann glanced over at me as she climbed the opposite bank. I held up the bottle. Seeing I wasn't lying, she stopped. "Toss it over here."

I shook my head. "I can't throw to save my life. Come over and get it."

She recognized a ploy when she heard one. "You can bring it up to the trailer."

"Where I can also tell your dad you're out here when you're supposed to be grounded. Your choice."

Warily, she came along the bank toward me. She had to anyway, to get to the path, but she stopped at the end of the bridge. "I don't care what you tell him."

"Should I tell him about last night, too?" A gamble, but her expression told me I'd hit pay dirt. I'd been kneeling up straight from the moment her foot went into the creek. Now I settled back down, bringing my legs around front, sitting cross-legged in an attempt to look less intimidating. I put the bottle in front of me like a lure. "I just want to talk, Beth Ann."

My use of her name startled her. Draping her knapsack over one shoulder, shoving her hands into her jeans pockets, she walked out onto the wood planks to within six feet of me. Her one wet foot made muddy prints on the wood. "What about?"

Not looking her in the eye, trying to keep my voice neutral, I said, "Someone threw a rock at me around eleven-thirty, quarter to twelve last night."

I could feel her muscles tightening, sensed her instinct to flee. She shifted her weight, arms plainly gesturing I-don't-care. "So?"

"I thought, since you spend so much time in these woods, you might have seen someone hanging around. Someone suspicious? But I didn't want to mention it in front of your dad, in case he'd think you had something to do with it."

Beth Ann digested my words with a frown. In the end, she merely said, "I haven't seen anyone."

An honest answer. At her age I would have jumped at the out I'd offered, making up a mysterious, evil trespasser, even giving him a couple of rocks to juggle. Beth Ann chose to leave herself under suspicion. Short of a confession, it was an honorable response, impressing me no end. Then again, it was also the strongest defense she could throw in my face.

Next topic. "Do you have a PC at home?"

Her forehead wrinkled up in what looked like sheer puzzlement. "No. And anyway, it's none of your business."

"Don't you ever use a computer for school projects?"

"Miss Maggie lets me use hers. Why?"

That stumped me. Beth Ann hadn't been inside the

house since I arrived. That meant if she was responsible for the printout, she planned it before she met me, so her feelings *were* personal, not based on my actions as I'd thought yesterday. Unless she'd used another printer. Where? School? But I'd assumed she'd put the paper inside the front screen before she caught the bus this morning.

I'd have to figure it out later. Right now, I didn't want to answer her question. Time to switch gears. I nodded to where I'd seen her on the right bank. "What were you doing over there?"

"Nothing." I didn't need to see her face to picture her pout.

"Are there mushrooms growing on that old stump?" I persisted.

"Too old." She shifted her weight again. "I was looking at the saplings next to it. They're chestnut trees."

Her words ignited another flash of my imagination. I saw a tall, graceful trunk leaning out over the creek, stretching high into the forest canopy. Both creek banks were carpeted with fallen chestnuts and empty husks. "That stump was a chestnut tree once, wasn't it?"

"Before the blight killed it." Her voice mixed bitterness with regret.

I vaguely remembered reading about the chestnut blight for a college course on the Great Depression. The disease had been brought into the country on an imported tree and killed every chestnut tree in America, ruining the economy of the Appalachians the way the Dust Bowl had ruined the Midwest. I'd never thought about the blight outside of economics or happening anywhere but the Appalachians. The saplings Beth Ann spoke of were little more than dead-looking twigs, with only a leaf or two each. "Where did the saplings come from?"

"They're all that's left of the old tree. A new sapling comes out every once in a while. They only live a few years before the blight gets them too, but they send up new shoots and the cycle starts again."

A pitiful existence for something once so majestic. I

hung one leg over the edge of the bridge, teasing the little crests of water with the sole of my sneaker. "Are there others around here?"

She laughed with contempt, a frightening sound coming from so young a throat. "There's a whole grove of them down in Richmond, protected inside one of the battlefield areas. So don't you let your conscience bother you when some bulldozer gets this one."

I wasn't troubled by the thought of bulldozers, but by Miss Maggie's comment about how they'd dam the creek.

Beth Ann, who'd run out of patience with me, grabbed her bug juice bottle and started back toward her house.

"What if I don't sell all the land?" *Good God, what was I saying?*

Beth Ann swept around, her jaw wide open, her eyes plainly mistrusting.

"I could live here," I said, the words coming spontaneously from some uncharted part of my brain. "Get a job in Fredericksburg. Sell enough of the land to pay the taxes on the rest—maybe over along the west border, where there's a parking lot anyway."

"You mean that?"

Did I? I realized the idea had been niggling around in my subconscious since yesterday when Miss Maggie mentioned the school groups. It might solve the easement problem, too. "I . . . I don't know. I mean, I have to look into it. See how feasible it is. See what I can afford."

Before she could react, a deep male voice rumbled down between the trees. "Beth Ann!"

"Oh, shit," she exclaimed. "I'm dead."

I hurried over to her side. Hugh was striding angrily down the hill. When he caught sight of me, his pace slowed by a fraction.

"It's my fault she's here," I sputtered, before he could get a word in edgewise. "I wanted to . . . to ask her about the property. Miss Maggie says she knows the woods better than anyone."

Hugh halted in front of me, close enough that I had to

strain my neck to look up into his face. "Beth Ann, go home. Wait for me in your bedroom."

That sounded ominous to me, but Beth Ann seemed anything but scared. "I came down here after I got off my bus. She had nothing to do with it."

"Beth Ann—"

"All right, I'm going." She tramped off up the hill, glancing occasionally back to see if her father was watching after her. He was, which left me free to make faces behind his back. Beth Ann caught one of them and cracked a half-smile.

Hugh swung around. Expecting it, I'd already returned my mouth muscles to their resting position. "Miss Montella—"

"Yes, *Mr.* Lee?"

"I want you to leave my daughter alone."

I felt the skin on the back of my neck tingle. "Why?"

"You upset her. She never cut school, or disobeyed me, before you came."

I wondered. Maybe I didn't know much about kids, but I remembered myself and my friends at that age. Some level of disobedience was the norm. A teen was *supposed* to push against boundaries. More likely, Beth Ann simply hadn't been caught before, which meant her actions were less calculated this week, more emotional.

Since my own actions all week had also been pretty emotional—oh, who was I kidding? They'd *always* been emotional, from the moment I spied the guy in green at the end of the birth canal and had mulishly refused to come out.

My reaction to Hugh's request was no exception. "Wow, I must be some bad influence. Here I've talked with her, what, fifteen minutes total? Already she's a juvenile delinquent. Tomorrow she'll be smoking. Teenage sex on Thursday, drugs on Friday, and—"

"No!" he yelled, his big fingers bunching into fists. "Just stay away from her!"

The fear I'd felt yesterday in the car with him was no

match for what washed over me now. At first I could say nothing—it was all I could do to breathe. His eyes stared directly down into mine. Flinching, I bent my head, trying to look anywhere but at him. Impossible, considering he pretty much took up my whole field of view.

I saw his fists relax, and one hand reached out towards me, possibly only in apology. Not about to find out, I bolted, across the bridge planks, up the hill, through the woods, across the yard, drawing my first gasp of air on the back porch.

My plan was to stay on the porch until I'd caught my breath and talked myself out of crying, but Miss Maggie was in the kitchen and heard me. She came crashing through the door as I sank down on the step.

"Pat, honey." She slipped her arms around me. "Calm down. Tell me what happened."

I spit out a garbled, condensed version as tears tumbled down my cheeks.

She pursed her lips. "He didn't hurt you, did he?"

"No. But I'm afraid he'll hurt Beth Ann." My Italian guilt genes were whipping that worry up into a froth. Not only had I done nothing to quiet Hugh's wrath, I'd made it worse. If he went home and—

"He won't. Hugh would never harm Beth Ann." Seeing the skepticism in my eyes, Miss Maggie gave me a reassuring squeeze. "I'm sure of it, Pat. The problem seems to be you. He wasn't his usual self yesterday when he dropped you off, or this morning in the post office." Putting her hands on my shoulders, she leaned back to survey me at arm's length, the step boards groaning as her weight shifted.

"I didn't *do* anything, Miss Maggie."

"Didn't have to." She nodded as if to answer some inward question. "I think you remind Hugh of his wife. Oh, not your personality—you're the exact opposite from Tanya—but she was dark like you. Though not as petite."

That made me laugh, relieving some of my tension. "By

clothing-store standards, you can't call anyone petite unless they wear size ten or less."

"You're also not supposed to wear anything but poly-ester stretch pants when you're over fifty. I have my own standards."

I wiped my tears with one hand, reaching down off the porch with the other to pick a clover blossom, twirling it between my fingers until all its tiny petals merged into a white blur. I was of an age where half the married people I knew were going through divorces. No matter how ami-cable they tried to make it seem, all were bitter to some degree. "I'm sorry I look like his ex, but—"

"Hugh's not divorced, Pat. His wife died. Long ago, while Beth Ann was a toddler."

"He's still mad that she left him to raise a daughter by himself?" I wasn't very good at this psychology stuff, but ten years seemed a long time to nurse that kind of grudge.

Miss Maggie shook her head. "Don't let it upset you, Pat. You'll be gone at the end of the week—"

"No. That's just it. I need to know because of what I said to Beth Ann." I told Miss Maggie about the chestnut tree episode and of my plan to live here and leave some of the land undeveloped.

She threw her arms around me ecstatically. "Oh, Pat. I'm so glad. I'd hoped you would—"

"*But*, if I'm going to have a neighbor—a tenant—who can't stand the sight of me—"

"Yes, I suppose you should know why." Miss Maggie sighed. "Hugh and Tanya married right out of college. Both got very good state jobs in Richmond—Hugh managing grant funding, Tanya designing tourism brochures. They bought a nice house, good neighborhood—"

"The whole American dream thing?"

Miss Maggie nodded. "Not long after Beth Ann was born, Tanya began taking drugs. I never asked all the de-tails, but I think it had something to do with postpartum depression and Hugh working long hours. God knows what else. Anyway, she became addicted. That's how she died—an overdose."

My guilt genes abandoned the old cause for this new one. "I made a stupid comment about drugs down by the bridge. That's what set him off. I should apologize." I stood up, ready to go back down at once.

"No." Miss Maggie grabbed my wrist. "For one thing, he'd know I told you, and I'd rather he didn't know I broke his confidence. For another, you have my supper to cook and a date to dress for."

Supper. Joel. I checked my watch. 5:17. Did I say my life was uncomplicated?

The crunching of tires against gravel reached our ears, accompanied by the familiar steel-drum ping.

"Beau—but it sounds like *two* cars," Miss Maggie mused. "Now who could he be bringing?" She was already heading around the side of the house.

"I'll be in the kitchen, Miss Maggie," I called after her, not wanting to face anyone with tear-streaked cheeks.

Splashing some water on my face until I felt human again, I then set to work, pouring the broth into a pot to warm. I was washing a fistful of spinach when Miss Maggie summoned me with a yell through the front screen door. I set the spinach to drain on a paper towel, wiped my hands, and lowered the burner under the soup before joining her.

"Pat—," Miss Maggie nudged me toward the two people sitting on the porch rockers, "—you know Beau—"

Today, his light grey, threadbare suit was topped off by a striped bow tie. As he stood, the wicker rocker relinquished his weight with an out-of-rhythm teeter. He did his bow-and-hand-squeeze routine. "You're looking fine, Miss Montella. Virginia living must be agreeing with you."

Knowing my eyes were probably still red gave a healthy blush to my cheeks, I'm sure, but before I could get over his reception, Miss Maggie was prodding me toward her other visitor, a woman, maybe ten years my senior. "Charlotte Garber, come all the way from California to look up her roots."

In one sense, she reminded me of my elementary school principal—kind, cordial, but don't let her catch you throwing stones in the school yard. Her clothes, though, seemed out of character. She was dressed in what's called "business casual"—you know, when they give you a dress-down day at work, and all the women show up in designer tweeds and Italian loafers. Me, I take dress-down days as a challenge, wearing clothes that make a statement. Like my K-Mart imitation L. L. Bean puddle waders.

Charlotte shook my hand with a wimpy, clammy grasp. "My great-great-grandfather was from this part of Virginia. Or, at least, my grandmother always said he was. All we knew of him was family tradition—word-of-mouth—like how he'd been in the Confederate Army when he was only a kid. I never expected to find out so much in only one day."

Beau sat again, stretching his long legs before him. "You're lucky to be looking up the Bell family. Like I was telling you down at the county archives today, Magnolia here has already done your legwork for you."

"The Bell family?" I repeated stupidly. My intuition had already begun to put the pieces together, but I didn't want to believe it.

"Her great-great-grandfather was Gabriel Bell, Pat." Miss Maggie seemed awfully reserved for someone who'd just had her life's work invigorated. Then again, I had a feeling those shrewd eyes of hers were transmitting a secret message to me: *Keep your mouth shut.* Did she know me already or what? "Gabriel was Pat's great-uncle, Charlotte. Looks like you two are cousins."

Charlotte leaned forward so fast, I thought the rocker would tip her right into us. "You're *kidding!*" she gushed like a teenager, adding yet another dimension to the school-principal/sophisticate melting pot. "Tell me, on the map that little stream is called Bell Run, and the housing tract across the main road—"

"Yes, yes, this was the original farm," Miss Maggie assured her.

"Gabe was a boy here," Charlotte sighed, standing, leaning out over the porch rail, studying what land she could see that wasn't blocked by the magnolia's limbs. I wondered what she *really* saw. The monster-matinee forest that had been my first impression? The dreamy woods I'd glimpsed today, complete with full-grown chestnut trees?

One landscape I was sure she didn't see—the wartime Bell Run of Gabriel Bell's adolescence: acres of tree stumps, burned-out scrub, and trampled, defiled farmland.

"It's too dark back under the trees to show you the family cemetery now," Miss Maggie was saying, though it wouldn't be that dark under them for another hour and a half. "If you come back tomorrow morning, I'd be glad to take you."

Charlotte willingly agreed but failed to recognize Miss Maggie's invitation as the dismissal it was.

Beau caught on, though I thought he wanted to stay longer. He stood and stretched. "I'd best be getting home. Miz Garber, you'll want to let me guide you back out to the main road. Might have some trouble maneuvering that big rental of yours." He nodded to a new Caddy parked behind his pickup.

Miss Maggie was silent until the cars were out of sight. Though the sun wouldn't set over the outside world for another few hours, here the birds were already noisily enjoying their evening meal. A single woodpecker, high enough up in a tree to make use of the light, was still hard at work, the sound reminding me of the rat-a-tat of a toy machine gun.

At last Miss Maggie turned to me. "Maybe you ought to tell me how to finish cooking that recipe. You'll never be ready by the time Joel gets here."

"Wait." I needed to know what, if anything, had changed. I nodded my chin toward the now empty rockers. "What does this mean, Miss Maggie?"

"Other questions to answer before that one, Pat. I had *you* investigated, remember?"

"You think she's a fake?"

Miss Maggie shrugged. "Plenty of veterans went west after the Civil War. No fancy hospitals to treat all the psychological aftereffects back then, but there was a big frontier where a person could take out his frustrations, start over. Gabriel Bell didn't have a home or family left here. If he deserted, or somehow escaped from the Federals, going west wouldn't have been a bad idea."

Reaching over the porch rail, she plucked a magnolia petal and took a deep whiff. "All the same, I find Charlotte Garber's timing interesting. Don't you?"

Inclosed you will find two or three pretty violets that I picked up on the very ground where my regiment stood and fought so splendidly. The ground was made rich by the blood of our brave soldiers. I thought the flowers would be a relic prised by you.

General Robert McAllister,
in a letter to his wife—May 1864

MAY 5, 1864—NORTHEAST OF SAUNDERS' FIELD

The fighting persevered not a hundred yards behind me, raging furiously the remainder of the day. I could hear the wounded all around, pleading for relief, but I lay as one dead, knowing I should be shot the moment I ventured forth.

I lost consciousness twice that I remember. On waking the first time, I found it dark. The chorus of musketry had abated, only fleeting eruptions of skirmish fire endured. New voices came to my ears: Yankee details sent to carry the wounded from the field. Thus I knew I was yet behind Union lines. In the darkness, with their lanterns casting as many shadows as they dispelled, I went unnoticed.

I fell into a restless slumber, my mind remaining agile yet knowing, in its instinct to survive, that my body must not stir. I was awakened anew by the perfumes of real coffee and cooking meat. The hushed rustling and murmuring raised by an assembly of thousands drifted upon the night air, but there was no activity in my proximity. Now was my opportunity.

Slowly, I worked my arms and legs, warming my blood, coaxing it into my extremities. Strapping my rifle on my shoulder, I crawled to the edge of the thicket.

Tiny campfires, like stars on a clear night, dotted this side of our morning trenches. What a hellish mockery of Creation's true firmament, even as the smoke from the day's havoc blotted out the sky above. Brush fires still blazed to the south, and I thanked the Almighty that my afternoon sanctuary had been spared that cleansing.

Keeping low, following alongside the refuge of underbrush as best I could, I stole away from the armies, stumbling in the gloom over the corpses. At the crest of the hill I left the battlefield behind. Unsure of my bearings, I made my way downhill through the dense growth, feeling through the darkness with all my limbs, expecting at any minute to blunder into Yankee reserves and be captured.

At last the welcome sound of water reached my ears. Since I'd not crossed the turnpike, I knew the stream to be Flat Run. Here I stopped to drink and eat a portion of bread, before filling my canteen and considering my direction.

The fulfillment of my mission lay upstream, with fifty thousand men between. Enlistment had not brought me closer to my target, as I'd hoped, but had provided me forty rounds of ammunition, only a fraction of which I'd spent that morning in battle. The canteen and haversack, too, would have their uses if I must make my way, in a wide berth, around both armies.

Downstream, a scant three miles in a straight line, was Bell Run. If the Yanks hadn't discovered my secret entrance to the cellar, I might yet find the apple butter and chestnuts I'd hidden last fall.

Even if that purpose went unrealized, if I found worse wreckage than before, it was still home. Sleep on the hard ground there would be sweeter than elsewhere. If only for one night.

I came upon the Yankee reserves before I'd gone but one mile. Shielded in the shadows of thicket along Flat Run, I watched them march down the plank road from Germanna Ford, heading south to join the melee. Row after row of them splashed across the creek, their column never ending, as if some infernal Northern factory were manufacturing them en masse.

At last all had crossed, and the echoes of their tramping feet were absorbed into the night. I knew there must be more to the north. They'd have left a guard at the ford and up along the railroad.

But as I presumed, no other Federals stood between me and my home. An impermanent condition, most likely. The Yanks had retreated across Bell Run twice before. Still, they'd brought supply wagons this time, as if they meant to stay awhile. One day more was all I desired.

I found the house plundered anew. In the gloom, I could see only the gaps where floorboards had covered joists. Taken for firewood, no doubt. Or to gain entry to the cellar, my last refuge. Tears came then, no longer to be held at bay.

Sick at heart, needing to know if my family's graves had also been despoiled, I picked my way across the rutted earth to their resting places. The starlight made silhouettes of their crosses, by some miracle all five still standing upright.

Relieved, exhausted, I lay down there, curled upon my mother's grave, cool Virginia clay against my cheek, and fell asleep.

10

"You've been quiet," Joel said as he tore open a third sugar packet to add to his coffee. "Didn't like the food?"

"I loved it." We'd ended up in a diner in Stoke. Casual, as he'd promised, but cozy enough for conversation and the food was wonderful. "Especially that cornbread pudding— spoonbread. I'm getting the recipe."

"I *thought* a good cook like you would want to try the local cuisine. What was that stuff you concocted for Magnolia tonight?"

"Bread soup with greens. My grandmother always made it with endive or escarole, but spinach works just as well." After the scene on the porch, I'd insisted on finishing what I'd begun, chopping the spinach, adding it to the steaming broth, before going upstairs to shower and change. It hadn't mattered how late I ran. As I surmised, Joel and Miss Maggie had been deep in conference in the war room when I came down. I'd retreated to the kitchen, not wanting to eavesdrop, afraid of what I might hear. Miss Maggie had dragged Joel in after me, saying she was too famished to talk business any longer. I'd added the bread cubes to the pot, making her promise to let them warm in the soup a good ten minutes before ladling any into a bowl and to sprinkle Locatelli over the soup before eating. She'd already been sampling from the pot as Joel had coaxed me out the door.

"Look," he said in his professional voice, bringing my attention back to the diner and the booth we sat in, "if you're worried about this Charlotte Garber person, don't be. First thing tomorrow morning, I'll be on the phone, checking her out. Commander Shelby's orders."

"What if she really is a descendent of Gabriel Bell?" I stared down at my reflection fluttering in the untouched cup of black coffee before me. The thick white cup, maroon-tinted along its rim—to hide lipstick stains?—was slightly chipped on the handle. "Will Miss Maggie change her will?"

"One piece of advice my father gave me before he died: Never try to second-guess Magnolia Shelby. Off the record? I think she'd want an equal split between Gabriel and Julia's descendants. So if Charlotte is legit and winds up having a hundred siblings and cousins, you'd still get half."

I hadn't even thought about Charlotte having relatives. And there was no way to draw a dividing line, north-south or east-west, that would include all of the stream, the family graveyard, and yes, I even wanted the jungle-encrusted ruin with the threatened historical easement.

Joel sipped his coffee, as if needing the cup as a blind from which to observe me. "Magnolia told me about your plans, Pat. She's thrilled you want to keep part of the land."

I shrugged. "Seemed the right thing to do at the time."

"And now?"

How could I explain that I was having more and more trouble reconciling the person I was, right at this minute, with the person who'd disembarked from that Amtrak train yesterday? Then again, the old Pat belonged to the real world. She still had a low-paying job, bills waiting for her at home, not enough skills, or ambition, to have a future worth anticipating. All these new idealistic ideas of mine didn't allow for poor casting. The heroine needed, if not independent wealth, at least a padded savings account. Could I hope for a decent-paying job in Fredericksburg when I hadn't been able to get another at home?

And now the stakes could very well be cut in half. Even if I managed to acquire all the choice sites on the property that I so possessively—irrationally—desired, I'd still have to sell *some* of it. I pictured Beth Ann and the rare smile she'd offered me today, and felt miserable. "I don't know," was the only response I could give.

Our waitress brought dessert, a slice of killer-dark-chocolate cake and a piece of fresh strawberry pie, overflowing with fruit and none of that gelatinous filler some places use. Each was cut in half so we could share both.

"No more business talk," Joel said. "I want to hear about you."

"You already know all about me." I gave up trying to decide which confection to attack first. Stabbing a forkful of strawberries, I skimmed them through the cake's rich icing.

"Not what I want to know." Elbows on the table, he leaned forward, so when I brought the fork to my mouth, raising my head, his eyes were there to capture mine. He grinned. "Who's watering your plants this week?"

I downed the berries with difficulty. Something about those gray eyes was causing my throat to shrink. "I don't keep houseplants. I always kill them. My thumbs are definitely brown."

Joel stretched out his arm, letting his fingertips brush the thumb of my free hand. "Seems okay to me. I bet your thumbs could work wonders."

His fingers settled lightly on the back of my hand, asking nothing, only sending warmth up my arm to spread around my neck and play hide-and-seek behind my ears. I told myself to respond, but it'd been so long since I'd done this sort of thing, I felt like I needed the game box lid to review the rules. Meanwhile, my hand was going into paralysis beneath his. "Maybe I haven't met the right plant yet."

"What's *wrong* with those Pennsylvania varieties? I'd have thought some nice begonia would have coaxed you into bringing him home ages ago."

The heck with physical flirting. I could hold my own in the verbal fray. "Begonias aren't my type."

"No? What *do* you like? Smooth, soothing aloe? Green, clingy ivy? Prickly cactus?" I shook my head for each, and he grimaced. "Don't tell me you go in for those artificial types that never lose their good looks?"

I shook my head again. "They collect dust, and they're *so* predictable."

"Ah. You like a sense of adventure?" His hand moved to envelop mine, the thumb tunneling underneath to massage my palm. "And a little danger maybe?"

I could feel the pulse in my neck and was sure Joel and everyone else in the diner could see it pounding away. Our waitress and another behind the counter were blatantly watching the two of us, whispering, probably taking bets as to how far his hand would get by the time we finished eating. "If you mean, do I tend to end up with the poisonous types? Story of my life."

"Know what I think?" Joel let go of my hand abruptly, leaving me to feel abandoned, though I kept telling myself he only wanted to drink his coffee. "I think you don't go anywhere you can meet nice plants. The ones at the office are wilting or dried out, right?"

"Big time." I returned my attention to my desserts. Chocolate would never let me down.

"And places like the supermarket, the plants have been up for sale way too long."

I nodded. "And around my apartment complex, there's an abundance of weeds."

He'd gulped all his pie in the last few sentences. "Now I'll bet you never take home flashy cut flowers that are gone after a day or two—"

"Yes, sir. My mother raised me to be a nice Italian girl."

"—though I wouldn't blame you if you indulged in a poinsettia for the Christmas season, to keep you company New Year's Eve."

"Nope. I watch Dick Clark alone in my bunny slippers."

Our waitress, probably wondering what the hold up in the seduction was, came over to ask if we wanted anything else and to slap our check facedown next to Joel's hand. I think she was trying to jump-start him.

As she walked away, Joel scooped up the last bite of

cake. "You need a change of pace. Try a Southern variety. They require a lot of tender care, but I think you'd get a wealth of pleasure in return."

He didn't even have to be looking at me now—I blushed every shade of crimson. "I don't doubt that."

"Finish up. We'll go plant shopping."

He wasn't kidding. Problem was, at almost ten-thirty on a Tuesday night, we couldn't find the right kind of store open, though we drove up Route 3 to Spotsylvania Mall outside Fredericksburg. I didn't care—both of us laughed the whole way out and back.

We were still giggling as he veered his car off the main road, into the inky forest near Bell Run. I rolled down my window, turning my face to the cool night air. Closing my eyes, I was aware of smells I'd never noticed before—flowers, moss, animals. They seemed to fill a void I didn't know I had.

I heard the car rattle across the bridge, crunch onto the gravel; felt it climb up to the house, before it came to a halt, and the engine died. Opening my eyes, I turned to Joel.

He was already out of the driver's seat, slamming his door, running around to open mine. "Oh, no," he said as he offered a hand. "I'm not saying good night to you in my car. Not when old Matchmaker Magnolia's likely spying on us through her bedroom windows."

The house was dark except for an upstairs hall light that I could see through the glass in the front door. "I think she's asleep, Joel."

"Don't kid yourself. That woman never sleeps. Come on." Squeezing my hand tighter, he led me up onto the porch, into the shadows between the door and rockers.

He started to speak, but I hushed him with a hand to his chest. "What's that sound?"

"Which one?"

He was right, the night was ringing with them: crickets beginning their summer concert, the murmuring of the breeze through the treetops, an owl hooting off to the west.

I hadn't heard them last night. Where had I been every other night of my life? Indoors, listening to TV? "The whistles, sort of like crickets, but different."

"They're spring peepers. Frogs. Down by the creek and in the muddy shallows of the river."

"They're so *loud*."

He laughed at the obvious delight in my voice. "You know, Pat, there's something else I want to know about you."

"What?"

His kiss wasn't unexpected, but it wasn't like any first kiss I'd known before. A polite inquiry, unassuming, undemanding. Or actually, he was letting me do the asking. More like he was auditioning, an interview where the applicant was putting forth his best effort. But damn, if this was the typing test, Joel was scoring ninety words a minute with no errors. I was ready to hire him on the spot.

He pulled back, grinning. "Now *that* answers my question."

"Satisfactorily?"

"Yes, ma'am." Joel let his hands wander down my arms until they found both my hands. "We still have to get you that plant. All right if I call you tomorrow?"

"I'll sic Miss Maggie on you if you don't."

"Ow! You Northern women play for keeps." He kissed me softly on the cheek. "Good night, Pat."

From inside the door, I watched him drive off before climbing the stairs. But I didn't get ready for bed right away. I sat by the open window, listening to the spring peepers.

Idyllic, huh? So wasn't I entitled to one dream of Joel that night? Preferably vivid, short on symbolism, long on satisfying repressed lust. In Sensurround.

But my subconscious was determined to revisit Saunders' Field, probably because I'd done my darndest all day to forget the morning's personalized *Twilight Zone* episode.

Each dream was a variation of the Zouave assault, me

behind the trenches, my attackers all giants with red hair and moustaches. Before any of them could get close though, soldiers on all sides shot them dead. As each fell, they metamorphosed, shrinking, their faces oozing into other shapes. Some became Miss Maggie, some Beth Ann, and all too many of them, me.

Against unnumbered foes;
Let courage rise with danger,
And strengh to strength oppose.
George Duffield, 1858

MAY 6, 1864—BELL RUN

I was awakened by the thunder of guns to the south. The sun was a bloody orb reclining on the eastern treetops, hazed over by the drifting smoke. It would go into hiding altogether before midday as it neared the sky o'er the battle. I, for one, would not call it coward for doing so.

The Rapidan swirled red-brown below, too many feet upon its banks having dislodged too great a load of soil into its waters. I would not drink from it.

My family's markers were starkly barren in the light of day. The very events that had created this assembly of crosses—that had caused the destruction of the souls they represented—also denied me flowers with which to decorate their last abodes.

I gathered up my rifle and kit, promising to return before the day was out.

At the house, I lowered myself through the joists into the cellar. The apple butter and chestnuts were gone, as I'd expected, but the few nubs of candles and sliver of soap, secreted beneath debris from the kitchen fireplace, were still present. From below I knocked a floorboard loose with the butt of the rifle, breaking the plank into smaller sections by leaning it against the foundation and throwing my weight, feet first, against it. The gray timber, having been made brittle by exposure to the elements, splintered easily.

Pocketing the soap and cradling the wood in my arms, I made my way down to Bell Run, to a knee-deep pool I knew of, protected by three large boulders. There I stripped and bathed, the icy spring water baptizing my members with exhilarating new life. Pulling my clothes in from the bank, I scrubbed them until the soap withered away. They'd not been off my person since I'd left to join the army, less than a fortnight ago. By their pungent aroma and profusion of tenants, one would presume them of greater age.

Shivering, I built a hot, smokeless fire on the bank. I dried myself and my clothes over the blaze, scorching the latter until I could hear the lice pop like kernels of corn over a flame. Soaking my blanket, I did likewise, revelling in anticipation of a day free of the incessant itch.

Swathing myself in my warm raiments, I drank deeply from Bell Run above where I'd bathed, where the water was sweet, then drew provisions from my bag. What the Army of Northern Virginia considered a day's ration wouldn't satisfy a grown man's hunger for even one meal. For my own part, I could have eaten all my victuals right then, and still wanted for more. Instead, I divided my bread into three portions, eating one, storing the rest away with my hardtack.

I would need these reserves, for the past days had demonstrated that no easy path lay between me and vengeance. I must circle the fighting, attacking from behind. Hadn't my own quarry proved this effective against greater odds?

But this wouldn't be one Rebel for every five Yanks. It'd be me alone against all the legions of Evil.

11

I wasn't smiling when I awoke.

Miss Maggie called up the stairs as I dragged myself into the bathroom. "Pat, Charlotte's on her way over to see the cemetery."

"I'll be right down." I tried to infuse a little enthusiasm, but it sounded like I was in line for a tetanus shot.

"Take your time. I'll take Charlotte out there by myself." Not an offer, a mandate.

She was gone by the time I came barefoot down the stairs. The day once again promised heat, though with less humidity. I cursed myself for bringing only two short-sleeved T-shirts. Today, I'd worn another long-sleeved top.

I steeped a cup of decaf tea, leaving the bag in until it practically begged to be removed, hoping strength would make up for the lack of chemical stimulant. Bringing the mug and my copy of *Wilderness Voices* into the war room, I settled back into a recliner.

Flipping absently through the text, I was ridiculously gratified to find several glossy pages of black and white photos. Can I help it if my inner child still judges books by how many pictures they contain?

The first was an old sepia portrait of Evan Bell, age eighteen, taken just after his enlistment in the cavalry. He wore a checkered shirt and his light, wavy hair curled about the short, rounded collar, framing an extraordinarily handsome face. A sensual, open-mouthed smile covered half his face, echoed by a laugh in his black eyes. I caught myself mentally labelling him a hunk, wondering if there was anything twisted in thinking that of an uncle. He'd broken hearts, I had no doubt.

On the flip side of Evan's picture was one of his brother Lane, also taken after enlistment, age twenty. He was the dark, brooding hero of Gothic novels. Well, maybe brooding was too strong a word, but he certainly wasn't smiling; it wouldn't have suited him if he had been. Lane wasn't as handsome as Evan, but his eyes were compassionate and perhaps a bit wiser. He'd joined a volunteer company which was absorbed into the infantry the next year. As part of the famous "Stonewall" brigade, he'd obtained the rank of First Sergeant before his death.

The photo opposite was of Julia seated, with Gabriel standing beside her. She favored Lane, her dark hair pulled back a little too severely, her dress plain, puritanical gray. I reminded myself that it could as easily be cornflower blue or dusky rose, that I was oriented to the world of color TV.

Her eyes—her eyes wouldn't let go of mine. I studied them with care, wondering what I was seeing there. Melancholy? Earnestness? Passion? All to some degree. Something purer. Truth? Yes, in her eyes and set into the line of her jaw. I felt troubled, unsure I could ever have loved this grandmother.

Gabriel was slightly out of focus, his hands blurred, as if unable to keep still for very long. He was fairer than Evan, in both hair and eyes, the latter reflective rather than piercing like the rest of his siblings. His smile was sincere and his face youthful—puberty had yet to hit with full force. I suspected his voice was still fairly high. This too disturbed me. If my experience at Saunders' Field had really been a message from Gabriel Bell, I found it hard to believe this callow, cheerful boy was the sender. Then again, he'd only been twelve when the photo was taken, and as Miss Maggie pointed out, the next two years would have been hell on him.

I compared him to Charlotte Garber, looking for some

resemblance. Silly. No reason she should look any more like Gabriel than I looked like Julia.

And I *didn't* look like Julia. Okay, she had dark hair and eyes, but that was more coincidence than anything else. My nose was one hundred percent Montella. You couldn't argue with that.

I felt Julia staring at me, like a painting whose eyes follow you around the room.

"I'm *not* like you," I said aloud. "Not at all."

My God. Here I was, talking to a book. Slamming it shut, I stood, restlessly pacing the distance to the windows.

Call Joel, I told myself. Ask him if he knows anything about Charlotte yet. Hear his voice. Salvage the day before it gets worse.

I faced Miss Maggie's desk, slightly daunted. Did she have a Rolodex under there someplace? An address book? I wasn't in the mood for excavation, even if I hadn't been afraid of getting something important out of order. Besides, knowing Miss Maggie, she probably had all phone numbers committed to memory.

What about a phone book? *Everyone* had a phone book.

After checking all the piled books for one with yellow pages, and after ransacking the kitchen and upstairs bedrooms (I didn't really search Miss Maggie's bedroom, just gave it a cursory scan), my quest for the phone book caused me to open the drawer of the hall table.

I didn't mean to snoop, but the letter was right there under my nose, "RE: FRANCIS J. SHELBY" in caps, on Veterans Administration letterhead.

Mrs. Shelby:

This is to confirm your appointment for Wednesday, May 6th, at 4 P.M. to discuss your son's release at the end of the month.

Signed by Dr. Schafer, Psychiatric Services, the VA Hospital in Richmond.

*   *   *

I was back in the recliner, book open, sipping tea when Miss Maggie and Charlotte came through the back door. I'd had plenty of warning—Charlotte caterwauled about pickers and insect bites from the edge of the forest all the way across the clearing to the porch.

For some jealous reason, I felt pleased, as if the forest had attacked her personally, though I was still scratching away at my own bites. I'd slapped on a thick layer of Beth Ann's bug goop this morning.

"Oh, there you are, Pat," Miss Maggie said when I came out to the kitchen. "I was just inviting Charlotte to join us when we go back to the Wilderness battlefield—"

"And I was just saying I wish I could," Charlotte simpered, dredging a quasi-Southern belle up out of her genetic pool, "but all that information you printed out for me is so *interesting*, Magnolia, I want to get right down to work."

Had she been all that anxious, she would have made her escape at once. Instead, she hung around, accepting a cup of instant coffee while I made some toast for my breakfast.

"It's so *sad* to think Gabriel had to leave his family behind," Charlotte lamented. "Of course, who could blame him, considering he'd been driven from his home?"

I wondered how much Miss Maggie had told her. If possible desertion had been mentioned, Charlotte was doing her best to gloss over it. Why not? Wasn't it natural to want to find heroes on the family tree? Still, I felt smug that I'd come down on Julia's side.

Miss Maggie, after a glance at me that once more requested my silence, asked Charlotte very specific questions about when and where her great-grandparents had been born.

"We aren't all that sure about Great-Grandpa, Gabriel's son, that is. He was already ten by the time the family settled in San Francisco. I had a great-aunt who said Gabriel met his wife in Texas, but I'm not sure exactly where they lived."

"Makes sense," Miss Maggie muttered after Charlotte

left. "Texas was Confederate during the war, a more likely new home for a Southerner than California, which sided with the Union." She came out of her musing abruptly. "Get ready, Pat. We've got a lot of ground to cover today."

We borrowed Hugh's Escort again. Miss Maggie went inside to fetch the keys while I waited outside, too embarrassed by yesterday's encounter with him to show my face. When she came out, she had the keys in one hand and a manila envelope in the other.

"This one's addressed to you," she said, putting the envelope in my hand as we walked over to the car. "Hugh said he found it in the overnight drop-off, so someone local sent it. I made him postmark it right away."

The envelope was bulky—maybe two inches thick in the middle. The mailing label had only my name, computer-printed and actually spelled correctly. No return address. The three first-class stamps had been manually postmarked.

Because Miss Maggie was clearly dying of curiosity, and because I was too curious myself to wait, I tore open the envelope. Inside was a quart-sized Ziploc bag and inside that, a small baby doll. I had one something like it when I was a tot, though mine had a grubby face within a week and lost half its blond hair the first month. This one looked hardly played with—that is, what I could see of it. Around its neck was a red yarn noose which apparently had been used to dip the torso into something black and gooey, then into a pile of down, until it looked like one of the ducks caught in the Exxon Valdez oil spill.

"What in blazes is that?" Miss Maggie wanted to rip the bag out of my hands for a better look, I could tell.

I handed envelope and all to her so I could dig into my handbag for the printout. "Read this."

"Read it to me, Pat. I don't have my glasses."

I did, and followed my recitation with a rundown of how I'd found the page yesterday and my deductions about a web site. "So I guess that doll represents my formal invitation to get out of town."

"Why didn't you tell me about this?"

"I thought Beth Ann had done it, and I wanted to talk to her first, before I got her into more trouble." Of course, all talking to her had achieved was to poke more holes in the case against her. "She said she uses your PC to research school projects."

"Does that paper have little specks in the right margin?"

I looked closer. "Like tiny sideways teardrops? About every two inches down the side of the page?"

"That's my printer, all right. Has a nick in the drum." Miss Maggie frowned thoughtfully. "Thing is, Beth Ann's not subtle enough to start with a note like this. If she doesn't like you, she'll let you know outright. Not to mention that down feathers and—," she opened one corner of the bag and took a whiff, "—what I suspect is driveway sealer aren't that cheap and, far as I know, Hugh doesn't keep either around. Plus, that young lady might be a frustrated, hormonal teenager, but she's not mean."

I knew what she meant by that. Rock throwing could be simple impulsive anger. The quote about Yankees, while loaded with implication, was harmless enough. Today's offering, on the other hand, felt malicious. The voodoo doll association, no doubt. I realized I didn't want Beth Ann to be the culprit. Still, a kid I could handle—or, at least, I could try to. I wasn't ready to admit the existence of a secret nonadmirer. And who else had access to Miss Maggie's PC?

Reading my mind, she said, "Now that it's warm, I'm always leaving the downstairs windows open. They're open now. Anyone could have pushed up one of those old screens, come in, printed that thing, and left the same way. But I agree we ought to ask Beth Ann first. I'll ask her myself tonight—she's never lied to me. Then we can decide if the sheriff needs to know about this. Okay with you?"

"Sounds like a plan."

"Still up for a history lesson this morning?"

I welcomed the diversion.

*   *   *

The Escort must not have been driven since yesterday—the driver's seat was still all the way forward. I made myself promise to push it back when we returned today, as my penance for yesterday's behavior.

We stayed in the car mostly, following the line of Rebel defenses south from Saunders' Field. Waving me into every pull-off, Miss Maggie hauled me from the car to point out overgrown trenches. After little more than a mile of this, I began to notice the rooftops of houses about a football field's length in through the trees to the left.

As if to answer my unasked question, Miss Maggie said, "The Park Service only owns the North and South entrenchments. In between, where the heaviest fighting took place, they dammed up Wilderness Creek and built houses. Named the lakes Lee and Grant."

I wrinkled my nose in distaste. "I wouldn't want my home on land where hundreds of people met violent deaths."

"No one's complained of a haunted house yet." Miss Maggie motioned me off the road again. "Actually, this sort of thing's pretty common. Fredericksburg outgrew its old town limits and now there's houses back to and beyond Marye's Heights—"

"Marye's Heights? Where Armstead Bell was killed?"

"Right. Pretty much all that remains of the first battle is a narrow strip, a few blocks long, less than a block wide, along the road where the Confederates made their stand. And in Gettysburg, there's a housing development over the north end of Pickett's Charge." Her voice became rich in irony. "When it came to preserving the battlefields, someone decided these bulwarks were more important than the flat spaces between, where most of the dying took place."

I studied the landscape, vaguely remembering that fourth-grade tour of Gettysburg. My teacher had been big into troop movements and strategies, treating the battle like a giant chess match. When you came right down to it, what had I learned? Not one blessed thing. And until now, I hadn't cared. "The history park Disney wanted to build, was that around here, Miss Maggie?"

"Manassas. Up near Washington."

"Near where Evan Bell died?"

"Not far."

"Were you against it? The Disney park?"

"I'm against the grass, Pat." Seeing my puzzlement, she took my hand. "If I had my way, this place would stay the way it looked on May 7, 1864. And every other battlefield, all over the world, would appear as it did the last day of the battle. War would have ended long ago if people had to view its ugly aftermath each day. Once the grass grows, once the horrors are gone, they can fool themselves into thinking it's worth fighting again."

Miss Maggie continued her discourse on history as we drove on, though that's all it was to me, a lecture like the one I'd endured in Gettysburg long ago. Not that Miss Maggie didn't crank out a better story. But I guess after the supernatural soundbites and Uncle Gabe's greeting card yesterday, I'd come to expect another psychic slap on the face.

"Turn right here, Pat. Park in that lot down the road." The sign read, "Stop #11: Widow Tapp Farm."

We hiked along a mowed trail around a field of grass, tracing, according to Miss Maggie, the Texas infantry movements. My mind wandered everywhere but the field: back to the doll in the envelope behind my seat, to the letter in the hall table, to Joel, Charlotte, Hugh, Beth Ann, and even to Beth Ann's bug repellent, which was working beautifully. Not one gnat buzzed around my ears. But abruptly, one phrase of Miss Maggie's brought me up short. "What did you say?"

"I said the Texans refused to advance while Lee was with them. They wanted him sent to the rear where he'd be safe. Which was reasonable, what with Stonewall Jackson gone. If anything happened to Lee—"

"Robert E. Lee? *He* was here? On this spot?"

Miss Maggie gazed keenly into my eyes. "Why, Pat? What do you see?"

"Nothing."

"Close your eyes—"

"No, it's not like yesterday." I took a deep breath, trying to figure out what it *was* like. "Just, the thought of him being here made me feel as if . . . as if I'd made some sort of discovery." That sounded lame. What was I talking about? Admittedly, my knowledge of history was hurting, but I knew Robert E. Lee was a general in the Civil War. Patrick Swayze may be visually arresting, but I did catch the name of his commander-in-chief, thank you. I laughed nervously. "I guess . . . I guess I didn't realize the big guys were so close to the action."

Miss Maggie was wearing her shrewd "never-try-to-con-a-teacher" frown. "Did Gabriel Bell want to know where Lee was?"

Strangely enough, the question made sense to me, but all I could do was shrug. "Only a feeling, Miss Maggie. No visions of fancy uniforms. No sounds, no smells. Nothing."

She looked so disappointed, I was tempted to make up an apparition on the spot.

"Let's go, Pat."

"Don't you want to hike the rest of the trail?"

"No point. You aren't seeing what happened here, are you?"

I shook my head. "Not like yesterday."

"I don't mean through some psychic force. I mean like Monday, when you pictured the Union army fording the river, felt what the Bell family would have felt."

"That was my imagination running wild."

Looping her arm through mine, Miss Maggie marched me back toward the car, our feet crunching against the dry grass. "You know, Pat, you have what it takes to be a historian. Most people think it's nothing more than memorizing a lot of facts. Would I have lived this long doing something that boring?"

I suspected the question wasn't meant to be answered. "What *do* you do then?"

"Take the facts and draw a picture—no, create a world. Fill in the blanks as best I can from what I do know. In the end, I've got a living, breathing image of what happened, an image I can see, hear, feel, as if I were an eyewitness. And the rush you get, that moment you actually fall into history—it's addictive." Her green eyes were glowing with excitement.

"But if it's partly imagined, Miss Maggie, you're not seeing what really took place."

She grinned. "Let me tell you about Mary Shelby's Rules for History, in fact, for Life in General: Number One—if you learn everything you can, you'll come as close to the truth as possible. Two—there's *always* something more to find out. And Three—truth ain't worth beans if you don't learn anything from it."

The last one, akin to what I'd been thinking earlier about my fourth-grade teacher, hit home.

The car was warm and stuffy from being closed up, with the faint, unsettling aroma of fresh tar. I lowered my window before starting the engine. "Miss Maggie, when you took Charlotte out to the cemetery, did you give her the same spiel you gave me Monday?"

"Yep. Standard two-bit tour."

"Did she . . . did she see anything?"

"Sure did. Her imagination's ten times worse than yours."

That's what I was afraid of. Charlotte had out-performed me. Almost as if we were siblings, I felt she'd end up being Miss Maggie's favorite.

"Yessiree," Miss Maggie continued. "Charlotte saw a whole grand parade stepping across that river. Men in crisp uniforms prancing in perfect step. Banners furled in the breeze. Sleek horses pulling big, shiny cannons. And all the neighborhood children lined up on the banks to watch and cheer."

"Sounds more like the Rose Bowl."

Miss Maggie nodded. "I was surprised she didn't throw in a float or two. Go straight, Pat. We'll go home a different way."

I obeyed, pulling off before the next intersection so she could tell me about Stonewall Jackson at Chancellorsville.

"Oh, I wish you could stay longer, Pat. I wanted to show you Chancellorsville and Spotsylvania and Fredericksburg this week, but it's Wednesday already and—"

"And you have an appointment this afternoon."

"Did Joel tell you?"

"No. I was searching for your phone book this morning. When I looked in the hall table, I saw the VA letter about your son."

Miss Maggie sat in silence, staring out the window at the gray battle map beside the car. I was afraid I'd made her angry, but when she said, "Turn left here, Pat," her voice was soft and somber.

I did as she asked and when the car was in motion, she spoke again.

"Frank turned eighteen toward the end of World War Two. Another eight months and maybe they wouldn't have bothered sending him overseas at all. He didn't want to go. Had his heart set on college, and who knew how much longer the war would last. When he got his draft notice, he decided to enlist in the Navy instead. Said the South Seas were warmer and the girls prettier.

She sighed as if exhausted. "They put him on a cruiser. Saw heavy action his first week. The kamikazes got to him. He couldn't fathom anyone wanting to kill that much. A few months later, one crashed his plane into Frank's ship. Killed a third of the crew. Wounded another third bad enough they were sent home, most of them burned and maimed. Frank came through it without a scratch."

"Physically," I murmured.

Miss Maggie nodded. "They don't give purple hearts for broken spirits. And he seemed fine until he came home. Even then, it was months before he began having waking nightmares, every time a plane flew over, every time he saw flames."

"Post-traumatic stress?"

"They didn't know what to call it back then. I could show you letters and diaries, all the way back to ancient Egypt, about men going crazy after wars, but nobody treated it like a true mental illness 'til after Vietnam. The VA doctors said Frank had schizophrenia. Their medications probably did as much harm as combat."

"He's been institutionalized ever since?"

"Off and on. Turn left here."

We'd reached Route 3. I recognized the landmarks.

Miss Maggie folded her arms across her bosom, as if she were cold. "They'd keep Frank in the hospital awhile, until they thought they had him on the right medication, then he'd come home to live with Jake and me. He couldn't drive, couldn't hold a job. Spent most of his time just walking through the woods. At night and on bad weather days, he'd pace the length of the hall like a caged animal. Chain-smoked from the moment he got up every morning. Then he'd start talking about people he saw on his walks, old friends he knew before the war. Said he'd call to them, and they were too stuck up to answer. Most of them had moved away years before, but you couldn't reason with him. Beau came over to spend time with him each week, even though Frank accused him of being a coward for not serving his country. Beau'd been 4-F 'cause of a rheumatic heart. But they'd been best friends since they were on the football team together in high school, and Beau stuck by him."

Which explained, at last, Beau's familiar but formal demeanor around Miss Maggie.

"Each time Frank got worse," Miss Maggie continued, "they'd hospitalize him again, play with his medication, send him home, and start the cycle over."

"Must have been rough on you," I said as I hit the turn signal to leave the highway.

"You can get used to anything, Pat. Problem was, after Jake died, I couldn't take care of Frank myself. They put him in a group home with other men for a spell. He did well there, better than before. The responsibility was good for him. But one of the men stole his medicine and, after a couple weeks, he had to be hospitalized again. Been there ever since."

I pulled up in front of the post office, pushing the seat back before I forgot. "The letter said they were releasing him at the end of the month."

"It's a game we play. As every new administration tries to cut the budget, I get a letter saying he's being released. I go show them I'm an old, old woman who can't take care of a totally dependent elderly man, and they change their minds."

"So far."

"Don't underestimate me until you've seen me in my helpless old lady outfit." She got out of the car as if to indicate an end to the conversation.

I grabbed my handbag and voodoo doll and caught up with her at the bottom of the post office steps. "You could sell some of your land to get better care for him."

"Private care?" She shook her head obstinately, the color rising in her cheeks. "The government sent Frank to war. They'd have preferred him to die on his ship. They'd just be out the price of a flag. As it happened, only his mind and soul were left in the South Pacific. He'll never have his name engraved on a memorial. Never receive a medal. But he's been giving his life for his country for half a century now. While I'm alive, the country will honor that debt."

"And after you're gone?"

Her anger drained from her. "I set up a trust fund. When I die, everything I own but the land gets added into it. Joel will make sure Frank's cared for. And Beau—Joel had me put him down as a second executor, to be on the safe side. Frank'll be all right."

I gave her a hug, the kind of big bear embrace I give to keep myself from crying, my whole heart going out to this woman I hadn't even known two days ago.

When I let her go, she took my hands, squeezing my fingers. "Besides, that land was never mine to sell."

I rolled my eyes. "*Cobadosta.*"

Miss Maggie frowned at my third-generation vernacular. "I'm not familiar with the dialect."

"Grandma Montella's favorite phrase. Dad said it meant 'stubborn as a goat.' " Of course, for all I knew, I could be saying something forbidden on network TV, or calling Miss Maggie a pencil eraser.

"Probably *capritèsta*, then. Goat head." Miss Maggie was pleased. "Why, thank you, Pat. I'll take that as a compliment."

Miss Maggie came downstairs at quarter to two, all decked out in her "helpless old lady outfit," complete with cotton-print dress and orthopedic shoes. I volunteered to drive, but she refused.

"Beau takes me. He gets Frank talking about fishing or football or whatever. Does Frank no end of good. We've been going every Wednesday afternoon for years, except the three months last summer when Beau's wife was completely bedridden, before she died. Beau'd promised her he wouldn't put her in a nursing home. Stayed right by her side to the end. Hugh took me to Richmond then, whenever he could, but Frank had a hard time adjusting. He doesn't do well around strangers."

"I'd upset him?"

Miss Maggie nodded.

"All right. I'll have dinner waiting for you."

"No, no. You've been feeding me like royalty. Take a night off. I've been treating Beau to supper in Richmond when he lets me. He stopped eating right after Helen got sick. And he can't afford to eat out much."

I remembered how his skin seemed to cling to his bones. "See if he'll come over for dinner tomorrow or Friday, Miss Maggie. Tell him I'm making something special for him."

A mischievous smile danced across her lips. "My mouth'll be watering the rest of the day just thinking about it. We'll get something fast tonight and get back early, so I can talk to Beth Ann about that thing you got in the mail. You'll be okay here by yourself, won't you?"

I assured her I would. Funny thing was, I felt more comfortable here in this house and on this land than I ever felt anywhere else, including the house where I grew up.

After Beau's old pickup took them off into the woods, I settled on a front-porch rocker, bare feet up on the rail, glass of iced tea balanced on the chair's wide armrest, and *Wilderness Voices* propped against my knees.

The time had come to meet my relatives. I thought about the Muscarellas, who loved working with their hands and an honest argument; the Montellas, with their ingenuity and off-the-wall sense of humor; the Giamos, penny-pinchers and good business people, except for Uncle Accursio who played the numbers faithfully and never held a steady job his whole life.

Who were the Bells? What had they contributed to my conglomerate?

I opened the book to the preface.

12

Histories of war are often told from the points of view of those involved: the politicians, the generals, and all too infrequently, the soldiers in the field.

I've chosen a different point of view, often forgotten, though more involved, more transfigured by war than all the others. This participant has displayed great bravery, suffered with dignity, yet never asked to be decorated or recognized.

My protagonist is the family. They've watched their sons and fathers go off to war or had war destroy their homes and livelihoods.

In the case of the Armstead Bell family, all of the above.

Wow, I thought. Way to go, Miss Maggie. I had chills already.

As she'd said, the rest of the preface gave a brief history. The bottom line was that the Shacklefords got the prize for first to set foot in the New World, though my particular branch of ancestors had staunchly avoided the American Revolution. I kissed my DAR membership goodbye.

The Bells showed up in 1803, immigrants from Scotland. Yeow! Kilts and bagpipes! The Montellas would get megajoke mileage out of that.

The brick house was originally built by the Shacklefords. The Bells were tenants, operating a grist mill along the creek. The rest was boy meets girl, boy marries girl, boy and girl move in with mother-in-law.

Next came the letters themselves, found by a Mathilda Howard of Richmond while cleaning her attic. Most were from Lane to his parents or sister, or back and forth between mother and daughter while Julia was in Richmond. Julia apparently had been a prolific writer, though her brothers saved few letters, putting them to other uses as paper became scarce. Evan only wrote a few times, evidently preferring to occupy his leisure with gambling, horse racing, and women.

Uncle Evan, you devil. I took a swig of my tea and turned the page.

September 16, 1861
Loudoun County, Virginia

Dear Julia,

I did not answer your letter promptly because I wanted to meditate on it and phrase my reply accordingly. I must participate in this war. To not do so would be a source of deep regret in my life. I cannot suffer others to fight my battles. While I am capable of bearing arms, I belong on the list of my country's defenders. Your Mr. Howard's words of peace are commendable, though I feel he could do more to bring the condition about by helping us render a swift end to the conflict. I do not fight against the abolitionists as you well know. Father's family never kept slaves and neither shall I. What I fight against is the invasion of Southern soil as at Sumter and Manassas.

I am glad you plan to spend the season in Richmond. Though I met John Howard but once, I am well acquainted with his Aunt Florence. No one is more capable of introducing you into society. I fear your choice of beaus this autumn will be limited to cantankerous old men and boys of Gabe's years. The war will not last long. Perhaps Evan and I will join you in the spring.

Your devoted brother,
Lane

Nov 5th—in camp, Falls Church
Father,

If only you had allowed me to enlist last spring, I might have fought in one battle. I do nothing but exercise horses. I am so impatient I feel as if ten thousand pins prick the whole of my body. I did not enlist to exercise horses but to fight Yankees. Every night I pray the next day to cross over the Potomac and meet the "grand army" on fair ground.

Very truly your son,
Evan

June 6, 1862
Near Richmond

Dear Mother and Father,

General Robert Lee was given General Johnson's command. He is well thought of and has the army's respect. Now it seems we are to attack. Talk in camp is that the Yanks sit at the mouth of the James and will march on Richmond. I am dispatching word to Julia to send her home if she has not already gone.

I saw Evan. He looks forward to the fight. I told him I was afraid that when the moment came to kill, I would be unable to do so. He is confident he will stand the gaff of battle and says that if he does not, he hopes our own men shoot him down. I will write afterwards.

Affectionately your loving son,
Lane

Bell Run—June 23, 1862
Dear Julia,

Your father is very angry and will not allow you to return home. I blame myself for thinking Florence Howard an adequate chaperon for one so young. You are my only daughter, and I have failed you.

You must not tell your brothers of your condition, Julia. They will be called into battle soon, if not already, and must not be distracted by worry for you. I fear Evan might try to harm Mr. Howard.

I do not like to think of you so close to the war, but your father will not relent. I will try to come if I can. Keep safe and well.

All my love,
Mother

July 3, 1862
Richmond

Dear Mother,

We heard the low rumble of cannon to the south and east for several days last week. I pray for Lane and Evan every minute. I wanted to go to the hospitals afterward, but Mrs. Howard assured me that if anything befell one of my brothers, the other would send word. I saw the list of the dead this morning. So many names. But among them neither Lane nor Evan.

Mother, you must not blame yourself for my transgression. Father is right. I have failed you. Neither should Mrs. Howard be held at fault. She is a good Christian, even now allowing me to remain beneath her roof. John and I will marry as soon as he returns from his parents' home in Maryland. He was to have come before now. The fighting has likely delayed him.

I have been helping to roll bandages. The other women make cartridges and uniforms, but I cannot bring myself to fashion the very instruments of killing and emblems of war. Mrs. Howard will not let the others chide me for it. Too soon I will be forced to forsake their company and spend my days alone.

Please come.

Believe that I am still your devoted daughter,
Julia

Feeling tears well up around my lashes, I raised my eyes from the page to the magnolia blossoms curling under the porch gutter. As accurate as my imagination had proved the last two days, it had totally struck out where Julia was concerned. I'd been picturing . . . well . . . a grandmother. Not in age or looks but in her thinking, her attitude. What I discovered was a frightened teen, only a few years older than Beth Ann, and in big trouble. She'd conceived her daughter out of wedlock in an era when society would shun her for it. Forever. She was feeling lonelier by the day, more and more afraid, wanting her mother above all else.

I could *feel* her, as if she were standing beside me.

The phone rang, startling me. Fortunately, my right hand had my glass of iced tea in a death grip.

Finding the phone was a challenge. The cord on the desk was attached to an empty cordless-phone cradle. Tracking the shrill electronic turkey gobbles—why can't they sound like bells anymore?—I at last located it on the floor near the TV, beneath a map of France.

The answering machine had clicked on so I told the caller to hold on while Miss Maggie's message played out. I wasn't about to enter into another game of hide-and-seek trying to find the machine.

After the beep, a very welcome voice said, "Pat? It's Joel."

I sank to the floor, feeling an unannounced smile invade my cheeks. "Hi."

"I had a great time last night."

Warmth spread from my ear down my neck. "Me, too. Want to come for dinner tonight? I'm on my own." I stretched out on the rug, flat on my back, closing my eyes to envision his face.

"Oh, right. It's Wednesday. Damn. I'm having an early dinner with a client in Fredericksburg. In fact, I'm supposed to leave work within the half hour. What if I stop by, say, around eight-thirty, nine o'clock?"

I pouted. Miss Maggie would be home by then, and I wanted Joel all to myself again.

As if he could read my mind, he added, "I'll pick you up. We'll go for ice cream."

"I'd like that." A click sounded, reminding me our every

word had been recorded. The mood faded. I opened my eyes. "Find out anything about Charlotte?"

"Just that she really is Charlotte Garber, and her church secretary verifies that she's been looking up her family's baptismal certificates and the like."

"You found which church she attends?"

"Not me. Magnolia. Must have given the poor woman the third degree this morning. Anyway, so far she checks out. I'll make a few more calls before heading out to Fredericksburg, okay?"

I could hear the impatience in his otherwise lazy southern tones. "Let it wait until tomorrow. Besides, the sooner you get to your client's place, the sooner you leave to come here. Right?"

"Yes, ma'am." His grin sounded loud and clear, and so eager, I closed my eyes again after hanging up, and lay there, remembering the teasing caress of his lips against mine.

But I was aware the whole time of something else nagging me, tugging at me, beckoning me to follow. I groped at the slippery directive, trying to get it into focus.

The phone gobbled again, right next to my ear. I pounced on it. "Joel?"

"This is Wilma Rae Boutchyard. I suppose this is Patrice?"

I wanted to yell "No! It's Pat!" and hang up on her, but I sat up, mustering all the politeness I could. Which wasn't much. "What can I do for you, Mrs. Boutchyard?"

"I will be coming by to drop off those recommendations shortly, Patrice."

Not today, I heard my inner voice whine. I couldn't handle her. Not without Miss Maggie here to keep me from mouthing off. "No, I . . . I won't be here. Sorry."

"Where are you going?" Meaning, what could be more important? Besides, she probably knew Miss Maggie was out and that I didn't have a car.

"I've begun a complete survey of the property," I said, congratulating myself for inventing a lie she couldn't refute. "I expect to be out the rest of the day. Why don't you call tomorrow, Mrs. Boutchyard?"

"I'll be there *today*. If you aren't about, I'll leave the package on the front porch." She slammed the phone down loudly.

I almost wondered, hearing the crunch of gravel outside, if Wilma Rae could make it here that fast. From my seat on the floor, I peeked over the window sill. Flora Shifflett's gray chariot pulled up out front. By the time I got through the screen door, she was walking around the car. The beige suit she wore looked as if it came off the same rack as her blue one. Must have been a blue-light special.

Her passenger was out of the car, too—a short man, fit-looking, with a silver mane. He removed the jacket of his black suit to reveal a pair of yellow suspenders that clashed with his hideous red tie. He wore a jeweled tie tack, gold cuff links, and three rings, the smallest of which was his wedding band. The message was, "Who needs taste when you've got money?"

"Pat, honey," Flora drooled. "Mr. Eastman was *so* interested, I just *had* to drive him right on out and show him the place."

I felt my hackles sit up, alert, sniffing the air for predators, as I descended to the bottom step.

"Darryl Eastman." Flora flung her hands at me, palm up, like she was Vanna White showing a vowel on *Wheel of Fortune*. "This is Patricia Montella. She'll be the new owner."

He spouted pleasantries and extended a hand which I didn't come forward to take. Even if I'd felt like it, I wasn't about to step down onto sharp gravel in my bare feet. "I won't be the owner for quite a while yet."

"Yes. Well. Mrs. Shelby *is* ninety-one." Flora had already told him this evidently. She repeated it with an air of reinforcement.

"I'd like to meet her," Mr. Eastman said. His universe-revolves-around-me ego probably figured he could talk the old biddy into selling.

I told him she wasn't home.

"Oh, that *is* a shame." Flora sounded genuinely put out, but I was willing to bet she knew of Miss Maggie's weekly visit to her son. She'd no doubt brought this client by this afternoon purposefully, to let him have at me alone. "What I've proposed to Mr. Eastman—and I know this is irregular, but it should work to our mutual advantages—I've proposed an escrow arrangement, Pat. You agree to sell to Mr. Eastman when the property's yours, and he'll set aside the payment—"

"Before you go on, Flora—" Mercy, I couldn't wait to squelch her scheme! "—some problems have come up. For one thing, there may be a second heir. Miss Maggie would have to split the land between us. For another, I haven't decided how much of my portion I'll be selling."

"But yesterday you said—"

"This place really grows on you. I want to keep at least half if I can."

Flora's paste-up smile quivered. "Oh. Well. I'm sure even fifty acres—"

Eastman cleared his throat. "I'd need some assurance the creek would be included."

I grinned, lunging in for the kill. "Sorry. If Bell Run's part of my inheritance, I'm keeping it. Nobody's going to dam it up as long as I can help it. And when I do sell, Eastman, I'm going with the highest bidder. Locking myself into a deal this early on is kind of stupid, don't you think?"

He huffed like a man who's had his time wasted. Flora was almost purple with indignation. Had I done wrong to make her an enemy?

I mulled it over for all of two seconds.

She *was* the enemy. Some little gremlin deep down in my gut told me so. I enjoyed watching her drive her pretty car too fast over the gravel, sending a geyser of stones into her doors and fenders.

I climbed onto the porch savoring the warmth of the sun-baked wood under my feet. My book lay closed on the rocker, but I had no further desire to read today. What was badgering me was a yearning, a summons, to visit the cemetery. Alone.

So the story I'd given Wilma Rae wouldn't be a lie after all.

I went inside to find my sneakers.

Bell House wasn't spooky at all. Maybe because today, I knew it for what it was. I could picture it in its heyday, not Wilma Rae's idealistic plantation manor but a stately house of orange brick, bulky rectangular chimneys anchoring each gable, and two, no three additions, all white clapboard. Outbuildings, too: barn, springhouse, root cellar.

I walked slowly around the ruin, shooing mosquitoes and flies from my hair. I hadn't worn Miss Maggie's hat, feeling a need to keep my lines of vision clear on all sides to allow my senses to absorb as much as possible.

A handful of yellow and black burst from the bramble, a feathered projectile streaking past my head, perching on a low tree limb. I don't know what kind of bird it was, like a sun-colored sparrow with black wings, but I watched him fly from one branch to another, deep into the forest where he was lost from sight.

The sun seemed to dim in those seconds, and I smelled wood smoke. Not like Monday night. Not a barbecue, or even a wood stove, but the acrid stench of burning leaves. Behind me, toward the river, I could have sworn I heard the snorting and whinnying of a horse.

The entreaty of the cemetery was stronger than ever, and I ran along the path toward the noises. When I came to the cross trail, the woods became silent. The horse had been to my right, toward the graveyard, I was positive, but the only animal I met was a gray squirrel sitting atop the stone wall. He scampered away as I entered the enclosure.

I dropped to my knees onto the cool, rough, weed-infested grass before the graves. A rush of familiarity swept over me, very like the Saunders' Field experience, but much more overwhelming. I had no urge to move. Apparently I was exactly where . . . where someone, some*thing*, wanted me to be. I froze in place, staring at the stones, wondering what to do next.

Then I remembered. Yesterday Miss Maggie had asked me to close my eyes. My heart thumped wildly as I did so now.

Immediately I saw five crosses, each with a pyramid of stones and broken brick supporting the base, keeping them upright. Evan's was most weathered, the wood silky gray, but it was also the most carefully constructed, the cross-pieces flush with each other, the lettering neat. With each successive burial, the crosses had been fashioned by less skilled hands until with Lane's and Julia's, they were merely broken boards, singed along the edges, probably carved by the same bent nails that held them together. A coffin-sized rectangle of earth in front of each marker was sunken in an inch or two. The ground was rutted, almost bare, with only a stubble of dry grass here and there.

No wall enclosed the plot, no forest stood beyond, only grayish, tangled growth. I clearly saw the Rapidan, its water a rusty café au lait, both banks barren, punctuated with tree stumps. The pungent odor of burning hung thick in the air.

Another faint scent made my nose itch, reminiscent of a local petting zoo back home. Damp animal fur. Horse shit.

And even as I thought it, the whinnying and snorting were back, loud this time, with the stamping of hooves.

Right behind me.

It seemed as though Christian men had turned to fiends, and hell itself had usurped the place of earth.

Lt. Colonel Horace Porter—May 6, 1864

MAY 6, 1864—BELL RUN

I saw the soldier long before he halted by my family's graves, recognizing him despite the straggly beard and moustache now hiding his chin and jaw.

He turned his head warily every few moments, but I remained as a statue, my garments blending with the dun-colored earth, and he, not expecting to see me, didn't.

Careless of him.

Dismounting, he examined the markers, one hand resting on a revolver slung below his navy-blue officer's vest. He'd left his coat folded across the back of his saddle, sword slung beside it. His trousers might have once been light blue and his boots shiny black, but both now carried old stains of blood and grass and the mud of many states. Two fingers pushed his kepi back from his forehead, then removed the hat altogether, freeing perspiration-soaked blond curls.

As he turned to remount, I came forward, leaving my gun, sack, and canteen behind. "Hello, John Howard."

He spun around, hat falling, revolver drawn, thumb curved over the hammer. Seeing me not ten yards away, dressed as I was, he could do nothing but gape at first. "I thought you were dead."

I disregarded his words. "Or should I call you General Howard?"

Smiling now, he eased the hammer forward and holstered his pistol. "Captain only. And that was Father's doing."

I advanced to within reach of my father's cross, running my fingers along the arm, prying a splinter loose. "What brings you?"

"I'm taking a message to Germanna Ford." His chest

puffed out, and his gaze wandered to his coat, as if he wished he'd worn it. To impress me, I suppose, since the air was much too warm to make a coat practical. "I volunteered as an excuse to come by Bell Run." Remembering the graves before him, he added uneasily, "I'm ... sorry ..."

Seeing his eyes linger on Julia's marker, I let my rage boil over. "Your Julia died when you never returned. She loved you. Enough to join with you before you could be wed. Enough to bear your child."

"Child?" He stood, stunned. It was true then. He didn't know.

"A daughter."

"If Aunt Florence wrote, my parents never said. Father stopped speaking to our Richmond kin when the fighting started." His smile became a proud smirk. "So I have a daughter, do I?" Abruptly though, the pride was replaced by consternation. "Father must never know."

"You returned home to speak to him of marriage, did you not?"

"Yes, but this war—"

"This war! It was *you* who spoke of peace. Of the immorality of killing at all, let alone one's countrymen, one's brothers." I felt a cruel laugh in my throat. "Julia believed you. And you left her to become an assassin yourself." I spat at his uniform.

He bore the indignity with an angry stiffening of his jaw. "I had no choice. My home came under fire. It was my duty to defend it."

"Your duty. Your home." My wrath hardened into a cold, hard lump in my heart. "Look around, General Howard. A hundred thousand men like yourself did this to *my* home. In defense of their own. What threat was Bell Run to them? How many other homes have you laid waste, General? Did you talk peace while your comrades burned and ravaged? Or are those lectures reserved for luring young girls to your bed?"

"Enough of this."

"How many others besides Julia have you seduced with your gentle words, General?"

He gripped my arm, bruising the flesh beneath my shirt. "What's wrong with you? Why do you persist—"

"Why did you come today? To tell Julia how you'd traded your convictions to become your father's pawn? To wear a fancy uniform and—"

I saw the blow coming but could not dodge his fist. My jaw met it squarely, loosing fire up behind my eyes, setting off a clamorous ringing of my ears. I shook my head vigorously to clear it, only to find myself flat against the earth, him astride me, his hands pinning my wrists.

"Stop this nonsense at once!" His shout set his mount to paw the soil anxiously.

"Go on, kill me, General. I won't be your first victim. How many have you killed? How many have you ordered to their deaths? Murderer!"

"One must kill in battle. You wouldn't understand."

"Wouldn't I? I stood with the Virginia Thirty-Third yesterday at the Orange Turnpike. I watched thousands meet their Maker, screaming for the loved ones they forsook to join the madness. Who will you summon in your final moment, General? Your father?"

Releasing my wrists, he clasped me by the shoulders, shaking me with all his strength. "I don't believe you. They'd never let you near the fighting."

I laughed. "Gabriel Bell isn't the youngest boy in Lee's army. I've seen youths of twelve, thirteen, shooting men dead as if Satan weaned them himself."

"My God—" His whisper was hoarse, tinged with horror, but the shaking stopped.

My laugh doubled, so I could hardly control it. "What a hypocrite you are. First preaching peace among brothers, then condoning the butchery, but only if all participants have felt the scrape of a razor across their chins. What will you allow next? The burning of mothers at their hearths if they bore any of the foe? The slaughter of their young children? The defilement of their daughters to fill the tedium between battles? Or was that always tolerable? Perhaps you left Julia because war was a more bewitching mistress."

He slammed me hard against the earth, throwing his full weight upon me, so full of fury he could barely speak. "I'll make you stop!"

The force had knocked all breath from me. I replenished it in one deep gasp. "If you would kill my body, General, have done with it. You can do no further harm to my soul. It roams even now amongst the damned. As does yours."

But he had no intention of killing me, only of teaching me a lesson. His greater bulk held me powerless as his hands tore at my flesh. Alarmed by the fervor of his attack, by the promise in his eyes of worse to follow, I fumbled for his revolver. He thought I merely struggled helpless beneath him, until he felt the barrel against his ribs.

"What in God's name—" He grabbed for the gun, trying to envelop my hand with his own.

I squeezed my eyes shut as I felt his palm slap down over the percussion mechanism, his finger hooking around mine even as I pulled the trigger. The whole of Creation exploded, the blast hoisting him so, that for one horrible moment, he seemed to hover above me. Then, plummeting back against me, his body shuddered in turbulent convulsions.

Terrified, panicked, I squirmed from beneath him, crawling swiftly out of his arm's reach. Cowering against my mother's marker, I watched John Howard die, his back, fittingly, to Heaven.

In his final breath, he murmured the name *Julia*.

13

Trembling uncontrollably, I opened my eyes, never so glad to see tombstones in all my life. I touched the green grass, combing my fingers through the clover and dandelions.

What I'd seen was as puzzling as it had been frightening. Had I imagined it all? A dream, fit together from the letters I'd read?

A twig snapped outside the wall, and I jumped. Beth Ann stood there, hands in her jeans, regarding me the way a bird regards a cat. "Were you praying or something?"

I tried to reassure her with a feeble smile. "Or something." What had she seen me do? What, if anything, had I said?

I shoved the memory of what I'd witnessed away. Time to talk to Beth Ann about that doll I received. But how, without putting her more on the defensive? Hesitantly, I ventured, "Won't you get in trouble for being here?"

She shrugged. "I wanted to—" Her gaze fell as her words came tumbling out, faster than a product disclaimer in a radio ad. "Dad didn't mean to scare you yesterday. He was just mad at me."

Allowing her the physical advantage had worked once, so I shifted my weight from my knees to sit on the grass. "Did he punish you when he got home?"

She put on her world's-out-to-get-me pout and nodded. "Made me stay in my room all night and no TV till Friday."

This seemed injustice enough to her. If she knew I meant child abuse, she gave no hint. Maybe Miss Maggie was right—only I incited Hugh to anger. "Yet, you're out again today. He's probably looking for you already."

"I don't care." Contrarily, it was evident she did. "Is it true there's another lady? That Miss Maggie might not leave you the whole forest?"

"Yes. Her name's Charlotte Garber, and she has as much right to the place as I have." I almost choked on the words, but if *I* didn't face facts, Beth Ann never would.

"Is she like you?" It was a challenge, heavy with suspicion, though I couldn't tell which side of the yes-no answer she wanted to hear.

"I don't know what she's like. I only met her once. She seems nice enough." I realized how much I wished I could call Charlotte a regular ogre. How I wanted Beth Ann to hate her and like me. I mentally shook away my jealousy, opting for positive action. "Okay if I walk you as far as Miss Maggie's house?"

She nodded, and I pushed myself up from the grass, starting toward her.

An explosion rang out. Something savagely jerked my arm, throwing me back to the ground before my brain got the notion I'd been shot.

A half beat of silent shock went by before Beth Ann screamed, seizing my good arm, yanking me to my feet with a superhuman burst of adrenaline. "Come on! Run! You have to!"

I didn't argue. We fled away from the sound, over the wall, head first into the brambles. Beth Ann still clutched my arm, swatting branches from in front of our eyes with her other hand. I felt the vines tangling around my feet, snagging at my clothes, scratching my face, but made myself lift my legs higher, matching her youthful strides, until I thought my lungs would rupture.

Abruptly, the thicket wall gave way. We were on the grass beside the ruin.

"Run!" Beth Ann urged. "You can't slow up now. I hear someone behind us."

I could hear nothing over the pounding in my ears, but

I didn't doubt her. She plunged directly into the wild jungle shrouding the house, dragging me after her. This time, though, a trail of sorts opened up before us, a dark tunnel of green tentacles surrounding packed earth. Before we'd gone a dozen steps, Beth Ann hauled me around in front of her.

"Jump!" I didn't need to ask what she meant. Her hands were at my back, propelling me, and suddenly, nothing was beneath my feet.

The landing, five feet down, jarred every bone in me. Slapping my hands down to balance myself, my left arm howling in agony, I found a brick floor. Beth Ann touched down lightly beside me, silently goading me forward into blackness. Hurdling down another high step, we sprinted along a cool, damp corridor, rounding a corner, collapsing onto the floor.

She was shaking so much, I wrapped my unhurt arm around her shoulders, holding her tight as I tried to catch my breath, both of us listening intently.

Someone was outside. The swish of underbrush grew near. I imagined bushes being whacked with a long branch in an attempt to flush us out of hiding. Beth Ann let out a panicky whimper.

I hugged her close, putting my mouth to her ear. "Shh. We'll be okay."

She leaned into me and, though her muscles remained taut, I felt her panic subside. Our pursuer moved on, the swishing noises fading away to silence.

"I need my arm back, Beth Ann," I said softly.

She sat up, whispering, "Are you . . . are you all right?"

Now that immediate danger had passed, my brain was checking its voice mail for pain messages. There were plenty, from every nerve ending, but my left arm demanded a monopoly, the throbbing just above my elbow shooting sharp arrows into my shoulder and wrist. I explored with my good hand, finding the whole sleeve wet and sticky, blood flowing freely, running down my forearm to drip from my fingers. Raising my arms above my head, I clamped three fingers over the wound, curling my thumb behind to maintain pressure. It hurt so much I really did see stars. And I'd thought that was just a saying.

"What are you doing?" Beth Ann asked, her voice quivering.

"They teach you this when you give blood, and some really clumsy nurse botches it." I was determined to keep my tones matter of fact, to keep her from panicking again. "Do me a favor, will you? Try to tear a strip of cloth off the bottom of my blouse. I need a bandage, and this blouse is headed for the trash anyway."

"I can do better than that." I felt her stir beside me. A flash of brilliance cut through the dark and, as my eyes adjusted, I saw in her palm a penlight on a keychain with a small Swiss Army knife. Beth Ann took the light from the chain, clenched it between her teeth, and pried a pair of miniature scissors from the knife. She looked to me for direction.

"Cut a two or three inch strip. That's good. Go all the way around back. The longer it is, the easier it'll be to knot." Leaning forward as she cut, my head decided to take a swim. I closed my eyes and talked myself out of fainting.

"Done," she mumbled around the light in her mouth.

I sank back against the wall, relieved. "I need you to put it on." Easing the pressure on the wound, I ran my fingertips lightly over it. The bleeding hadn't stopped completely but had slowed significantly. "Wrap it around a couple times and pull it tight, gently, until I tell you to stop. Go on. Don't be afraid. My blood won't hurt you. No HIV. Swear to God."

I kept up the chatter. It helped keep her hands steady.

Beth Ann neatly knotted the ends, cringing at the blood on her fingers, wiping them on her jeans before taking the light from her teeth. "Aren't you going to put your arm down now?"

"Won't hurt to leave it up for a while." My fingers had already gone numb, but I couldn't risk giving new life to the bleeding.

"There's so much blood." In the dim light, I could see the alarm in her eyes. "Maybe I should go for help."

"No." We hadn't heard anything for a while, but I wasn't taking chances. The loony who shot at us might still be out there, waiting. "Someone will come looking for us."

"My dad will," she said, trying to convince herself as much as me.

"Where are we?"

"The cellar of the Bell House." Beth Ann moved the light across the floor and up the wall across from us. Both were of brick, the floor worn smooth and satiny by generations of feet. The air smelled the way old cellars do: a little moldy, a little stale, a little earthy, like fresh potatoes. I felt safe here. Protected. The way I used to feel when I was little and Mom held me after a nightmare. Of course, if being shot didn't qualify as a nightmare, I don't know what would.

"I think where we jumped used to be the outside steps," Beth Ann was saying. "There's holes in the bricks where wooden stairs must have been."

"Great hideout. Come here often?"

"Only found it last summer."

"How far in have you gone?" I was picturing the whole thing falling on her in a destruction scene reminiscent of a dynamited skyscraper.

"This is it." She swung her light around to reveal a floor-to-ceiling pile of bricks and rubble blocking the passage.

My muscles were beginning to spasm painfully. I relaxed my shoulder, resting my arm across my knees in an effort to keep it elevated.

"You're sure you're all right?" Beth Ann toggled her light between my arm and face.

"I'm fine." Damn light. Couldn't even wince. I forced a grin. "Tell me about school. Your classes, what clubs you're in, everything."

After a bit more prodding, once I got her talking, she was like a spigot with a broken washer. I heard how she loved science and hated English. How her biology teacher

let her care for the class guinea pigs. How she played clar-
inet in the school band and was president of Ecology Club.
Each time she tried to change the subject back to my arm,
I'd prompt her with more questions. I didn't mind listening—it took my mind off the throbbing and creeping cold
in my bones, though I was sweating like an NBA player
after ten minutes in a game. That association gave me my
next cue.

"Ever go out for any sports?"

"Well . . . I was manager of the hockey team last fall."

I asked her what managers do.

"Run the clock and keep score for games. Cut up or-
anges for halftime. A couple times during practice scrim-
mages Mrs. Barnes even let me help officiate."

"Sounds like a lot of responsibility."

"Yeah . . ." she grinned. "But the cool part is, you get
to wear a whistle. And—" All at once she went tense, gripping my wrist.

I heard it, too. Someone outside.

"Beth Ann!" The bellow was deep and thoroughly annoyed.

"Dad!" She was on her feet and around the corner before
I could draw my next breath. "Dad, over here!"

She'd left the pen light. I picked it up, rising to my feet
until the passageway went topsy-turvy. Leaning my back
against the bricks, I waited for the world to right itself, then
I slowly staggered around the corner, down the hall, out
into the stairwell. Knowing there was no climbing out
alone, I propped myself up against the wall to wait for Beth
Ann to bring her father back.

A bright light made me squint. The beam slowly descended, taking in my arm, the whole sleeve deep crimson,
along with the bandage and most of the shirt's left side.
Raising my head, I saw only a giant shadow lurking behind
the glare.

Setting the light on the ground, the specter thrust a burly
hand down in front of my face. "Grab my wrist."

Pocketing the penlight, I obeyed, thinking with his support, I could easily use the footholds in the brick to climb out. Had I known he intended to lift me out like one of his mail sacks, I would have asked for another rescuer.

He set me down beside him, clamping his arm about my waist to hold me upright. "Beth Ann. Run back to Miss Maggie's and call 911. We'll be right behind you. Here, take the flashlight."

"Oh, Dad, it isn't even dark yet." Her voice was back in normal teen exasperation range.

Before I could even think about following her, Hugh scooped me up into his arms as if I weighed no more than a load of laundry, taking away what little breath I had left.

"What the hell are you doing? Put me down."

"You're hurt." The vise of his arms tightened against my struggles.

"My *arm*, not my legs." My kicks were of no use. He didn't intend to let go.

Since keeping Beth Ann calm was no longer an issue, all my suppressed fears were free to come rushing out of the closet. I'd been talking to his daughter, walking toward her, the moment I was shot, and yesterday Hugh had warned me to stay away from her. Had *he* pulled the trigger?

"Let me go or I'll scream," I said, trying to keep my voice from quaking, though I don't think I had the energy to make good the threat.

He lowered me slowly back to my feet. "Yes, ma'am. After you," he said, waving me on with a gallant sweep of the flashlight, his voice sarcastically polite.

I stumbled down the low trail. If I had to stoop, Hugh must have been bent in half, but the beam bobbed steadily behind me.

I emerged onto the mown path. The sky above was streaked with pink clouds, the sun completely gone from the treetops, the ruin, one big, spooky silhouette. I started off to the left, but Hugh, with a heavy hand on my shoulder, swung me around to the right.

My head was turning traitor on me. The surrounding

forest became an inky blob; the grass seemed to drag at my feet. When I passed the trail without seeing it, Hugh lifted me once again. I didn't have the strength to fight him.

His arms felt solid and warm.

Safe.

Letting my head fall against his chest, hypnotized by the sway of his walk and sound of his heartbeat, I allowed myself to pass out.

If people raise a howl against my barbarity or cruelty, I will answer that war is war and not popularity seeking.
General William Tecumseh Sherman, 1864

MAY 6, 1864—BELL RUN

As I gazed down upon the lifeless form that had once been John Howard, I wound my arms tightly around my knees and willed my trembling to cease. The shot might have been heard, or another messenger might come looking for John, so I knew I must leave soon. When I thought my legs could again support me, I pushed myself to my feet.

War-hardened, the mare had only trotted off a short distance at the pistol shot. I approached her slowly, downwind so as not to frighten her by the smell of blood on my shirt, though that also seemed of little concern to her. She let me take her reins, offering her nose to the caress of my palm, following me back to where I'd left my things.

Loosing the coat, sword, and rolled blanket from behind the saddle, I shook out the latter, finding a clean shirt and a ration of salt pork concealed within. The pork made my mouth water, so great was my hunger, but I made do with the promise of a meal later, when I was safely away. For the shirt, I gladly traded my own raiment, rent and gory from the struggle. Tucked into my trousers, the sleeves rolled to my wrists, it concealed my torso well in thick gathers of homespun cotton.

Toting the rest, I returned to John Howard's mortal remains. I'd never wished to take life in this fashion—selfishly, in defense of myself alone. Killing John had not rescued his soul, unless I'd saved him further punishment by preventing the augmentation of his sins.

Rolling him to his back, refusing to let my eyes stray to his wound or face, I undid his gun belt, then restored him to the attitude of his passing, freeing the belt from his hip. Retrieving the pistol from my mother's grave, I wiped the repugnant evidence of the deed from both weapon and belt upon the blanket before sheathing the revolver in its holster.

Covering John's face with his coat, I placed the sword beside him, shrouding the rest of him with the blanket. I had no time to dig another grave. Even if I had, I couldn't bring myself to bury him in proximity to my parents, who'd received such sorrow from his act, or near my brothers, to whom he'd turned traitor. And certainly not beside the cross bearing the name of Julia. Nor beneath the once fertile soil of Bell Run.

I buckled the sidearm about my waist, feeling its weight tug at my trousers. Eight rounds remained in the belt, another four in the gun itself.

Returning to the mare, I raised her stirrups for the length of my legs. With a mount, I could journey many miles tonight, perhaps making up lost ground, perhaps coming closer to my goal. I'd have to make a wide circuit of both armies, forced to make my path along streambeds and roads, across fields, forsaking the better cloak of the thickets, but haste seemed worth the hazard.

Slipping my own rolled blanket and rifle over one shoulder, my sack and canteen over the other, I mounted. With a final canvass of the forest, the river, the weathering crosses, I prodded the mare forward, bidding silent farewell to my family, never expecting to set eyes upon home again.

Dusk was settling in early, the battle smoke hanging thick in the air, obstructing the sun's drama with its own farce, dimming the forest to gray sameness.

I proceeded slowly at first, taking more than an hour to retrace my previous route along Flat Run, across Germanna Plank Road, and on to the battlefield. I'd no knowledge as to where the day's fighting had placed each army, and I did not relish the thought of coming upon either as they prepared their evening rations. Once around both flanks I could increase my speed on the roads further south.

So I crept nearer to where I'd begun yesterday, listening with all my being for noises other than the muffled clop of the mare's hooves along the stream bank.

All at once, not two hundred yards before me to my left,

came a piercing Rebel yell and instantaneous musket play. The mare started, side-stepping, and I reined her in, reaching down to stroke her neck.

A renewed attack with no more than an hour's light lingering? It was lunacy, a mere excuse for the spilling of blood. Had the gods not tasted their quota for one day?

To my right, a crashing of dead wood and leaves led me to expect a stampede. A single bluecoat emerged, rifle in one hand, a full, heavy sack in the other—some manner of plunder, no doubt, from the farmhouses to the west. He was more amazed to confront me than I him, though scarce the blink of an eye passed before he dropped his sack.

I didn't wait for him to raise his weapon, but dug my heels hard into the mare. Responding to my panic as well as my command, she surged forward as I crouched low over her mane, curling into the smallest target possible.

The rifle's report sent a bullet whistling past my shoulder; a second lifted my haversack from my hip. It flopped back against me as I urged my mount on, clinging fast against the wild contractions of animal flesh below.

No other shots rang out, but I maintained the gallop over the uneven ground until the mare stumbled, nearly pitching me over her shoulder. Shoving my heels forward, I reined her to a halt. The rattle of musketry was behind me now and, over it, I detected no sign of pursuit.

Walking the horse, I found her gait irregular and slid from the saddle to examine her. Speaking soothingly to her in the dim light, running my fingers over her sweaty calves and around each hoof, I found a sharp rock wedged into her right front shoe. I was able to dislodge it, but the foot beneath was tender.

Patting her muzzle to reassure her, I coaxed her forward. Her gait was improved, but my ear detected a hair's breadth hesitation as the hoof took her weight. I wouldn't ride her if I thought she felt any pain at all.

"Such is how I reward you for saving my life," I murmured, the irony in my voice lost on my companion. "I wish I had an apple for you, but perhaps we'll find grass further along." I knew of meadows lining either side of Flat Run's west branch. If the land had come through this last campaign undefiled, I'd set the mare free, where she'd have food and water until one army or the other captured her.

As if guessing my thoughts, she gave a low snort of approval, nuzzling my shoulder—the closest I'd come to a fond gesture since Lane died.

Sliding my palm along her jaw, I remembered Father saying once that animals could not enter Heaven.

This horse had not one evil bone within her when taken to become an instrument of war. She'd since witnessed carnage and plundering and God knows what else, yet remained giving in her nature. She'd watched me murder her late master, yet bore me willingly, saving my wretched skin, now showing me affection. Forgiveness, servitude, charity—I wondered if Father didn't begrudge these beasts their Christian virtues.

But unlike animals, men are transformed by Evil. I'd known this, yet seeing John today, seeing no trace of that once tender youth, seeing only selfish pride and savagery—

This last he likely called, in his conceit, virility.

No, the devoted, caring John Howard, Clarissa's father, died long ago. Perished as Julia had perished. This world, so scandalized by the offspring of their love, yet so willing to embrace hate, was no fit place for them.

~~⊲~~ 14 ~~⊳~~

When I opened my eyes, I was lying on my bed in Miss Maggie's back room, with two alien creatures dressed as paramedics hovering over me.

One was shouting my name in a loud stadium voice. I wondered if she had a mike hidden behind her mask and safety glasses. She looked triumphant when I lifted my eyelids, as if she alone had brought me back from the dead. She didn't know how accustomed I was to loud voices. At Muscarella reunions I'd sat amidst two hundred people all talking like they had bad long-distance connections. No, what woke me was her cohort swabbing my arm with acid.

They'd taken the blouse off me, so I was lying there breeding goosebumps in my bra. The pillows that should have been under my head were propping up my knees, and a blood-pressure cuff was strapped to my right biceps. They'd washed most of the blood from my left side, painting a third of that arm a grotesque shade of jaundice.

Iodine. No wonder it burned like hell.

I raised my head for a better view of the wound, a cigar-shaped scrape maybe two inches long. Didn't look a tenth as bad as it hurt but, considering the pain ratio of a tiny paper cut, I guess it could have smarted a lot worse. At least the throbbing had subsided.

"Just winged you," the medic with the iodine said. I got the impression he was grinning under his mask. Happy because I was conscious? Or half naked?

The other pumped up the pressure gauge until my right

arm hurt as much as my left. Sticking an icy stethoscope under the cuff, she slowly let the air out. "Her blood pressure's returning to normal," she said in her ordinary voice, reserved for talking about the patient as if she weren't there. "Still on the low side though."

"You lost a little blood." The guy was apparently the spokesperson of the two. He tossed the swab on the floor while his colleague ripped open a single-serving gauze pack. "The bullet nicked a vein slightly. Kid downstairs says you stopped the bleeding yourself."

Beth Ann. I was glad she was still here. I wanted to see her, make sure she was okay. I described to the paramedic my service in the front lines at annual blood drives.

"Well, it worked." Folding the gauze to the size of the wound, he held it in place while his partner taped it down. Then he stripped off his gloves and glasses, yanking the mask down below his chin. A human after all. Kind of cute, too, though way too young for me. "Try sitting up."

They hoisted me upright, all of us expecting my head to do a crash dive any moment. I felt woozy but didn't return to la-la land.

"We'll take you to the hospital," the cutie said. "Get a doctor to check you out, but I doubt you need stitches."

I considered spending the night in an emergency room trying to explain Dawkins-Greenway's excuse for medical insurance, which insisted on treatment at a preapproved hospital, of which I swear there were three in the whole country. "Couldn't you just tag me DOA now instead?"

"You don't want to go to the hospital?"

"It's against my religion." I glanced at my arm. With the blood cleaned off and the bandage covering the wound, the limb didn't seem like it would fall off soon. My medical plan only paid if they carried you in half-dead.

"You could develop an infection."

With all that iodine coursing through my veins? As far as the germ community was concerned, I was a Superfund toxic-waste dump. "I promise if I do, I'll come to the hospital myself. I'll even have them page the two of you so you can say 'Told you so' in person. Okay?"

"You'll have to sign a waiver. And we'll give you a tetanus shot." As his partner prepared the injection, he rattled off the standard blood-donor instructions: Leave the bandage on overnight, don't get it wet, drink plenty of liquids tonight and tomorrow, and don't herd elephants with that arm until at least Friday. Then they took off the blood-pressure cuff and jabbed the right arm with a hypo, making it hurt as much as the left.

Miss Maggie walked in bearing two glasses, water in one, some kind of orange-red liquid in the other. A plate of chocolate chip cookies was balanced on the latter. She was breathing hard, as if she'd climbed the stairs once too often and, still in her old-lady getup, she looked every inch her age. The medic with the big mouth rushed over to give her a hand.

When she saw me awake, she smiled. "Pat. How do you feel?"

Seeing her brought back the episode at the cemetery. I needed to tell her about it, ask her what it might mean. But first I had to do something to erase the deep lines of worry on her face. "I feel cold. Somebody want to hand me my nightshirt?"

I'd stashed it under the pillows. Now it was in a heap at the bottom of the bed. The cute medic helped me on with it while the other started packing stuff away. She'd also peeled off her gloves and face protection, though, unlike her colleague, it wasn't an improvement.

"And I feel thirsty," I continued. "Either of those drinks for me?"

"Both." Miss Maggie set the glasses and plate on the nightstand. "This first," she said, placing the glass of water in my hand. It felt so cold she must have melted a glacier.

The male paramedic pulled out a clipboard. "Ma'am? I need to see that card again."

"I left it in my bedroom." Miss Maggie bustled out and was back in less than a minute, handing him what looked like my plastic health-insurance card. "I took it out of your wallet, Pat. Everything's taken care of."

She didn't explain how she'd worked that miracle, or why the card had been in her bedroom, but I was more concerned that she was still running around. I made her sit beside me while I signed his papers. When she wanted to walk them to the front door, I grabbed her hand. "They found their way in, Miss Maggie. Trust them to find their way out."

She relented, and we listened to them march down the stairs. I heard both Hugh and Beau speak to them but couldn't make out the conversation. The front screen slammed, and the murmur of voices moved outside.

Miss Maggie pushed the plate of cookies at me. "Here. Replenish your sugars."

Cookies? In this house? "Where'd these come from?"

"The package says they come from elves but—"

"You know what I mean, Miss Low-Everything-Diet."

She grinned sheepishly. "I keep a secret stash. For when Beth Ann comes over, of course."

I'd grill her about its location later. "Is Beth Ann still here? Will Hugh let me talk to her before he takes her home?"

Miss Maggie laughed. "She refuses to leave until she's seen you."

I nibbled a cookie between gulps of water. "Did anyone call the police?"

"The sheriff was here. Took Beth Ann's statement. Said he'd be back tomorrow for yours—"

She broke off as we both heard sneakered feet vaulting the stairs at Olympic speed. Beth Ann skidded to a stop at the door, looking awkwardly apprehensive. Her clothes were filthy and bloodstained, but she'd washed her hands and face.

I grinned at her. "You smelled the cookies, right?"

She relaxed, seemingly at a loss for words, her features softening almost into a smile.

"Come over here and help me eat these things," I said,

setting my now empty water glass on the nightstand.

Beth Ann took a few tentative steps into the room. "I . . . I can't. I haven't had supper yet. Dad would—"

"I think it's time to tell her, Miss Maggie," I said somberly. "She's old enough to know."

One thing about Miss Maggie. She jumps right in and plays along with the best of them. "Oh, I agree."

"Know what?" Beth Ann looked scared now, but she inched nearer.

"One of the deep, dark secrets of womanhood." I waved her onto the bed, beckoning her to lean closer, whispering, "Something you'll never hear from your father."

I had her hooked, her eyes wide with fascination. "What?"

"Beth Ann, anytime you have a day like we had today, chocolate *is* supper."

Miss Maggie nodded sagely.

Beth Ann sat back, the angle of her head raining pure cynicism. "You're kidding, right?"

"Swear to God." I crossed my heart and held up my hand.

Miss Maggie shoved the plate under her nose. "Go on. We won't tell your dad."

Grinning now, entering into the conspiracy, she took two.

Miss Maggie stood. "Speaking of supper, I'll go see if Hugh wants any. We still have leftovers from Monday that'll do."

After she left, Beth Ann broke a chunk off one cookie and rolled it around her tongue. "How's your arm?"

I pushed up my sleeve so she could see the bandage. "I won't be able to milk any sympathy out of it. The bullet didn't go in."

"I know." She broke another chunk. "I saw it hit a tree. Knocked a big splinter off."

"You're observant." I reached for the juice glass. Sipping, I tasted strawberry, banana, and orange. Typical of

Miss Maggie. Plain O.J. would have been too mundane for
her. "Did the sheriff talk to you?"

Beth Ann nodded, frowning. "Dad and Mr. Dillard think
it was the same kid the sheriff caught deer hunting on Miss
Maggie's property last December. The sheriff's going to
question him and his friends."

Which explained why no posse was out combing the
woods. But a kid would probably have run like hell, not
taken up the chase. "Did you tell them the person came
after us?"

"Yes." Beth Ann lowered her gaze. "Dad says I just
panicked, that I must have imagined hearing someone."

That angered me. Bad enough she was bound to get the
hysterical female treatment down the road from doctors and
car mechanics—she didn't need it now from her own father. "Does he think I imagined it, too?"

"I *was* scared." She blinked uncertainly. "I've never
been that frightened before."

"Me neither." I almost burst out laughing at her skeptical
frown. "It's true, Beth Ann. My heart was pounding so
loud, I thought it would give us away. But no matter how
scared we were, someone *was* out there. I'm positive."

She dispatched the last of one cookie thoughtfully.
"Maybe whoever fired the shot wanted to see if we needed
help."

I couldn't blame her for holding fast to the accidental
shooting theory. I preferred it myself. If not that, the only
choices were an armed neighborhood psycho or someone
who wanted me dead—probably the someone who loathed
me enough to send hate mail. I decided to think about that
possibility later. "Regardless, you thought you were saving
my life today, and for that I'm grateful."

Beth Ann's blush was one of shame. "Don't be. I . . .
I . . ."

I let her stammer another half minute before deciding to
help her out. "Are you trying to tell me about that rock you
threw the other night?"

Her eyes widened, half in misgivings, half in deeper guilt, but she nodded.

"You always have such lousy aim?"

"I wouldn't have hit you," she said hastily. "I thought . . . I mean . . ."

"You didn't know how else to deal with me turning your forest into another housing development?"

She nodded again, more timidly, then fervently added, "But I didn't do that other stuff—the doll and that paper. Miss Maggie asked me, and I swore to her I didn't."

"I know." I'd come to believe that in the course of the afternoon. Like Miss Maggie said, Beth Ann wasn't mean.

"I'm sorry about the rock," she mumbled, her whole attitude sincere, repentant.

The old softy in me almost gave in to the urge to tell her all was forgiven. Almost. "Beth Ann, if I *ever* catch you sneaking around the forest in the middle of the night again, I'll skip telling your father and spank you myself. Understand?"

I wasn't kidding, and she knew it. Her eyes practically came out of her head. "Yes, ma'am. I won't. I promise."

I set my juice back on the night table. "But I'm still grateful for today, and my family always says thank you by hugging."

Her blush deepened until it could have humiliated a rose in full bloom. "You don't have to—"

"Sure I do. It's an Italian thing." I held out my arms. "You might as well get it over with."

She came into my embrace shyly, but once there, wound her own limbs around my back and nearly squeezed the breath out of me. I got the feeling I was the one being thanked.

I also got the feeling we were being watched. Letting her go, my eyes locked on those of her father, who was standing in the doorway, filling it completely. Neither of us had heard him mount the stairs. He moved like a cat. By association, I pictured a cougar on the hunt. Hugh's forest-green polo was streaked with my blood, reinforcing the predatory image. And seeing my blood there brought back the memory of him lifting me, carrying me, the snug haven of his arms and chest. I felt the blood rush into my cheeks.

Hugh shifted his gaze, settling on the cookie remaining in Beth Ann's hand.

Embarrassment made me confrontational. "I wouldn't be much of a bad influence if I couldn't talk her into spoiling her appetite, would I?"

Hugh seemed to chew the bait before rejecting it. "Sugar's good for shock."

Beth Ann swung her head back and forth like a judge at a tennis match, unsure who had the advantage. "You mean I can have more, Dad?"

"After supper. Miss Maggie's going to heat up something for us, down in the kitchen. Go give her a hand."

Accepting that, she stood.

"Beth Ann," I said, "promise me you won't go out into the woods by yourself for a few days. In case the kid with the bad eyesight comes back looking for deer." This last was to let her father know what I thought of his theory.

"She won't be going anywhere except to and from school," he said, turning to her. "You're still grounded, remember? And since you've ignored me the past two days, I'm extending it through Sunday."

"Dad!" Feeling persecuted, Beth Ann looked to me for support.

"What do *you* think you deserve?" I asked.

Her eyes told me she was thinking about our little secret of her late-night sojourn and target practice. Jamming her hands in her jeans pockets, she studied the floor. "I guess I can live with it."

"Good. Do me a favor? Take some of these dishes downstairs so Miss Maggie won't have to make an extra trip later." I grabbed my juice and the last two cookies so Beth Ann could clear away the water glass and plate.

Hugh stepped aside to let her through the door, never taking his eyes from me. I responded with one of the looks

I use on Burt when letting him know what I think of his management skills.

Then, at last, I was alone. It had been dark outside when I awoke, and I wondered what time it was. My watch sat on the far corner of the night table, its band and face caked with dried blood. I could wait until tomorrow to clean it and see if it still worked.

Two car engines started up, the ping of Beau's pickup and something bigger, the ambulance or whatever vehicle the paramedics had come in. In the silence after they left, I was once more aware of the night sounds. I wanted to go to the window, poke my head outside, breathe in the honey-suckled air. But even if I could have trusted my weak knees, I couldn't help imagining an assassin lurking in the forest shadows, waiting to take aim at my head in the window.

I sat sipping and nibbling, wondering if someone had truly, purposefully, taken a shot at me. If this had been a *Murder, She Wrote* episode, the obvious suspect would be the next in line for the inheritance. Charlotte.

Did Charlotte know I'd be alone this afternoon? And had she sent me the doll? Maybe to try to scare me away first, so she could have the inheritance to herself? But had she even been in town yesterday morning when the printout had been left inside the door?

Another car pulled up. The front screen door slammed and Joel's good-natured tenor cried out, "Anybody home?"

I opened my mouth to reply, but Miss Maggie beat me to it, calling him out to the kitchen. After a few moments, I heard him exclaim, "What?", then after another interval came slow footfalls on the stairs. If it was Joel, he sure wasn't eager to get to me.

He was dressed in another disheveled three-piece suit, and I saw why he'd taken his time. Miss Maggie had loaded him down with a second glass of juice and a small, steaming bowl with a spoon balanced on a saucer beneath.

He smiled kind of weakly when he saw me. "Miss Maggie told me to make sure you eat all of this."

"Put them here on the table." I set my glass down, too, and sat upright, patting the spread. "Sit."

He complied. "This is nothing but a plot to get me into your bed."

"Damn right." Clutching his lapels, I pulled him closer until his lips met mine. My right hand found its way up over his shoulder, fingers tracing the contour of one ear, the texture of his hair.

His hands, maddeningly, parked themselves at my waist. Trying to inspire him, I leaned back against the pillows, pulling him along. He came willingly enough, until his chest lightly rested against mine, and I could feel his agitated heartbeat. His kiss became more playful, but playful was obviously as far as we were going tonight. I told myself it was only our second kiss, that I should be glad I'd finally landed a gentleman. My rattled nerves, however, would have much preferred the emotional release a bout of frenzied passion would provide. You don't give a starving person nouvelle cuisine.

Pouring a mental bucket of ice water over my hot Italian blood, I let him pull his mouth away.

"My, my." He drew a spacious lungful of air but didn't move otherwise. Exhaling, his breath warmed my face. "If I knew you were serving up sweets here tonight, I'd have skipped dessert and hurried on over."

"That was only the appetizer. I haven't gotten to the main course yet, let alone the sweets."

He sat up primly. "You are a dangerous woman. Better eat your soup before it gets cold. Though God knows what you'll be like once you get your strength back." He reached for the bowl, which I could now see contained leftover bread soup.

I stayed his hand. "No more liquids 'til I take a bathroom break. Want to escort me?"

Standing, he gallantly offered his arm. "My pleasure, ma'am."

As I rose to my feet, my equilibrium took its good old time deciding which way was up. I swayed, clawing at

Joel's arm as he snaked his other around my back. He was barely touching me, not supporting me nearly as much as I would have liked, as if he were handling delicate china.

Closing the bathroom door on his face, I turned to the medicine-chest mirror and there saw a reason for his restraint. My face was about three shades lighter than my normal Mediterranean melanin, with so many scratches, I looked like I'd made enemies of a dozen cats. Joel was either thoroughly repulsed or afraid of breaking me. I hoped fervently for the latter.

He helped me back to bed, insisting on holding the bowl while I ate, though I convinced him I'd prefer to manipulate the spoon myself. Not that his feeding me wouldn't have been terribly romantic, but I'd had enough sticky wetness on me for one day.

"So what happened?" he asked.

"Didn't they tell you downstairs?"

"We lawyers like to hear all sides of an argument."

I felt a snort coming on and quickly repressed it. "No lawyer I've ever known."

"The witness is directed to quit stalling and answer the question."

"Counsel is directed to say 'please.' "

Joel sighed. "Now I understand. All your houseplants died of sheer frustration."

This was the only entertainment I'd had all day, but I relented. I told him about the shooting, starting, of course, *after* my historical infomercial.

"Neither you nor Beth Ann saw the shooter?" he asked when I'd finished.

"I didn't. I'm pretty sure Beth Ann didn't either. She would have said." I took the bowl from him to slurp up the dregs from the bottom.

"You said Beth Ann heard someone behind you after you both ran through the woods. You didn't hear anything?"

"No, but—"

"But the blood was pounding in your ears," he repeated,

taking the empty bowl to return to the saucer on the table. "Why wouldn't Beth Ann's ears have had the same problem?"

My own blood started to pound again, this time in vexation. "Because she's twenty years younger than me. With longer legs and a higher center of gravity. And I *did* hear someone searching the bushes around the ruin."

He said almost apologetically, "Might have been a deer."

I pushed myself up at that, sticking the outrage on my face within inches of his nose. "It wasn't!"

He brought his hands up to gently cup my shoulders, his eyes sad. "Can you prove it?"

"Why do I need to?" I was irked that he wouldn't return my anger, as if I were some ranting little kid. Of course, my last comment had had a distinctly whiny quality to it. Bullets bring out the cranky brat in me. "Why won't you believe me?"

Joel pulled me into a hug. Fatherly, complete with pats on the back. Surprisingly, it felt wonderful. Benign and undemanding. I rested my head on his shoulder.

"I never said I don't believe you," he said soothingly, "but it's the sheriff who matters, not me."

"This isn't like *Matlock*? You aren't going to rush out and uncover the truth?"

I felt him chuckle. "Pretty much all I do is write wills and settle divorces."

The back screen door slammed. I listened to Hugh thank Miss Maggie for supper, saying they had to get home because Beth Ann still had to do homework. As Miss Maggie said something about a storm brewing, I saw faint sheet lightning silhouetting the trees to the north.

Turning my head from the window, facing in toward Joel's neck, I closed my eyes and snuggled against him until I could feel the artery in his neck pumping away. Hesitantly, he ran the back of his fingers gingerly across my cheek and when they'd retraced their course, his thumb continued along my bottom lip, so lightly it tickled. I did my best to accommodate him, turning my head, opening my lips—

15

"I'm coming up," Miss Maggie yelled from the bottom of the stairs, "so whatever you two are doing, cut it out."

By the time Miss Maggie came through the doorway, our pose was chastely Victorian, me reclining delicately against my pillows, Joel holding my hand courteously.

Miss Maggie took it in suspiciously. "Has he been a perfect gentleman?"

I nodded, red-faced, though he'd done no more than stroke my face and neck. Red-faced because I'd been fantasizing where it might have led had Miss Maggie not interrupted.

"Too bad. No fun at all." She waved him off the bed. "Give an old lady your seat, Joel. I need to talk to Pat. No, no. I want you to sit in. Pull over the desk chair."

Joel obeyed, setting the straight, torture-chamber-style chair so its back was to the bed, then straddling the seat, his arms folded along the carved wood of its spine.

Miss Maggie patted my forearm. "Gave us a scare, missy. Came home to find Beth Ann on the phone with 911 and Hugh carrying you out of the woods, blood all over the three of you. I thought Beau was going to have a heart attack right there, he got so upset."

"Is he okay?"

"I made him sit downstairs 'til his color came back. Kept going on about how the sheriff ought to do something about illegal poachers. Hugh got him calmed down, reassured him you were going to be all right—"

"But this *wasn't* a hunter, Miss Maggie—"

"I know that. Gave the sheriff the doll and—"

"What doll?" Joel piped in.

Miss Maggie did the explaining, and he responded with a stunned "Good Lord" and a "Why didn't you say you were getting threats?" directed at me.

I didn't want to mention Beth Ann, so instead of replying, I asked Miss Maggie, "If the sheriff knows about the doll, why's he still stuck on the poacher theory?"

"Because he doesn't want to bring in the Feds unless he's sure. That package came through the U.S. mail, making it federal jurisdiction."

"But—"

"Hush now, Pat. We can hash this out later. Got other things I need to discuss first." She sighed. "That health-care card of yours—the back said something about calling for preapproval of emergency care if you were able to do so. Had an eight-hundred number. Stupidest thing I ever heard, having to get permission before someone can save your life."

"Dawkins-Greenway doesn't believe in name-brand medical plans," I explained. "They found the cheapest, fly-by-night operation in the country. You ought to see what I have to go through for an annual GYN exam. Did you call?"

She nodded. "No answer."

This was so ironic, I laughed. "Figures."

"Oh, I didn't give up. I called Information and got the number for Dawkins-Greenway. Tried to get hold of your personnel department, hoping not everyone had gone home for the day."

"And you were told, 'We don't have a personnel department.' They laid them all off last year. Hired a benefits company that sends in temps."

Miss Maggie smiled. "I now understand your case against the place. Anyway, I asked for anyone who worked with you and ended up talking to someone named Denise. She was the only one still at her desk by that time."

"My cube mate. I bet Burt's got her working overtime this week because I'm out."

"Something like that." Miss Maggie had sobered abruptly, patting my arm again, to the point of distraction.

I put my hand over hers. "What?"

She sighed. "Your department was downsized this week. One from each team."

"Downsized," I repeated obtusely, knowing exactly what she was trying to say but refusing to believe it.

"Denise said Burt left a message on your home phone. I thought you'd rather hear it from me."

Downsized. Let go. Terminated. Unemployed. Sure, I'd hated my job, but as in any relationship, I wanted to be the one to break it off, on my terms; not be discarded like unsold yard-sale junk. And Burt The Coward, had waited until I was safely away on vacation. I felt hot tears threatening to spill over.

"I asked about severance," Miss Maggie continued. "You get eight weeks."

"Eight weeks! I've been there twelve years!" The tears wouldn't be held back then. They flowed uninhibited down my cheeks while I swore a blue streak.

Miss Maggie shoved a wad of tissues into my palm. "That's why I asked Joel to stay while I talked to you. I'm going to sign half the land over to you this week, Pat—"

"Magnolia!" Joel practically fell off the chair.

"Hush up, Joel. The property's mine to dispose of as I please. I won't make her wait until I die when she needs help now. You can sell it right away, Pat. Invest the money, give yourself a cushion. Or hold onto it 'til you really need it."

I rubbed the tears from my eyes. "Miss Maggie, I . . . I wouldn't feel right—"

Her exclamation sounded almost like an old-fashioned "pshaw!" "Wouldn't feel right taking what belongs to you? I've seen you looking at the forest, the river, at the creek this morning. Tell me you don't feel like it's yours already."

Thunder rumbled low in the distance, so much on cue, it sent chills up my spine. Joel was sulking the way he had the first night, when he couldn't get his way over that stupid agreement he wanted me to sign.

"And you're welcome to live here," she said. "I don't know how much longer the lease on your apartment goes, but—"

"No. I won't come live with you for free." Demoralizing enough to have to collect unemployment without accepting charity, too.

"I didn't say 'free.' I'll hire you as my personal cook and dietician. If Oprah can do it, why can't I?"

Joel grunted. " 'Cause you can't afford to pay her, that's why."

"I wish I could. But it'll give you a home base, Pat, while you look for work. That is, if you're still thinking of moving to Virginia. I realize it's sooner than you expected. You still have family back in Pennsylvania. Friends you might not want to leave."

"I'll think about it, Miss Maggie." One thing I knew. I couldn't totally rearrange my life in one night, even if I weren't in pain.

"We'll let you get some sleep," she said, patting my arm once more. "Been a long day." As she and Joel stood, thunder echoed again, louder and closer.

"Miss Maggie?" I had to get that cemetery scene off my chest before trying to sleep, but I didn't want Joel listening in. I could imagine the misgivings he already had about me. "I'll need help getting ready for bed. Maybe Joel could take the dishes down to the kitchen for you."

Joel came to the bedside, standing over me with a frown, but he merely said, "If you don't need me anymore, Magnolia, I'll lock up for you. Might as well not have to make the steps again."

I could have kissed him for that—not that I needed an excuse—but he never gave me the chance. Picking up the dishes, he turned away. Not even a platonic peck on the forehead.

Miss Maggie walked him to the doorway. "I closed all the windows. Just lock the front door. And Joel, I'll call you tomorrow morning about the deed transfer."

"Yes, ma'am," he replied, like a kid called to the blackboard for a tough problem. With a nod to each of us, he murmured goodnight.

Sitting up on my bed, I pulled my legs up to cross them in front of me. "Miss Maggie, what do you know of John Howard?"

She returned to her seat on the bed. "He was your great-great-great-grandfather."

"Not by marriage, though."

"No. You've been reading *Wilderness Voices*?"

"I didn't get very far. Only to Julia's response to her mother's letter saying her father wouldn't let her come home, even though Richmond was under attack." Even now, it put a lump in my throat.

Miss Maggie smiled. "You feel for her."

I swallowed, blinking my vision back into focus. Now wasn't the time to go all mushy. "I need to know what happened to John Howard."

"He left Richmond in the spring of sixty-two. Went home to Maryland. I don't know if he ever intended to return to Julia or not. I *do* know his father, John Sr., was an abolitionist who stopped speaking to his brother in Richmond at the outbreak of the war. Likely he threatened to disinherit his son if he returned to the South. And the Howards *were* fairly well off. John Jr. was given a commission in the Union army, possibly his father's doing."

The front door slammed below, signalling Joel's departure.

"But he never tried to get word to Julia?" A roll of thunder made the window blinds buzz in sympathy. I couldn't help flinching.

"Probably figured he'd never see her again."

"He ruined her life," I said bitterly. This morning I

hadn't even known who the man was. Now I would have yanked the trigger of that pistol myself.

"Pat . . ." Miss Maggie placed a comforting hand on my knee. "John Howard wasn't some horrible monster. He was Julia's age, sixteen in the fall of 1861, and about the *only* boy not gone off to war. He was probably as innocent, curious, and impulsive as she. Romeo and Juliet. Only this time Romeo gave in to his family. Romeos usually do, or did, back when I was teaching."

I thought about girls in my high school who'd gotten pregnant before graduating. Sometimes the boy's family forked over child care, but all except one of those girls had ended up as single mothers, their consorts going on to college or whatever, leaving the consequences of their act behind.

"And," Miss Maggie added, "there's no proof he ever knew about Clarissa."

Which brought me back to my next question. "Did John Howard survive the war?" I wanted to hear he'd lived a long life, had oodles of grandkids, so I could call my experience a dream and forget it.

But Miss Maggie shook her head. "Killed in battle."

"Which one?" Please, I prayed, let it be Gettysburg or—

"Wilderness."

A bright flash of lightning made the lamps flicker, as if they were as jittery as I felt. I braced myself for the thunder clap, following seconds later, as if the sky had ripped itself open.

"What a coincidence," I mumbled.

Miss Maggie scowled. "I'd like to think it wasn't. The letter home to his family said he'd been ambushed by a sniper while delivering information between corps. Pat, you aren't going to faint, are you?"

She looked so alarmed, I guessed what little color there was in my face must have drained out, which explained the whirling of the room and trembling of my hands. I had to gulp several deep breaths before sputtering, "I saw his murder."

She steadied me by touching my face, getting my full attention. "Slowly, Pat."

I related the whole incident, even how I'd felt drawn to the cemetery all afternoon. "It was like a vivid dream. I thought maybe that's what it was because—"

"You say Gabriel Bell shot John Howard in self-defense? Or as revenge for his sister perhaps?"

"That's what it sounded like." I hugged my good arm around my waist. "But I *must* have dreamt it. You know how there's always at least one part of a dream that just can't be? That's how I know, Miss Maggie—"

A blinding streak of lightning filled the sky, the instantaneous boom wrenching my gut. The lamps went out, jet blackness instantly pressing against my eyes.

I found Miss Maggie's hands holding mine. "Pat, calm down. Lightning hit the transformer is all. The power'll come back eventually."

Only then did I realize I was shivering violently, whimpering. Taking another deep, steadying breath, I made myself sit up. "I'm okay."

"What part of your, er, dream didn't ring true, Pat?"

In the darkness, I could see it again, explicitly. "Gabriel Bell . . . Uncle Gabe." I mentally dredged up the portrait in the book, setting it beside my memory to compare them. No, I wasn't mistaken. "He had dark hair and eyes."

This war is horrid. . . . Everything looks dark.
                    from the diary of Horatio Soule—May 6, 1864

MAY 6, 1864—WEST BRANCH OF FLAT RUN

I waited until night fell completely before passing through the clearing above Flat Run, within sight of the Reynolds' house. Likely some general was quartered within, possibly with sentries on watch. Candles glowed brightly in one front room, strengthening my assumption. In these days of short supply, no one would waste tallow. Except the military, who wasted everything.

Grateful for the smoke-filled sky blotting out moon and stars, I led the mare along the bare creek bank, shielding myself with her body.

When we came to a small protected lea some distance away, I freed my mount of saddle and bridle. As she grazed, I settled myself beneath a tree at the edge of the meadow, my own supper much overdue.

The minié ball had pierced one square of hardtack, wedging itself into the next. The taste, I thought with a laugh, could only be improved, but the crackers would wait until my other victuals were spent. I broke off a piece of salt pork, eating it with half my remaining ration. My jaw ached mightily as I nibbled each morsel, the leathery meat bringing me almost to tears. John had left his mark once more and, as with all his endeavors on my part, it could not be easily disregarded. I'd have to soak the hardtack thoroughly if I could find no other nourishment.

My plan was to proceed through the woods into Locust Grove during the evening, where I hoped to obtain knowledge and food. Though with two weapons and a bedroll, I looked too much like a soldier, one noticeably absent from his brigade.

Aware of a further predicament, I removed my shirt. As I feared, John had rent more than the garment I'd discarded. The strip of petticoat with which I'd bound my breasts now hung loose from one side, tearing a bit more each time I stretched. Folding my blanket lengthwise, I wound it tightly about my bosom, lashing it securely with the rope that had slung it from my shoulder.

I paused before donning the shirt once more. It was so white, in it I'd be conspicuous from any distance. To dull the shirt's radiance, I rubbed it in the dirt around the tree roots, though the cloth stayed lighter than I liked.

With the shirt on, untucked, hanging about my knees to hide the revolver, I hoped I looked like nothing more than a fat boy off on a day of hunting. One with a fondness for rough play, I thought, rubbing my bruised jaw. If anyone questioned me, I could say I took the haversack and canteen from a dead soldier. True, at any rate.

Our family was known in Locust Grove, so I dared not show my face. However, in the balmy spring evening, windows were left open and conversations were easily overheard. What amazed me, with the world in chaos, people were yet more interested in their own insignificant troubles. Those that spoke of the butchery not two miles to the east were mostly old men who thought themselves more knowledgeable than any general.

Any save Lee, that is.

Some said if Jackson had lived, the war would have ended at Gettysburg. To a man, they blamed Pickett for that folly, not the one who'd ordered Pickett's men forward. No one would malign the name of Robert Edward Lee.

One teamster, who'd arrived from Parker's Store within the half hour, carried the most news. Lee's second in command, Longstreet, had been brought down near the farm of Widow Tapp. Some said he was already dead, some said not. Other generals had met the same fate, among them General Stafford, whose rash charge of the previous afternoon had rewarded him with a minié ball in his spine.

Before today, had Lee met Jackson's fate, Longstreet would likely have been appointed commander, though everyone thought him too slow. A. P. Hill was sickly, could barely lead the Second Corps, and Ewell had become increasingly indecisive, though no one knew whether to blame that on the loss of his leg or his recent marriage. "Jeb" Stuart, though Evan had sung his praises, was rumored to be too brash and unreliable to lead the whole army.

Unlike the North, who seemed to have no shortage of replacements for supreme commanders, the South wouldn't last another month without Lee.

The war would end.

I surmised, without a commander for his Third Corps, Lee would be forced to tarry close to Longstreet's line. If his troops still occupied Widow Tapp's land, Lee would likely be quartered in a house some little ways back, or in Parker's Store itself.

Now I had my direction, but in order to obtain food, I resolved to wait until the village slept. Even so, I found most root cellars empty, others securely bolted. Crawling into a springhouse where the spring flowed from beneath its north side, I found milk, which I sampled on the spot, and a quarter wheel of cheese. I broke a small chunk from the latter, stowing it in my sack, removing five rounds of ammunition for payment. I would not steal.

Before leaving Locust Grove, I gathered a handful of young carrots from one garden and two runty potatoes from another, paying once more with cartridges, the only barter I had.

Parker's Store was little more than three miles walk to the southeast, but nearly half the journey followed well-travelled road. Even at this late hour, traffic chanced by. I walked, hunched over in the tall grass, or in the cover of the trees where they lined my path. Each time my ear detected horsemen or a wagon, I threw myself to the earth and kept still until they passed out of sight. Each time the growing exhaustion of my limbs made it more difficult to rise.

My feet seemed to gain weight, and I dragged them forward with effort. Though my body ached for rest, I could not waste the black night in sleep.

Not far past the turnoff for New Hope Church, I came upon a dirt trace leading off to the south. I knew the road would turn toward the Webb farm not much further along and, though the Webb house was as likely a place for Lee's quarters as any, I was reluctant to venture closer until I knew for certain. The trace, I recollected, should bring me out to the Orange Plank Road not far from Parker's Store. And unless I met up with pickets, the way should prove safer.

The first blush, a deep purplish-scarlet, tinted the low eastern sky as I neared Orange Plank Road. A rooster crowed in the distance and, to my left, birds in a thick stand of trees began their morning chants. But no gun play welcomed the sun, as it had the last two dawns.

Too weary to think what this might portend, I staggered into the copse beneath the trees, slithering under its concealing patch quilt of leaves and thorns, falling asleep before my head touched the ground.

16

I awoke feeling strangely adrift, the result of sleeping on the king-sized water bed in Miss Maggie's front bedroom.

She'd met my proclamation about Uncle Gabe with silence, then a tighter grip on my hands and, "Your nerves are shot, Pat." I hadn't been able to see her expression in the dark to know if she thought me completely off my noodle, but she'd insisted I bunk in with her for the night, so I guess she figured I was harmless, at least.

I'd been too exhausted to protest. Even if I hadn't been, my nerves *were* shot, and having someone with maternal instincts nearby during the night helped. Especially since I didn't sleep much, what with all the leftover adrenaline in my system.

Miss Maggie's side of the bed was already vacant, though her digital clock read only seven-ten. Fighting the tide, I managed to swim to shore and swing my legs over the edge of the bed. My wooziness was gone, but every memory of the previous afternoon was flagged by an achy muscle. Inspecting my left arm, I found a huge black-and-blue mark surrounding the bandage. Color-enhanced by the film of dried iodine, its shape reminded me of New Jersey—Cape May halfway down my forearm, Newark halfway up my biceps.

Soaking in a hot bath eased my back and legs, but the left arm muscles, violated by the bullet, and the right shoulder muscles, violated by Hugh's manhandling and tetanus shot, refused to unwind. The best therapy was the aroma of brewing coffee that slapped me in the face as I opened the bathroom door. Easing on a T-shirt and my white pants, I hurried downstairs.

Miss Maggie was standing in the middle of the kitchen floor, inspecting two maps taped to the freezer and refrigerator doors. An assortment of magnets formed two parallel diagonal lines, ten o'clock to four o'clock, across the top, smaller map. "Pat, you look much better. Your color's back."

"In more ways than one," I said, holding up my arm. "Can you help me put this bandage on?" She'd left a clean one out for me, not the one-inch strips most people keep around the house but the big square patches grammar-school nurses use on kids' mutilated knees.

As Miss Maggie stretched the bandage over my dark, angry-looking lesion, my gaze wandered over to the coffeemaker and left-handed grinder beside it. "I thought you didn't brew coffee in the morning."

"Decided to break out the decaf Kona beans today. Pour yourself a cup."

I did, taking my time, looking out the window, sensing the need for a peaceful interlude before facing whatever Miss Maggie had planned for the day. Runoff trickled from the eaves, creating a sporadic curtain across my vision, but the sun shone on the treetops opposite, dressing them scantily in a frilly mist. The sky above was brilliant blue. My two deer were back, the fawn bolder today, closer to the house. I heard a bird chirping lustily, changing his melody every few seconds, like a prima donna giving her audience the first line of each song in her repertoire. Scanning the forest, I located the showoff, perched on a dead branch sticking out from one of the tallest trees. I sipped my coffee, warming my fingers around the mug, inhaling the fragrance, trying to awaken all my senses at once.

Miss Maggie came to my side and slipped her arm around my waist. "Going to be a gorgeous day. Cooler. Ready to get started?"

"Where today? Chancellorsville? Fredericksburg?"

"Oh, no. We've got to pick up the trail while it's hot."

"What trail?" Pulling my gaze from the window, I eyed the fridge warily. "What are you up to?"

Miss Maggie pointed to a lined notepad on the table as she shoved a pen into my hand. "We need to make a list of questions."

"What, no laptop?"

"Sometimes technology gets in the way." Back at the fridge, she was ogling her maps once more, moving a magnet here and there. "Let's start with 'Who was Gabriel Bell really?' "

"Miss Maggie, you're not taking what I told you last night as gospel truth?"

"Put yourself in my place, Pat. I've got two choices." Taking up a magnet shaped like an Oreo, she placed it to the west of the parallel lines. "The logical explanation of your Saunders' Field experience is that you lied about your ignorance of the Civil War; that you were trying to set me up for yesterday's story, to make me wonder if Gabriel Bell was in fact at Saunders' Field at all. Logically, your next step would be to have a vision in which you see Gabriel's death, long before he went west and raised a family, proving Charlotte a fake and ensuring the whole estate for yourself."

It made sense, depressingly so. I sat down at the table. "But if you believe that—"

"Who said I believe it? I simply said it's logical." She plunked a Hershey's-kiss magnet on the lower map. "Ever heard of Moberly and Jourdain?"

"Sounds like a law firm."

"Charlotte Anne Moberly was principal of a women's college in Oxford. In 1901, she was looking to hire a new vice principal. Offered the post to Eleanor Jourdain who, by the by, was about your age at the time. Not that it matters. Miss Moberly wanted to make sure they'd get along— she'd gone through a slew of vice principals already—so she suggested they spend a week together. Miss Jourdain had an apartment in Paris and invited her prospective employer to visit. While touring Versailles, they witnessed, apparently, scenes from the 1780s. Each wrote a separate account of their experience, compared reports, then went on to compare their sightings to historic records. Published everything in a book called *An Adventure*. They spent the rest of their lives investigating the affair, but no *logical* explanation was ever found."

I mulled it over as I poured more coffee down my throat. "You think something similar happened to me?"

"Maybe." Miss Maggie was a teacher again, giving me a look that said she would not patiently wait for the answer to problem one. "Who *is* Gabriel Bell, Pat?"

"How would I know?"

"Aside from the fact that you're the eyewitness? The person, A—had to have a motive for assuming Gabriel's identity, B—was someone John Howard recognized, C— has some reason for reaching out to you—"

"Maybe Gabe, whoever, isn't reaching out at all. Maybe I'm just—"

"Tuned into the right station?"

I shrugged, setting down my mug. "Something like that."

"However you look at it, Pat, it's the same reason. Who else are you likely to be tuned into if not Julia? That *was* Julia you saw, wasn't it?"

Reluctantly, I nodded, still not wanting to admit my great-great-great-grandparents were an egocentric macho jerk and a transvestite psycho. One killed by the other. I heard myself rationalizing aloud, "He would have raped her, beat her. She *had* to shoot him." But somehow I knew it went deeper than that. Julia had been thinking of murder before that afternoon. Before Saunders' Field. Now I knew where I'd acquired that particular strand of DNA. Julia was right. We *were* alike.

"If *Gabriel* is the skeleton that my grandfather rein-terred," Miss Maggie was saying, "Julia must have buried her brother under her own name so she could assume his.

To join the army evidently. Odd. In her letters, she sounds very much against war."

"Maybe she was trying to get back at the Yankees for killing her family."

"She deserted after her first battle."

"She'd only need to shoot five soldiers to even the score." I sipped my coffee again.

"Possible. But remember your 'discovery'—," she put it in finger quotes, "—yesterday at the Widow Tapp Farm?"

I took a moment to recall. "That Lee was there?"

She nodded. "I think Julia's enlistment had something to do with finding Lee."

"What for? To get his autograph?"

"I don't know, but look here." Miss Maggie moved the Oreo magnet to the top of the paper. "This map is Wilderness Battlefield in 1864. Up here is Bell Run. Down here is Lee's headquarters tent. If we assume Julia was in the cemetery late in the afternoon of May sixth, having just shot a Union officer, I doubt she'd hang around. But if she still needed to find Lee, she'd have to circle back behind the Confederate line." Miss Maggie propelled the Oreo counterclockwise around the parallels. "That'll be our route this morning."

I wondered why she wasn't hassling me to hurry, though I suspected, if it hadn't been for the storm, she would have had me out there last night. Suddenly, I sat upright, stunned by a realization, a faint glimmer of hope kindling in my gut. "If Uncle Gabe is buried in Julia's grave, then Charlotte can't be—"

"Maybe." Miss Maggie said this so firmly, my glimmer was snuffed out like a birthday candle. "Two explanations for her story. One, that Julia herself perpetuated the Gabriel Bell myth. Perhaps she had another child out of wedlock, in Texas, say. That's why she had to leave."

"Meaning Charlotte and I might be even closer cousins." Deciding I needed more coffee, I crossed to the pot. "What's explanation number two?"

"Charlotte, or whoever put her up to it, wants to stop you from inheriting the land. Meaning she, or whoever put her up to it, also tried to kill you yesterday."

I nearly dropped my mug.

"I'd send you home, Pat, if I thought you'd be any safer there, but as long as my will stands—"

"That's why you want to give me the land all of a sudden. You're trying to protect me. It's got nothing to do with my job."

"Sure it does. Your layoff gave me the excuse." Miss Maggie was tossing a magnet shaped like a banana from one hand to the other. I wondered if I'd have manual dexterity like that at her age.

If I lived past today. "But what if . . . what if your will has nothing to do with it?"

"Who've you got in mind?"

Since my life was at stake, I didn't see any point in being tactful. "Hugh."

"Hugh? Pshaw! Hugh wouldn't hurt anybody."

"I bet he would if Beth Ann was in trouble."

Miss Maggie pressed her lips together to consider it. "Maybe. Let's say you're right, Pat. Weren't you only *talking* to Beth Ann when you were shot? She wasn't 'in trouble,' was she?"

Put that way, my accusation sounded stupid.

"I asked Hugh if he heard the shot," Miss Maggie continued. "He thought it probably happened the same time the mail truck arrived for the day's pickup, around quarter to five. The sound of the engine and that slight rise on the far side of Bell Run would have muffled the noise."

"But he didn't come looking for Beth Ann until dusk," I said, incredulous.

Miss Maggie grinned. "She's figured out how to lock the bathroom door from the outside. Hugh knocked but got no answer, of course. He thought she was giving him her silent treatment at first. Finally got worried and tripped the lock with a screwdriver. By then—"

A low " 'Morning" came from the direction of the screen

door. Hugh let himself in. "Didn't want to track mud through the house, so I came around back."

Over his uniform, a lightweight rain slicker hung loose from his shoulders. On his feet were rubber boots, like what I call "my puddle waders," but knee-high and caked with mud. His were probably authentic L. L. Bean.

"The car's out front, Miss Maggie. Here's your mail."

She took the bundle from him, car keys on top. "Thanks for bringing it up, Hugh. How's the creek?"

"The drive's fine. Footbridge is under about six inches yet but receding fast. Should be okay by lunchtime."

"If you can wait ten minutes or so, we'll drive you back down."

"No need, Miss Maggie. I don't mind walking."

"Nonsense. Look how much mud you got on you just walking alongside my house. Pat, pour him some coffee."

I turned to do her bidding. When I turned back, Miss Maggie had left the kitchen, and I not only found myself alone with him, but he was standing directly behind me. I jumped, sloshing hot coffee onto my left hand.

Hugh snatched up a towel, swathing my fingers in it as he took the mug. "Sorry. Didn't mean to startle you."

I pulled away as if he'd wrapped a snake around my limb. Then, feeling foolish, I said, "You didn't. It was only a spasm. Sore muscles."

His gaze was making its way up my arm. "Looks painful."

I'm not sure why his ogling irritated me, but something about him always made me want to pick a fight. "Nothing compared to what you did to my other shoulder when you yanked me out of that pit."

"Where, here?" His massive hand swallowed up my right shoulder, the fingertips pushing against the muscle connecting the blade and joint.

I flinched, not because it hurt, but like all his movements, it scared the hell out of me. Actually, he seemed to know exactly how to manipulate that muscle. I felt the knots letting go despite my own tension.

"Sorry if I hurt you," Hugh was saying, his gaze now fixed on my shoulder as if he could somehow examine my joint with X-ray vision. "I got one look at all that blood on you and . . . and forgot my own strength, I guess. Been a long time since I handled . . . since I touched . . ."

I quickly shrugged out from under his grip. Nothing had changed in the character of his massage, but my shoulder had suddenly gone simultaneously cold and hot under his fingertips, as though he'd smothered it in Ben-Gay.

"What, did I hurt you again?" His eyes showed surprise, impatience, annoyance, but not . . . not what I expected to see there.

Not that I had any idea what that was. Feeling really stupid now, more so when I realized I was disappointed, I said hastily, "No. It's better. Thanks."

To my relief, Miss Maggie returned. "Pat, go get your sneakers on. I swear, you must have been one of those kids who always kicked off her shoes under her desk."

Miss Maggie directed me to the right at Route 3. She had both maps, sans magnets, spread across her lap. The second map, I discovered, was a current county-road map. "Take the next left, into that development."

I mumbled a curse for the third time as my foot slipped on the brake pedal. Hugh hadn't acquired all that mud from Miss Maggie's side yard. The pedals were coated with it. But, though he'd driven the car up to the house, the driver's seat had already been pushed forward when I got in.

Miss Maggie had me turn a quick right. A long lake spread away from a dam on my left.

"Flat Run," Miss Maggie said. "Called 'Lake of the Woods' now. We'll follow the west shore as best we can. Maybe something'll come to you."

I was being used as a sort of human Geiger counter. How would I list that skill on my new resume?

The west shore amounted to more than seven miles of mazelike streets lined with trees and expensive-looking houses. All I got was this guilty impression that I was trespassing. None of my ancestors popped into my head for a visit. In fact, I found it impossible to picture the landscape as anything but lakeshore. If there was any history left here, they'd hidden it under water. I told Miss Maggie as much.

"Let me get you out of this development. I know a couple other roads we could try."

Getting out of the development involved another two miles of maze, but I recognized the road. "Route 20. Saunders' Field is behind us."

"Right."

Maybe the reference helped to anchor me. My eerie come-and-get-it urges didn't return, but the road, land shapes, forest, all seemed sort of familiar again. I pulled off the highway.

"Let me see your map, Miss Maggie. The old one." I didn't know if Julia had ever viewed a map in her lifetime, but I wasn't looking for her to pinpoint her location from the beyond. I merely wanted to try guessing her decisions. "I think she would have followed this branch of the creek."

"Did you see something?"

I shook my head. "I'm thinking that if I wanted to avoid the army, I'd stay off the main road as long as possible. That other branch crosses over way too close to the action."

"Actually the map's wrong. Your branch doesn't cross at all. See here on the road map?"

I leaned over, straining against my seat belt, to study the other map. "It comes out closer to Locust Grove. Even better."

"Maybe we should stay in the car, Miss Maggie," I said as I cut the engine. I'd pulled off onto the grass beyond a small bridge spanning Flat Run. "I'm partly blocking the road." Truth was, after yesterday, I was afraid to leave the shelter of the car.

Miss Maggie saw right through me. "No one'll try to shoot you with me close by, Pat. If I die first, my will kicks in, and since I haven't altered it yet to include Charlotte, she'd be out of luck."

She coaxed me out, then, slipping her hand into the crook of my right elbow, led me down to the creek bank. "So Pat, what do you think?"

"I'm not getting hailing signals from 'the Dark Side,' if that's what you mean." I gazed downstream, away from the bridge, the road, the cultivated fields beyond Hugh's car.

"Let's try the other side of the road," Miss Maggie suggested. "Julia would have been headed upstream."

I agreed, but felt no different there.

Miss Maggie kept walking, me in tow. "Close your eyes, Pat. I'll guide you."

So we strolled, me thinking if Julia had been here, she was long gone. Another inner voice, definitely Muscarella in character, said sensibly, *Of course she's long gone. It's been more than a hundred and thirty years.* The practical Giamo faction piped in, *If she was ever here at all.*

But another part of me, maybe my Bell psyche, was lulled by the gurgling of the stream, the perfume of wildflowers, the breeze on my face, the grass brushing against my ankles.

I stopped abruptly.

"What?" Miss Maggie asked.

I shushed her. On the very fringe of my hearing, I thought I'd caught footsteps. Muffled, sort of hollow-sounding thuds, slightly uneven. I stood listening intently, but they were gone. Opening my eyes, I found Miss Maggie's eager face close to mine.

Shaking my head, I repeated what I'd heard.

"Hollow? Like a horse hoof?"

"I guess." Try as I might, I was having trouble re-creating the memory.

"Julia might have taken John Howard's horse. Uneven, you said?"

I shrugged, feeling guilty that I couldn't confirm anything.

She patted my arm. "Don't be so hard on yourself, Pat. You've given us a lead."

"Miss Maggie, you can't assume that every little trick

my mind plays on me is based in historical fact."

She laughed, gently pivoting me around and walking me back toward the car. "Historical fact is as much an oxymoron as military intelligence. History is only our *interpretation* of what happened."

"Based on documents, archaeological evidence—"

"Never trust a piece of paper or a pottery shard more than yourself, Pat."

"Shelby's Fourth Rule of History? Or Life in General?"

"Either. Both."

We climbed up to the road, crossing to the car, but before I could slide the key into the lock, Miss Maggie pulled at my arm, turning me to face her.

"Each time you've glimpsed the past, Pat, you've . . . you've left yourself open, let it come to you. Today you tried to snatch at those footsteps, didn't you?"

I nodded.

"Don't. Observe only."

"Yes, ma'am." She was absolutely right. This wasn't a butterfly hunt. The more I'd strained to hear those footsteps, the faster they'd faded away. "Don't worry, Miss Maggie. If it happens again, I'll bring back a full report."

But the pinch of anxiety on her lips lingered. "Just make sure you come back."

🖎 17 🖎

"Pat, that must be the tenth time you've yawned since our last stop."

"Sorry, Miss Maggie. I didn't sleep well last night." The yawning was actually the only thing keeping me awake. Without the extra oxygen, I already would have driven into a ditch.

The map said we were on county road 611 between Locust Grove and a red crossroads labeled "Parker." Miss Maggie had induced me to stop about every half mile, hauling me out of the car and walking me, eyes closed, for a hundred feet or so. I was beginning to feel like a French poodle with a bladder problem.

I hadn't seen, heard, smelled, or otherwise sensed any piece of history on those little expeditions, but at the first three stops I felt a twinge of paranoia each time I heard traffic approaching. I could feel the gravel of the shoulder beneath my feet, so I knew we were safe, unless, of course, any of the drivers were DWI. After the third stop, I began to relax, so much so that I became sleepy. The routine of it all, combined with a restless night, I supposed. When I closed my eyes during our last walk, I even dozed for a moment.

"You haven't been drinking your liquids like you should," Miss Maggie scolded. "Maybe we should head home."

I knew how much finding Julia's trail meant to her, so I protested. "I'm fine. Just a late morning slump." The last word bent itself around another yawn.

"We should get back anyway. We're meeting Beth Ann's bus."

My questions hovered between "Why?" and "What's the rush?", but I was too tired to decide which line of inquiry to pursue.

"She's got half days today and tomorrow," Miss Maggie continued, answering my second question. "Achievement tests."

"So we're escorting her home?" Remembering the promise I'd forced on Beth Ann last night, not to go anywhere alone, I wondered whose idea this was.

"Only to drop off the car. She's coming to my place for the afternoon. I convinced Hugh she'd get into less trouble around us than alone in the trailer."

"Around us? Or around you?" I could picture his reaction to any suggestion of me as a sitter.

"Doesn't matter. I told Hugh I need her help this afternoon. That is, if you're not too tired after lunch."

What prompted that last comment was still another yawn on my part. "Maybe I'll take a quick catnap when we get home."

I saw her smile out of the corner of my eye. "Home?"

It was a nudge, to show me how naturally I'd used the word. I purposefully misunderstood it to be a direction. "Want me to turn around here? Or keep going until I hit the next road?"

"Turn around. We'll save the next stretch for tomorrow morning." The smug grin stayed on her lips all the way back to Route 3.

The school bus stopped before the gates of the Bell Run development. I'd parked a few car lengths further on and watched the rearview mirror for Beth Ann to disembark. She jumped out, wearing another black T-shirt, this one showing a school of gray and white dolphins. While the black helped set off the picture, I couldn't help thinking that a blue or green top would better set off her complexion.

I tapped the horn. Beth Ann looked up and, seeing the

Escort, her brow clouded. When she spied Miss Maggie and me inside, she slid eagerly into the back seat. "What are you guys doing in Dad's car?"

Miss Maggie explained her plans for the afternoon as I drove the short distance to the post office. "Unless you'd rather stay in the trailer?"

"What, are you kidding? You're sure this is okay with my dad?"

Hugh assured her himself when we took the keys inside, if *assure* was the right word. "You're to do any homework right after lunch, and you'll stay at Miss Maggie's until I come for you tonight. Understood?"

"I don't have homework. We only did tests this morning."

"Don't you have some kind of report due Monday?"

"Yes, but—"

"Start it today." He freed a notebook from the knapsack she'd tossed on the counter.

"But I—"

"Today," he held the notebook out uncompromisingly, "or you'll stay in your room instead."

Miss Maggie snatched it out of his hand. "I'll see that she does, Hugh. Come on, you two, time's a-wasting."

Beth Ann and I followed her out, me with a backward glance from the doorway. The look on Hugh's face was—I didn't know what to make of it. Sort of like Dumbo's mom when they took the little guy away from her.

"She'll be fine," I said with exasperation. "I won't exert my wiles today. Promise."

He produced his unique half-snort–half-grunt as his face turned red and his knuckles white. Feeling instantly sorry for my comment, I murmured, "Happy postmarking," and got myself out of there.

Miss Maggie and Beth Ann waited at the bottom of the steps. Before we'd gone ten feet, I noticed an empty beer can lying in the grass beside the gravel lot and automatically stooped to pick it up. Beth Ann and I bumped heads as both our hands closed on the can.

Miss Maggie laughed. "Forgot to tell you, Pat. Beth Ann's as much a militant recycler as you are. Maybe worse."

I let go of my loot, electing instead to rub the sore spot on my head. "Yeah? I'm pretty fanatical about it. Half my kitchen's a recycling center."

Beth Ann grinned as she pinched the aluminum between her fingers, pouring the rainwater and beer dregs out onto the grass. "Wait 'til I show you what I have set up in Miss Maggie's basement. Come on." She took my hand, tugging on it almost as hard as her father had the day before.

For some reason, I glanced back at the trailer before it was lost from view behind the trees. Hugh watched from a window—too far for me to read his expression, but one thing was certain. He wasn't smiling.

I'd only seen one end of Miss Maggie's basement, when I'd helped her put our stash of tomato sauce into the freezer at the bottom of the steps. At the other end, near the outside door, were utility shelves stacked with corrugated cardboard boxes, each neatly labeled: NEWSPAPER, PLAIN PAPER, GLOSSY PAPER, BROWN PAPER, GLASS, TIN CANS, ALUMINUM FOIL & PLATES, BATTERIES, GROCERY BAGS, and boxes numbered one through six marked PLASTIC. To one side was a bigger box labeled CARDBOARD. On the other was a thirty-gallon trash can half-filled with flattened soda and beer cans. Mounted on the wall above was a crusher. Beth Ann slipped her new acquisition inside and yanked down the lever.

I expressed my awe. "My apologies, Beth Ann. You've got me beat by four kinds of plastic and two kinds of aluminum."

"She does motor oil and old tires, too," Miss Maggie said proudly.

Beth Ann blushed at all the praise. "Soon as school's out, I'm going to build an earthworm compost box." She dropped the crushed metal disk into the trash can. "You could help, if you want. If you're going to stick around."

I glanced at Miss Maggie, wondering if she'd mentioned my layoff to Hugh or Beth Ann. She shrugged innocently enough.

"I need to take care of some things at work," I said hesitantly, "but I'll be coming back, maybe before the end of the month."

Beth Ann's awkward smile made me want to throw my arms around her in another embarrassing hug. I locked my hands behind my back to quell the urge.

Upstairs, someone knocked and hollered, "Miz Shelby?"

"Sounds like the sheriff," Miss Maggie said, making a beeline for the stairs. "I forgot he was coming to talk to you about yesterday, Pat."

All three of us went out to the front porch. Miss Maggie introduced Sheriff Brackin, who wasn't much older than me. His stomach muscles seemed tense, as if he had a habit of sucking in his gut. The brown Stetson he seemed determined to keep on his head had me wondering if the hat was hiding a receding hairline. Not that he wasn't attractive, but with it went an aura of harmlessness that didn't fit his uniform. I supposed, though, the trait could be to his advantage.

He scanned my bruised arm. "Hope you're feeling better this morning, ma'am."

"I am, thank you. You're here for my statement?"

"Truth is, I have some questions for both you and Miz Shelby." He drew a notebook and pen from his shirt pocket.

Miss Maggie gestured us all toward the rockers. I was the only one who sat down on one. Beth Ann perched on the railing. Miss Maggie elected herself spokesperson. "What can we do for you, Dennis?"

"Miz Shelby, ever heard of a Charlotte Garber?"

"She came to see me Tuesday afternoon and again yesterday morning."

"What about?" His politeness was gone as he concentrated on whatever he was writing on his pad.

"She's researching her family tree. Seems she might be related to the Bells."

"Which explains what your books and papers were doing in her motel room."

My stomach lurched. On TV, the cops only searched rooms if you were wanted or . . .

Miss Maggie must have been thinking the same thing. I felt her lean heavily against the back of my rocker. "What happened, Dennis?"

"She's dead, Miz Shelby. Fisherman saw the top of a car sticking out of the river this morning. She was behind the wheel when we hauled it out."

"An accident?" The high, scared whisper was my voice.

He paused a little too long. "Possible. She might have come out this way during the storm last night. Missed the turnoff to Miz Shelby's in the dark. Drove off the boat ramp before she realized the road ended."

"Then she wasn't shot?" Miss Maggie asked.

"Just a contusion on the back of her head, ma'am." He pushed up the brim of his hat with his pen, watching me as he spoke.

"Did you find a gun among her belongings?" Miss Maggie persisted.

"No, ma'am. Now why would you ask that?"

"You already know, Dennis Brackin." I'd wondered if he was another of her former students. The scowl Miss Maggie gave him clinched it. Somehow I was certain he'd smart-mouthed her once too often. "Everyone in the county knows Pat here is the rightful heir of this property, and I suspect the gossip's made its way around about me possibly cutting Charlotte in for half. I didn't know beans about the woman, but she sure had motive for trying to kill Pat yesterday."

"Funny thing about that, Miz Shelby. That motive works both ways." He was still eyeing me, like a hungry man watching his dinner come out of the oven.

I sat upright. "But what about that tar-and-feathered doll, and—"

"Maybe you thought Miz Garber was threatening you. Or maybe you sent those things to yourself, so you wouldn't look suspicious. The paper was printed on Miz Shelby's laser printer. Now how would Miz Garber do *that*?"

Miss Maggie clamped a hand onto my shoulder. "Pat didn't leave the house all last night. I can vouch for her."

Nodding, he made a note. "Last time the victim was seen, far as I can tell, she was leaving her motel room yesterday around noon. Mind telling me your whereabouts, Miz Montella? Between noon and the time you were allegedly shot?"

Allegedly? The word meant I was in deep doodoo. "I was sitting here on the porch. Miss Maggie left around two. I spoke to Joel Peyton on the phone. I don't know what time. Three-thirty, maybe. Then—" I made a quick decision to skip the Wilma Rae phone call. No package of recommendations had been left, so she must have changed her mind about coming. Or came, didn't find me enthusiastically awaiting her, and changed her mind about leaving her Precious. I didn't need her telling the sheriff the gist of our phone call. "Then Flora Shifflett came by. And right after she left, I took a walk out to the old Bell House and cemetery."

"Where you stayed until Miz Lee came by?" He jabbed his pen in Beth Ann's direction.

Glancing at her, I saw fear on her face as I replied, "Yes, Sheriff. I sat on the grass there."

"How long?"

"I don't know." How long did it usually take to travel back a century and a third, witness a murder, and pop back to the present? "I lost track of time."

"Not more than a few minutes," Beth Ann said. "I got there at quarter to four. Went straight to the cemetery from my bus and stayed with her until my father came."

I knew that was a lie. Beth Ann hadn't had her backpack with her, and Miss Maggie said she'd rigged the bathroom door in the trailer. Also, she'd been looking for me, so I assumed she stopped at Miss Maggie's house first, possibly even searched the woods along the creek. Still, I kept my mouth shut. If Sheriff Brackin knew she was lying about the time, he might suspect she was lying about the shooting, deducing I somehow set it up to give myself an alibi.

But I reached forward, overlaying her hand with mine, hoping she'd get the message to clam up before digging herself in too far. Flinching, her eyes met mine. I saw anguish there. She wasn't sure if I'd killed Charlotte or not.

"Planning on visiting with Miz Shelby a few more days, Miz Montella?" Sheriff Brackin had pocketed the pad and pen, parking his empty hands on his hips.

"I was supposed to go home Saturday . . ." *Home.* I didn't know where that was anymore. ". . . but I can stay longer."

He nodded. "Might be a smart idea. I got your home address from Miz Shelby last night, though, in case I need you."

Didn't take much brain power to sort the warning out of that one.

"I'll be in touch after the medical report's done, and we know the time of death." Sheriff Brackin clomped loudly down the porch steps and halfway to his chocolate-brown patrol car before Miss Maggie called to him.

"Don't you want Pat's statement about the shooting?"

"No time now. Be back later."

Who could blame him? He had a homicide to investigate. If I wanted all the attention, I should have gotten myself killed yesterday. Funny how his priorities work. Rubbing my forehead as the sheriff drove away, I said, "I think I'll go lie down a while, Miss Maggie."

"Not 'til you've had a glass of juice, you won't. Beth Ann, go fetch it for her."

Miss Maggie propelled me into the front hall while Beth Ann ran ahead to the kitchen. "You said Flora was here yesterday?"

"I forgot all about it later." I related the gist of the encounter. "She essentially wanted to put the land on layaway."

"Sounds like she's real desperate for a commission," Miss Maggie mused.

"She wouldn't get any money until settlement, would she?" I leaned wearily against the bannister post as Beth Ann appeared with my elixir.

Miss Maggie shook her head. "But with the funds in escrow, she could get any would-be creditors off her back. Bet she's got one doozie of a payment on that fancy car of hers. And she knew you were alone yesterday afternoon."

I tried to picture Flora in her ubiquitous business suit, stalking me through the forest, up on her tiptoes to keep her heels out of the loose dirt. The only part of the image that struck a chord was the rage on her face. "She *was* pretty upset when she left here, but I can't see her sending the threats. Until yesterday afternoon, she thought I was selling Bell Run. She wouldn't have wanted to scare me off."

"I'll get Joel to check into her finances anyhow. In fact, I'll give him a call right now. Go on upstairs, Pat. You look all in."

Beth Ann followed Miss Maggie into the war room without a backwards glance. The tension in her young shoulders gave me a sick feeling inside.

On the hall table, next to Beth Ann's notebook and Miss Maggie's stack of mail, was my copy of *Wilderness Voices*. Scooping it up, I climbed the stairs.

I drank half my juice before setting the glass on the night stand. Bunching my pillows up, I settled back against the headboard.

I was tired, but the sleepiness was gone. Besides, with thoughts of Charlotte and Flora—and Hugh—floating around my cranium, the last thing I wanted to do was encourage nightmares by napping. I decided to concentrate on the enigma of Julia.

I flipped through the book, finding where I'd left off, but impatient for answers, I began skimming. The name Fitzhugh Lee caught my eye.

Bell Run—September 5, 1862
Dear Julia,

Evan was killed ten days ago. General Fitzhugh Lee himself sent word and has arranged for Lane to bring his brother home. As I understand it, his company was attempting to derail a Northern supply train at Bristoe Station. The locomotive arrived before their task was finished. Evan worked courageously beside his comrades until the last moment, but the train broke through, killing and wounding several. General Fitz Lee spoke highly of Evan's valor and named him a true son of the Confederacy. We laid him where the slope was highest, overlooking the river.

Lane asked after you. When told you were yet in Richmond, he determined to come to you and bring you home for Evan's memorial. I told him you were ill and discouraged him from calling on you. He is very troubled by Evan's passing and seeing you now would only upset him further. I do not want family cares to distract him in time of battle.

Father and Gabe will need my help at the mill for harvest this year. I will come to you as soon after as I may. Keep Lane in your prayers.

Always and affectionately,
Mother

Just like Uncle Evan to take on a whole train. Except 'courageous' wasn't the word I'd use. I skipped the next letter, from Lane to Julia about Evan, filled with the same sort of b.s., followed by glowing descriptions of Robert E. Lee as if he were virtually the Second Coming. Why did men feel they should fight their way out of trouble instead of think their way out? And why did they assume words like "valor" would console mothers and sisters? Might as well be honest and call it "stupidity."

Richmond—November 22, 1862
Dear Armstead,

Our granddaughter was born early this morning. Julia has named her Clarissa, after me. The infant seems very frail, yet the doctor believes she will survive.

Our daughter is still not well. The fit of melancholy that took her when Evan passed on has worsened. She eats little and is so weak, she is unable to care for Clarissa herself. Mrs. Howard has found a nurse among her servants, though it pains Julia to have the child taken from her arms.

It would mean much to her if you could write some assurance that she and Clarissa would be welcomed home once they are fit to travel, perhaps in the spring when the roads are dry. Please, Armstead. One son is gone, and Lane lives in grave danger each moment. I cannot also sacrifice my daughter.

All my love,
Clara

There was no date or address on the next letter. Miss Maggie's footnote said it was probably written on the fourteenth or fifteenth of December, scrawled almost illegibly over the faded print of a handwritten recipe. She also noted her corrections to the spelling and punctuation, to make it comprehensible.

Mother, come home. Father went to Fredericksburg to fight the Yankees what come a fortnight ago. They brung him home shot. The doctor took off his arm but he has fever bad. He wouldn't let me go in his stead, Ma. I wanted to.

Gabe

December 24, 1862
Bell Run

Dearest Julia,

Father died last night, with Mother, Gabe, and me at his bedside. In his delirium, he has been aware of no one for two days, yet in the end, opened his eyes and said our names clearly, even you and Evan, as if you both sat with us.

How different is this Christmas from last. Gabe helps to cheer us, but I wish you were here. Mother says you are yet too ill to travel home for Father's burial next week. I promise to come to you before my leave is up. You must get well, sister.

Your loving brother,
Lane

And that, sports fans, was how Lane found out about Clarissa. His mother's fears were groundless. Far from condemning Julia or the baby, he fell in love with his little niece the second he laid eyes on her. To quote Julia: "He would wander about the Howard residence with Clarissa tucked into the crook of his arm or reclining upon his shoulder, carrying on the most nonsensical conversations with her, at which she would coo and smile, encouraging him further." What a guy. A wonder some Southern belle hadn't snatched him up long ago.

I remembered Lane had less than a year to live. Better he hadn't left a wife and kids with no means of support. Then again, Julia would have had a sister-in-law to share her grief.

I thumbed ahead, looking for "Gettysburg" or some such reference. A little inner voice—I suspect Giamo since it had to do with taking things in order—reminded me that I'd skipped over Clara's death. I paused, half ready to turn back, but something stopped me. A feeling that I wasn't prepared to face that episode yet. A feeling accompanied by an agonizing twisting of my stomach and tears in my eyes. Julia had been devastated by the loss of both mother and home. Even now, she couldn't bear to think about—

Even now. I quickly lifted my eyes from the page. For a moment, it had seemed perfectly natural to think about Julia in present tense.

If the soldiers were allowed to settle the matter, peace would be made in short order.

John Crittenden, Alabama infantry—1863

MAY 7, 1864—PARKER'S STORE

I awoke not to the rattle of musketry but to the rattle of a wagon over the Orange Plank Road.

Smoke still flavored the air, yet bright, hazy sunbeams from directly overhead bathed my hiding place, raising steam from my skin. I was drenched with perspiration, the blanket hot, sticky, scratchy against my middle, though I dared not remove it.

Moving to a shadier spot, I brought out the small piece of cheese for my breakfast. Softened by the heat, it caused little distress to my still painful jaw. The sweltering day and saltiness of the cheese produced a powerful thirst. I drank deeply from my canteen.

Evidently, the battle was over. The question remained, had the armies marched on during the night? It seemed unlikely. Lane had written after many battles, describing the carrying of the wounded from the field, the burial details, the scavengers from both sides preying on the possessions of the dead like vultures. Some soldiers gifted with an artist's eye would sketch the battlefield the day after, filling in remembered tableaus of the bloodshed.

Everyone would rest, their rations reissued and, if more fighting was expected, ammunition. Letters would be written to assure those at home that the Reaper had been cheated once more.

A day of living in peace beside an enemy whose blood you'd craved only a few hours earlier. But, as Lane had written, hunger and exhaustion could make a man stow duty in his pocket for another day.

"You, boy! What are you doing there?"

Startled, I spun around, one hand halfway to my revolver. Eyes wrinkled with age squinted through the trees at me, and I cursed John's bleached white shirt for giving me away. But my inquisitor held no weapon. He was a bent old man, the white homespun of his clothes emphasizing his brown spotted skin. I envied him his hat for, though it boasted only a short brim, it shaded his eyes.

Corking my canteen and picking the last crumbs of cheese from my shirt, I approached the man warily. "I was resting, sir. Is this your land?"

He scanned me, and though his eyesight seemed clouded, his review was so acute as to bring further uneasiness. "Come to join the army, have you?"

"What if I have?"

This amused him no end. "How many Yanks you figure on shooting with that old rifle, boy?"

"All of them, sir." That would give him an anecdote for his cronies.

"You're polite, I'll say that for you." Still puzzling over my appearance, giving special regard to my bruised face and generous torso, he asked, "Where're you from, boy?"

I abhorred lying but there was nothing for it, considering my situation. "South of here. Down toward Carolina. I saw smoke up this way as I was walking yesterday. Reckoned the battle was nearabouts."

"Nearabouts? It was *here*, boy. Right on t'other side of that old barn yonder, two days ago." He pointed to what now was no more than a pile of burned sticks west of the crossroads. "Our boys pushed them Yanks back up the Plank Road like they was willows in a storm."

"Is the Army of Northern Virginia still up that way?"

"Not two miles up this here road."

"Then that's where I'm headed. Can you tell me where I might find General Robert E. Lee so's I can tell him I'm here?"

As I suspected, that set the old coot howling with laughter. "Mighty glad Marse Robert'll be for your help. You just make your way toward that thick column of smoke, boy. You'll find him all right. And all the Yankees you can shoot."

I thanked him and left him laughing behind me as I made for the road. I knew better than to trust his words, though they'd told me one thing. The army was still nearby.

My father had also done business at this place, and though I'd never accompanied him, I would not mention the name Bell. I'd give myself no name at all if I could help it, to avoid bearing false witness. Calling myself Gabriel Bell had never felt like a lie. Some part of Gabriel lived within me, as do the spirits of all my family, though I lamented that my little brother's good name should be associated with the foul sinner I'd become.

Still, I would accept my punishment come Judgment Day, comforted that from my wicked deeds had sprung some measure of good. Clarissa, though formed of an unholy union, had a pure and loving heart. Gabriel's innocent, unblemished soul had joined Mother's in Heaven, safe for all eternity. And God willing, I would stop this evil war.

A soft tapping at the doorway made me start. Beth Ann came into the room, slowly, as if she expected she might have to leave in a hurry. Her hands were jammed into her jeans pockets, elbows straight, shoulders two inches higher than normal. "Miss Maggie said to ask if you want lunch."

Somewhere down in my digestive regions a growl responded favorably, almost desperately. I realized I had yet to put food in my mouth that day. Wiping my eyes with the swipe of one hand, I closed the book and swung my feet off the bed. "Lunch sounds great."

"Does your arm hurt that much?" She was looking for a reason for my tears, preferring physical pain over anything she didn't understand.

I shook my head. "This map of New Jersey's called a hematoma. Latin for 'looks worse than it feels.'"

That got a feeble smile out of her. "No, it isn't. 'Hema' means blood. And I think it's Greek or something."

"I forgot, you're a scientist. Anyway, it doesn't hurt much. The muscles are sore, that's all."

"You were crying." She blushed, probably wondering if she should have blurted it out.

"I was reading a sad book." Remembering how my thirteen-year-old self would have viewed crying over a dumb story a one-way ticket to sissydom, I felt the need to underscore the word "sad." "It's about a girl who lost her parents and brothers in the Civil War."

Beth Ann's eyes darted to the book in my hands. "Miss

Maggie said you had a brother who died in a war." Still looking for a reasonable explanation for the tears, she assumed the story reminded me of Lou.

But I hadn't thought of my brother at all. Funny how Julia's family seemed more real to me than my own. "He went overseas when I was four," I said, reverting to my old excuse. "I never . . ."

Miss Maggie's book seemed to burn in my hands. I remembered the box on the top shelf of the linen closet in my apartment. In it were military medals, a flag folded into a triangle, maybe fifty letters. I'd found the box among Ma's things after she died, but I never lifted the lid since then, never read the letters. Now I wanted to.

"I don't remember my mother either," Beth Ann mumbled. She regretted saying it immediately, sinking inside herself, taking an involuntary step backwards.

Uncertain whether she wanted me to probe further or not, I told myself to take it slow. Standing up, I tossed the book on the bed. "Want to keep me company while I eat?"

"I have to do my homework." She backed away, still disconcerted, still unsure of me.

"Beth Ann, wait." The take-it-slow decision maker in me would have been content to let her go, let her sort things out by herself. The speaker was my impulsive side, the loudmouth who had to know what she was thinking.

"I know you couldn't have come straight from your bus yesterday." Seeing a protest coming, I headed her off. "Miss Maggie said the most likely time for the shot was around quarter-to-five. We hadn't been talking that long before it. Why did you lie to the sheriff?"

Beth Ann tried for an aloof shrug, but her cheekbones went crimson, her eyes shifting in embarrassment. "I didn't want him to arrest you."

Good Lord, she'd been protecting me. I felt my own face grow warm, competing with her blush for Best in Show. Touched as I was, I forced a matter-of-fact voice. "He can't without more evidence. Don't you watch detective shows on TV? Or only the scientific stuff on PBS?"

She refused to be lured into another smile. "He said you had a reason for killing that lady."

"He also said it might have been an accident."

With a "How-dumb-do-you-think-I-am?" roll of her eyes, she shifted her weight from one leg to the other and, still not meeting my gaze, said, "Look, when I saw you at the cemetery yesterday, you were ... you looked sort of ..."

I could imagine what I must have looked like, a pathological killer who'd just punched the time clock at day's end. "Beth Ann, I *swear*, I didn't murder anyone."

Blinking in surprise, she looked up. "I know. I thought whoever shot at us yesterday must have killed that woman, too."

I was speechless, and that's rare for me. This girl, after knowing me all of four days, one of which was spent throwing insults and rocks in my general direction, now trusted me without question.

"But I ..." she mumbled, her gaze finding the floor once more, "I don't want you to ... to go away."

She didn't add "like my mother," but I knew that's what she was thinking.

"Miss Maggie, all I'm having for lunch is some of your nonfat ricotta cheese on toast."

She followed me over to the pantry, a terrier on the scent. "A family recipe?"

Taking two slices of the local version of Italian bread— roundish soft white bread with sesame seeds on top—I brought them to the toaster, vowing to bring Miss Maggie a loaf of the genuine article from Corpolese's Bakery back in Pennsylvania. "My mother used to give this to me for lunch every time I faked a stomachache to stay home from school. Does that count?"

"Drat, the laptop's in the war room." She took up the pen and lined pad we'd used that morning. "What do you call it?"

"The recipe? How do you say 'Poor Man's Bagel and

Cream Cheese' in Italian?" I retrieved the one-pound tub of ricotta from the fridge, doing a quick inspection while I had the door open. "How about if I make Sicilian manicotti for dinner with the rest of this cheese and the eggplant you've got in here?"

She smacked her chops in anticipation, but then stopped, jaw open in mid-smack. "Oh, but Pat, you're supposed to be resting your arm today. Save it for tomorrow. Beau promised he'd come. We'll probably get back too late to get it started today anyhow."

The toast popped up, and I slapped a heaping tablespoon of cheese on each slice. "Get back from where?" I remembered she'd said something about needing Beth Ann's help.

"You'll see. Is that cinnamon you're putting on top?"

"Secret ingredient. My grandmother swore by this." Actually, I added cinnamon or sometimes jelly because nonfat ricotta has about as much flavor as air. Maybe less. But Miss Maggie beamed as she scribbled away.

After lunch, we looked in on Beth Ann in the war room. She was sitting on the floor, using the tartan recliner as a table. Having gnawed a neat little band of teethmarks just below the eraser of her pencil, she was scowling at a blank page in her notebook.

"How's it coming?" Odd question for a teacher of Miss Maggie's experience to ask. Even I could tell it wasn't coming at all. I wondered if Beth Ann's block had to do with everything else cluttering up her mind, all of which could be traced directly to my doorstep. Maybe I *was* a rotten influence.

"Pat'll help you with it later," Miss Maggie said impatiently. "Right now I need you for something. Bring your pencil. And Pat, get your shoes on."

Saddling Beth Ann with a bulging tote bag, she led us, to my growing anxiety, back to the scene of the crime. At Miss Maggie's bidding, we walked single file, close order, me in the middle. Far from making me feel safer, I was reminded of those rows of metal ducks people shoot at in an arcade. The ground was considerably drier this afternoon, but the residue of mud still sucked at my sneaker soles, like in dreams where someone's chasing me and my feet feel like they're glued down.

Miss Maggie called a halt to our little parade at the cemetery gateway. "Beth Ann, did you come up from the river trail yesterday?"

She nodded. For the first time I noticed another trail into the woods to the right of the front wall, which explained how Beth Ann had appeared there without passing me first. Not that I would have noticed her.

"Where were you, Pat?"

I pointed. Nothing could induce me to leave the security of the pack.

"Which tree did the bullet strike?"

"Over here." Beth Ann didn't point, but instead scampered across the yard to the southeast corner, with Miss Maggie and I scampering a lot slower right behind.

Just outside the wall was a tree the diameter of a telephone pole, a creamy vertical gash scarring its bark. The victim, a foot-and-a-half-long splinter, lay on its back atop the wall. The tree's wound ran from my eye-level down to about elbow height. I could clearly see how the bullet had acted as a horizontal wedge halfway between the splinter and tree. I could also see where the bullet had finally lost momentum and stopped. What I couldn't see was the bullet itself.

"Someone dug it out!" Beth Ann said in amazement.

Miss Maggie didn't seem surprised. "See anything else funny?"

I stared blankly, too busy imagining the sinister hand that had come back to remove the evidence, but Beth Ann saw what Miss Maggie meant. "The splinter. The force of the impact should have thrown it to the other side of—Hey, look!"

She was leaning over the wall, excitedly pointing to the ground where a single footprint was cast in mud. Not Flora's dainty heels either. This sucker belonged to Bigfoot.

And the imprint was that familiar ripply pattern from the bottom of my puddle waders.

I felt sick.

If Miss Maggie recognized the print, she said nothing. "Let's get to work. Beth Ann, dig into that bag and find my yarn."

I wondered why she'd brought along a pale yellow skein. Taking Beth Ann's pencil, she looped the end of the yarn around it and stuck the eraser end in the tree, in the rut made by the bullet. "Hold this tight, Beth Ann. I'll be pulling on it. Keep it lined up with the scar in the wood. Come on, Pat."

Unraveling the skein, we walked over to where I'd been hit.

"Stand exactly as you were yesterday," Miss Maggie ordered.

Sounds simple, right? I'd been moving forward at the time, toward the cemetery's exit. If this yarn was correctly pinpointing the angle of trajectory, I couldn't see how the bullet had hit me where it did. It should have missed me completely or gone straight through my body right about heart level. Not that I wasn't grateful it hadn't.

A second bullet? A second gunman? Warily, I looked around for a grassy knoll.

Miss Maggie came up with a more likely explanation. "I assume you don't get up from sitting on the ground without using one or both hands? Sit down the way you were yesterday, Pat."

I obeyed, though the grass was still damp.

"Now get up and walk like you would have."

I did, automatically pushing off with my right hand, my left flailing through the air for balance. As I shifted my weight to walk forward, my left arm, still up at an angle in front of me, came in contact with Miss Maggie's yarn, right over my bandage. I stared at it, the worst-case scenario running through my head. "Another half second and—"

"Come on, Pat. Let's find out where the shot was fired from." She moved to the west wall, turning to check the tension of the yarn. "Beth Ann," she called, "yell if you see us go crooked."

Beth Ann nodded from her position at the tree. To my eye, she looked vulnerable there, but if that footprint was any indication, she, at least, was safe enough.

Miss Maggie let me help her over the wall, but we couldn't go much further because of a squatty, dense thicket. "I'll go around the other side, Pat. Hand the yarn over to me."

The height of the trajectory had been gradually dropping. By the time I joined Miss Maggie around the other side, the yarn was about even with my waist. A few more steps, around a patch of knee-high white flowers, brought us back to the trail, beside a light gray, smooth-barked tree.

"I think our would-be murderer crouched here," Miss Maggie said, hunkering down slightly, holding onto the tree to support her stiff joints. "Anyone standing up would have been in plain view had you turned this way. But the top of your head would have been hardly visible over the wall, so—"

"So I had to stand up to make a decent target."

"Right. And see, Beth Ann wasn't in sight at all."

Sure enough, the trail curved a few feet further on, where two big trees and more underbrush blocked the view of the whole front wall. "The murderer must be deaf then. I was talking to Beth Ann when—"

"You might also have been talking before she came." Meaning to myself, while I watched the Time Tunnel rerun.

I admitted that I didn't know if I'd done or said anything.

Miss Maggie hollered across the cemetery. "Beth Ann, say something in your normal tone of voice, like you did when you talked to Pat yesterday."

Her voice was barely audible. I couldn't make out the words at all, and it wasn't sufficiently different from mine in pitch to tell the difference.

I nodded my acquiescence. "So we can assume the shot was fired from here and maybe the person didn't know Beth

Ann was present." Which made me feel better. I'd hate to think anyone would commit murder with an innocent kid watching. And I'd like to think, if Hugh had anything to do with it, he cared enough about Beth Ann to keep that kind of ugliness far away from her. Although, his motive assumed he'd seen me talking to his daughter.

Miss Maggie yelled to Beth Ann to let go of the yarn, and she shoved the skein into my hands. "Reel it in, Pat." With her back to the cemetery, she gazed down the trail. "I figure the killer either followed you out here, or came from the direction of the parking lot over at the industrial park."

"I must have been followed, Miss Maggie. I didn't know I was coming here until Flora left."

"Then why weren't you shot in the back along the trail?"

No use dwelling on that one unless I wanted nightmares.

"If I'd planned to shoot you yesterday," Miss Maggie continued, "I'd have felt safer driving up to an abandoned lot than turning into the drive. Let's say I walked down the road to the house, coming out of the woods just in time to see you cross the clearing. I'd say to myself, 'Pat's going out to the Bell House or the cemetery.' I can follow her, taking the chance she'd look back and see me, maybe get suspicious. Especially if I know I'm not the best shot in the world and might miss the first time."

I grinned at that. "Oh, sure, Miss Maggie. An assassin who can't hit the side of a barn."

"Why not? Just because everyone who fires a gun on TV has deadly aim doesn't mean it happens in real life. You know how many people in this country buy guns and never bother to learn how to use them? Not to mention the number of people with a plain case of bad eye-hand coordination. And if the person never did anything like this before, you can figure on shaky hands."

I pictured this new adversary, as much a klutz as me. A reassuring thought or another worry?

Miss Maggie led me back toward the cemetery. "We're

dealing with a careful individual, Pat. Careful enough to return and pry that bullet out."

I caught her arm before we were close enough for Beth Ann to hear. "That's Hugh's footprint under the tree."

"I know. Made this morning, *after* the rain. A cautious person would have come back as soon as possible, while you two were hiding in the cellar, or after we were all back at my house. Hugh probably just came out here to do a little investigating himself this morning. Wouldn't you, if it were your daughter?"

Beth Ann climbed over the wall to join us, so I dropped the subject. Miss Maggie wanted us to show her our escape route, though she mercifully didn't make us do it again. After indicating where we'd vaulted the wall, we took the trail around to the ruin.

Broken branches showed where Beth Ann and I had erupted from the forest. I hadn't known it at the time, but we were only a few feet from the trail.

"You heard someone behind you?" Miss Maggie asked Beth Ann.

"I thought I did." She bit her lip uncertainly, looking around for some clue. Today the setting was serene. The sun warmed our skin, birds chirped in the trees, the breeze toyed with the tall grass. Yesterday's evil had evaporated, making it impossible to replay the scene in our heads.

"Could you have heard someone coming down the trail instead?" Miss Maggie suggested.

Beth Ann considered the possibility. That's where we differ most. Her scientific mind considers possibilities. My stubborn one sticks to my first story no matter what. Pride, I guess. Truth is less important than being thought a liar. Or worse yet, *mistaken*. And lawyers think my kind make good witnesses. Ha! I could learn a lot from Beth Ann.

"Maybe," she conceded. "Does it make a difference?"

Miss Maggie stepped back to study the angle between our escape route and the trail. "Someone right behind you would see where you went from here. Since we assume you weren't seen, you either had a big head start, or your assailant decided to take the trail, to avoid ripped clothing and scratched skin."

I brushed my fingers over the scabs on my cheek. Beth Ann's face boasted only the usual adolescent acne. "Where are your scratches? You were ahead of me. You should have more."

She twisted her right arm around to show the soft underside between elbow and wrist, which looked like she'd scraped it over a bed of nails. Several times. I remembered how she'd kept that arm up in front of her while her other hand had held me in a death grip. Granted, her tendency to keep her hands in her pockets hid the damage, but I felt guilty for not noticing the cuts earlier.

Miss Maggie took a last look around. "Show me how you got into the house."

Beth Ann led the way. I couldn't have found the path again if my life depended on it. I'd been on autopilot going in, in zombieville coming out.

As we reached the cellarway, Miss Maggie put her hand out like a surgeon. "Beth Ann, the flashlight."

Sure enough, the magic tote produced a torch with a three-inch lamp. Miss Maggie moved the beam over every inch of our surroundings. "Good choice, Beth Ann. Easy to get into and far enough off the trail to screen your retreat. You'd have been caught using the other entrance."

"Other entrance?" we echoed in unison, Beth Ann intrigued by a new discovery, me amazed Miss Maggie knew about our hiding place at all.

"Beth Ann's not the only kid to grow up on this land," Miss Maggie said, answering the question on my face first. "I explored every inch of this ruin when I was her age. Every inch I could see by daylight anyway. No flashlights then, and I didn't dare take one of Pa's lanterns. There's only so far I'll go into a spooky place with a candle." Miss Maggie turned to Beth Ann. "Do you mean to tell me you don't know about the well?"

"Will you show me?" She was expecting a negative

comeback, but the sparkle in her eyes said she'd already thought of a way around it.

"She'll only come looking for it by herself if you don't, Miss Maggie. But maybe she'll promise only to explore it if an adult's with her. And with safety equipment—a helmet, at least."

"I promise," Beth Ann said, a little too hastily for my liking, but it sounded sincere. To Miss Maggie, she added, "Pat'll come with me. She'd never let me get hurt."

I sighed. How did I get into these situations? Although I had to admit I was curious about the ruin. Julia had grown up here; her mother had died here. But that didn't change the fact that a thirteen-year-old was playing me for a soft touch. "Your father should be the one to—"

"Are you kidding? He'd *never* let me. He chewed me out last night for climbing around this part of the cellar. You saw how safe it was."

"I wouldn't go with you without his permission." God knows I'd already put her in enough danger behind Hugh's back.

"Would you ask him?"

"Me?" I sniffed. "He'd sooner say yes to a door-to-door evangelist."

"Miss Maggie then." Beth Ann turned those puppy dog eyes on her new quarry. "Please? He never says no to you."

Miss Maggie's sigh mimicked mine. "Come on. I'll show you both where it is, and I'll talk to Hugh tonight."

She led us around to the south side of the house, wading through chest-high grass where the building formed an ell. "If you look close, between the vines, you can see flat stone slabs."

I saw them, about five feet ahead, in front of a big pile of moss-covered rubble, lush thicket forming a dainty curtain over the entire corner.

"Beth Ann, the hatchet," Miss Maggie instructed and from the tote came a deadly looking weapon. "If you want to get in closer, I suggest you start chopping your way in."

"You couldn't fit a weedwhacker in there?" I asked, as

Beth Ann tossed the bag aside and slashed in earnest. "Watch you don't take your ankle off, Beth Ann."

Apparently though, she'd hacked her way through jungles before. A path quickly opened up in front of her. Miss Maggie and I followed in her wake. The stones, when unveiled, were rectangles of gray slate, each about two feet long, a third as wide, bumped up against each other in a row.

"The slabs aren't too heavy," Miss Maggie said. "I used to move them myself. Don't use your bad arm, Pat."

I'd leaned over to give Beth Ann a hand, obediently lifting with only my right arm. The stone was weighty, but Miss Maggie was right—anyone in reasonable shape could hoist them.

I was vaguely aware of another twinge of déjà vu. Nothing so powerful as what I'd felt at Saunders' Field. This was subtle, like someone blowing across the back of my neck. Gave me the same kind of chills, too.

When we'd removed all five slabs, Miss Maggie aimed the flashlight beam into the opening beneath. About four feet down I could see a wet brick floor, a round drainage hole to one side.

"Used to be a well," Miss Maggie explained. "When I was little, a rusted cast-iron pump was still standing here next to it. I figure it must have been open originally, with a bucket on a rope. They probably added the pump and filled in the rest sometime during the nineteenth century."

"Why didn't they fill it all the way to the top?" I asked.

She handed me the flashlight. "Look for yourself."

"You mean, climb down there?" I wanted to, I realized. Or anyway, my Bell side was all for it. The Giamos were urging caution. The Montellas were laughing at the very notion. The Muscarellas were saying Hail Marys.

"I'll go," Beth Ann volunteered eagerly, dropping to her butt, her legs dangling over the edge.

I fastened a hand to her shoulder. "Not so fast, Kemo Sabe. Me first."

"What did you call me?" Beth Ann asked as I lowered myself down onto the wet bricks.

"I'll explain when you're older." Cool, clammy air enveloped my arm. The smell was more than musty. Stale, dank. Like a grave.

Bending down, I trained the light on that wall. There was a sort of window, or actually, a tunnel, though only a few feet long. I tried to see something beyond it, but with me coming in from the bright sun, the flashlight didn't seem to have enough potency.

Or was that it? As I stared, my vision cleared. I was somewhere up high, looking out across a road paved with wooden planks, over a barren field. There, two, three hundred yards away, a row of fenced-in shacks stood before a big white house. Between the house and shacks was a cluster of large tents. The sun was hot, uncomfortable. My nose twitched as the mixed odors of heavy smoke, manure, and decaying roadkill reached it.

Several horsemen, all in gray uniforms, approached the tents on a road behind the house, one riding a beautiful pale steed. As he dismounted, I caught a view of his thin face, eyes shaded by the brim of his hat, but a full, neatly trimmed white beard gleaming in the sun. I knew him instantly.

Robert E. Lee.

Whatever happens, there will be no turning back.
General Grant to President Lincoln—May 6, 1864

MAY 7, 1864—FARM OF THE WIDOW TAPP

I'd found him.

Yet I was still too far away. My rifle might, perhaps, perform the deed at this distance, but I couldn't see his eyes. I wished him to see mine at the critical moment.

And a tree limb was not the steadiest post from which to take aim.

I'd learned that Lee was quartered not in a house like many of his generals but in a tent in Widow Tapp's farmyard, nearly underfoot of the fighting. I'd tramped out along Orange Plank Road, its wooded fringe still vile in the aftermath of combat. Nearing the site with caution, I'd clambered up an old maple to survey the terrain ahead in moderate safety.

I'd watched for hours as the sun slipped from its crest to hang even with my left shoulder. There'd been much activity, yet no one entered or emerged from the tents. Beyond the farmyard, I could see the field of yesterday's contest, littered with the carcasses of men and horses. A wagon, its mule team straining against the full load, slowly made its way between the rows of blue and gray dead, delivering another harvest to a mass grave.

I'd glimpsed dust rising on the path from the Chewning farm: horsemen, though bedraggled and dirty, but with better uniforms than most. One pale horse fit Lane's description of Lee's mount, Traveller, its white-bearded rider straight and august in his saddle, though thinner than I'd envisioned. He'd probably been visiting his corps commanders along the line, perhaps, ironically, coming in close proximity to the Thirty-Third Virginia. Perhaps closer than he was to me now.

One rider continued past the farmyard, crossing Orange Plank Road at a gallop. To my right, opposite a meadow,

I could see fortifications this side of the boundary of thicket. An officer emerged as the horseman reined his steed. Leaning down from his mount, the rider excitedly conveyed his message, gesturing to the thick forest to the southeast.

Back at his headquarters, Lee stood, conversing with three other officers. One followed him inside the near tent, the second took to his horse once more, retracing his steps toward the Chewning farm. The third barked orders to those nearby, and activity around the tent doubled. A wagon was dragged across the yard by four soldiers, who began loading crates and barrels.

It looked like a move. And soon. Overnight, most likely, lest the Yankees get wind of their plans.

Or perhaps the bluecoats were retreating, and Lee was giving chase. If so, they wouldn't wait until nightfall.

I was in a quandary, for I dared not attempt to steal past the pickets in daylight. Yet if I waited, I might miss my chance entirely.

Behind and to my right came the clamor of chopping and trees being felled. I feared for my lookout at first but realized the "soldier beavers" were only concerned with the woods to the southeast, along the unfinished railroad. Extending their defenses? Not if they planned to leave soon. A ruse to make the Yanks think they were digging in further perhaps?

Or possibly they were clearing a path. Why southeast? To bring the army around for a rear assault on the retreating Yanks? A slow, clumsy plan. Why not simply march up Orange Plank Road to Brock Road?

Unless . . .

Unless Lee needed to defend the capital.

Suddenly I understood why the Yanks had brought their supply wagons this time, and why John had been headed for Germanna. He was to have brought up the rear guard. They'd never meant to retreat. Lincoln's army was at last pushing on toward Richmond.

Toward Clarissa.

Was I too late? The South might be dissuaded by the

loss of their godlike commander. The North though, this close to Richmond, instilled with the hatred bred in the last decade, might devastate and ransack the capital, regardless.

I would return to Parker's Store at once, send word to Florence Howard with the next teamster on the road to Richmond. Then I vowed, I would come back to face Lee.

Tonight, if Providence obliged.

⚜ 19 ⚜

The scene faded, replaced by dolphins in an earthquake.

Only the dolphins weren't shaking. I was.

I blinked, mystified, until I realized the seismic activity was due to the dolphins' wearer moving her arms rapidly back and forth while her hands gripped my shoulders.

She was calling my name, too.

"Beth Ann," I said, as her face came into focus.

The earthquake stopped.

I was sitting on the wet, sunken floor of the well, facing the window into the Abyss, my arms resting casually on my knees. Beth Ann was hunkered down beside me, her back against the opposite wall. Her eyes were now so wide with relief, I could readily imagine how scared she'd been a moment before. I tried to pat her arm reassuringly, but I found the flashlight in my hand, still on. I switched it off.

"Pat?" I looked up to find Miss Maggie anxiously peering over the edge.

"I'm okay," I said for both their benefits.

"I told Beth Ann you were prone to seizures." Miss Maggie's tone was a warning to watch what I said.

"A girl in my class has them," Beth Ann said, fingers still gripping my shoulders. "She has epilepsy. Not the kind where you get convulsions. The other kind, where you stare into space. But her seizures don't last near as long as yours." She was babbling nervously. Now that she was over her relief, she was replaying the episode in her head.

"Let me up, Beth Ann." I pulled my legs under me in

anticipation of standing. Beth Ann let go, sliding her back up along the wall as she straightened up, offering a timid hand which I accepted.

"How long was I out?" I asked as I stood.

"Almost five minutes," Miss Maggie replied grimly.

Beth Ann stuffed her hands back into her jeans pockets. "I wanted to shake you sooner. Miss Maggie said not to. But you were . . . you didn't—"

"Did I say anything?"

Beth Ann glanced uncertainly at Miss Maggie, who did the talking. "You said *Robert E. Lee* and *Richmond* and *Clarissa*. Come up out of there, Pat. Let's go back to the house."

For a woman who'd been all gung-ho about picking up the trail this morning, she'd cooled off big time. I would have volunteered to try again if Beth Ann hadn't been there. This had been my most vivid experience yet, as if this hole in the wall were some kind of amplifier of Julia's memories. My cemetery vision had lasted longer, but no one had physically shaken me out of it either.

I felt cheated. I hadn't wanted to come back to the present when I did.

Without thinking twice about it, I knew I'd return to Bell House as soon as Beth Ann went home.

When we came out of the forest, the headlights and grill of the Boutchyards' sedan were visible in front of the house. Elliott was leaning against the far fender, cigarette ember showing beneath his baseball cap, smoke curling around the red insignia above the bill. I wondered what he did for a living. Lab animal for the American Lung Cancer Association? Poster boy for Phillip Morris? Cigar store Indian? Smokestack?

"My appearance won't endear me to Wilma Rae, Miss Maggie." Let alone that the breeze across my wet backside made a dandy surrogate air conditioner. "Can you keep her entertained while I go change?"

"Take your time, Pat. I'll try to get rid of her."

Beth Ann and I ducked in the back door and tiptoed up the stairs. Hearing Wilma Rae's Chairperson-of-the-Board baritone demanding to speak with me personally, I made up my mind to change clothes in world-record slow motion.

Beth Ann flopped stomach-down onto my bed, her fingers playing with the chenille pom-poms while she watched me trade filthy, wet white pants for filthy, bloodstained jeans.

"So, what's the problem with your report?" I asked, trying to get her mind off me and my "seizures."

"It's for Social Studies. We're supposed to interview our parents."

"About what?"

"Anything, as long as they talk about themselves and not about us."

I wiggled out of my T-shirt, which was white and now muddy in back, then struggled into a navy pullover jersey. Sort of like a sweatshirt, it had a big pocket in front and a hood, plus roomy sleeves that could be rolled up without feeling like a tourniquet against my bandage. "You can't exactly write it until you talk to your dad, can you?"

"I was trying to come up with questions to ask him. Got any suggestions?"

I was at a loss. Not only was I not a parent, at Beth Ann's age I'd never asked my mom or dad anything that didn't have to do with staying up to watch TV or permission to go somewhere with friends. They would have considered anything about themselves prying, which a nice Italian girl doesn't do.

Still, I'd always promised myself, if I ever had kids, I'd raise them to believe they could ask me anything. And I'd give them honest answers. "What do you *want* to ask him?"

Beth Ann shrugged. "I guess I want to ask about my mother."

"So do it."

She shook her head. "Dad won't talk about her. Miss Maggie told me a little. She sounded nice. I think, well, sometimes I think what it'd be like if she hadn't . . ." Anger and hurt filled her eyes like tears. "I want to know why she killed herself. Why she left us."

I wanted to gather her into my arms, hold her, tell her everything would be all right, like I'd done yesterday after the shooting. But she didn't want comfort now. She wanted answers. And I didn't have any. "Do you know she was addicted to drugs?"

Beth Ann nodded. "I have to be extra careful to stay away from them. Chemical dependencies can be genetic."

I felt myself smile, loving the scientific bent of her mind that dredged facts like that to the surface. "People on drugs don't always do things that make sense."

"I know, but I can't help wondering if there was a reason." Her head tilted down, her attention seemingly absorbed in the bedspread pattern. "I think . . . I think something happened the night she died. Something bad."

Beth Ann had only been a few years old at the time, but she'd been there. And she might have witnessed her mother's death. "Like what?"

"I'm not sure. Just a feeling I have. I wish . . ." She looked straight at me, analytically, as if I were a frog ready for dissection. "You like Mr. Peyton, don't you?"

Talk about out of left field. Honesty, I reminded myself. "Yes."

"Did you fall in love as soon as you saw him?"

"I'm not in love with him, Beth Ann. Not yet. I don't believe in love at first sight." Sitting on the floor, I pulled my suitcase over and began removing my other dirty, whitish clothes, tossing them atop the pants. If I had to stay extra days, I'd need to do a load of laundry.

"But you must like him more than . . . more than other guys you meet on the street. You were attracted to him somehow, right?"

I nodded. "That's the way it works. You start out liking the way a guy looks, or smiles, or acts, so you go out with him. Then, usually, the more time you spend together, the less you like him, and vice versa, until one of you breaks it off." Was I really that cynical? Did I have to ask myself the obvious?

"But you *still* like Mr. Peyton?"

"I only met him Monday, Beth Ann. Early days yet." Denise would have said I was setting myself up for failure. Sure, I'd only known Joel a few days, but hadn't he already gotten past the proverbial first base? Not far past. And he sure didn't seem in a hurry to steal second. I told myself it was a Southern thing, that men seduce the way I'd seen people drive down here: politely. And I assured myself that, like drivers, Southern beaus eventually get where they're going.

"I don't think men are like us," Beth Ann said pensively.

I couldn't help laughing. "Understatement of the millennium."

She wasn't in the mood for my witticisms. "What I mean is . . . Dad said you're . . . He thinks you . . . When he saw you with me . . ."

"I know what your father thinks of me, Beth Ann." I had to stop and draw in a deep breath. Just thinking about Hugh got my dander up. "There's nothing I can do about it."

"You don't hate him, do you?"

"No, of course not." That, I felt, came out a little too glib. Wasn't it true? I knew what hate felt like. I hated Burt and Dawkins-Greenway and every one of their holier-than-thou clients. Hugh and I just had conflicting personalities.

Right. Like conflicting personalities churned up my stomach the way the mere sight of him did.

But that wasn't hate. I didn't know what it *was*, but it wasn't hate.

I told myself I'd better make more of an effort to get along with him. Not only because of Beth Ann. He'd be my mailman, for Pete's sake. I'd have to trust my unemployment checks to him.

Beth Ann's elusive half-smile made an abrupt appearance. "How old are you, Pat?"

I hesitated out of habit, until my scruples insisted honesty had to apply here, too. "Thirty-six."

"How many boyfriends have you had?"

I grinned. "According to my friend Denise, not nearly enough."

Her eyes snapped down to the mess her fingers were making of the bedspread, her face turned Kool-Aid red. "How many were . . . you know . . . lovers?"

Mother of God. I was in way over my head. Heat soared up the back of my neck, igniting my cheekbones. "Beth Ann . . . I . . . I . . ."

"Sorry. That was dumb." She bounced off the bed, making a dash for the exit.

Had I had time to think, I probably would have let her go, but I flew across the room on impulse, heading her off at the doorway, having no idea what to say. In the awkward silence, I could hear Wilma Rae, still mouthing off down on the porch. My conscience gave me an out, I could go rescue Miss Maggie. What a choice: listen to Wilma Rae's narrow-minded rantings or talk sex with a teenager.

"Candid questions are never dumb," I said at last. "Just unexpected. Come sit down."

We settled on the bed, crossing our legs and facing each other like we were about to play patty-cake. I found it impossible to look her in the eye. Even if I'd ever imagined myself having "The Discussion" with a daughter of my own, I figured on having a dozen years or so to write the script. I couldn't simply repeat what my mom told me because she hadn't—that nice Italian girl stigma again. Had I asked, I'm sure Mom would have brought me straight to the parish priest for an exorcism.

So I'd have to wing it. What was I afraid of? That Beth Ann knew more than me? Likely as not, she did. "Maybe you'd better tell me what exactly you want to know."

Beth Ann twisted her fingers nervously, rocking herself gently to and fro. "You're not married, so I thought . . . I assumed you had a lot of . . . a lot of . . ."

"Boyfriends?" The word "lover" had been difficult for

her to spit out, but I couldn't get my mouth around it at all. "You think I'm some sort of femme fatale?" The notion of me slinking around like some daytime-soap starlet sent me into a sudden fit of jittery giggles.

Beth Ann was pouting, convinced I was laughing at her. I gulped my hysterics back down, though I couldn't stop grinning for the life of me. "Real life isn't like the movies, Beth Ann. Just 'cause I'm single doesn't mean I spend all my free time trying to pick up guys in bars."

"You don't have to try. Men like you." She said it so sincerely, with so much frank puzzlement, I resisted another burst of uncontrolled mirth.

"What, you mean Joel? Joel's a fluke." She started to interrupt, but I cut her off. "No, really, he is. Before this week, the last date I had was a year ago December. That so-called friend I mentioned, Denise? She set me up with one of her brother-in-law's buddies for our office Christmas party." It'd been such a memorable experience, I'd opted to stay home this past year, drinking hot cocoa and watching *It's a Wonderful Life.* "Let's see . . . since college, I've gone out with five guys. Only two made it past the first date, only one of them survived the second. He lasted three whole months."

"Were you in love with him?"

I shook my head. "That was during my I-must-have-a-man-or-be-considered-a-failure phase. Italian aunts can do that to you. Listen, Beth Ann, never let anyone say you need a man to succeed. If the right guy comes along, fine, but don't ever stop being yourself." Which was my problem. I had no idea who I was.

"Are you going to marry Mr. Peyton?"

I sighed. "It takes longer than a few days to figure that out." I'd always wanted to believe somebody out there had my name tattooed on his heart. Was Joel the one? He *was* different. Maybe he'd stay different. "Did I answer any of your questions, Beth Ann? I only talked about myself. What about you? Any boys you like at school?"

A self-conscious smile teased the corners of her usually somber mouth.

"Out with it," I coaxed. "I was honest with you."

I might as well have been prying open a tamper-proof aspirin bottle, but finally she let loose the name Pete—a blue-eyed, raven-haired hunk who played trumpet in band. I remembered boys like that. At my last reunion, they'd all been fat and bald, but I didn't tell her that.

"He hates girls," Beth Ann said, the situation hopeless.

"He will for another year or so. Boys are slow like that." The word "slow" made me think of Joel. "And they don't evolve very far beyond that stage either. Have you told your father you're interested in boys?"

"No!" I could have asked if she ate slugs for breakfast and gotten a less emphatic response. "He'd ground me to my room until college."

"My father tried to do that. In fact, he thought I was too young to date while I was *at* college. What I was thinking was, if you told your dad now, it would give him a chance to get used to the idea before your senior prom, at lea—"

The sound of raised voices, Miss Maggie's in particular, broke in. I was off the bed, out of the room, running down the stairs, vaguely aware of Beth Ann's footfalls right behind me.

Miss Maggie was bristling like a pit bull, yelling, no, *shrieking* at Wilma Rae to take her "small-minded, stiff-assed, antebellum bullshit" off the porch and off the property this minute. Wilma Rae was making a valiant stand by the rockers, firmly entrenched, showing no signs of retreat.

Much as I would have liked to hear Miss Maggie's extended vocabulary on the subject, I could tell the clash was doing a number on her blood pressure. The back of her neck was scarlet, and her whole body was shaking. I slipped an arm about her, softly urging her to calm down.

When Miss Maggie paused for a breath, Wilma Rae sniffed her high and mighty opinion. "I know you'll talk some sense into her, Patrice."

"My name's Pat." The drop of her jaw made it all worthwhile. "And as for me talking sense to Miss Maggie, it'd be like a frog teaching a bird to sing. She's got more sense than anyone I know."

Miss Maggie snaked her arm around my waist and squeezed. I glanced at her to see if it was a warning. The fire in her eyes said she was egging me on. I might have been tempted to really lay into Wilma Rae, but the little pulsing artery in Miss Maggie's neck had me worried. I squeezed back. She felt small and frail.

"There are the recommendations." Wilma Rae levelled one manicured nail at the far rocker, at an accordion folder resting there, stuffed with about a ream of paper.

I smiled wickedly. "Feeding time for your recycling boxes, Beth Ann."

I could feel Beth Ann's apprehension melt as she sprung into action, snickering as she stepped around me to get to the rocker.

Wilma Rae snatched up the folder, hugging it to her as if we were threatening her only child. Though I suspected she had quite a litter of brats just like it, giving people *agita* all over the county.

"You might as well leave, Wilma Rae," I said evenly. "Miss Maggie and I have decided never to restore Bell House. And no developer's going to demolish it as long as I'm alive. It'll stay as it is, as a memorial to every family shattered by the Civil War. By any war. *Capisce?*"

You'd think I'd slapped her across the face, the way she recoiled. Though I'm sure her reaction wasn't so much to my declaration of intent as to my slip into Italian. She marched off the porch as if heading for Jerusalem with the Crusaders. Elliott, who hadn't even glanced curiously in our direction during the fray, dropped his cigarette and snuffed it out with the toe of his shoe as he opened his driver's door.

"And please," I called, not content until I got a rise out of him too, "don't leave your cigarette butts all over the ground. We're environmentally conscious around here."

Bending to pick them up was his only response, but

Wilma Rae threw me a scowl that would have turned Mother Teresa to stone. Slamming her car door shut, Wilma Rae swiveled her chin until it pointed haughtily straight ahead. If we'd mounted her on the hood, she'd have passed for a Viking figurehead.

⊠ 20 ⊠

"Come inside, Miss Maggie." My arm was still around her as the Boutchyards drove off, and I took a step toward the door. "You'd better rest awhile."

"Don't you treat me like an old lady, Patricia Montella. I was standing up to Wilma Rae before you were born. Called me a heretic the day I told her class George Washington never chopped down a cherry tree."

But she didn't fight me as I guided her inside. In the war room, I coaxed her into the paisley recliner. I'd have made her go lie down on her bed, but weak as she seemed, I was afraid the climb up the stairs might bring on a heart attack.

"Do you want me to call your doctor, Miss Maggie? Or I could go get Hugh's car and take you to the hospital."

"Lord, no. I'll be all right if I just sit a spell." She patted my hand, but the feebleness of the gesture didn't reassure me. "Beth Ann, run upstairs and get my water pills for me. I forgot to take them after lunch."

Beth Ann, anxious to help, bolted for the hall. I heard her take the stairs two at a time.

"Sit down, Pat." Miss Maggie gestured to the blue recliner, but I sank down on the floor beside her, propping my elbows on the armrest, settling my chin on my arms.

"I should have come out sooner, Miss Maggie. I'm sorry."

Her fingers stroked my hair. "That was quite an impassioned little speech you gave, Pat."

"One of my best," I said sarcastically. "I'd make a great politician. Almost had everyone believing I could turn this place into a shrine. Let's see what else I can promise that I can't deliver."

"Close your eyes, Pat. Look into the future this time. What do you see?"

I tried. Maybe I had some weird latent gift for seeing into the past, but when it came to looking the other way, the overhead mirror was flipped to night vision. Nothing but darkness. Even my hyper imagination refused to co-operate. Nope, precognition was not on the menu. "I see the insides of my eyelids, Miss Maggie, and there's nothing interesting on them. Should have stared at bright lights first."

The weight of her palm settled on top of my head. "What do you *want* to see, Pat?"

The image of Beth Ann crouching beside the chestnut saplings faded in. What did *that* mean? That I wanted to keep Bell Run as it was for her? I did, but my vision went beyond that. If I ever had kids of my own, I'd want them to grow up as she had, exploring every inch of this forest, looking for animal prints in the snow, splashing through Bell Run on a hot July afternoon. And learning the tragedy of those five graves on the hill above the Rapidan.

"I want kids, Miss Maggie. Five thousand like you had." I lifted my head to look at her, but her attention, her smile, was focused across the room.

"I think Beth Ann's wondering how either of us could possibly have five thousand children, Pat."

Beth Ann had paused on the threshold, pill bottle in one hand, glass of water in the other, eyebrows up.

I couldn't help grinning. "I've heard multiple births are common with induced fertilization, but I guess I'd still have to adopt a few hundred or so."

"Make sure they give you a lifetime supply of antacid," Miss Maggie added, "especially if any of them are like this one here."

Beth Ann set her cargo on the table beside the recliner. "You're both kidding, right?"

I sighed, nodding dejectedly, letting my head drop back down on my arms. "Unless I win the lottery in the next ten weeks."

Miss Maggie patted my head like I was her prize Great Dane. "King Midas syndrome. Never fall in love with your fixed assets."

"Don't throw your pearls of wisdom at me, Magnolia Shelby. You wouldn't sell Bell Run either, even if they took away everything else you owned."

"I'll tell you a secret, Pat. I stopped driving because I had to sell my car to pay the taxes. Slow year in the publishing world. Sold my family's antique furniture one other time." My jaw dropped in disbelief as she snapped open the pill bottle and dumped a dose into her palm. "Oh, they'd have understood. Sometimes I wonder if there isn't a curse on this place. No one's been able to give it up for the past four generations."

"More than that," I pointed out. "At least since the Shacklefords settled here."

"Then let's find a way to keep it, Pat." She swallowed the pill with a gulp of water. "Starting with Charlotte. The more I hear about her, the less I'm inclined to leave her side of the family anything."

"What have you heard?"

Miss Maggie set down her glass, settling back with a thoughtful pout. "Seems Charlotte had herself a little tête-à-tête with Wilma Rae. The sheriff questioned Wilma Rae about a folder of her recommendations found in Charlotte's motel room. Wilma Rae claims Charlotte showed up at the Boutchyard door yesterday morning. Same time Charlotte was here, though I didn't mention that to her."

"Why would she lie?"

"Probably afraid of admitting she might have been the last to see Charlotte alive. But she did say Charlotte was convinced you were a fraud, Pat."

"Me?" I tried to remember my encounters with Charlotte, tried to think what I'd said to give her that impression. My meager conversations with her weren't the sort that took root in long-term memory. Wondering if it had to do with Wilma Rae's threatened visit yesterday, I told Miss Maggie the gist of her phone call. "I didn't tell the sheriff. Thought it'd hurt my alibi more than help it."

Beth Ann had been fidgeting beside Miss Maggie's table. Now she dropped down in front of the recliner, pulling her legs up to cross them. "The Boutchyard's car passed my bus yesterday afternoon just before we stopped. Turned onto your drive, Miss Maggie. That's why I didn't come up to your house right away after I left my trailer. I don't like Mrs. Boutchyard."

"So she *did* come," I murmured into the chair's upholstery. "I wonder why she didn't leave her folder like she said."

"Did this Charlotte person drive a big, black car?" Beth Ann asked.

Miss Maggie and I said, "Yes!" in unison.

"I noticed a car waiting behind the bus as I got off. I didn't think about it at the time, but it didn't pass me as I walked home. So it either turned into the development or—"

"Or down my drive." Miss Maggie tugged her chair's lever and sprang forward.

I was on my feet, a hand on her shoulder before she could stand. "Don't even think about getting up, Miss Maggie."

"Oh . . . oh, all right." With an effort, she restrained herself. "But don't you see, Pat? If Wilma Rae met Charlotte here and gave her your copy of that blasted folder, she can prove Charlotte was alive and in the vicinity when you were shot."

"But she'd have told the sheriff—"

"Don't you believe it. Marrying into the Boutchyard family was a major coup for Wilma Rae, and she's not about to soil the name by getting involved in Charlotte's death or your shooting." Miss Maggie paused, her eyes darting, her frenzied thoughts almost tangible. "If Charlotte didn't shoot you, maybe she saw who did."

"Which explains why *she* was murdered," I mused.

"Right. And Wilma Rae becomes prime suspect."

"Why would she try to kill me? Because Charlotte said I was a fraud?" As motive for murder, it seemed flimsy.

"Pat, honey." Miss Maggie leaned back, taking in as broad a view of me as she could with me standing over her. "That tiny drop of Southern blood in you was the *only* reason Wilma Rae brought her royal backside over here to look you over this week. Granted, she wants something out of you, but she would have tried a back door first—me, or Joel, maybe even Beth Ann here—if she didn't think you worthy of her presence. Without your Southern lineage, in Wilma Rae's eyes, you're not only a Yankee carpetbagger—"

"You think *she* sent the doll?" No way could I picture Wilma Rae crawling through one of the downstairs windows to use the computer. Oh, she might fit through one of the larger windows, but action wasn't her style. Then again, ordering people around *was* her style, and I *could* picture Elliott climbing through a window.

"It fits her thinking, Pat. She sees you not only as a Yankee, but as a foreigner. Doesn't matter that the Montellas have been paying taxes in the U.S. for over a hundred years. Far as she's concerned, your boat docked at Ellis Island last week. Wouldn't have taken much for Charlotte to convince her you're no daughter of the South. Why, shooting you would have been a sacred duty."

I'd run into prejudice before, though more in the form of stereotypes. Heck, every Italian on TV is either a crook or an idiot. And I've weathered some pretty nasty looks when I check the "other" box under "Race" on official forms. One registrar at college even crossed it out and checked "white" while I stood watching. If she didn't want the truth, why ask?

I've never felt "white." In my experience, white people don't nail bull horns to their garage gables to ward off the

Evil Eye. They don't eat smelts on Christmas Eve. They don't kiss every single person at a family gathering of five hundred. They don't place two crossed silver knives outside during thunderstorms. This last, mind you, my family had been doing generations before Ben Franklin took credit for inventing the lightning rod.

But until now, no one had hauled me in front of a firing squad for it. "Did Wilma Rae say that?"

"She said everything but. Why do you think I got so gosh-darn mad at her, Pat?"

Smiling, I leaned down and planted a big kiss on her forehead. "For defending my family honor, I'll cook you all the macaroni you can eat." I turned to Beth Ann. "Did you tell the sheriff about seeing the Boutchyard's car earlier?"

"He didn't ask."

Of course not. He'd been convinced my assailant had been poaching deer. "Did you see any other cars? Like Flora Shifflett's Mercedes?"

"No *cars*."

"What, Beth Ann? It could be important."

"There was a lady in the woods. Down on the river trail. She told me you were up at the cemetery. That's how I knew where to find you."

Miss Maggie almost erupted out of her chair again. "What did she look like?"

Beth Ann shrugged. "She looked poor. I felt sorry for her. I think maybe she was a homeless person." She searched both our faces, obviously trying to gauge how much stock we'd put in her observations. "I don't think she was the one who shot you. She was headed the other way, toward the creek. And even if she intended to circle around, she wouldn't have told me where you were."

I mulled it over. "I guess a vagrant could have passed by while I was . . . while I was having one of my seizures."

Miss Maggie wasn't convinced. "Beth Ann, what exactly did the woman say?"

"She said, 'Hello' first. I'd been walking with my head

down, and I didn't notice her until she spoke. Then she said, 'Go on up to the cemetery. Pat's there.' I thanked her, and she said I was welcome and walked off down the trail."

"She called me by name?" I began to pace. This made no sense.

"*Must* have been Charlotte," Miss Maggie said. "You haven't met anyone else who Beth Ann doesn't know."

I couldn't for the life of me imagine mistaking Charlotte for a homeless person. Unless, after her clash with the brambles that morning, she'd put on scrungy clothes before braving the jungle again. Or unless she was in disguise while stalking me. But if she knew where I was, why was she headed the other way?

"Let's get Joel on the phone. See if he's found out anything yet." Miss Maggie stood before I could stop her. "Sorry, Pat. I need to be at my desk for this."

"I could have brought the phone to you."

"Not if you want to listen in." She was already across the room, shoving papers and books aside. Next to the empty phone cradle, she unearthed a speaker hookup.

"Now, where did I leave the handset?" Miss Maggie pressed a button on the cradle, and the shrill gobble sounded in the front hall. "Beth Ann, fetch it in off the hall table, will you?"

Beth Ann sprang off her chair and was back in a few seconds with the itinerant phone. Miss Maggie punched the talk button and hit number four on the speed dial. I should have guessed she'd have Joel programmed in, not that she'd felt the need to write his name next to the proper button.

He picked it up on the third ring. When Miss Maggie identified herself, he said, "Magnolia, you know I hate it when you use your speaker."

I hated them, too. The on-off clicking with every pause, the amputated sentences, drove me nuts.

"No help for it. I want Pat to hear us. And watch your language, Joel Peyton. Beth Ann's here, too."

"All right, but don't go shuffling papers like you always

do. Sounds like a giant bloodsucker devouring Toledo in a wind tunnel through this thing."

I couldn't resist. Snatching up one of Miss Maggie's books, I fanned the pages in front of the mike.

"Cut that out!"

"Wasn't me, Joel." Miss Maggie chuckled. "Pat's got a mean streak in her."

"Don't I know it." He didn't, though. This was mild compared to the noises Denise and I had broadcast regularly over Herb's speaker phone. We used to patch him through to fax machines at least once a day.

"Find out anything on Charlotte Garber, Joel?"

"The sheriff's still looking for her next of kin. She wasn't married. Lived by herself in an apartment complex."

That sounded too much like me. I felt a twinge of empathy for Charlotte. Glancing down at my bandage, I wondered, if the bullet had angled a few inches to the right, who would have mourned me? Next of kin wouldn't be a problem in my case. A whole passel of Montella, Muscarella, and Giamo cousins would show up for my wake, if only to get invited back to Aunt Lydia's afterward for porchetta sandwiches, tomato pie, cannoli, and cream cake. Aunt Sophie would probably have a mass said on my one-year anniversary. But would anyone miss me?

"Does it hurt?" Beth Ann whispered, looking concerned.

I shook my head, dislodging all thoughts of my own demise.

Joel was still talking. "Dwight Pearson down in the sheriff's office promised to give me a buzz soon as they find out where Charlotte worked." After a hesitation, he added, "He did say they sent her and the car down to Richmond."

Miss Maggie looked grim, and I asked what it meant.

"Means Dennis Brackin threw his accident theory out the window. It's a full-blown homicide now. Why, Joel? They find more evidence?"

"If they did, it's locked up tight. Couldn't even get Dwight to drop his usual hints."

Miss Maggie pursed her lips as she absently drummed her fingers on the desk.

Joel cleared his throat. "I don't want to appear picky, Magnolia, but whatever you're doing that sounds like the Four Horsemen of the Apocalypse is getting on my nerves."

She stilled her fingers by pulling them into a fist. "What about Flora?"

"I checked her credit. All her bills are current. Likewise with the mortgage on her house. She's leasing that fancy car. Probably the only way she can afford it. Only thing interesting is that she was turned down for a personal loan last week."

Miss Maggie's terrier nose twitched. "Loan? What for?"

"Don't know. Though, I don't imagine with all her other expenses, Flora has much left over for food at the end of a month."

"Let alone hundred-and-fifty-dollar business suits," I said. "I thought *I* was living on the edge. At least I only stick to the basic food, shelter, and used Plymouth."

Miss Maggie frowned. "Sounds almost like she's out to impress someone."

"A man?" I guessed, remembering Denise's clothing binges with each new beau.

Miss Maggie's eyebrows went up. "That's a thought. She *was* married. Still is, actually. Only been separated a few months."

"I checked that, too," Joel put in. "Neither one's filed for divorce yet."

"Doesn't explain why she wants the extra money," Miss Maggie said. "Joe Shifflett sure wouldn't be impressed. He'd know her financial situation better than anyone."

I had a brainstorm. "Maybe it's bait. Pretending to be rich to lure a new man."

"That's disgusting." Beth Ann's ideals had been offended.

Remembering the touchy conversation we'd had earlier, I hastened to reassure her. "I'm not saying she's that desperate. Or that she's right in what she's doing. I think she either wants to make her husband jealous, to get him back, or she's trying to give him a reason to agree to a divorce. Unfortunately, Beth Ann, people use people all the time to get what they want."

"Lordy, you women do love these soap opera plots," Joel huffed. "More likely Flora's expecting a lull in commissions. Rumor has it the deal with the farm next door might fall through. Developer's having trouble pulling together the cash."

That didn't sound dire enough to commit murder, no matter how mad I'd made her the day before. And anyway, Charlotte didn't fit in.

"Much as I'm enjoying this little dialogue with y'all, ladies, I do have work to do." He was impatient again. What, I wondered, could I do to siphon his impatience away from law, into matters of romance? I made a mental note to ask Denise, though I suspected her suggestions would be decidedly kinky—wrap my naked self in legal writs or something.

"Magnolia," he said gently, "in light of Charlotte Garber's murder, I'm going to advise you to hold off signing anything over to Pat yet. Brackin's bound to read something into it."

"Doesn't matter, Joel." With a sad smile, she took my hand. "The land would only be a burden to her right now. Best I pay the taxes and upkeep for a while."

"I'll help. Somehow." I couldn't take her charity, no matter what form it took. Damn, damn, damn.

"Me, too," Beth Ann volunteered. "I already help Dad with the trails and mowing and stuff. I can do more."

"Hush up, you two." Miss Maggie took up the receiver and shut off the speaker. "Coming by tonight, Joel? We've got some suspicions about another person, too, but I'd rather not talk about them on the phone." Meaning Wilma Rae and not mentioning names since the woman had her tentacles spread all over the county. Smart.

I couldn't hear Joel's response, but my ego was hoping he couldn't get through a whole day without seeing me.

Then some little voice deep inside whispered, *No, not tonight. Too much to do.* Abruptly, Julia came to mind, along with everything I'd seen during my last family reunion with her. Which I'd yet to recount to Miss Maggie.

She caught my eye and seemed to guess what I was thinking. "Got to run, Joel. Talk to you tonight." She punched the talk button as she set the phone on the desk. "Says he'll be over after dinner, same as last night. Claims he owes you ice cream and a plant and he's paying up." She stood. "Beth Ann, you'd better get something down in that notebook before your father gets here."

We left Beth Ann chewing her pencil in the war room. I followed my host out to the kitchen. "How are you feeling, Miss Maggie?"

"Fine, Pat. Takes more than Wilma Rae to keep me down. Come out on the back porch."

We sat on the step. The afternoon was warm but not humid. The breeze smelled wonderful: clean and fresh, no car exhaust, no stale air conditioning, no scorching smell of dust in the heating vents. I breathed deeply, trying to get my fill before the time came to take another job in an office where the "fresh air" passed through machinery and grimy ducts before reaching my nostrils.

"Tell me what you saw, Pat. Did Julia return to Bell House?"

I shook my head. "She found Robert E. Lee at Widow Tapp's farm. I don't know why I could see it from Bell House, but it was the most vivid scene yet." I described the landscape.

"How do you know you were seeing the Widow Tapp's farm?"

I shrugged. "Beats me."

"You didn't hear anyone speak. In fact, the way you tell it, you might have been looking right out of Julia's eyes this time. That didn't happen in the cemetery, did it? You were an observer there, or you couldn't have seen her hair and eyes."

True. So why did I feel like she'd caught me cheating

on a test? "I saw what Julia saw at Saunders' Field."

"Yes, but you weren't party to her thoughts. You must have been this time, Pat." This was not the Miss Maggie who'd almost dragged me in front of a Winnebago on Tuesday in her enthusiasm. This was the one who gave detentions. She wasn't pleased at all. I wondered why.

"What did Julia do in today's vision?" Miss Maggie asked.

"Nothing. She couldn't get close enough."

"Close enough for what?"

I wet my lips, feeling like a snitch in a bad cop movie. "To shoot him."

"Shoot him! Shoot Robert E. Lee?" she exclaimed.

"This kills my chances of getting into the Daughters of the Confederacy, doesn't it?"

She couldn't help smiling. "Wilma Rae can't prove a thing. Lee wasn't even wounded at Wilderness. But why, Pat? Why Lee and not a Union general?"

"All Julia cares about is ending the war. She's sure that, without Lee, the South will stop fighting. Is that true?"

Miss Maggie frowned intently at me, and I realized I'd slipped into present tense again. But to my question she merely shrugged. "Possibly. Killing a Federal general wouldn't have made a difference. Lincoln would simply appoint someone new. The Confederates were running out of capable officers. And while the army would follow Lee anywhere, they were getting pretty disgruntled over the lack of supplies and the worthlessness of Confederate money."

My gaze followed a flash of red across the clearing. The cardinal perched on a thick vine, the bird's shrill chirp cutting through the forest undertones. "But you said Lee wasn't even wounded, meaning Julia must have been caught or killed before she could try."

"What was her plan?"

"At first, she was going to wait until nightfall and sneak up on the tent. Then she noticed the army was getting ready to move, toward Richmond she thinks, so she's headed back to Parker's Store to send a message to the Howards, to warn them. I mean, she *sent* a message."

If Miss Maggie noticed my present tense again, she let it go. "There's no record of any message received, but the household did up and move to Lynchburg suddenly. Came back to Richmond a year later and found their house had been spared. Here I thought they'd only grown tired of having the war on their doorstep."

"After sending the message, Julia planned to go back to Widow Tapp's farm. If the army's still there—*was* still there, she plans to kill Lee tonight. I mean—" Never mind the tenses. The drama was playing out as I saw it. I couldn't think of it any other way. "We can go back after Beth Ann goes home. I'm sure I'll be able to see everything from Bell House again."

"No." Miss Maggie wound her fingers around my hand urgently. "I don't want you trying to look into the past again."

"But we'll lose Julia's trail. This morning you said—"

"I know." She squeezed my fingers until the tips turned red. "I didn't realize the danger then. Julia's got some sort of hold on you."

"No, she doesn't." It came out whiny, which I knew wouldn't get me anywhere. Miss Maggie had been exposed to too many moody teens not to be immune. "What danger?"

"If Julia had been captured attempting to assassinate the commanding general, the military reports of the time would have mentioned it. Like as not, she was killed. What if you're in her body, looking out of her eyes, when it happens?"

"I'll come back and tell you all about it," I said as confidently as I could. Actually, the notion gave me the willies. I tried to wiggle my trapped fingers to get the blood moving again.

"Beth Ann shook you for two full minutes today. If she hadn't, you might still be there. The next one could put you in a coma, Pat. Or kill you."

"Miss Maggie, my fingers are numb." I guessed right. The diversion worked. She relaxed her grip, bringing her other hand around to massage the life back into my digits. Blood surged into them in sharp pricks.

"Pat, you're like a daughter to me."

I was moved by this curt admission, but something inside shied away from it. "You don't want to adopt me, Miss Maggie. I come with hundreds of cousins, all of whom are liable to show up when they're broke."

Instead of laughing, her eyes filled with tears. "I don't want to lose you."

I slipped my arms around her, thinking about her son. I didn't believe the encounters would kill me, but was there any chance I'd end up like him? In a mental institution, babbling away about how I wanted to assassinate Robert E. Lee? Or worse yet, I already had Julia's homicidal blood in me. Would it trigger the killing spree of my fantasies?

I flinched away from the thought, telling myself to laugh at my paranoia. So what if I had bloodthirsty genes? I wasn't about to buy a gun. Knowing my heritage, I could avoid guns like recovering alcoholics avoid drink. Unless, of course, the NRA got Congress to make them as mandatory as social security numbers.

To the woman I was rocking in my arms, I offered love the way my family always did, asking, "What do you want for dinner tonight, Miss Maggie?"

She smiled, wiping her tears with the back of her hand. "I'll cook for you. Chicken Fricassee."

"You can't fool me. That's Italian for 'throw everything from the fridge into the frying pan.'"

"It's French, Miss Smarty-Pants."

"Then maybe you don't want an Italian side dish to go with it. There's this old Giamo recipe that would—"

She was on her feet the next instant. Her usual energy had rekindled, making those green eyes sparkle.

I allowed Miss Maggie to coax me inside, but not before I stole a last glance at the trees. *My* forest. Beckoning, promising cool respite from the warm afternoon. Promising soothing fragrances and pleasant murmurs.

Who was I trying to fool? I knew it wasn't the woods calling me. It was Julia.

I am going to send you a trophie that came off the battlefield at Gettysburg. I got three pictures out of a dead Yankees knapsack and I am going to send you one.... The pictures are wraped up in a letter from the person whose image they are.

Georgian, Harmon Martin, to his sister—1863

MAY 7, 1864—PARKER'S STORE CROSSROADS

Procuring the means with which to send a message was a chore. Paper had been more readily available when last I had need of it, in Richmond nearly eleven months ago. Now, in this corner of the world, it seemed scarce and valuable.

At last though, I found a woman at a farm along the road to Shady Grove who, while unwilling to trust me to enter her house, let me sit upon her porch step with her pen and meager bottle of ink, writing on the back of an old envelope. She'd had a son, she said, who'd sent words of solace after each battle, after each skirmish no matter how insignificant. His letters had given her hope, until she'd received none after Gettysburg.

On the envelope's upper corner was written "Sharpsburg, Maryland." I too had saved all Lane's letters in their original sleeves, so I understood the sacrifice this woman had made on my behalf.

My missive was brief: "Leave Richmond at once. Delay no more than three days, else the war will be on your threshold." I signed it merely, "A friend." Florence Howard would not take to heart a communication from my brother Gabriel, and by now likely presumed me dead. Why else would I stay away from my daughter? Neglect her this way?

Clarissa.

She'd been ten months old when I saw her last. Now she'd be walking on her own, tottering about the Howard household, perhaps stretching her tiny arms up to be lifted.

How I missed her.

A tear fell, washing out the end of the last word I'd written. I hastily wiped my eyes with my sleeve.

When the ink had dried—it did so quickly beneath the hot sun—I folded the envelope in thirds, sealing it with a drop of precious wax from the woman's supply. I wrote the Howards' name and location over top the faded ink, then thanked my benefactor, and went in search of an obliging carrier.

This was a nearly effortless task. Demand for almost every commodity had increased, especially in Richmond, the wealthy not inclined to give up their comforts because of the war. Where commerce still existed, teamsters were making frenzied runs to keep up with this demand. Many were more than willing to deliver letters from soldiers. One, his wagon loaded with herbs and berries for Richmond pharmacists and cloth dyers, agreed readily when he spied the name Howard, knowing the family to be well off and likely to reward him.

And so, my business at the Parker's Store crossroads achieved by late afternoon, I set off to find a shady refuge, deep in the woods, where I might cook a potato and wait for nightfall.

21

I needed some thinking time alone, so I cashed in my laundry excuse. Down in the cellar, unrolling socks and turning undies inside out by the light of a bare incandescent bulb, I mulled over my options.

Even without the supernatural "magnet" pulling me toward Bell House, I felt a need to go there. I had to know if Julia had actually tried to carry out her plan. How would you feel, finding a Lizzie Borden in your family tree yet never knowing if she swung her axe? Sure, I knew Julia killed John Howard, but his murder was self-defense. The question was, had she ever pulled that trigger in cold blood?

What would it mean to me if she had?

I told myself to find out first, then worry about it.

Spraying stain remover on the knees and cheeks of my white pants, I played through the most uncomplicated scenario—me slinking away to Bell House alone. Problem one: If I slipped into an even deeper trance, which seemed to be the emerging trend, no one would be around to shake me out of it. True, I still didn't believe it would do me physical harm, even if Julia were to die in the next sequence, but I wasn't sure I could get back on my own. Not that I'd had anything to do with getting back the other times. For that matter, I'd had nothing to do with going either.

Problem two: The person who'd shot me, on finding me alone in the woods again, wouldn't botch a second chance. Unless, of course, Charlotte did it. If we're talking most-to-gain-from-my-death-at-the-time, she still won hands down. But that would mean whoever murdered her—

New thought: What if someone knew Charlotte took that pot shot and killed her so she couldn't do it again? Killed her to protect me? Did anyone care that much about me? Miss Maggie? Joel? . . . Beth Ann?

Beth Ann *couldn't* have done it, I assured myself. *I* was her alibi, from the time of the shot virtually until Hugh took her home last night.

On the other hand, I knew she was perfectly capable of sneaking out of the trailer in the middle of the night. What if she'd seen Charlotte take aim at me? What if she recognized Charlotte's car, not because she'd seen it in the afternoon, but because she'd been at the boat ramp just before—

Oddly enough, I felt more anxiety picturing Beth Ann out in that storm than picturing her shoving a car into the river.

While my brain was sifting through all my irrational conjectures, my fingers were sifting absently through pockets. In the shirt I'd worn Monday, I found Flora's business card. Staring at it, I thought of a solution to both problems.

First, why go out to Bell House alone? Just because Miss Maggie had been my faithful sidekick all the other times didn't mean I couldn't ask Joel. Could the Don Juan in him resist the offer of a lovers' tryst in the woods?

On second thought—

Maybe I could go with the "damsel in distress" approach and appeal to his Southern sense of duty. If he still turned me down, there was always Beth Ann, who I was sure would follow me anywhere. Though I didn't want to expose her to danger again.

But I intended to minimize the risk by keeping the suspects occupied. Flora was easy. I'd seen several of her realty signs while driving through Lake of the Woods this morning. If we were right in guessing she was desperate for money, she wouldn't turn down the chance to show a house.

Wilma Rae would be more of a challenge. Like Flora, I ought to focus on her weaknesses. Hit her in her recommendations. Or a frontal attack on the Confederacy. After thirty-six years of TV watching, I must have absorbed a few satirical plot ideas. I'd come up with something.

Hugh was iffy. His weak spot was Beth Ann, but sending him off on some wild goose chase for worry of her seemed cruel. One simple solution did occur to me, but it depended on whether Hugh was willing to look at me across a table while he ate. Maybe if Beth Ann asked him.

Dumping the last of my laundry into the washer along with an eyeball-estimate of soap powder, I started the heavy-duty cycle and went upstairs.

Miss Maggie was at the kitchen sink, one hand on the faucet and in the other hand, a deboned, de-skinned chicken breast. "Bad timing, Pat. I had the chicken half-washed when you turned on the washer."

"Sorry."

"No problem. Doesn't take long for the tank to fill."

"Is Beth Ann staying for dinner?"

"She can if she wants. I'll defrost another breast in the microwave."

"I'll go ask her."

She was stretched out on the war-room carpet, scribbling frantically in her notebook.

"You look like you're on a roll," I said from the doorway.

Startled, she looked up sheepishly. "It's not my report. I spotted a wildflower I couldn't identify in the woods today. I'm writing a description to show my biology teacher."

Crossing the room for a better look, I saw three fairly good drawings of the flower, leaf, and whole plant. Her write-up was so detailed it belonged in a field guide. At her age, my notebook doodling had consisted of uncomplimentary teacher caricatures and sarcastic poetry. The closest I'd come to non-homework science had been "Ode to a Dissected Earthworm." One of my best, actually.

"I came in to ask if you wanted to stay for supper." I

heard the ulterior motives in my voice. A few days away from D-G and my bluffing aptitude was already fading.

Beth Ann didn't notice. Her mouth grew a disappointed pout. "Better not. It's my turn to cook at home. Dad would have a fit."

"You can cook? What's on tonight's menu?"

She shrugged. "Frozen dinners, probably. I can make great omelettes, but I think we're low on eggs."

"Tell you what. Do your cooking here tonight and invite your dad. I'll teach you how to make Italian rice."

Her eyes widened hopefully as she sat up. "Really?"

"Yes, really. I'm looking for an excuse to make brownies. Help me out, Beth Ann."

She grinned. "I'll call him right now."

"Tell him we're having chicken fricassee and risotto Giamo." I hadn't known a man yet to turn down a home-cooked dinner for the frozen kind. Or a woman, for that matter, unless it was Denise during one of her diet binges. "We'll need a vegetable, too. What do you and your dad like?"

Her nose wrinkled up. "Dad likes everything."

"While you like nothing?" I did a quick mental scan of the veggie bin in Miss Maggie's fridge. "Will you at least try whatever I make?"

"Depends." The wrinkles on her nose had now spread to her upper lip. I was tempted to warn her, as my mom had always warned me, that her face would gel that way permanently.

"I want a promise," I said. "One itty-bitty taste. You can have a big glass of water to wash it down."

"I'll need it." Beth Ann held her facade of disgust for another moment. "Okay. One taste." She fetched the telephone from Miss Maggie's desk and punched speed-dial number one. "What time should I tell Dad to show up?"

The question knocked me off balance. Time, I realized, would be the trickiest part of my plan. Everything hinged on what time Joel could meet me, if he would. Then again, I couldn't make dinner too late, or Miss Maggie would get suspicious. "Seven o'clock," I compromised, hoping I could get away with the excuse of a late start on the side dish.

I threw together a batch of my "code-red scratch brownies" first, so named because of their medicinal qualities after a bad day at work. My only rule for them is that you can't substitute carob powder for the cocoa. Anything else goes. I've made them with oatmeal, nonfat dry milk, pear juice, you name it. As long as they come out of the oven or microwave smelling and tasting of chocolate, nothing else matters.

While Beth Ann was whisking the batter smooth and Miss Maggie was busy browning chicken, I begged off for a potty break, sneaking the phone with me into the powder room.

"Pat?" At least Joel didn't sound impatient. Just confused. "I told Magnolia—"

"This is something else. I need—"

"Speak up. I can hardly hear you."

"I can't. I don't want Miss Maggie to hear." As it was, I was as jumpy as a bank robber with dye on his hands.

"Why?" His lawyerly caution was kicking in. Time to get to the point. Sort of.

"Joel, I need you to do me a really, really big favor."

"One too many *really*s for my liking. Especially if you don't want Magnolia to know about it."

"Listen. I need to go out to the Bell House tonight, but I don't want to go alone. I think—" How could I explain without mentioning my little private seances? They'd scare him off for sure. "There's something I have to know about my Grandmother Julia. I think I can find out at Bell House."

"What problem's Magnolia got with that?"

Why couldn't he be impulsive and say yes? "I guess, after yesterday, she's afraid to let me out of the house. I see her point—that's why I don't want to go alone. If I had—if *you* came with me, I'd feel safer." I almost said "if I had a big, strong man along," but that seemed to be laying it on too thick. "Can you meet me out by the ruin before you come up to the house? Just for a few minutes."

"Why not go out in broad daylight? I could come over Saturday—"

"No." I'd practically shouted it and, wincing, I listened for questions at the door. Nothing. "I have to go tonight. I'd go right now if I could, but I'd have to take Beth Ann and after yesterday—Please, Joel?"

"Well, I suppose we could always tell Magnolia we were looking for some privacy. That wouldn't be a bad idea anyway. Anytime she's within fifty yards, I feel like we've got a chaperone."

So that's why he'd been on good behavior last night. "I'll make it worth your while, Joel Peyton."

"Yes, ma'am. I don't doubt that. I suppose you don't want me parking in front of the house?"

"No. You can park at the post office. Hugh and Beth Ann will be here for dinner. Or over at the industrial park, if you want. What's the earliest you can come?"

He made humming sounds through the receiver while he thought about it. "If you're all fired up about us prowling through the woods, I guess I ought to change clothes. How about eight-thirty?"

I knew I couldn't wait that long. Just standing here by the small powder-room window, I could feel Julia's lure. Even if that wasn't a problem, Hugh was coming at seven. I wanted to make sure he was in the middle of dinner and couldn't up and leave without seeming rude. Even if that's what *I* intended to do. "Can't you make it closer to seven-thirty?"

"Lordy. You sound mighty anxious to get your hands on me."

Whatever worked. "I am. Pretty please?"

"Eight. Meet you at the ruin."

I agreed, and we said our good-byes. Before going on with my plan, I cracked the powder-room door an inch. The smell of frying chicken tickled my nose. Beth Ann and Miss Maggie were talking in the kitchen, but the topic hadn't gotten around to missing persons yet.

Closing the door, I dug Flora's card out of my jeans pocket and punched in the number. Flora herself answered, and if the background noise meant anything—a radio playing country-western and the muffled, irate blare of a horn— she was in her car.

I laid the thickest Southern accent I could manage atop my Philadelphia mumble. "Ah'm calling to inquire about one of y'all's houses?"

"Yes, of course. Hold on a sec."

I pictured her pulling off the road. She'd want to catch every one of my simpering, half-whispered words.

She killed the radio. "All right, ma'am. Your name, please?"

I should have expected that. I suppose it was my accent that made me spit out, "Ellie May—" I almost said "Clampett," though if I was right in placing Flora in Denise's generation, it wouldn't have mattered. Only one other old TV show came to mind. "Ellie May Rockford."

"And which property are you interested in, Mrs. Rockford?"

It always irks me when people assume I'm married. I was willing to bet Flora was damn politically correct in all her other utterances. Couldn't she say "Ms."? Or did she want me to come back and say I wasn't married, so she could mark me down as "don't take seriously?" I'd show her. I'd make Ellie May a rich widow. "Well, now, I'm not sure. Did you say your name was Flora, honey? I was driving along this right purdy lake this morning, Flora—Lake of the Woods, that was it—when I saw the cutest li'l ol' house. I wrote down your phone number but clean forgot to make a note of the address. You know which place I mean, honey?"

"We have several in the area. Perhaps the two bedroom bungalow with the blue shutters—"

"Two bedrooms? That sounds so *puny*."

"Oh, you're looking for something bigger?" I could almost hear her smack her chops hungrily. "We have a four bedroom, three bath, country kitchen—"

"Was that the one with the big, circular driveway out front? I do so *love* circular driveways."

"Why, no, but—"

"Tell you what, honey. You show me all you've got. We're bound to hit on one. Can you meet me over there tonight?"

"Yes. Yes, of course—"

"Say, around eight? You'd better give me directions." I let her drone on, repeating her directions back as if I were writing them down.

"You're not from around here, are you, Mrs. Rockford?"

Oops. Had I given myself away somehow? "Fancy your knowing that."

"Your accent seems very, uh, Texan, perhaps?"

"Right on target. Flora, honey, we're going to get *along*. Bye now." I thumbed the talk button quickly. Had she suspected? I didn't think so. I hoped not.

One to go.

A timid knock sounded at the door. "Pat?" Beth Ann asked worriedly. "You're okay, aren't you?"

"I'm fine," I shouted.

"You were talking."

I did a silent three-word tour of my cuss vocab before opening the door and showing her the phone. "I had to make a private call."

Embarrassment crowded all the anxiety off her face. "I'm sorry. I thought you were . . . you know."

"I don't get the seizures that often." I heard the washing-machine buzzer, signalling the end of my load and giving me an idea. "Do me a favor? Don't mention the phone call to Miss Maggie. It was about my job, and I don't want her to worry."

Beth Ann promised. "The brownies are all mixed."

"I have to throw my clothes in the dryer. You can go onto the next step." I rattled off oven instructions. "Ask Miss Maggie for a pan—nine by eleven or the closest she's got. Don't forget to grease it. Lightly. Okay?"

She saluted with a grin. "Got it."

I started down the hall toward the stairs. "I'm going to fetch my good blouse from upstairs so I can handwash it. Be right down."

It was an extra chore, but I needed something to hide the phone in when I walked through the kitchen.

Miss Maggie didn't look up. She couldn't without burning herself on the hot oil she was pouring from the frying pan into a tin can in the sink. "Pat, can you wait till I finish the chicken to do your side dish? I want to type the recipe into the laptop."

This played into my time schedule perfectly. I had to resist the mad-scientist laugh bubbling up the back of my throat. "Have to anyway, Miss Maggie. Both my risotto and the asparagus have to be cooked on top of the stove. Be easier if I have it all to myself."

"Asparagus!" Beth Ann moaned. Her hand froze halfway out of the Crisco can, a huge glob of shortening clinging to the small scrap of wax paper she held.

I pointed to her hand. "I said 'lightly.' And smile. You might even like it." I reiterated how I was going to handwash the blouse in my hand and bolted for the cellar stairs.

Since I sincerely doubted Wilma Rae would be programmed into the speed dial, I called Information first, using my fingernail to scratch the number into a bar of brown soap at the utility sink.

I'd been rehearsing a groveling apology, the prelude to a shocking disclosure about how Charlotte was an industrial spy for a New England hazardous-waste company in the market for a dump site. I figured I wouldn't have to invent much more, Wilma Rae being an expert at jumping to conclusions. Besides, I'd imply that it wasn't safe to divulge more over the phone and make an appointment to go by her house at eight. That was the weak spot in the plan, though. Wilma Rae wouldn't be as desperately patient as Flora. She'd ring up Miss Maggie's at 8:01 to find out why I was late.

As it turned out, Wilma Rae herself solved the problem for me. She must have still been out terrorizing the community because her answering system picked up. And I do mean *system*. A wonder she hadn't put in for an 800 technical assistance number.

Prerecorded, her voice lost some of its intimidating resonance. "For information on school-board meetings, press one. For the St. George's Episcopal Vestry, press two. For the Daughters of the Confederacy, press three. For the Ladies' Christian Values League, press . . ." She offered eight choices in all.

I listened to each one, phone propped between my shoulder and ear, as I transferred my laundry from washer to dryer. Sure enough, I got lucky on number seven.

"The Society for the Preservation of Southern Ideals meets every Thursday evening from eight to ten at the American Legion Hall. New members are always welcome. To leave a message, press one. For further inf—"

Dropping the last sock into the dryer, I jabbed one, glad to be rid of her migraine-inducing babble. She deserved the perfect new member. "Hey, y'all. Ellie May Rockford, here, all the way from Texas. I'm fixing to put down roots in your li'l ol' state, and I'd be pleased as a penguin in a meat locker to join your li'l ol' club. I'll be at your soiree tonight. Better yet, I'll come by extra early so's we can all get acquainted. 'Round about seven-forty-five? See y'all then."

Unless I missed my guess, Wilma Rae probably interviewed new blood personally. I hoped I was convincing. The "penguin in a meat locker" line hadn't sounded very Southern, but my Montella inventiveness was working overtime as it was.

So, my plan was in place. Now, what was I forgetting? A way out of the house.

I pictured the local rescue squad using the jaws of life to pry my hips from the powder-room window. No good.

Could I climb out my second-floor bedroom window? If the porch roof didn't collapse under me, how would I get down? Unlike the rest of the property, Miss Maggie's house didn't have a vine clinging to it anywhere.

I wandered across the cellar, past Beth Ann's recycling center to the outside door, a single unit of painted wood and vertical beading where the slats were joined, locked by a modest steel bolt on one side.

Gingerly testing the bolt, expecting the squeaks and groans of old metal, I found it well-oiled and silent. The hinges, too, offered no protest as I pushed the door open a foot. Peeking out, I saw I was on the house's east side, right around the corner from the back porch.

My longing to return to Bell House quadrupled; it was a supreme test of will not to go right away. Like not eating donuts at work during Lent. (For the record, a Boston cream almost always has me doing penance by the third week.) I forced my legs back down the steps, letting the door close gently behind me. Even then, the yearning stayed with me, a physical ache in my gut.

"Patience, Grandmother," I whispered. "Just a couple more hours."

My left brain sent me an FYI, reminding me that I was talking to a woman long dead, fighting off a thoroughly illogical temptation. "Dwell on more important things," my logic center suggested, like who killed Charlotte and would kill me, given the golden opportunity I was devising.

I decided instead to think about the mundane, i.e., laundry. Or at least, what excuse I could conjure up for coming downstairs around eight o'clock.

All my adult life, I'd used coin-operated dryers. There isn't a lot of skill involved, just one rule: One coin is never enough. Almost always took three—that is, one hour—for a light load, more for jeans and such, though I'm sure those machines were inferior to Miss Maggie's Maytag.

I had no idea how long a standard house dryer took to complete a run. Mom never used hers. Even in the dead of winter, she'd hang her wash outside or from lines strung all around the basement. Wet socks smacked me in the face whenever I went down there on a rainy day.

Still, it looked like my timing depended on when my laundry was done. And no way should it take two hours.

My good blouse came to the rescue. I usually dried it on a hanger over my bathtub drain, but the tag said tumble dry low, so that's what I'd do, after the regular load was done. Then if it was still too early, I'd play it by ear.

My originally simple plan was getting more complicated by the minute.

In the midst of this awful scene, General Lee rode to the front ... The fierce soldiers with their faces blackened with the smoke of battle, the wounded, crawling with feeble limbs from the fury of devouring flames, all seemed possessed with a common impulse. One long, unbroken cheer ... rose high above the roar of battle and hailed the presence of the victorious chief.

Colonel Charles Marshall, at Chancellorsville—1863

MAY 7, 1864—ALONG THE ORANGE PLANK ROAD

The setting sun bathed the drifting plumes of smoke, lining them with rosy fleece.

I stood on the edge of the forest, caught in the beauty of the twilight, even over so grotesque a canvas. I wondered how many soldiers noticed this crimson smoke? This gentle mockery of their handiwork? How many generals paid heed to this manifest of greater power?

None, I imagined. All were too occupied in their preparations for the next day's bloodshed. Perhaps I alone beheld this token of Creation.

As I stood watching the sunset, wagons began to roll by from the direction of the battlefield. Heavy wagons, loaded with provisions and ammunition. Looking to the northeast, I could see the glow of brushfires rekindled by the evening breezes. Perhaps the wagons were sent ahead to remove them from the path of the flames. Or perhaps the army was using the diversion of the fires to steal away from their trenches.

Shrinking back into the shadow of the trees, I began to make my way toward the flickering radiance. I'd not gone far when I heard the sound of slow-approaching horse hooves upon the planks. Stopping to reconnoiter, I identified the same group of riders I'd seen earlier in the day: Lee's staff, the almighty general himself in their lead.

Tilting his head to one side, Lee listened to the officer beside him. One fist, carelessly perched on the saddle's pommel, held the reins, but his manner seemed stiff and uncomfortable. His other hand he kept inside his undone coat, as if pressing against his ribs.

Without taking my eyes from him, I drew a cartridge from my sack, bringing the rifle up under my arm. I had the cartridge paper between my teeth, ready to tear away one end, when I paused.

Lee was no more aware of his peril than a chicken before its neck is wrung. Even if he raised his head, met my eyes at the moment I pulled the trigger, he'd have no notion why I should be his deliverer. I wished him to look me in the face, to hear what my family had suffered. Wanted him to die with the name Bell foremost in his thoughts.

I made my way back through the woods, following the horsemen to the crossroads. The wagons turned south, toward Shady Grove, confirming my fears that the contest was to move closer to the capital, but Lee's men halted before Parker's Store.

The general spoke to one rider, who then took off north at a gallop, toward the Chewning farm. The rest of the officers dismounted, some entering the store, some sitting upon the step. Lee and two others remained standing, one pacing, unable to keep still.

Lee removed his hat, placing the other hand back inside his coat. Even in the last light of evening, I could see the glistening sweat on his brow, the curling of his drenched white hair. After a moment, he left the company of his staff, proceeding alone around to the rear yard of the store.

Seeing my chance, I stole across the road as fast as I could. As I'd told Cobb, they were all men, even high-and-mighty General Lee. All put their pants on the same. All occasionally sought out the privy.

The store had taken minor damage from the battle, windows broken, pickets missing in the fence. I could see the top of the privy behind a grape arbor at the very end of the yard. It would be safest to approach from the other side, making certain no one else was about, appearing to be merely another visitor to the necessary.

I'd pictured myself using Pa's rifle to do the deed. It seemed more chaste than John's revolver. Who knew how many victims had succumbed to the pistol's blast? The rifle had only been used for hunting. Until last November.

Remembering, I faltered. No, I'd not use the rifle. Did Lee deserve a nobler weapon than John?

Discarding my rifle and kit, I scanned the alley hastily. No one had followed Lee from the store's front. No one came from the opposite direction. Stealing around behind the yard, my hand beneath the hem of my shirt, clutching the revolver, gaining courage from it, I came upon the open door of an empty privy.

Beside it though, on a bench beneath the grape arbor, I found my quarry seated, coat off, hand pressed to his chest. I drew my sidearm, levelling it just above his fingers.

My moment had come at last.

22

I realized I'd left myself no way to sneak the phone back up through the kitchen.

The washer was chugging away, the blouse soaking in a bucket, Miss Maggie calling from above that she was ready for me, and here I was, with a turkey in my hand liable to gobble and give me away at any moment.

I made a mental note to scratch "the Spy Division" of the CIA off my list of prospective employers.

"Be up in a minute, Miss Maggie," I yelled. I hurried over to the outside door, climbing the steps as I pushed it open, then running the short distance to the powder-room window. Reaching up, I balanced the phone on the sill and dashed back to the cellar before the urge to keep going toward Bell House became irresistible.

I paused to catch my breath after I shut the door, knowing the next time I set foot outside Julia wouldn't let go. The feeling wasn't a pleasant cajoling any longer; it had mutated into a emotional itch that demanded scratching.

Upstairs, I begged another potty break, saying the cinnamon I had for lunch was playing havoc with my stomach.

Miss Maggie nodded from where she stood washing utensils at the sink. "Fetch the laptop from the war room on your way back, will you, Pat?"

I could have kissed her. "Sure thing."

After I'd reinstated the phone and set up the laptop on the kitchen table, I drew my first full breath. It was rich with chocolate. Beth Ann was taking the brownies from the oven.

I joined her at the stove, lifting the lid on the skillet simmering on the back burner. Golden chicken swimming in wine, green peppers, canned tomatoes, and mushrooms, doing a number on my salivary glands. "You're good, Miss Maggie. I want the recipe."

With a grin, she donned her reading glasses and flexed her fingers over the laptop's keyboard. "What are *you* making?"

"When I was Beth Ann's age," I explained as I raided the fridge, bringing forth asparagus, grated Locatelli, and egg substitute leftover from Tuesday, "the only veggie I'd touch was *caduna*. Spelled *C-A-R-D-O-N-E*. It's actually a weed. Every spring, Uncle Pasq used to go out to some secret place only he knew and pick a bushel. The closet thing I've seen to it in a market is Swiss chard, but you can cook asparagus the same way."

Miss Maggie was enthralled. Nothing like a good story to spice up a recipe. I chopped off about five inches of the tender stalks, trimmed the ferny growth around the tips, and gave them to Beth Ann to wash. Omelette expert that she was, she had no trouble mixing the egg and cheese, then dunking the stalks in before coating them with bread crumbs. I let her start frying them while I worked on the risotto.

Miss Maggie was thrilled. She'd heard of risotto. Had she been less excited, she might have wondered why I didn't pronounce it in dialect. All of my relatives boil rice like normal people. In risotto, you sauté the rice first, then add broth a little at a time to swell it slowly. I'd learned the recipe from an Italian cookbook, so it was likely a northern technique. Most Italian cookbooks treat the southern provinces like poor cousins.

The problem with risotto, though, is that you have to keep your mind on it. Between Miss Maggie's questions, checking on Beth Ann's progress, and holding Julia's high-pressure nagging at bay, I wasn't at my best. The rice kept sticking despite my constant stirring. Still, it turned out edible, the onion and red pepper giving it the right flavor, the mozzarella melted into it at the last minute, hiding the slightly pasty texture. And luckily, none of my guinea pigs would know the difference anyway.

As he had that morning, Hugh appeared at the back screen door silently, without warning. Startled, I glanced at my watch, ready to ream him out for showing up early.

Six-fifty-five. Already.

Pride in my cooking warred with my need to stall. Risotto should be eaten the minute it's done, or it'll turn into a glob of glue.

Then I remembered the excuse that was supposed to have kept me on schedule. "My laundry. I forgot all about it."

"Relax, Pat," Miss Maggie said, sampling some asparagus and rolling her eyes in ecstasy. "The dryer buzzer went off ten minutes ago."

"I didn't hear it. Let me go check—"

"Eat first. Your clothes aren't going anywhere."

"The shirts will wrinkle. I'll only be a minute. Back by the time you set the table." I dashed downstairs before she could say anything else, worried that my laundry obsession was making her suspicious.

To my delight, all the clothes were still damp. I clutched a fistful of the shirts and undies, running them under cold water to get them wet again, and added the soaking blouse without bothering to wring it out. Then I set the machine for the delicate cycle. If Miss Maggie was right about the buzzer's timing, I estimated at least another thirty minutes before the next blast. I thought about letting it go a full cycle, but if I ruined this batch of clothes, I wouldn't have much left to wear except the ones on my back. And the blouse had cost me half a week's pay.

Hugh and Beth Ann were putting the last touches on the table setting, Miss Maggie filling the plates from the stove—a wise choice since the table wasn't all that big. I went over to help her, listening with one ear as Hugh grilled Beth Ann on the status of her report. She was fudging, making excuses. I wondered when she'd drop the bomb-shell that he was the subject.

"Here, Pat." Miss Maggie handed me a plate. "Dish out your rice. I'll get a little basket for the asparagus."

I loaded up four plates with rice and chicken, calling Beth Ann to take them to the table. She looked relieved to be out from under "the Inquisition."

Miss Maggie lined a small plastic basket with napkins, transferring the fried stalks from the paper towel where they were draining. "You know, I've been thinking about your *cardone*, Pat. You say it's like Swiss chard?"

I nodded as we all sat down, Beth Ann and I side-by-side facing the wall, me on a card-table chair replacing the one Beau had taken away. Hugh and Miss Maggie sat fac-ing each other on the ends.

She turned to Beth Ann. "What's the name of the plant that grows on that patch of sandy soil, down where we thought the Bells' kitchen garden might have been?"

Beth Ann wrinkled her brow in concentration. "The one with the big leaves? The stems that look kind of like cel-ery?"

"That's it."

"It's a wild artichoke. Not native. Planted originally by early Europeans."

Wide-eyed, I turned to Miss Maggie. "You mean there might be *cadunas* here at Bell Run? I haven't had the real thing since Uncle Pasq took off for Florida with his second wife."

"We'll take a look at it tomorrow, Pat," Miss Maggie said with a grin.

Beth Ann made a face. "Asparagus is bad enough. Ar-tichokes are truly disgusting."

"My family doesn't eat the artichoke part. Just the stems." Picking up the basket, I held it under her nose. "Come on, you said you'd try."

She selected the smallest stalk, examining it as if it were a microdisease growing in a petri dish.

"Are you going to eat it or dissect it?"

Beth Ann cut a tiny portion with her fork, getting mostly fried coating. "You promised me a glass of water to wash it down."

I jumped up to fetch the largest cup in Miss Maggie's cabinet, one of those thirty-two ouncers that you get at junk food places. Filling it with ice and water from the refrigerator-door dispenser, I set it before her. "Here. Go for it, kid."

Beth Ann treated me to a withering glance before stabbing her prey and bringing it to her mouth, which remained resolutely shut.

"She won't eat it." Hugh, who'd been silently working his way through the food on his plate, eyes lowered, didn't look up as he made the cynical prediction.

Looking like she was forcing down medicine, Beth Ann shoved the fork into her mouth. After a few seconds of reluctant munching, the corners of her mouth twitched.

"My God, Pat," Miss Maggie said. "I think she *likes* it."

"It's *okay*." Beth Ann tried to infuse ultimate indifference into her voice, but the twitch became a real smile. And she didn't touch her water.

I saw the same smile on Hugh's lips. He'd known exactly which button to push to get her to try the stuff.

Both Miss Maggie and I sensed the need to change the subject, before Beth Ann went totally self-conscious and couldn't eat at all. We spoke in unison, praising each other's cooking. Since that lasted all of two minutes, I soon needed to opt for another topic.

"I was reading your book today, Miss Maggie, and I came across the name Fitzhugh Lee."

Hugh's fork froze halfway up the ascent from his dish. He raised his eyes so I could see the distrust in them.

Miss Maggie scooped up the last of her first helping of risotto. "Fitzhugh was a popular name in the family, but that particular one was Robert E.'s nephew. He was a general in the cavalry, Evan's commanding officer. From what I've heard, he had a great sense of humor."

Struck by another whim to get on Hugh's nerves, I

swung my gaze over toward him, giving what I hoped was the impression that I was comparing him to his namesake and finding him wanting. "A relation of yours?"

He laughed—the first I'd heard that tremulous sound since Monday. The vibration rattled the flatware against the plates. "My mother loved the old names. I've got brothers named Richard Henry, Francis Lightfoot, and believe it or not, Lighthorse Harry."

"I call him Uncle Horse," Beth Ann volunteered around a mouthful of asparagus.

I pictured a whole clan of red-haired giants. *Madonne.* "What, no Robert E.?"

"The youngest was supposed to be named that," Hugh said. "Mom got a girl instead. Named her Ann Carter, after the general's mother."

"Dad says we're an obscure branch of the family," Beth Ann explained. "Robert E. Lee's something like my fifth cousin, eight times removed."

The discussion had begun to really whip up that heckling in my gut. At the mention of Lee's full name, it practically overwhelmed me. I wanted desperately to turn toward the window. Julia was there. I *knew* she was. After holding her at bay all afternoon, I felt myself being dragged into her grasp.

"What wrong, Pat?" Miss Maggie asked, alarmed. "You're pale all of a sudden."

"Nothing." I drew in a lungful of air. "Just that stomach ache I had earlier. I'll be all right." To Julia I sent the telepathic message: *I'm coming. You've waited for me over a hundred years, Grandmother. One more half hour is all I ask.*

As if in response, the dryer buzzer went off.

Miss Maggie's eyebrows rose. "What did you set it on, Pat? It hasn't even been twenty minutes."

Goosebumps broke out on my arms like a time-lapse video of paint blistering. I tried to persuade myself the timer was my doing, not Julia playing poltergeist. My lack of fear before, I realized, stemmed from the fact that she'd never influenced *my* world. Or, at least, no one in it but me. My travels to the past had been like reading a book—you could put it down and go on with your life. That's why it hadn't felt dangerous. Now . . . "I must have set it wrong, Miss Maggie. I'll be right back."

She called after me, but I sputtered assurances as I ran down the cellar steps. Sure enough, the dryer was off and not even its warm breath could dispel the cold dread I felt. My clothes were *absolutely dry*. All of them, even the ones that'd been dripping wet twenty minutes ago.

I wondered what else Julia's homicidal mind, dormant for a century and a third, was capable of?

"Look," I whispered, low and shaky, "I'll come right now. Just keep Beth Ann and Miss Maggie out of this. Please." Leaving the dryer open, I made a beeline for the outer door.

The sky above was still bright blue, though the sun had long ago sunk below the treetops. The clearing was shrouded in gray shade, but it was still too light to cross without the risk of being spotted from the kitchen window. Julia obviously wasn't working on daylight saving time.

The only path into the woods on this side of the house was the trail down to Bell Run, the opposite direction from where I needed to go. Then I remembered Miss Maggie and Beth Ann mentioning a river trail. In my mind's eye, I saw bluebells bursting from the underbrush on a path leading away from the trailer.

Worth a try.

Only when I was beneath the shadow of the trees did I notice I'd forgotten a flashlight. Turning back wasn't an option. The trail was dim at first, but my eyes seemed to adjust faster than usual.

The forest was stone silent, except for the occasional mournful cry of some bird so far up in the canopy he might as well belong to the next galaxy. The silence only served to enhance the loneliness. This evening there were no chipmunks, no squirrels, and the peepers had yet to commence their nightly gig.

I was almost at the bridge before the welcome gurgling of Bell Run reached my ears. Regretting that I couldn't stop to harass tadpoles tonight, I breathed in its mossy perfume as I ran over the wood planks, still damp and dirty from the morning's flood.

I found myself shying away from the partial clearing around the trailer, now feeling thoroughly coupled with the gloom. Crossing the grassy expanse swiftly, I slipped back into the protective embrace of the forest, startling a young doe who crashed away into the thicket, vanishing almost instantly.

This path, less trodden and narrower than the trail to Bell House, led into denser woods. I waded through leafy tentacles, my arms raised to avoid the thorns. The track recrossed Bell Run below the rocks Miss Maggie had pointed out. Nothing so accommodating as a bridge here, but the boulders formed stepping stones, two logs spanning the widest gaps. My Giamo prudence urged further study, citing my not-so-great sense of balance and the higher than usual water level of the creek. Ignoring it, I plunged ahead, reaching the other side with passably dry sneakers and no turned ankles.

The trail paralleled the creek now, though I stopped after I'd gone only a few yards. I knew in my heart I'd come to the site of Armstead Bell's grist mill. There were no ruins. From what I could see, nature had completely reclaimed it. Not that I could see much. The stream banks were higher here, the gully sunken, seeming to recoil from the bright sky silhouetting the trees far above.

But I felt Julia's hostility. The Yankees had completely dismantled the mill, burning the remains to ash. The fire had spread, raging through the parched woods that night, until it found Clara Shackleford in her home.

My sense of urgency surged and instinctively I climbed the steep bank behind the site. This was where the original path from the house had been. Still was, unless I'd once more penetrated into the past. In the darkness, deep in this woodland, maybe time didn't exist at all. My senses seemed useless. All I was aware of were the beads of sweat clinging to every inch of me, making me shiver.

I'd thought the stream was a good distance from the ruin, but the way seemed short, Bell House appearing before me sooner than expected. The trail emerged from the forest almost directly opposite the L-shaped addition and pile of broken bricks marking the location of the old well.

I held back once more, not so much from the light of the clearing as from a feeling that someone was out there waiting.

Glancing at my watch, I saw it was only twenty-five after seven. Too early for Joel. Also too early to be convinced all likely assailants were busy elsewhere.

There was no movement in the clearing, no sound. I ran across the grass to the stone slabs, expecting to hear gunfire, ears straining for sounds of pursuit.

Nothing.

Crouching, leaning against the broken bricks, I caught my breath, then set to work removing the slabs. My left arm balked, the muscle cramping in agony against the weight.

Tears welled up in my eyes. I couldn't have come this far to be stopped by my stupid arm.

Neither could I lift the stones one-handed.

A twig cracked around the corner of the addition. I fell to the ground, thankful for the tall grass and camouflaging neutrality of the twilight. The figure that came into view wore a dark green windbreaker, sleeves pushed up to the elbow. One hand held a flashlight, the other was out of sight in his jacket pocket.

"Joel!" I ran over to him and planted a quick kiss on his cheek. I admit, I was interested most in his brawn at that moment. "You don't know how glad I am that you're here early. I need your help—"

I'd tugged his elbow in the direction of the ruin. His hand came part way out of his pocket, far enough for me to see the square butt of a semiautomatic pistol.

Joel's eyes widened as much as mine. "After what happened to you yesterday, it seemed like a good idea to bring it along tonight."

For believing me last night, for feeling the need to protect me, I kissed him again, on the lips this time. "Leave the gun in your pocket. I need both your hands free."

He grinned. "God Almighty, I've met some aggressive women in my day, but—"

"No. I mean, not now. Later. Come on." I led him back to the ruin. "I need you to move these slabs."

He scanned the pieces of slate. "What for?"

"There's an old well underneath. It leads into the cellar."

"You're going inside?" He sounded dubious.

"Not all the way. Just . . . just as far as I have to."

Flicking on his flashlight, he inspected the rubble and vine-covered foundation beyond.

"It's too far back to collapse into the well," I assured him, doing my utmost to console myself at the same time. "Please, Joel."

"Well, let go of my arm then, so I can get to work." Handing me the flashlight, he bent down to lift the first stone. "You want all of them off?"

"Two's probably enough." Then remembering my hips, I added, "Make it three to be on the safe side."

He moved them easily, stepping back with a chivalrous wave of both hands. "All yours."

I looked into the yawning blackness of the well. Never had I been so frightened of a place, yet so ready to plunge in. I made myself use caution. "I need you to come with me. I'm going to . . . to go into a sort of trance. I may need you to bring me out of it."

Even in the diminishing light, I could see the utter disbelief on his face.

"Please, Joel. Please trust me. I can't explain now. It'd take too long."

His eyes drifted to the opening and back to me. His jaw, open in skepticism, closed into a frown as he searched my face. "What do you want me to do?"

"Just stay with me. If I'm under longer than—" How

long this time? I wanted to see everything, wanted to know
everything there was to know about Julia. But like Miss
Maggie, I was now apprehensive. "—longer than, say, fifteen minutes, shake me hard. If I don't come back, go get
Miss Maggie. Okay?"

He shrugged. "Whatever you say."

Using my good arm for balance, I jumped into the well,
flashing the light into the side tunnel. Dankness once more
assaulted my nostrils. I could see about five feet of damp
passageway, then a short drop to a dirty brick floor and,
beyond that, another brick wall. All in a present-century
state of crumbling.

Julia wanted me inside this time. There was a promise
associated with the other end of this passage, like the come-
on from a carnival fortune teller: "All will be revealed."
Only this time I knew the claim was genuine.

As Joel dropped lightly to the bricks beside me, I
crawled through. The shaft was roomy enough for me to
swing my legs around to let myself down the last couple
feet into the room. A little inner voice told me I was nearing
the right spot, but I made myself wait for Joel, grasping his
hand securely as he emerged from the well.

"It's going to happen soon, Joel." His hand felt so warm
compared to mine. I tried to control my shivering as I
towed him to the center of the room. God, I was scared.
"Promise you'll stay."

"I'm right here, Pat. Don't worry."

We both heard the next sound. Someone outside, calling
my name. A deep, booming voice.

"Hugh," I whispered, feeling Julia slipping into my
mind. "No, he can't find me. Not now."

But it was too late. Even as the landscape slowly altered
before my eyes, a second flashlight backlit the tunnel. I was
only vaguely aware of my hand, with a life of its own,
fumbling into Joel's pocket, bringing out the gun, aiming
it at the mouth of the opening as Hugh's head came into
view.

No, not Hugh. Robert E. Lee himself. My impatient finger nuzzled the trigger. . . .

I saw battle-corpses, myriads of them,
And the white skeletons of young men, I saw them,
I saw the debris and debris of all the slain soldiers of the war,
But I saw they were not as was thought,
They themselves were fully at rest, they suffr'd not,
The living remain'd and suffer'd.

      from *When Lilacs Last in the Dooryard Bloom'd,*
                    Walt Whitman

MAY 7, 1864—PARKER'S STORE

"My name is Julia Bell."

Had I been in his place, my gaze would have been fixed on the pistol, on the finger which held my life beneath that first knuckle.

Lee's gaze met mine. Melancholy eyes, on a face red and gaunt. "Miss Bell," he said with a polite nod, his breath labored. He began to rise, but before his full weight could shift to his legs, his jaw clenched as if trying to mask great discomfort. His shirt, I observed, was drenched with perspiration as he stiffly resumed his seat. "Will you excuse me if I fail to rise?"

"Are you hurt?" It sounded a pointless query to my ear, considering what I meant to do, but I'd seen myself as a David slaying Goliath. This was no giant before me, though his struggle to maintain dignity seemed almost beyond human bounds.

"No, Miss Bell." His mouth looked as if it had never known a smile, but his eyes seemed sadly amused by my remark. "Merely an old man with an old heart."

To hear the great General Lee describe himself thus was disconcerting. My arm quivered beneath the weight of the gun. I brought my other hand up to help steady it.

He kneaded his chest gently, still intent upon my gaze. "Do you live nearabouts, Miss Bell?"

I felt my insides harden: "I did once, before the war destroyed my home."

He disregarded the challenge in my voice. "I thought you a Virginian by your speech. Have you ever kept a pet squirrel, Miss Bell?"

Presuming the question a part of some metaphorical rebuttal to my earlier provocation, I said, "Squirrels should not be denied their homes in the forest any more than people should be denied theirs."

He nodded gravely. "We're agreed on that point. My daughter, however, insists on keeping one. And the squirrel insists on biting everyone who comes near."

I wondered if I'd made some mistake. Perhaps this wasn't Lee after all. He wore no insignia. He might not even be a general. "Are you Robert E. Lee?"

"Yes, child." His eyes moved now, barely, taking in only my weapon before returning to my face. "What caused your doubt? You didn't know of my daughters?"

I hadn't imagined him with family, picturing only the war monger, tall in his saddle, dictating men's destinies.

"I have three," he continued, his stare becoming hollow. "Four before my Annie died a year and a half ago. She wasn't much older than you." He drew in his breath sharply, holding it a moment before letting it go slowly, as if willing some deep ache to float out of him upon its current. His hand pressed tighter against his ribs.

"Perhaps it was your punishment." I heard, truly for the first time, the bitterness which had colored my voice this past year, in all its cruelty. My pain could not be disposed of in so unhurried a manner as his.

The general seemed not to notice but considered my comment as an opinion honestly set forth. "The notion has struck me before, with each death of a loved one—my son's wife most recently. And since the war began, both my grandchildren. Yet I can't envision a merciful God taking innocents for the sole purpose of my chastisement." Recognition came to his eyes once more as they explored every inch of my face. "You've also lost someone to the war?"

"Both my parents—" My words were fierce, spat at him in rage, "—and all three brothers."

The natural downward curve of his mouth increased, as if in reflection of my own misery. "All killed in battle?"

I began to tremble, tears clouding my vision. "My two elder brothers and my father. My mother died in the Chancellorsville fires."

"You're from Bell Run, then, along the Rapidan. I read of the incident afterwards. The house and mill were destroyed. Your mother was a Shackleford. I knew her father." He made a low moan, as if grieved. "Are you alone, child? What of your third brother?"

Tears coursed down my cheeks as I remembered him, unable to fathom evil and ill will, never coveting lofty ideals. "Gabe was simple. He didn't understand. . . . He died because . . ." Because he'd loved and trusted everyone, even strangers, freely sharing anything he had. Always smiling. If anyone on this earth was ever assured a place in Heaven, Gabe was.

I blamed myself. We should have returned directly to Richmond after burying Lane. But I knew when I left Bell Run, it would be for the last time. Those four graves above the river—the land itself—seemed to hold me captive. When the army returned, Gabe determined to enlist. He'd no idea what soldiering meant, only that Evan and Lane and Pa had done it. Nothing I could say would dissuade him.

I'd thought of my mother, alone in Heaven, the rest of us damned as murderers and adulterers. Gabe, at least, should join her there. What was one more sin on my soul as long as his remained spotless?

As he marched away toward the army camp, I'd raised Pa's rifle and shot him. He never sensed my betrayal nor saw the anguish on my face. He'd died straightaway, his smile still on his lips.

Overcome by grief, I lowered the revolver, my resolve

shattered. Sobs shook my being, weeping such as I had not experienced since Evan's death, cleansing the anger and hatred from my heart.

I felt a warm, heavy hand settle on my shoulder. The pistol was taken from me and a clean handkerchief pressed into that palm. "God help you, child." His whisper was heartfelt. "I know my deepest sympathy can do nothing to ease your sorrow."

I was drained at last of rancor, and my tears ceased. My heart felt empty now, numb, lifeless. Wiping my eyes and face with the bit of linen he'd provided, I breathed in its aura of strong soap and salty perspiration.

Lee had once more sunk onto the bench, expelling his breath to lessen his discomfort, before drawing himself upright to his former dignity. He removed the bullets from the revolver's chamber. "Do you have kin? A neighbor, perhaps? Someone who'll take you in?"

He intended to let me go, I realized, astounded. "I have friends in Richmond."

"One of my officers will escort you." General Lee offered the empty revolver, butt first.

I stared at the weapon. "You're giving it back to me?"

"Perhaps you still wish to shoot me?"

"I never *wished* to harm anyone. I merely wished an end to this war."

"And you thought my death would bring it about?" With a tremulous breath, General Lee turned his gaze from me, his eyes centering on some distant vision. "These men did not leave their homes to follow me. Had there been no generals, they would have done so. Men take up arms when they want what they can never have. Or more often, when they fear that what they *do* have will be taken from them. And then they themselves destroy all that's worth having."

I realized the truth in his words. Evan wanted no more than to live life to its fullest, yet never saw his twentieth year. Father had feared for his home when the armies first visited our part of Virginia. His sacrifice left Bell Run defenseless. Lane . . . I couldn't think of him without conjuring his image when last he held Clarissa and laughed with her. Lane's thoughts had always been for others. He'd entered into the fray to sustain his share of the burden, as he would have helped a neighbor shore up a sagging chicken coop. His colonel said he'd taken a bullet meant for another. In doing so, he left Gabe and me a burden neither of us were prepared to shoulder.

Not that I blame him for Gabe's death. Like the rest, I took up arms when I feared my little brother would also be taken from me. Gabe rests now in a better place, but I can never again look upon his smile.

And what of my latest transgression? Had I truly killed John in defense of myself? I'd stopped fearing death long ago, and the pain he'd inflicted was trifling compared to what I expected to endure throughout eternity. Nor did I fear joining with him again—our prior unions had brought joy such as I'd never known. What I realized I'd wanted—what I could never have—was John's love. He'd put on a uniform to please his father. In doing so, he'd forsaken his beliefs, abandoned all that had made him an individual. Love was no longer his to give. And perhaps what I'd feared losing most was what little memory I had left of the real John.

Yet my action hadn't destroyed all. Even now when I thought of John, I saw not the swaggering Union officer who'd struck me to the ground yesterday. I saw only the beautiful youth who'd walked with me so many winter afternoons. Who, late at night in the garden, would hold me close in his arms and tease my lips with his own. Who, in a deserted root cellar we'd discovered, had first awkwardly made love to me. And when I remembered the feel of his body pressed against my own, it wasn't the demanding clenches of a cruel man trying to take what he could, but the ardent caresses of a tender lover, giving all he had within to give.

⚞ 23 ⚟

I felt intensely warm. My body was in a vise, something heavy pushing against the front of me, pinning my back to a cold, hard surface, sharp edges jutting into my spine. Breathing seemed just about impossible, my mouth gagged by—

My God! *I was being kissed*!

And I was kissing back! Zealously!

This was no polite inquiry either, no playful volley. This kiss meant *business*! Somehow, while I was off in my time machine, Joel had not only managed to steal second base but was rounding third, heading for home. And I wasn't even attempting to field the ball.

He couldn't possibly have as many hands as I felt, my body welcoming them no matter where they roamed, starved for the tingle left in their wake. Our legs were becoming entwined, our thighs in concert as they skimmed against each other. His mouth gave lavishly, indulging, stoking up my inner boiler. I felt myself expanding, trying to accommodate more of him, my lips probing for the outer limits of his, finding—

Hair.

A moustache!

I froze, my eyes flying open. All I could see were the shadows of his bent head and hunched shoulder, silhouetted by an eerie light. But it *was* Hugh—his size told me that right off. I should have known. Joel could never be that . . . that . . . abundant.

I twisted my mouth away, pushing against his chest. "What do you think you're doing?" I'd meant to sound indignant, but my voice cracked as I tried to catch my breath.

He mumbled something unintelligible as, denied my mouth, he went for my jugular, turning my knees into sun-softened Jell-O.

I shoved harder, my old panic giving me strength, as frightened of my own responses as of him. "No, please. Please don't—"

Hugh raised his head abruptly, his labored breathing like a hot blow dryer on my forehead. He gave the impression that he was scrutinizing my face, though I knew he could no more see my expression than I could make out his in the darkness. His body was still pressed into mine, still holding me captive against what I assumed was a brick wall. And his hands had come to a standstill on two extremely sensitive parts of my anatomy, distracting me no end.

"Please," I gasped. "Let me go. I don't want—"

He stepped back, disengaging his thigh, his hands seeking more neutral territory, namely, my upper arms. Even there, my flesh turned traitor, rising to receive him. He felt it, too. "What kind of game are you playing?"

My eyes darted, exploring my extended line of vision. The source of light seemed to be a flashlight beam, pointed diagonally up at old rotted joists supported by dry, barren vines, so tightly interwoven there was no space between. The tunnel was ten feet away. With Hugh barring my path, my arms locked in his grasp, it might as well have been a hundred miles.

I mustered all my Muscarella grit. "You took advantage of me while I was—"

"*I* took advantage of *you*?" he boomed. "All I did was put my arm around you when you started crying. You led the way from there."

Crying? My eyes had that itchy, wrung-dry tautness you get after a heart-wrenching sob. When Julia broke down, I

must have, too. As for the rest of his claim, when Julia
began reminiscing about John, I guess I—

"I . . . I wasn't myself. My subconscious must have
thought you were Joel."

His grip tightened. Not painfully, but there was no
longer pleasure in it. It dawned on me then . . . okay, I
should have noticed sooner, but my brain can only sort out
so much data at once . . . *Joel wasn't there*. Unless he was
prone on the floor, blocked from my sight by Hugh's bulk.

I struggled to see. "Where's Joel? What did you do to
him?"

"Calm down!" There wasn't a whole lot of patience left
in his tone, so I stopped squirming. "Your lover ran off to
get help. At least, that's why he *said* he left. I think he got
spooked when you slipped back into the past."

"You know about my . . . my . . . ?"

"Miss Maggie half-explained it before she sent me out
looking for you." Hugh paused, his hold changing again,
easing. "I didn't believe any of it, until I saw you."

My brain whipped up a mental picture of what his face
must have looked like, and I couldn't help laughing, sorry
to have missed the live performance. "Scared you, too,
didn't I?"

He inhaled angrily. "You *were* pointing a gun at me."
His voice was strained, tense. Dangerous.

I sobered immediately, reminding myself I was likely
dealing with a murderer. "I want to go back to Miss Maggie's."

He sighed, his thumbs moving ever so slightly in a caress. I dug my fingernails into my palms, holding myself
rigid against the wave of pure delirium it produced.

"Please," I begged. "You're hurting my arm." A lie, but
it worked. He dropped his hands, backing away even further.

I saw the flashlight now—Miss Maggie's beacon, not
Joel's—and there on the floor at my feet, Joel's gun. I
swooped, snatching it up, waving it menacingly toward
Hugh. "I just want to leave. Get out of my way."

Hugh hadn't lifted a finger to prevent it. Head lowered, he thrust his hands deep into his pockets, stepping aside. "Go on. I won't try to stop you. Tell Miss Maggie I'll be back to get Beth Ann in a while."

I didn't like his defeated manner, but it could as easily be a ploy. Not taking my eyes from him, I backed quickly toward the tunnel. He didn't watch, but I knew he was listening, waiting for me to leave.

I was dismayed to hear the sound of rain beating against the bricks out in the well, but better to get caught in a downpour than stay here.

Then the fumes hit me. *Gasoline.*

"Shit!"

Hugh turned at my exclamation, but I didn't elaborate further. Scooping up the flashlight, I raked its beam around the room. On the far wall, the light was sucked through a black doorway. "That way!" I shouted. "Hurry!"

Hugh stood dazed. I threw my whole weight against him, expecting him to feel like a steel wall. Amazingly enough, he budged, putting his arm around my waist and pulling me after him. Not so much in response to my nudge as to the fumes, which were now unmistakable on this side of the chamber.

As we lunged across the threshold, Hugh shoved me in front of him because I still held the flashlight. There was a hallway to our right, and I fled down it, stumbling over the uneven floor littered with pieces of brick. Hugh was so close behind me I could feel his breath on the top of my head.

I expected a big explosion. It was more of a *whoosh,* stale air rushing into my face, being sucked into the vacuum created by the flare-up. The flashlight's gleam dimmed as sooty smoke began to billow around us. My nose already recoiled from its stench.

Hugh saw it, too. "Move! Faster!"

I didn't need his hands urging me forward, though their solid weight renewed my courage. I had to get him out of here, for Beth Ann's sake.

We came to a wall of rubble, completely blocking the passage. I scrambled up to the top. The smoke was thickest there, stinging my throat and eyes. I could hear Hugh coughing behind me. He was more than a head taller, probably had already inhaled twice as much as me.

The gun was still in my right hand. I jammed it into my big shirt pocket, then focused my strength on forcing bricks from below the joist in one corner, aiming the beacon through the resulting peephole. The smoke was thinner on the other side, sweet, fresh air being sucked into my face through the small gap.

"It's where Beth Ann and I hid yesterday." I said. "If we can clear enough of an opening, we can get out."

Hugh was already up beside me, using both hands like bulldozers. I helped with my right, my left supporting the light. I was choking, trying to hold my breath against the ever increasing density of the smoke, but Hugh was working like a horse, breathing ponderously, wheezing.

Balancing the light in front of me, I put my left hand to work. The arm balked again, but I gritted my teeth, telling myself the pain could be no worse than childbirth. And if I ever wanted the chance to compare the two, I'd better work harder.

Without warning, Hugh grasped me about my waist, launching me through the opening with all his might. It was like trying to squeeze into a pair of Lycra shorts, junior petite at that, but his two hundred-some pounds of thrust muscled my butt through. I heard something rip, a jeans pocket I think, but I seemed in one piece.

"Get out," Hugh was trying to yell, between his choking and gasping. "Go for help."

I scrambled back up the opposite side, shoving bricks down between my legs. "Those joists and vines will catch soon. You have to get out now."

He was leaning on his arms, his eyes glazed over, the flashlight illuminating his face like a low-budget haunted house stunt. "Can't—"

"Hugh!" I dug faster, my arm throbbing in agony, my

hands bloody. "Dammit! Think about Beth Ann. You want me to tell her you gave up?"

"Miss Maggie can take care of Beth Ann," he murmured. "Or you. She likes you."

"I won't be around, you jerk!" I screamed. "I can't climb out of the stairwell alone. My arm's bleeding again." Not like yesterday, not yet anyway, but the bandage under my rolled-up sleeve was already soaked.

That spurred him to action; I hoped in time. I could feel the heat of the fire now, its crackling getting closer. The smoke was surging through the cranny, so thick I could hardly see Hugh just a few feet away. The light was my only guide. I transferred it to my side, my head pounding for lack of oxygen. If I felt this bad, I knew Hugh was in danger of passing out. And if he did, I'd never get him out.

"Try to get through," I urged. The opening still didn't look big enough for him, but we couldn't delay any longer. "Come on, hands first. I'll help you." We clasped each other's wrists—his grip felt horribly frail—and I tugged at him, throwing my weight backwards. We made progress until his shoulders snagged.

Wrapping his hands behind my back, I seized his shirt, placing my feet up near the opening so I could use all my lower-body strength. "Pull your shoulders in tight, Hugh. Push with your legs. Please."

His eyes were squeezed shut, wincing as he strove to twist his joints to their tiniest diameter. All I could think was, thank God we weren't both female. If we'd had to deal with a womanly pair of hips his size, no power on earth could cram them through.

I hooked my fingers into his armpits, doubling my efforts as he doubled his, and he slithered over the bricks at last.

With my right arm around his back, I crooked his left over my shoulder, compelling him to stay bent over and on his feet. "Keep low. The air's better."

"The light . . ."

It was still up above, but so much smoke swept through

now, I could barely see it. "We don't need it. I'll feel my
way along the wall."

We felt our way around the corner, down the hall, into
the stairwell. He was too weak to climb out by himself, let
alone lift me, though he tried both before leaning heavily
against the wall. The smoke hugged the wall here, rising
straight up, like a chimney, and we both breathed in the
fresher air.

I screamed for help with every last bit of stamina in me.
I was able to sustain it only a few seconds, the roar and
crackle of the fire growing ever closer and louder as I weakened. At last, spent, I sagged against Hugh, tears streaming
down my cheeks. His arms came around me in a feeble
hug.

Then, high and shrill above the fire came a panicked
shriek, "Dad! Pat!"

Beth Ann. She could never help me lift Hugh out, probably didn't even have the body weight to hoist me. I knew
I'd be putting her in danger. The brambles around the stairwell would flare up soon, possibly trapping us all. But she
was the only hope left. Mustering energy reserves I didn't
know I had, I screamed in answer until I was hoarse.

She came running along the passage of vines, another
figure right behind her, shining a big, bright light in our
faces.

Miss Maggie? No, too tall.

The light was set on the ground, and the figure hopped
down beside us. His black baseball cap sported an oval
patch with STOKE COUNTY FIRE AND RESCUE em-
broidered in bright red. Reeking of smoke himself, Elliott
Boutchyard didn't say a word as he boosted me out of the
stairwell.

"Dad!" Beth Ann dropped to her knees beside her father.
We were on the southwest side of the ruin, upwind, away
from the smoke. "Dad, are you? . . . Is he? . . ."

"I'm all right, honey," Hugh muttered, punctuating it
with a fit of raspy coughing. Bad as he looked and sounded,

he smiled up at her, placing his large, sooty hand over hers.

More volunteer fire fighters were arriving, bringing equipment, and Elliott went off to join them.

"The paramedics are on their way," Beth Ann said, holding tight to her father's hand. "Miss Maggie called 911 as soon as we saw the fire. She stayed back at the house to direct them."

I stood watching the flames inside the brick structure, illuminating the great billowing clouds of smoke from below. As the joists and vines were consumed, the black, noxious gasoline smoke had given way to the white, cottony variety, dispersing the glow evenly throughout the clearing. The surrounding forest was black in contrast, the sky above a lustrous sapphire. Where the smoke rose above the treetops, it soaked up the sunset, turning an intense scarlet.

Realizing I was exhausted, I lowered myself to the ground, my hand settling onto Hugh's arm. His head swung around abruptly and, even in the dim light, the look in his eyes brought back the memory of that kiss in the cellar. My stomach, my whole body, reacted with an almost painful contraction.

Hugh shifted his arm from under my touch, turning his eyes away from me as he cleared his throat, resting his hand on his chest. His face, in the shimmering of the firelight, was still flushed. In that moment, he reminded me very much of his famous cousin, just as Julia had seen him last.

"Look." Beth Ann, her voice rich with awe, rose to her feet, pointing.

Following the line of her outstretched arm, I saw four figures in front of Bell House. Two Union soldiers each held an arm of a hysterical young woman in a plain black mourning dress.

Julia.

There was no sound. I didn't need any. My mind filled in her screams as she fought against them in vain, trying to enter her own house, now engulfed in flames. Trying to save her mother.

Behind her, prostrate on the ground, his body convulsing in grief, was a teenage boy. Uncle Gabe. No perpetual smile animated his face now, only horrible contortions of emotion. Imagining his half-changed voice, howling in misery, I bit my lip to control the lump in my throat.

"It's her," Beth Ann whispered. "The woman down at the river. The one who told me Pat was at the cemetery."

Julia? The spectral scene faded until only one figure remained. She wasn't struggling now, but stood calmly, facing me, slowly nodding. She'd known of my danger yesterday and had sent Beth Ann.

"They were right there in front of the house." Beth Ann took a step forward, as if she could bring the scene back. "They were! You believe me, don't you, Dad? Pat?"

Hugh had pushed himself up on his elbows. There was no disbelief in his expression, though it was obvious he hadn't seen a thing. He was gazing at me, waiting for me to answer his daughter's question.

"Chancellorsville," I replied, my voice quivering with emotion. "Clara had gotten Gabe out of the house. She went back in to look for her daughter, not knowing Julia was down at the grist mill, trying to save it. By the time Julia came back . . . She never forgave herself."

Beth Ann dropped to her knees once more, trembling, encircling her father with one arm, leaning her head against his chest. "What does it *mean*? Why did we see it?"

I turned back to Bell House. Julia was still standing there patiently, though apparently I was the only one who now saw her. She began to walk forward, her determined black eyes boring right through me. I wasn't afraid. To Julia, I was the embodiment of Clarissa. How could I be afraid of someone who loved me that much?

I rose to my feet as she neared. She turned to her right, looking over her shoulder to make sure I understood her meaning. I was to follow her.

Hugh touched my leg. "Where are you go—?" He cut himself off with a cough.

I slipped my limb easily from his weak grasp, sighing.

Did it matter what I said, or what they thought of me? "My grandmother needs me. Beth Ann, stay with your father until help comes."

I walked toward the cemetery slowly but deliberately. The trail was completely lost in the inky forest, though some extra sense kept me on it, maybe Julia herself. I could no longer see her. I didn't need to. I knew what this was all about. And I was only too willing to comply.

A bouncing light appeared through the trees off to my left. Wading into the brush, crouching down, I drew the handgun from my pocket. It felt heavier than before, the metal warm from resting against my stomach.

I waited for the beacon to pass my hiding place. Rising to my feet, the gun cradled comfortably in both hands, I uttered the words I'd said to Burt a hundred times in my fantasies.

"Freeze, turkey."

24

Joel froze. "Pat?" His voice was a paradox of relief and foreboding. "Thank God. I thought you were caught in the fire."

I stepped out onto the trail, now faintly outlined in the boundaries of his flashlight beam. "I've got your gun aimed right between your shoulder blades, Joel. Walk backward until I tell you to stop. Then we'll take the trail toward the cemetery, you in the lead. Got it?"

My first mistake. Questions gave the lawyer in him a chance for rebuttal. "I'm not sure I understand. What's this all about, Pat?"

"Joel. *Sweetie*. Do you really think I have much tolerance left? I'd just as soon shoot you and get it over with."

He shifted the light to his other hand and said, "The cemetery sounds like the perfect place for that private rendezvous you wanted. What are we waiting for?"

He backed down the path cautiously. When he was on my left, I stepped out onto the trail and told him to turn around before directing him onto the cross trail. Neither of us spoke again until we were inside the cemetery wall.

Joel stopped. "What now?"

"Move over there, behind Armstead's stone." The gun's weight was becoming a problem. My wound had never quit throbbing. Both my arms ached, and the skin of my palms was torn and sensitive. But it wouldn't be much longer now. I ran my tongue over my dry lips, tasting salt and ash. "Turn to face me."

He did, raising his beam immediately to get a good look. "Shine that thing in my face, and I pull the trigger! I mean it!"

He knew I did. His torch beam lingered on the gun instead, which I'm sure concerned him more anyway. Not that he hadn't run a full visual inspection of me first, taking an especially long squint into what he could see of my eyes. They no doubt reminded him of what he'd seen there last— Julia, with a maniacal gleam in her eye. Only this time, no Julia.

I still didn't like the distraction of the glare. "Put the flashlight on the ground, Joel. Point it toward yourself."

He seemed relieved to be able to rid himself of it. Crossing his arms over his chest, he looked at ease, but his apprehension was obvious in the careful way he chose his words. "When you said you wanted to meet me in the woods tonight, I was imagining something more pleasurable, Pat."

"Miss Maggie wrote her will long before your father died, and you took over her affairs."

That threw him. "What's that got to do with—"

"You saw your chance to bleed her trust fund but to get the rest of the estate, you had to locate me before she died or—"

"Don't be silly." Even with the flashlight throwing long shadows up onto his face, the wariness stealing into those gray eyes was evident. "I can't touch Magnolia's money."

"You can after she's gone. And after all, she *is* ninety-one. How long would you have to wait until you have full power of attorney? With no one to challenge you but an elderly psychiatric patient in a VA hospital. Or did you plan to murder Miss Maggie, too, after I was out of the—"

A sharp cramp hit my left arm. I bit my lip against the pain, taking that hand from the gun grip so I could shake out the muscle. The weapon seemed heavier by the second. I tilted my right hand to get more palm support underneath.

Joel had noticed, of course. His gaze hadn't left the gun. He started forward.

I jabbed the muzzle at him. "Don't!" He froze, and I told myself to keep talking. The sooner I found out what I wanted to know, the sooner I could get this over with. "You knew if I died, the land would pass to the trust."

"I never wanted to hurt you, Pat."

How could he still sound so sincere? I reminded myself how desperate he was, looking down the barrel of the gun that could end his life. "Next you'll be telling me how you didn't hide back there on the trail yesterday and shoot at me."

His Adam's apple, enhanced by the oblique light, bobbed grotesquely in his throat. "But I didn't *kill* you, Pat. I couldn't go through with it."

"So you gave me this big nick in my arm instead? Out of the kindness of your heart?"

He blinked, fear of making me angrier warring with something like regret in his eyes. "The gun went off as I jerked it away. I didn't mean for you to get hurt. If you hadn't moved forward—"

Miss Maggie had been right, in a way. Shaky hands. Klutzy murderer. His incompetence rankled me almost as much as his greed. "You could have hit Beth Ann."

"I didn't know she was there! I heard you talking but—"

I cut him off, not wanting to hear how I'd been talking all along to myself, how it was partially my fault Beth Ann had been in danger. "You came after us, Joel. We both heard you."

"Only to make sure you were all right." He wiped his sweaty palms on his jacket. "If I'd wanted to kill you, I would have kept firing that thing until . . . Look, I don't deny the rest of it. Yes, I planned to take money from Magnolia's trust fund after her death. I made it legal. There's a loophole in the agreement that lets me withdraw more than the normal allowance without having to justify the need, as long as Frank's cared for. That's all Magnolia's concerned about anyway. And I *will* make sure he's cared for, Pat. Think of it as my fee."

"Miss Maggie didn't object?"

"I don't think she saw how I could misuse it. She's shrewd, but she's no lawyer. I admit all of that, even trying to figure a way to sell some of the land to boost the principal of the fund. The allowance is based on a percentage of the interest. The higher the principal—"

"So you planned to murder me."

"No! There were other ways. Safer ways."

Other ways. "That paper you wanted me to sign Monday night. Was there a loophole in that, too?"

Joel nodded reluctantly. "It said you weren't guaranteed the entire acreage, and gave Magnolia the right to sell any of the land before she died, or the executor, me, the same right on her death in order to settle the estate."

My legs felt weak, the rest of me nauseated. I sank to my knees beside Julia's marker, propping the gun on top of her tombstone to relieve my arms. "When I refused to sign, you tried scaring me away with that tar-and-feathered doll."

"No, I didn't know anything about that. Scaring you away wouldn't have worked. Magnolia wouldn't have changed her will." His hands relaxed, fingers flexing. "What I did was hire an actress to play the second heir."

"Charlotte Garber."

"She thought *you* were the imposter, that I was trying to keep you from swindling Frank out of Magnolia's land. The deal was, if Magnolia split the property, we'd sell Charlotte's half, and she'd get fifteen percent."

"And when Miss Maggie asked you to check into her background, all you had to do was make up believable answers. What went wrong that you had to get rid of her, too?"

A wave of anguish crossed his face. "I didn't lay a hand on her, Pat. You have to believe that. Please. I'm no murderer."

He was pathetic.

I glanced at the column of white smoke above the tree-tops, remembering the smell of the gas fumes, the sight of that toxic black cloud swallowing up the corridor, my own terror in trying to free Hugh, watching him struggle against each poisonous breath. The cold granite beneath my wrists was no match for the cold loathing seeping into my heart. "How can you stand there and say that? Bad enough Charlotte's dead, bad enough you tried to kill me twice, but Hugh had nothing to do with your scheme. Yet you set that fire—"

"I didn't!" He stepped forward again, this time without thinking. I raised the pistol, and he paused, licking his lips nervously. "I had a very good reason for keeping you alive. I decided today to . . . to marry you. Eventually."

Good thing I was already off my feet. As it was, I almost dropped the gun. "Marry me? To get Miss Maggie's land?" I'd told Beth Ann that Joel was a fluke. How naive could I get? After years of guys ignoring me in favor of women like Denise, it never even dawned on me that all Joel was after was my inheritance. "And then you'd murder me after Miss Maggie dies."

"No, no!" He paused for a deep breath. "I gave up that plan. The idea was to share the estate with you, manage it for you. But I thought . . . I *still* think . . . we could be happy together."

I opened my mouth, but nothing would come out. My brain was stuck in a loop, a thousand emotions wanting to respond, none positive, most purely malicious. But I was so flabbergasted by his ego, which assumed I'd throw myself at his feet in joy at such a proposal, all I could do was stare.

Joel pressed his advantage. "I don't blame you for not trusting me, knowing I shot at you. You don't know how relieved I was after I botched it. I wouldn't get another chance. Wednesday was the only day I could be sure of finding you alone. But I was glad because I knew I couldn't hurt you. Then you called today, asking me to meet you—"

"Handing you a second opportunity on a platter," I said stonily. "I should have realized what you really intended as soon as I saw this gun sticking out of your pocket."

"Pat, you don't understand! If I wanted you dead, I

wouldn't have come at all. I would have made certain I had an alibi. But you said you'd go alone or with Beth Ann. . . . I knew you'd be vulnerable. I brought my nine millimeter to protect you. Just like I said."

I don't know why I even tried to make sense of his babbling, but I did. "Protect me? From who?"

"From me, Miss Montella."

The voice had come out of the darkness beyond the cemetery entrance. I turned my head toward it, puzzled, forgetting even the weapon in my hands.

Joel didn't take advantage of my distraction. He stood motionless, the blood draining from his face as he uttered panicky oaths under his breath.

"Come into the light so I can see you," I shouted, recognizing the voice but needing to see the face that belonged to it before I'd believe the theory my brain was scraping together.

"No need to holler." As he ambled forward, the first thing to reflect the light was the little bit of white around his collar not covered by his dark trench coat or ubiquitous bow tie. The second was the double barrel of his shotgun. Beau carried it indifferently, tilted toward the ground, but the hand wrapped around the grip was tense, the trigger finger poised.

Coming fully awake to the danger, I staggered to my feet, impulsively swinging my gun toward him, sheer adrenaline supporting my arms now.

Beau seemed unconcerned. "I was waiting out there, hoping you'd shoot Joel. I'm real disappointed in him. Thought we were on the same side."

"We are, Mr. Dillard," Joel said hastily, his words spilling out too fast. "I was just bluffing until I could get my gun away from her—"

"Son, why don't you move a few feet closer to the lady, so I can keep an eye on the both of you for the time being?" Beau used the shotgun like a classroom pointer, and Joel, sweat glistening on his forehead, quickly obeyed.

"Miss Maggie trusts you," I sputtered, shaken. "You're Frank's best friend. Why would—"

"Frank Shelby's been living scot-free off the taxpayers for fifty years now, with a military pension on top of it. Never had to work a day in his life, let alone pay off a mortgage and put kids through college. Never had to use up all his savings on his wife's cancer treatments because Medicare didn't cover enough." This wasn't the polite Southern gentleman I'd met Tuesday. His words were edged with contempt.

Beau relaxed, laughing softly. "All I had to do was get Joel here to convince Magnolia to list me as second executor. Despite everything he just told you, that loophole was my suggestion, though he was eager enough to go along at the time." Using his "pointer" again, this time waving it toward me, he added, "Why don't you toss that weapon over to me, Miss Montella, before you hurt yourself?"

"No." I brought the semiautomatic's sights in line with his chest, my hand far from steady.

"Do as he says, Pat." Joel's voice was as jittery as I felt. "You don't know how dangerous he is. I didn't know he intended to hurt anyone. By the time I did. . . . Shooting you was his idea. He set the fire tonight, and he killed Charlotte yesterday."

"Whose fault's that?" Beau asked angrily. "You should have shot this one like you were supposed to and left. Those threats I sent her would've had the sheriff looking all over the county for some hate-crime lunatic, giving us plenty of time to get rid of any evidence. But, no, you wander all around Bell Run looking for your wounded doe, and you let that Garber woman see you carrying a firearm after she heard the shot. You should have shut her up right then and there. Instead you always call me to come get you out of your messes. Like this one. The gun, Miss Montella?"

I clutched it tighter. *I could do this.* I could shoot him and save both Joel and myself. Beau had no idea whom he was dealing with. I came from a whole family of murderers.

I had it in my blood. So why did my finger refuse to pull the trigger?

"Pat," Joel murmured. "If you're serious about using that thing, take the safety off and cock it. The lever on the side."

Safety? No one on TV ever fooled with a safety before blowing away the bad guy, did they? That took the spontaneity out of the drama. Of course, had I posed a real threat to the Clint Eastwoods of the world, I would have studied up on these things. And I wouldn't be hesitating to flip the lever, yank the hammer back, and shoot.

"I was kind of hoping you wouldn't point that out to her, Joel." Beau raised the tip of his shotgun now, until I could see into the abyss of its twin muzzles. "Toss the gun over here, Miss Montella. Last time I'll ask nicely."

Mind poker, I thought desperately. That was something I was good at. "You don't want any shooting, Mr. Dillard. The noise would bring all the firefighters running."

His eyes narrowed. "Don't think I couldn't get away. There's a rowboat waiting for me right at the bottom of this bank."

"Wouldn't take a forensics genius to trace our murders back to you if you use your own shotgun. You only want Joel's gun so you can make it look like a murder-suicide."

Joel fidgeted beside me. "Let's not give him any ideas, Pat."

"I have no intention of making it easy for him, Joel. He'll have to kill me to get it."

Joel was horrified. "Don't back him into a corner."

"You're very brave when your own life's at stake, Miss Montella." Beau swiveled the shotgun until Joel had the million-dollar view. "You don't want to make me do this. Ever seen what buckshot can do to a person?"

"Pat, please," Joel pleaded, sweat dripping off his chin. "Give him the gun."

I saw what was happening then. Beau was baiting me. He *wanted* me to reach for that lever. Then he'd shoot me and claim self-defense. The sheriff already believed I was Charlotte's murderer. Miss Maggie might protest, but she'd known Beau all his life and Joel, the wimp, would back up his story. And in the end, they'd have the land, the trust fund, everything.

Funny thing was, I realized I had no intention of releasing that safety. I wasn't ever going to fire this gun, or any other. I couldn't murder anyone. Even in self-defense. Because, unlike Joel, unlike Beau, I couldn't shrug off the blame and say someone else forced me to pull the trigger. I'd be obliged to watch my bullet tear through human flesh, accepting responsibility for its path of destruction. And living with that the rest of my life would drive me insane. As it had my great-great-great-grandmother.

In my mind's eye, I saw Julia, an uncommon smile on her lips. That had been her point all along. To save me from my dark side. From myself.

I lowered the gun, relaxing my tired arms at my sides. "People only have power over you if you give it to them, Joel. Mr. Dillard, even if you stand there threatening us all night, I'm not giving up this gun voluntarily."

Beau turned his weapon back on me, raising it to his shoulder to take aim, though I suspect it was merely another attempt to intimidate me. I never found out. His gaze shifted beyond my shoulder. At the same time, I felt a cold draft on my back, like a freezer door had opened right behind me. I didn't turn around, knowing who was there.

I imagined Julia could look awfully scary if she put her mind to it.

Beau's face paled to match his shirt. The shotgun was lowered slowly, until it hung limp from his hands.

"Beau," came the sad voice of a teacher who'd just caught her star pupil cheating. Miss Maggie stood on the path beyond the cemetery wall, her yellow sweats barely visible at the forest's edge. The freezer door behind me closed abruptly.

"Put your gun down," Miss Maggie continued. "I've got Elliott Boutchyard with me, and he's a better shot than you any day."

"Got that right," came a deep, grating voice from the

shadows. "Why don't you set that puny thing on the ground and put your hands on the wall, Beau? You too, Joel Peyton."

Joel hastily complied. Beau moved as if in a daze, still staring in my general direction.

"Pat," Miss Maggie added, "come here while Elliott makes a couple of citizen's arrests."

When I joined them on the trail, I saw the reason for Miss Maggie's request.

"I'll take that gun you've got," Elliott said in a whisper. "Beau and Joel are likely to pay more respect with me waving that around than this old fire ax." Sure enough, it was the only weapon in his hands. "Pretty impressive the way you talked Beau into putting his gun down like that. Never saw anything like it. And I thought I saw everything in 'Nam."

As Elliott walked away, Miss Maggie threw her arms around my waist and hugged the wind out of me. "Oh, Pat, you were wonderful."

So neither of them had seen Julia.

Miss Maggie's further adulations were cut off by a whirlwind of red hair and black T-shirt bursting from the brush.

Beth Ann had new scratches all over her arms. "Pat, are you . . . ?"

"I'm all right. I told you to stay with your father."

" 'Until help comes.' Those were your exact words." She grinned. "So when help came, I brought Miss Maggie and Mr. Boutchyard out here. Miss Maggie sent me back to guide the sheriff through the woods without a light. He's right behind me."

"About time, too," Elliott said loudly. "Get your butt over here, Dennis. I need a cigarette."

25

The stench of stale smoke hung over Bell House the next morning.

I'd come out early, after still another glimpse into the past, in the form of a vivid dream just before waking. Miss Maggie had understood my need to come alone.

I could see the brick walls now, only the singed remains of vines lining their base. A wide expanse of churned up dirt, already parched by the sun, blocked my path to the ruin, as it had blocked the fire's path to the forest last night. From this vantage point, there seemed little lost except the thick overgrowth, most of which had been green and, therefore, poor tinder. The previous night's rain must have helped, too, seeping into the dead wood, slowing the fire's progress, and the brick wall had, like a fireplace, contained the worst of the blaze.

I walked around the fire break, then back to a mound of debris at the southeast corner. The broken bricks were still warm beneath my hands as I climbed to the top, moving with care in case the wall had been weakened. What I was seeking had to be at this end of the house, in the part of the cellar where I'd felt Julia's presence most strongly.

Looking over the wall, I could see that all the vines and most of the joists were gone, reduced to a layer of powdery gray ash covering the floor of the now visible cellar. In the room on the opposite corner, the chamber right off the well where Hugh and I had first smelled gas fumes, the walls had been baked to a shiny sable.

"What the hell are you doing up there?"

Startled, I lost my precarious balance. Hugh was at my side at once, arm around my waist, keeping me upright. And he was wheezing from the exertion.

"What are you doing out of bed?" I nagged, annoyed with him for ignoring his doctor's orders. "You're supposed to be resting."

"I *am* resting." Just as annoyed with my nagging, he removed his arm. "Locust Grove sent a sub to do the mail. I was taking a nice, relaxing stroll. If you hadn't been up here—"

"If you hadn't yelled, I wouldn't have stumbled."

"Fine. Let's at least finish the debate on the ground before one of us breaks a leg."

I turned back to the wall. "You can go down. I need to look for something."

A frustrated sigh. "What now?"

Even as he said it, I saw, amidst the ash and ruins, lengths of bone, part of a skull. I pointed, unable to speak, tears dribbling over my eyelids to roll down my cheeks.

"Who is it?" Hugh asked.

"Julia Bell."

"But she's buried in the cemetery."

I told him, haltingly, about all my visions, ending with this morning's, in which Julia went to Richmond, only to find the Howards already gone. She'd made her way back to Bell Run where, deciding Clarissa was in safe hands and better off without her, she'd killed herself..

I didn't look at Hugh when I finished, not wanting to see the doubt on his face. Easy enough to picture it, as I listened to him draw out his breath slowly in the silence.

"Well," he said at last, "we'll have to figure a way to get her out of there. Once we bury her alongside the rest of her family, maybe she'll stop haunting you."

I smiled. Hugh didn't understand. My relationship with Julia was much more permanent than a simple haunting. But he hadn't scoffed, and that was enough. And maybe he was right. Once we reunited Julia with her family, perhaps she'd find peace. I hoped so.

Hugh ran his palm along the old brick wall as he lifted his chin and surveyed the ruin. His gaze, though, seemed to take in all two hundred acres, all of it as much under his skin as mine. I asked him what he was thinking.

"I was wondering what you'll do with the place once its yours," he said. "Have you decided?"

My smile shriveled as I shook my head. "I don't see how I can possibly keep it."

"I think you'll *have* to give it up. That's the only way to get what you want." His Mr. Know-It-All inflections irritated me big time, all the more because I knew he was right. Even if what I wanted had done a complete turnaround in the past five days.

"You can't hope to own it yourself," he continued. "It'll be enough work as it is, getting a foundation off the ground, soliciting memberships, applying for grants, without—"

Foundation? "What are you talking about?"

"Miss Maggie said you wanted to turn Bell Run into a sort of education center. The only way to make that work is to form a charitable organization and turn the estate over to it."

I felt as if he'd kicked me in the head and actually got some brain cells working. "What do I need to start one?"

Hugh produced his unique half-snort. "Guts. Though you seem to have more than your share already. Stamina. A good percentage of nonprofit groups give up in their first year or two. And a cheap lawyer. Maybe you can get the judge to make it part of Joel's sentence."

Had I been hanging on his every word, I might have read more into the insinuation in his tone. But I was hardly listening at all, my mind racing ahead, envisioning the whole thing. I'd promised myself a life and, suddenly—poof—here it was. I didn't care how much hard work went with it. This was worth doing.

"Miss Maggie might know someone," I mused, my thoughts leaping ahead. "Somehow I'll have to get Wilma

Rae involved without her bossing everyone. That'll ensure half the county's help. And grants . . . *you* know about grants. You used to do that for the state—"

"A long time ago," he said, acidly implying that it belonged to a past that was shut up tight, with no likelihood of ever being pried open again.

My Giamo side told me I'd better change the subject fast, the Montellas were scrambling for a joke to diffuse the tension, but the Muscarellas, as usual, were looking for an argument. He wanted guts. I'd show him. "Miss Maggie told me about your wife. You want me to stay away from Beth Ann because I remind you too much of her mother, right?"

He turned his back, all ready to stomp down to the ground and off into the forest.

I let him get about ten feet away. "Beth Ann needs answers to her questions."

He stopped, his neck crimson, his shoulder muscles twitching ominously beneath his polo. I almost apologized. Almost. For once, I was perceptive enough to keep my mouth shut.

"I left the trailer this morning," Hugh said, his back still turned, "because Beth Ann asked about her mother. And I got mad at her."

"What do you want? Pity? No problem. Come back after you talk to your daughter."

The silence between us practically throbbed as I waited for his explosion, ready to blast back with equal force. I had to strain my ears to reassure myself the birds were still singing in the trees, that all creation wasn't waiting along with me.

"You're not at all like Tanya," Hugh said at last, though his voice, cold and rigidly controlled, was not heartening. "She was an artist. She wrote poetry. She didn't have a realistic bone in her body. After we had Beth Ann . . ."

Again the silence, so empty I yearned to fill it with more verbal prodding. I bit my tongue.

He swung around without warning, with such a turbulent

look in his eyes, it was like looking down the crater of a volcano about to erupt. "You do have one thing in common. You've both pointed guns at me. At least *you* thought I was Robert E. Lee. Tanya knew damn well it was me, even if she was stoned out of her mind."

My own outrage turned back on myself, calling me all sorts of well-deserved profanities. No matter what I did, I hurt this man. Though I couldn't have stopped Julia, even if I'd known. Not really expecting an answer, I murmured, "What did you do?"

Shoulders sagging, intensity gone, his eyes scanned the forest indifferently. "I grabbed Beth Ann and ran. I should have called the police, but I didn't. Because she was my wife. Because I would have felt humiliated. I would have felt like I'd failed her. But I did anyway. She OD'd that night."

I didn't want to see him this way, giving up, as he almost had in the cellar last night. "That's why you haven't told Beth Ann. Not because of what her mother did. Because of what you didn't do. Let her judge for herself, Hugh. She'll surprise you."

His eyes came around to meet mine again, not convinced, but suddenly his spirit was back, along with a conniving gleam in his eye. "If you understand Beth Ann so well, she should spend more time with you. At her age, she probably needs a woman to talk to now and then."

Recognizing a fellow con artist, I laughed. "She's begun asking questions about sex, right?"

The way he rolled his eyes was answer enough, though I was willing to bet he didn't know about Pete, the trumpet player. Daughters don't discuss hunks with their fathers.

"Tell you what," I said, "I'll help you with Beth Ann's hormones if you teach me everything you know about grants."

That slow grin of his surfaced. "You'd be getting the worst side of that arrangement."

"Hey, I got her to eat asparagus, didn't I?"

His eyebrows went up as he nodded. "Okay, you've got

a deal. Shake on it?" He offered his hand, and I took it. His big warm paw completely enveloped mine, which felt nice, especially since he didn't let go after the normal deal-clinching interval.

It dawned on me that every time I'd been scared around him, I hadn't really been afraid of him physically—I'd been afraid of what he was liable to do to my heart. A foreign sensation for me.

Not that I wanted that sort of complication right now, what with everything else topsy-turvy in my life.

So, when he asked if I'd keep him company on the rest of his walk, I only went along for the exercise.

Swear to God.

ᴁ EPILOGUE ᴁ

MAY 22—BELL RUN

I plunge my fingers into the cold, clear water of Bell Run. A tadpole, a stubborn one this time, butts his head against them.

The cool, quiet forest is like heaven after the last five sweaty, nail-biting hours of fighting traffic all the way from Philly. I have yet to unpack my car. My entire wardrobe's stacked up on the back seat, half blocking the rearview mirror, and everything else I can't live without is inside the trunk. The only things I'd carried into the house were the goodies brought from Corpolese's Bakery—Italian bread, tomato pie, white pizza, homestyle pasta, and chocolate biscotti—and the box of Lou's stuff from Vietnam.

I've read his letters more than once during the past two weeks, so that I now know some of the passages by heart. Lou and I would have hit it off. He had that quirky Montella sense of humor. And in every one of his letters, he'd questioned the war, not politically like everyone else in the '60s, but as his Grandmother Julia had a century earlier. Questioned that people actually believed it a solution.

Anyway, Miss Maggie had met me at the door with news of Flora. "She sold a fifty-acre tract over on the other side of Stoke, so that should solve her financial woes for the time being. Turns out she needed the money for a baby."

"She's pregnant?"

"No, and that's what was tearing her marriage apart. She wasn't trying to impress another man, Pat; she was trying to impress an adoption agency." Miss Maggie had snatched up the bag of biscotti. "Put your brother's letters in the war room. I want to get right to work on them. I think I'll title this book *NO BORDERS FROM ABOVE: The Vietnam War Letters of Louis Montella.* Sound good to you?"

I'd kissed her cheek to show my overwhelming approval, then let her shoo me away so she could read in peace, which was fine by me. All I'd wanted was to come out here and get tangled up in the forest—not in the vines, but in the speckled sunlight and muggy stillness. In the earthy smells. In the memories, both mine and Julia's.

Shaking the water from my fingers, I retrace my steps to take a narrow trail Hugh showed me, that parallels the creek to the river trail. I stop to skim a flat rock out over the placid flow of the Rapidan before continuing my hike up to the cemetery.

There, wildflowers have already begun to fill in the rectangle of red clay where we'd buried Julia. A new stone for Gabriel is on order. When it's ready, we'll move Julia's stone to her grave.

I sit on the wall, its fieldstone warmed by the sun. The breeze plays with my hair as I listen to a fugue of bird songs from the surrounding trees.

I close my eyes, and the strong aroma of bread baking reaches my nostrils, so tantalizing I can't help but smile, but I'm puzzled because the breeze is coming from the direction of the house, and I know Miss Maggie isn't baking.

The moment I open my eyes, the scent disappears. When I drop my lids again, it's back, hardy and intoxicating. I realize this is simply another of my great-great-great-grandmother's recollections. A happy one this time.

Julia's way of saying, "Welcome home."

Hang My Head and Cry

⚑ 1. WHO'LL BE A WITNESS? ⚐

I have been forty years a slave and forty years free and would be here forty years more to have equal rights for all.

—Sojourner Truth

JULY 2, 1871—CHURCH HILL, EAST OF STOKE, VIRGINIA

Demon Fire. That's how I describe it to Preacher Moses. Wasn't all yellow like a regular blaze, not at first. The belly of these flames be glowing eerie blue, and they dance atop the church floor without consuming, like that bush in the Bible what Preacher tell us 'bout. I heared a fierce wind, too, but didn't feel more than the summer breeze where I stood, and I smelled the breath of the devil hisself, sweet and tempting as the candy sticks Mama sometimes bring me from Fletcher's Drug Store.

By the time I wake up everybody and we all come running back up the hill, the night was lit up brighter than noon and the church be already half gone. No hearth fire ever burned that fast or fierce.

This morning Preacher stand listening to me and surveying the smoldering mound that only yesterday served as our church, supper hall, schoolhouse, and general gathering place. In the first light of day, the charred wood be shiny as the satiny coat on Colonel Gilbert's black mare.

"You've never seen a whole building burn, Mance," Preacher say. "They all go up that quickly. This church was built of old boards, already dried out. Good tinder."

"But I seen the horseman," I told him. "The one from Pockalisp."

"The Apocalypse," he corrected. "And what you *saw*, not seen, was one of those same white men who always ride out here to cause trouble."

Preacher Moses ain't often wrong, so I questioned my own eyes first. True, I seen only one horseman, not four like in the Bible. Also true, both horse and rider be covered with plain white sheets, like the five men what rode out here the night 'fore the last election and gave old Uncle Henry such a whipping as he ain't walked right since. We all knew four of those men be the three Harris brothers and Jack Soyers, on account we recognized their voices, though the sheriff say he can't accuse them since none of us actually seen their faces.

But last night's rider never spoke and, fact was, nobody but me seen him close up this time, so Preacher Moses was just assuming. I shut my eyes, picturing the horseman again as he tossed his torch through the church doorway, and I felt sure something be different about that man.

"Go home, Mance," the preacher say to me. "Get some sleep."

My eyes felt heavy from being up all night, and scratchy from all the smoke—like a pair of rusty horseshoes was weighing down my lids—but I didn't want to miss anything important. "You calling a meeting tonight, like you did last time?"

Preacher Moses faced me then, and I can tell he weren't pleased. "How do you know about that?"

"I seen you and some of the menfolk late that night, walking out toward where them Rebel graves sit looking over the river. Heard you tell everybody they had to go vote, and not let white trash scare them away."

The preacher's jaw got stiff as the statue of George Washington in front of the courthouse down in Stoke. "The laws are on our side, Mance. The Fifteenth Amendment. The two Force Acts. The Ku Klux Klan Act only last April. President Grant'll send the army down here if it keeps up. Voting's the only way we're going to stay free, the only way we can put colored men in the legislature to vote for more laws to help us. You know that."

"Yessuh, I do." I also knew that laws didn't seem to mean much where us dark folk were concerned. True, them first horsemen didn't make good their threats after our men voted, but that was only 'cause the very next night, their ringleader, Jack Soyers met his Maker. They say he was throwed by his horse down on the Orange Turnpike, where it passes by what's left of the battle trenches. Uncle Henry say Yankee ghosts spooked his mount.

Preacher Moses hunkered down to look me in the eye, then reached up and touched his warm, moist fingers to the skin above my left eyebrow, where I got a birthmark the size and shape of a robin's egg. "The Lord placed His thumbprint on you, Emancipation Jackson, so I know I can trust you. I need you to stay with your mama tonight, to protect her, in case those riders come back. Will you do that, Mance?"

I promised I would. Them Yankee ghosts might not be so obliging this time.

JULY 1, PRESENT DAY

I sat on the brick foundation of Miss Maggie's outside cellar door, swatting at the mosquitos feasting on various parts of my anatomy. My scalp, still wet from a quick shower, was the only cool part of me. The night was so hot I might as well have been standing in front of the ovens at my cousin Angelo's pizza parlor. At least there, the heady aroma of pepperoni was a perk.

Out in front of the house, one of two patrol cars the color of milk chocolate still had its lights on, twin beams of red and white pulsing across the edge of Bell Run's forest every half second, giving me that queasy feeling my stomach always gets when I look at strobe lights.

I tried gazing up at the sky instead, which was violet-blue in the last glow of twilight. Stars were trying to cut through the haze, their light flickering like fluorescent lamps in need of new starters. A solitary bat fluttered by, headed for the river and supper. The dope. All the mosquitos were right here, eating me alive.

Across the sideyard, Deputy Dwight Pearson turned on a portable floodlight, washing out sky and stars and attracting an instant cloud of moths. The beam silhouetted the sheriff's precise but ineffectual-looking posture and Miss Maggie's bent-over but dynamic one. Dynamic even in baggy shorts with her bony knees showing.

"Use your head, Dennis," she was saying. "This ground hasn't been disturbed for as long as I can remember." She jabbed an arthritic forefinger at the small strip of churned-up dirt between them—churned up nearly three hours earlier by me, using only a gardening fork and visions of juicy homegrown tomatoes. The two-foot deep hole at one end of the strip was my doing, too, after unearthing what I'd thought was a piece of odd-shaped tree root. Until I noticed that it had teeth.

"That skull belongs to a life lived at least nine decades ago," Miss Maggie concluded, her estimate based on the fact that she'd called this piece of real estate home all of her ninety-one years and she had a black hole of a memory. "Considering all the action Bell Run saw during the Civil War, we've probably got a soldier here. I'm not going to let you ruin a possible archaeological site."

"We'll wait to hear what the M. E. says, Miz Shelby," Brackin replied, being above all a man who liked to form his own opinions. I'll allow that's not a bad trait for the guru of local law enforcement, but Stoke County had a low crime rate and Brackin didn't get to form opinions often enough to stay in practice. His stubbornness tended to be less motivated by objectivity than by a desire to stall, so as not to resume his Maytag-repairmanlike existence any sooner than he had to.

I stood up, hoping the mosquitos wouldn't be able to find the part of me farthest from the ground, which worked for all of five seconds. From my new vantage point, I surveyed the county's two deputies, now leaning against the side rail of our front porch, shovels in their hand, waiting for the go-ahead. From this distance, Dwight Pearson and Brenda Owens looked like twins—both tall, blond and big-boned, wearing identical uniforms, which tonight were equally wilted with the heat, though Brenda had come on duty for the night shift less than fifteen minutes ago. Neither deputy appeared terribly anxious to do hard labor in this weather.

During Miss Maggie's lifetime, she'd taught eighth grade history to just about every native of this part of Virginia, including Brackin, and now she gave him one of her teacher glares, guaranteed to make any kid admit to throwing spitballs. Brackin didn't admit to anything, but he did shut up. And luckily, the cell phone hanging on his belt let out an electronic cackle at that moment. He walked a dozen steps away from her as he answered.

Miss Maggie turned her attention back to the hole, grinning down into it like a proud parent. "This is *so* cool, Pat." I'd lost count of how many times she'd said that in the last two-plus hours. If I'd struck gold, I couldn't have made her happier. Historians are odd that way.

When I'd spotted the teeth on the jawbone—after dropping it in horror, then gingerly scooping it into my little trowel and holding it at arm's length—I'd taken it inside to show Miss Maggie. She'd hauled me back outside and had me show her the exact position of the bone as I'd found it, which probably wasn't as accurate as I could have been because I wasn't willing to touch the thing with more than two fingertips. Then she'd made me help her get down on her knees—not an easy movement given her arthritis—where she took up the trowel and gently scraped the dirt away until a bony face seemed to float to the surface. That's when she'd said it was time to bring in experts.

"I still don't understand why you called the sheriff," I

said, inching closer. My Italian superstitions were warring with my curiosity and my superstitions were the odds-on favorite, so I stopped inching when I could see the raised eye ridges of the skull. They were almost the same shade of gray-beige as the surrounding soil.

"Law says you have to file a police report if you find human remains. Figured I'd get the formalities out of the way before Emmy shows up."

Emmy was Dr. Emmaline Brewster, an anthropologist from the University of Virginia and another former student of Miss Maggie's. She'd phoned Emmy first to give her the details, and within the half hour we'd gotten a call back from her that everything was arranged. She and one of her lab assistants would be here later tonight.

I glanced up at Brackin, but he, still on the phone, was heading over to his deputies. "You didn't tell the sheriff you already contacted the university, did you?"

"No use complicating the matter. I'll tell Elwood when he shows up." Elwood was the doctor the sheriff summoned whenever he needed a medical examiner. For Miss Maggie, everyone in the county was on a first name basis.

Miss Maggie let a spontaneous giggle bubble up out of her insides, a pretty scary sound coming through her raspy old vocal cords. "This is the first historic find for the Julia Bell Foundation, Pat. Aren't you excited?"

I hadn't thought of it that way. The whole concept of the Foundation—that is, setting aside the majority of Bell Run's acreage as a historical and environmental classroom—was only six weeks old. The ink had barely dried on the preliminary paperwork. Yet here we were with our first project. It *was* exciting, but I wished I'd found something more along the lines of a lost city. Finding bones *had* to be a bad omen.

"Once word gets out," Miss Maggie was saying, "this is bound to bring in donations—"

My ears pricked up. Bad omen or not, the Bell Foundation needed bucks. I wondered if Yorick would take offense at being a poster child.

"I can't get over it," she continued, a regular motor-mouth in her enthusiasm. "All the years I've lived in this house and never knew this was here. Then you come along and—what made you dig here, Pat? Weren't you going to put your garden on the other side of the house?"

I nodded. "I thought I wanted a spot that gets sun most of the day." And, I didn't say aloud, the lazy couch-potato inside me wanted a bare piece of ground, where I wouldn't have to chop up sod now or fight weeds later on. "But I couldn't get my fork more than a few inches down into the soil over there."

"Well, what with the drought we've been having these last three weeks, the ground's probably baked into adobe."

Too true. When I'd come here to Bell Run in May, wild-flowers had been at high tide, filling every inch of clearing between the house and surrounding forest. Now only tidal pools of white clover and buttercups remained in the shad-ier areas, like here on the east side of the house. Every-where else was matted brown straw.

Miss Maggie had been tolerant of my gardening whim. After living in an apartment all my adult life, I'd felt almost obligated to plant a few tomatoes and peppers, though I was way late in the season to expect much of a crop, even down here in Virginia where the first frost might hold off an extra week or two.

A cynical little inner voice kept whispering that I was really marking my territory.

I justified it by telling myself I was honoring my Italian heritage by continuing one of my family's traditions. Thing was, where Dad put his veggies had never been decided by soil or sun or drainage. No, Mom said he had to plant down the end of our small yard because the garden attracted spar-rows—they nibbled the lettuce and took daily dust baths between the rows of basil sprouts. And Mom didn't want birds pooping anywhere near her clotheslines.

This, I explained to Miss Maggie, was the extent of my landscaping knowledge. "Then this morning I realized that if the wildflowers had dried up and died out back, my plants probably would, too. Actually, I had this recurring dream about it the past few nights: I'm trying to loosen up the hard ground when one of the local farm boys comes up the path from the creek and tells me I should dig over here instead. So I decided to see if my subconscious knew more about gardening than I did."

Miss Maggie raised her eyebrows. "Good thing it was *your* dream. I wouldn't take farming advice from any of the local kids. Football advice maybe. Or drinking and girls."

I shook my head. "No, he wasn't anyone I've met. He was young—eight, ten maybe. A black kid. Real skinny, light complexion. Big mole over one eyebrow."

"Mole?" Magnolia Shelby wasn't easy to shock, but that made her jaw go slack. She grabbed at my forearm, but our combined sweat made her hand slip to my wrist. "This boy in your dream, what was his name?"

Her reaction spooked me and my stomach roiled from more than the strobe effect of the siren lights. "I don't know. He didn't say."

She let go my arm, but now *I* got her teacher look. "I guess Beth Ann must have told you."

Beth Ann Lee and her father, Hugh, were our closest neighbors, over on the other side of the creek. Even though I was nearly three times her thirteen years, Beth Ann and I had a sort of big and little sis relationship. "Told me what?"

Miss Maggie shifted her eyes from me back to Yorick. "Told you about Mance. Because if she didn't, it means Bell Run has itself another ghost."

A chilling new mystery from the
Edgar Award-winning author of
A Cold Day in Paradise

WINTER
OF THE
WOLF MOON

AN ALEX MCKNIGHT NOVEL
Steve Hamilton

On Michigan's northern peninsula, ex-cop Alex
McKnight enjoys the solitude of his log cabin. But when
a young Native American woman comes to him asking
for help, his peace is shattered. And when she suddenly
disappears, McKnight is plunged into a dangerous inves-
tigation that will reveal the dark secrets and evil motives
hidden in a town called Paradise...

"The isolated, wintry location jives well with
Hamilton's pristine prose, independent protagonist,
and ingenious plot. An inviting sequel to his
Edgar Award-winning first novel."
—*Library Journal*

NOW AVAILABLE FROM ST. MARTIN'S PRESS

Winner of the Edgar Award for Best First Novel, author Eliot Pattison masterfully scales the heights of the genre with this gripping thriller that follows the tradition of *Gorky Park* and *Smilla's Sense of Snow*.

THE SKULL MANTRA

Edgar Award Winner

ELIOT PATTISON

When the grisly remains of a corpse are discovered, the case is handed to veteran police inspector Shan Tao Yun, a prisoner deported to Tibet for offending Beijing. Granted a temporary release, Shan is soon pulled into the Tibetan people's desperate fight for its sacred mountains and the Chinese regime's blood-soaked policies when a Buddhist priest, whom Shan knows is innocent, is arrested. Now, the time is running out for Shan to find the real killer ... An astonishing, emotionally charged story that will change the way you think about Tibet—and freedom—forever.